IT IS WHAT IT IS?

Steven Hall
Hey Buddy - How You Doing?

Garrison L. Moreland

First Edition

NEWMAN SPRINGS PUBLISHING
320 Broad Street
Red Bank, NJ 07701

First originally published by Newman Springs Publishing 2020

ISBN 978-1-64801-722-3 (Paperback)
ISBN 978-1-64801-723-0 (Digital)

Printed in the United States of America

Dedicated to Jerry Balram and Sammuel E. Borden.
Thank you for all your support.

Wanna-Be Lovers

You wanted to be satisfied,
With a butt-naked emotion
In the fire of a season.
To make the magnitude
Of a golden smile baffling,
As you continued to look for love
In an upside-down environment deleted
Without a diary,
Which included a window for a scene
Of dreams coughing.
The first of that is to entertain,
And wasn't abandoned
For an astonishing new language in your display.
But instead,
The gift was never outside your fears on your Sabbath day.
It was a guide to another desire,
Which was still there for a preview,
And with more ugly predictions than however.
But on the other side of deception and conspiracies.
I asked for your love with legitimate returns,

And without the mesmerizing episodes,
That would side kick me
In the benefit of my ass for your love.
And also recalling,
Any asylum of a different X-ray we are in,
Which has been seen before?
But a new generation is revealing,
That love means less—
And without the knowledge to know more
Is still generated from above—
Like an outrageous sight of illusions.
When you and I will be kissing myths,
Or legends for a noble kiss in heat?
When you have recovered
From another triple cross by your emotions.
When I have touched and felt the vague nasty
In your entangled world.
A forbidden alias for no more captivating confessions
Of love between you and I.
To cut each other's throat for someone we loved,
And believed,
Who was real when there was no real.
Garrison L. Moreland

Prologue

WAITING FOR SHIT TO HAPPEN is an amazing and mind-blowing concept, which is fulfilled with excitement, curiosity, and unpredictable results for a human being.

Since we are human beings with many faults, it's amazing how innocence is eventually born into faults with growth, because we are successfully waiting for more shit to happen. While we are constructing our life to be better human beings, without the assistance of faults, but it doesn't happen, because this is our human nature.

The purpose of who we become as a person, and being with a person in love, is a difficult development of reality in any life we live. We do not always become someone we want to be, or treat other people with the respect and consideration they deserve for love.

Based on the knowledge and experience we consume and confront, but are left with false hypocrisy and judge mentality to criticize anyone else, which has accumulated throughout our lives, with an unfocused purpose to condemn others. Like your opinion is more significant than your compassion and civility is?

The difficult process of living with ourselves on a daily basis is no answer to provide us with a better way to love someone else. Since living with ourselves and who we are? When love and the person has been destroyed—which has prevented us from seeing one of the most important viewpoints about living with ourselves and who we are?

This is why secrets are born, kept, and are hidden as a salvation for another way, than to oppose the damaging process of searching for everlasting love, with someone else for compatibility in another face book of romance.

But for many people, it only takes one unfortunate experience with love and romance to change the destiny of their mentality and emotional fiber. When a relationship, or marriage, or family has failed to be a success for its own destiny.

Then love and romance has become more destructive in our daily lives for the purpose of being what? And yet, all the mysteries about love and romance are like no other, with a wonder of surprise and jubilation to pursue the unknown of what with someone?

Or any emotion will lead you to be with another fickle-minded individual. Who admires the possible prospect of excitement with, and the mystery that has entered their life. While always looking forward to seeing what is to come? Or the new stuff that is given to you now.

But surprisingly, the thing about love and romance is? It doesn't matter how much you feel, care, or what you think you have with someone. It is not enough to prevent you from crossing a line, or doing something else with someone else.

Because you will see someone else more attractive and enticing enough to do something with, when you are clearly in love with someone else? But this continues to confuse the hell out of you? Or are you one of these people where this makes complete sense to you, when it doesn't make sense at all?

This is the mystery of love and romance. It seems that it will always put you in the mix with your emotions, and your behavior for temptation to do something you shouldn't do. But you know what the deal is, blame it all on love.

When control, discipline, principals, judgment, reasoning, and your character becomes blissful, with no rationality to explain. Because some excuses don't have excuses for love and romance when it comes to someone else, or their misgivings. When it's time for your heart to be broken.

Or clearly lacking the understanding of how, something so wonderful, beautiful, daring, giving, and strong can change so rapidly to hate, and countless misgivings to evaluate your emotions with regret.

Then at some point and time, men and women realize they are unable to give each other everything they want, need, and expect in a relationship. Considering, what expectations are within people and life these days.

It's like a brief description. Or a type of joy for a protection terminal—which is a glass enclosure provided under a yield sign. Whether right is wrong, or whether wrong is right, it's really about the way people introduce their beliefs.

Like tears falling from your eyes are forthcoming to another person's eyes. And recalling will not bring back the taste of eliminating misfortune again. But raindrops continue to hurt when they come down, and express themselves directly and powerful as a storm.

When it comes to love, relationships, marriage, and family, it's amazing how so few of us really get it, and the rest of us don't seem to have a clue as to what it's really all about? When so many relationships, marriages, and families fail because of love.

What you believe in today, you may not believe in tomorrow. Or as oppose to the way emotions can change according to life, and about what is new, different, experienced, and happening within yourself.

Unfortunately, we don't get any better as human beings, because family, religion, ourselves, love, marriage, people, money, jobs, and children all come into view. It's like the spectrum of colors in the realm of a prism. Everything you see in not revealed or is real.

Or like love? It comes and goes without you knowing what happened. Or believe what you experienced and have gone through in your heart and in your life was real.

The longer time passes, and the more and more you have a relationship with a person. Somehow you come to the same conclusion eventually about relationships—they don't last—and they don't work. But to convince yourself that they do work. You continue to try with someone else who is presumably different? Always believing in the same thing, but with a different person as a new ray of hope.

Or you continue to go through the same thing with someone else. No matter how much you want to deny it. There isn't much of a difference when you are with someone else going through the same thing, except for a heighten elevation in your feelings for a new attraction for someone else.

Or what you seem to convince yourself of, and having a problem with true companionship. Playing games of chance with each other's heart, with fear in each other's emotions that we pursue and gets us nowhere.

In many relationships, there is a percentage of people who stay together for an unknown over flow of reasons. That no one else can figure out why they are together in the first place?

Like when she cursed him out real bad. Since he wasn't paying attention to her? But quite a few other people heard her loud and clear. So he couldn't wait until 8:00 p.m. So he could be with this other woman and show her respect and love, as he walked away from the dragon who set him on fire.

Like he wished he could burn more than her ass in return, but it wasn't the time or place for this to happen?

Like the more you try to believe in something you are involved in. The more you find out how unreal it is. When something happens in a relationship, it may seem as illicit, as you believing you are the last red hot lover.

Because your ego, and your dreams have spoken to you about someone else? Or being without the act of fornication—not to be judgmental? But how many of us are conceived out of wedlock? Not as many as out of fornication, I bet? Or is that a trick question? Since we live in a world besieged with monkey business.

But as far as men are concerned, it would have helped, if God could have created another alternative to women—to take the edge off along with the pressure, which never seems to disappear from their constant preoccupation with women.

There is no doubt that men are weaker to the competition of woman. Especially if you have to heed to punishment from laughter? Women possess a visual power a man could never have, and her femininity is second to none.

Her looks and body are defined and definite within itself. Life becomes a forum to it when you think of something you need or want more, than a woman or a man. When your insatiable fantasies and dreams can be turned on exclusively.

Unfortunately, men frequently want what a woman has rather than what she is? And wishing for that sexual pleasure doesn't show a concrete feeling, which is hot-wired by a true anxiety of no way to be beyond emotion and betrayal.

But why women want men is a mystery to them. It's never for the same reasons why men want them, because of the way men do unto themselves?

Like if you were a person who could see tomorrow, with a hostile intention taken away with romance at first sight?

Or if man's biggest weakness is still his libido—since the muscle of pleasure is always stiff—and it never calms down whether you wanted it to or not. But if touching a woman's sex in a day is so much notorious, then a man can give her a reason to believe?

Continues to make a mockery out of romance with relationships, and everyone knows this? This is why relationships are more difficult to deal with from person to person, after you have met someone.

And what would be the other alternative for people to come out into the streets to volunteer, and begin their own trademark of universal hoe-hopping. Especially when people don't want to do anything right, right for love?

If it wasn't for the belief that we try and hold on to family, religion, ourselves, love, marriage, people, money, jobs, and children to show some balance of value in life? Then a heart in happy endings will cause you to accomplish more suffering.

Not to mention, that many people would still like to believe in a relationship when it comes to romance. In spite of the fact, there are many people who seem to get lost alone the way.

Or recalling, if you consider falling in love again? It will always change things somehow, and after a while the hurt begins, then followed by the constant pain. The one emotion you can never seem to escape whether its good pain or bad pain. You can only feel the pain in relationship to its loss?

There was a time when a man would die for his pride and honor. There was a time when a woman would die with her legs closed to display her courage?

But there was no doubt, it reminded him of searching for footsteps in the dark, and wondering what this is about concerning anything? He thought about the difference and the change in things, as he had become older. And he is sorry to say, he is now in the mix.

Marshall Blake Abbott wasn't going to see anything he wanted to see. But if you laugh before he did, then take a little off the top because he will be laughing without you in the wind, y' know.

He had been involved with this woman for the better part of ten years. A woman he loved. A woman he married. And now, he is involved with other people who know each other and are involved with themselves. And because of this whole situation experience—it has become his bad.

So with each passing day, there isn't a bare ass uncovered up by the truth. When he turned the corner of sin, in which, he saw from the jealousy, that didn't appear behind a hidden door of congratulations for him, and for some other people. Whenever his or her butt doesn't touch the red pepper of love, then this is the madness that occurred, when you are in love with someone.

Not to mention, another one of loves mysteries is a lack of equally in love or loving someone. When two people are in love, and adamantly claim how much they love each other, and within their journey to bond with each other.

Then after countless experiences together, and unknown confrontations provided by life, then the setting begins where it appears, that one person loves the other person more than the person loves them.

This amazing event of how, love and the other person always comes up short in their evaluation of love, with reference to their meaning. When you know, that based on your separation and experience with this person, that they didn't love you the way you loved them, with a true conviction and meaning for giving? But taking from you was their true smart-drive for closing things out.

1

"DAMN YOU, JADE! I DON'T understand? Why you won't talk to me? What happened? Won't you explain this to me? What is going on?" She stood there like a zombie. Then she got her coat and left.

He was standing in the living room looking foolish. He couldn't believe she walked out. She was sitting in her car, breathing heavily, and trying to regain her composure.

She suffered from asthma. Her excitement needed to be kept to a minimum. She cried. She retrieved her phone from her bag. She called him. He waited for her to answer while she tried to stop crying.

"I am sorry for walking out on you. I am at the end of my rope. I don't know what to say to you, or know what to do?"

"Then how about the truth, Jade?"

"Marshall, I don't know what the truth is anymore?"

She cried, hung up abruptly, before she left the apartment. It was like he was talking to himself for the entire evening.

Regardless of the changes she was going through, she had to know he was lost in never-never land. How could he understand what was going on inside her?

Her behavior was provocative to say the least. He couldn't begin to endow any of it seriously, pertinent or not, it was her talk. And to understand her aim as to why, she would hurt him with all her negativity?

If he didn't know any better, he would have to say? He felt like a sewer rat hidden underneath the ground, with a touch of evil running away from all of this? But mainly to relay a message to her while leaving, which he didn't get?

Before she drove away in a painful state, he thought, he knew what was going on with her. He would have offered her all the comfort he had to give.

It was obvious anyone can see she was in a lot of pain. However, she wasn't trying to solicit him for any of his help. Now he is like an epidemic with death looking at time, or never reawakening his dreams within her again.

Because of everything that had happened, and wishing he could be there for her, when they fought through the obstacles in the past to get to where they were now. But not as two opposing forces, with hostile feelings toward one another.

He realized, she didn't want to hear this from him or anyone else. And then again, he didn't want to be truly insensitive. Although there was still a big hole in the chair she sat in, which didn't support her problems?

2

IT WAS A SERIOUS SITUATION for him and her to be admitting to, without a light to see it had all come to an end for them. He didn't know why, the real illness was caused by an over exposure to life, before the lunatics were at array?

She was aware of what it meant to her—in her own mind without telling anyone. It meant he had to realize, she may have lost another child before he came into her life.

It didn't matter whether or not he knew about it. It's just the fact she didn't tell him about it. He hoped one day the despair in her heart will be gone, like he told her. And on this day, she could feel the reward of free pain in her heart.

It was never his intention or desire to hurt her in return for the way she hurt him, but this was his problem to deal with.

He thought about taking her down the way she took him down and judging from the way he cared about her and loved her, it brought him more of a heartache than some peace of mind when it came to an end with her.

He could have saved himself more misery then by not being there for her and moving on with his life. He was trying to save something that couldn't be saved. He wished he had known this in advance.

So whatever he believed they felt for one another and had established with each other. He asked himself over and over. How could he berate her at the level she slowly applied to him?

When he thought about the women in his life before her, and after they became a couple, there were many opportunities available for him to be with other women and sleep with them. Only if he had a change of heart and wanted to make it possible, based on his personality and past behavior?

But it wasn't going to happen. He maintained his faithfulness in their relationship and marriage. His control was more than good, before he would ever think about selecting another woman over her, or cheat on her, or trying to cover it up with a legitimate reason later?

Not that it doesn't happen every day. Or would be a brief description of cruelty like she volunteered to him, with more special effects he couldn't describe from her layout.

Jade could have definitely been a much better bitch about what she was doing. Or the way she did it to the both of them, if this was her point to eliminate them, he thought.

Shit! He could have come up with something a lot more creative than this? If that's what she needed to better justify herself with?

His love for her was undisturbed. He wanted to give her anything he had to offer. And yet, a woman continues with the bullshit about how there are no good men out here, unless they are married or gay?

Maybe they should stop to think and reconsider; perhaps there aren't a lot of good women out here either?

Maybe there are too many women out here to try and trust, based on a woman's ratio to men? The problem still continues when a man is having trouble in his life because his woman is out there cheating on him?

Or when a woman is experiencing the same kind of betrayal in her life because her man is out there cheating on her? But when you look at it all…it is always either one or the other when it comes to men and women.

Like when things changed between him and her. She offered him pure hell with attachments.

He continued to love her everlasting smile in the day dreams of a winter's breeze. When no one else was watching him. When he couldn't find a reason to sleep, because he couldn't get her off of his mind.

She is an extraordinarily beautiful woman. When he considered not too many things could be compared. The intolerance of love he felt was eternal torment and pain for him, and with the implication of being without her for the rest of his life. It was just a strange turn of events.

Although from a psychological torment of hate brewing from inside of him. And feeling what she did to herself, and did to them in the solitude of their loneliness brought out the worse in him? Being without one another was already difficult enough to conceive.

But he continued to believe in the unorthodox hope of their love they once shared. The pain could never stop approaching him more, and as real as the word was? He couldn't seem to catch up with her anymore, or the lies she told him, and tried to pimp him out with.

There could be no confusion that could have confused him more than to throw his life away for a woman he loved. When he finally realized unreasonable limits must end.

3

She was unable to take a bad mistake back, and there was no voice coming back to her, without a sound from inside of her. Her love would be explicit to Marshall in the course of a complex way. She made a horrible mistake. He was the best thing in her life she claimed.

She didn't have to play psychology with him, or games about their relationship. Being in love with him was peaceful, as fanning beautiful colors all day long. She was kissing the butterflies of a different color too. He was a magnificent warm lust of seductive poetry in motion to her.

She wholeheartedly loved him. He was a restive sunset shinning into her life, which took more than her breath away. It was the most painful thing she ever had to deal with. She didn't want to give him a picture of happiness, as if it was all an illusion.

She also couldn't explain the water that was left on her brain, which definitely affected her reasoning and logic. Or made her feel pressured to do absolutely nothing about her situation.

It was in the daylight, when her good judgment was lost. When her relationship with him began to wither away gradually, and before she was able to come in from out of the rain and changed things between them.

The years of happiness she enjoyed had succumbed to a memory of a childhood dream—in the sensitivity of her being another woman—and listening to another man talk about his non-impact feelings for her. She was lost in a memory of her lost.

She was unsatisfied with all of the hellos, which were in her life. Why did the midnight whispers of her soul make her cry into her sleep?

It wasn't enough for her, when her dream became as bad as another persons American Dream, which didn't materialize for her but fell apart. How could she explain to him how much she still loved him, when she cheated on him?

She felt like killing herself for the mistakes she made. She couldn't take back how bad she felt, and screwed up after hurting him, she claimed. She didn't understand her reasoning for cheating on him the way she did.

It wasn't about anything that was going on with him, or he did specifically, or didn't do for her. It was about her, or about her being a woman, and she decided not to tell him about anything going on with her?

It didn't make sense to her, after she did what she did. Her whole smile was no longer laughing every day with her emotions again. He on the other hand, didn't want anyone to know his business? How could he explain this to himself or anyone else? He wanted to keep this catastrophe, which happened between them in control.

Or hope that the present day would disappear. Since it was her intention not to talk to him about this face to face? It was another thing that didn't make any sense about her.

She could tell him details about her personal secrets, but she couldn't tell him about how she lost her mind? And did what she did to bring their relationship and marriage to an end.

No one is going to tell him that this is a woman's prerogative. Life without her was like trying to maintain a good sense of humor, when it was killing him inside.

Even though he knew it was going to hurt like hell, when this was happening. There really wasn't shit to laugh about. When you are getting your heart handed to you, and you have no reason why she pulled it out in the first place?

He couldn't forget about enjoying the pastimes memories of her. He couldn't stop thinking about her before he thought about himself, and it wasn't getting better. They were two people who were buried into each other's collective dust once.

Like he tried rolling around in her madness for a while, after he applied stitches to his heart to keep it from coming apart, which was damn near impossible? She didn't seem to care anymore, as far as whether his heart was repaired, or remained with a hole in.

She was like a person standing behind him, with corroded eyes. Who didn't care about her own business any more. She didn't realize this was like a slow death she was putting them through. She was either killing their hearts together, or she was being murdered by their hearts not being together?

Either way, he didn't want to be a fool in the name of her salvation? They were definitely dead. He didn't know what else to do. He was lost with her in his life now.

Everyone else they knew, and didn't know admired them. They were jealous and envied the relationship and marriage they had, but also had the nerve to tell them. There was always someone else there making a pitch. Someone else who wanted her, or someone who wanted to sleep with him.

He thought about it over and over. He had to let her go for good, with all that had happened between them didn't make a difference. When he first discovered her cheating and betrayal. He knew then it was over between them. It was something he couldn't forget or accept.

It's like someone you love trying to do a number on you. The trust and the commitment to each other is the essence in any relationship, and obviously those elements were no longer there as far as he was concerned.

There could be no more marriage, if she was going to be with another man behind his back. Like it was something being done all out of spite, it was nonsense to him. She and him were more than a spiritual treasure to each other, he thought.

No one tried to help them when they saw the changes in them, and the fact they were sacrificing something different between them wasn't a concern for anyone. It was as if they wanted them to fail, plain and simple. Why should they be happy?

They had a real tenderness between them. He thought if he could step over her body in his mind; then anything could be forgiven. But there wasn't enough satisfaction or revenge in that for him.

It's like something he once read and it said, "Whenever you give someone unconditional love, and that love is betrayed, then the damage can never be repaired."

4

SHE IS NO LONGER SEEING the man she was involved with. But she is cutting the ribbon with someone else? He had given the best he could. It was as if she went off the deep end, and was addicted to some different kind of stuff.

It didn't feel right, when there was nowhere for him to run, or hide from her, which was a large part of the problem. Just dealing with everything you give away to someone else emotionally, and everything that you are and are frightened of?

Hoping, someone you loved didn't put your exposed emotions all out there, and leave them out there to show how unimportant you really are to them. Since someone else gave them the best advice about moving on without each other, and basically all it is, is a crock?

He could only imagined, if he could squeeze a devastating little woman from out of a bottle. So she could show him where to put his ideas someplace else? Or she could make it all go away, and wipe away his memory of the whole event.

If he could only do this with a wish, it would offer him another peace of mind. So she could move voluntarily into the night alone without him. But she would come back from time to time to visit him for another night of familiar history between them.

It was her mistake well, if she woke up in the morning to table-talk abuse from him, she imagined. Nor did she feel the intimacy in her personality, and because of all the emotions she didn't have any more. She could see a widespread of smoke with words unspoken from the ashes.

It was strange to him how she could be a rewarding familiar kiss at times, which led to her wetness for him. And her polite anger that is unspoken, and foreign to a dear result from her view of love. Whether it is him or any other man for that matter?

Who could put his measly hands on an old woman's behind, as it becomes genetically painful after hesitating for a while, before they really do it. She could have figured out another way to make someone else cry for her mistakes.

He couldn't love her by her new index any more, or who she had become. Nothing more could be pointed out by the truth. His imagination caused him to wish he could fill her glass up with holy water, because clear water definitely wasn't working.

It would be an undertaking to snap her out of this emotional turmoil. So she could stop speaking hypocritically to herself. There was nothing to laugh about inside. He loved her, as painful as it was to admit, and feel after their disaster.

But looking at her sometimes, like she was a different day, with a sunset for a smile, when she was that good with it. He would ask her to come here, so they could negotiate together. He would ask her to come here and lie down beside him.

So she could forget about those exasperating moments of her day, which was worse than a black cat crossing her path more than once in a day. She was superstitious as hell too?

But on occasion, she would still get together with him for a night of prevailing sex, which was something that was messing up the mix for them, also. He shouldn't have been doing it with her, but his excuse was that he was still coming down off his high with her.

He wasn't sure what her excuse was for doing it. All he knew is that his impeccable head was tired, and her gorgeous breast weren't quite fully stimulated.

He wondered how this other guy would feel, if he knew she was still coming to see him. Like how he knew after she made love to him. She would be going back to him. For some reason it didn't faze him anymore based on what he felt, but he knew it was still wrong between them.

It wasn't really good for any one of them to continue with this? Since she wouldn't work out her problems with him, or talk to him about it. Like when she moved out just before he discovered she was having an affair with someone else.

They went through changes for a year, and what she was saying to him about the image of her love being a false issue? It was a selected type of life, located in a negative picture. Where the rebirth of her feelings had become unexplained things.

The unfamiliar looks which continued to come from her? Which surrendered her love as terminal in their relationship, and to be shown as succumbed punishment for her or him.

The danger was breeding from within them, not knowing if it will be there for them to co-habitat again? Consequently, not on this earth, but he knew he should never say never just from experience.

He knew there will be other men in her life, without a heart of love for her to cover up their repulsive behavior, with eyes of prey from someone else wanting her. A reason for his thoughts to be unnamed in his mind. If he were to let it rise defensively, let it fall easily from his concern, and let it say what it wants to say.

A vague mystery of ill-advised lies, it was also bad when she poured her own boric acid into the mix. He dreamt about uncomfortably walking into a symbolic night on the streets with her.

He could see himself, as a dead man not returning to life. He could see a stranger who wasn't her, and appearing out of nowhere, cursing the night birds appearing in her sight. Now that their relationship has disappeared.

Even the lack of communication about things between them was hidden behind fears of hers. The sweet and bitter emotions of romance from their relationship were now considered a bitch in disguise.

Being without her was also like—kissing her frantically for her advice on any given day. Also the sun in the sky was losing its fulfillment to him.

Pieces of his mind were all laid out on a mimic table with nothing to say. So he could sit down all alone, and take a walk and think about having sex with his next door neighbor. He needed to mead with her regardless of their separation.

Just like many beautiful things have been in as much damned. When different things were born from old things. And now, you have a problem talking about it with this person, all of a sudden?

5

MARSHALL WANTED TO KICK SOMETHING, or violate something in order to deal with the uncertainty of things. He thought about everyone else in his dreams who had someplace else to go. Or if he was expecting a visit from a fat, funny little angel. Who was caught kissing in heaven, and fooling around without permission from you know who?

Who became another person's fool, as he thought about maybe another? Who was standing a long side a mysterious shadow, which couldn't be seen or heard of?

She continued to escape him for a different kind of intimacy in her heart. He didn't stop liking or loving her, in the early morning view of another person being ridiculed.

She was once the personal essence of his enjoyment, but on the same track of disappointment. Her memory didn't seem to remember the real picture that wasn't there for them. His eyes were closed, and he couldn't see through her eyelids.

He could no longer feel her at random, or the nipples of her breast rippling through his mind. When she would lay her nude body on top of his back and fall a sleep? Life never seems to come out of fairness when you are searching for sincerity to ask about pleasure or please?

Then they came all this way to struggle without success. Then superstition is better than the sun at early morning light, and her thoughts disappeared in reality which he missed. She was no longer close to his emotions the way she once was.

He could see hate exercising a terrible description in him. There was only one kind of conversation between them now. Her talk was inferior pertaining to the side effects she left him with. His thoughts remembered when it came to this subject? It will be a long life without her.

With caution, he tried again and again before he fell hard, and saw the pain coming back to him. He didn't deal with this situation well. Personally his hurt and pain was about anger. It wasn't about lost or being so lost without her.

She took away all the rationality of their relationship and marriage, when she had a melt down on herself. And all he wanted to know was why? It pissed him off that she couldn't offer him an answer to something, and as a result, he still didn't deal with his composure well.

When he and her had separated, it was good that they were good to one another. It's not like they didn't disagree about a lot either? He still didn't understand what was all the betrayal about?

If she wanted to go and leave and communicate, or interact with another species from out of space? All she had to do was let him know this is what she wanted to do.

And if it was without him, then no problem. She knew that he wouldn't stand in her way. If she ever wanted to do anything with or without him? Because he always encouraged her to do what she wanted to do.

She also understood he would do anything he could to help her. He understood what it was about concerning her feelings, but it didn't mean he agreed with her. It was simple, why screw over someone when someone is not trying to screw over you?

All she had to do was say she didn't want to be together any more. She knew she could talk to him about anything, but he guess he was wrong. This could have made a lot more sense, than what she put them through, and for what, to give someone else another impression of the truth or a lie about them?

Because all her deception didn't accomplish one constructive thing? People do separate for good reason, as well as bad reasons quite frequently.

But all she was saying was check this out with no warning or explanation? Then he was saying—yeah right! I don't think so, not down this river?

Hoping to hinder her this time before it repeats itself again. He was the outside man in her life. He will give it to her, like she gave it to him for one good last emotion between them.

When you spoil a woman you love because of love. How much of your love is taken for granted, because of what she expects from you always? And not realizing you are doing everything to please her, even when you are not being pleased in return as a result of expectations.

When there is no morsel of grief, or innocence to tame the hope to do her better, than wearing a perfect nose job to cover up the truth in their relationship.

If he didn't fight back for her with roses from sage dirt, then there would be no more confident smiles to give out for love, which would cry out in hell without a fucking pack of Band-Aids.

She would be off in her premium, just walking away and saying the hell with it? Just like whatever she felt was on her mind, floating around free with no time to be real anymore. It became about her selfishness, or her everyday goal of self-destructive behavior, and how she was punishing herself for her mistakes and convictions.

He guessed he was supposed to feel bad for her and take her back. Someone she didn't know or recognized anymore. The shame was still in her game. Her eyes were no longer in public for him, if they were seen together.

He noticed the problems in her behavior, like surfing through the internet for a serial killer. Or searching for the truth when it is bad, and lasted, then they were interrupted. Since what, save what, neither one of them would come back from this mistake in a past reality, he thought.

They were affected by it personally. Like they were thieves with more hidden alibis. He thought about being around for the way this went down. When love doesn't love you or anyone else back for that matter, y' know?

One day he remembered. He took a gift from her soft hands, and he wanted to kiss her behind on both sides of her cheek. Yesterday and today would never come together, when he needed it to be for some misunderstandings between them.

She took the gift back from him, and walked away to show him the back of her behind politely. He understood then, he was no smarter for whatever he went down to kiss her behind for his taste of choice.

Often with confident people falling down on their way up, you want them to blame the wrong person in life. He wanted her help to open his eye, as to where the pleasure was going to come from. It wasn't her problem anymore.

6

SHE KNEW HE COULD NO longer feel her nude body in the way they used to touch each other. He guess she would smile and laugh with him in a rainbow of no justice now? And by day dreaming about his connection to be with her, after ten years have disappeared with every passing day?

The low self-esteem he had about this wasn't covered. He knew people took chances by opening up a big box they knew nothing about. When you know it is a mystery within it-self, but wall-la!

It captivates you with a wonderful moment. When you recall you were in a beautiful relationship, and happy for over a long period of time. Then out of nowhere, and with no possible warning.

Something incredibly horrible happens to the person you love, they changed—and there is never an explanation offered—as to why something like this would happen to her, which drove him crazy.

What can you do, when your love means nothing for the beginning of another day, or the light in the morning sky? Like when you walk onto hasty grass to avoid the shit, which was left there by someone else for you to step in?

Since they didn't pick up after their dog? But will complain about the person who left a load in front of their house, and didn't pick it up?

Or if you tell a bad joke which feels better than an irritating rub down. Or given to you by the person you made love to the night before?

He wanted to make love to her every day they were apart in the beginning, rather than have sex with someone else. Wishing it wouldn't take away from his tunnel vision, and the person he loved every day he slept without. A false sense of hope, and what could he celebrate about?

He was unsure about what to do for his meaning of this? When he couldn't seem to find a way to eliminate his emotions for this person, after the pain and suffering he felt from her. He expected all the irrelevant stuff to roll off of him into a thousand pieces and go someplace else.

His feelings didn't make him feel subpar. He gave a precious gift away with answers which were prejudice, and judgmental by other people.

Now his relationship and marriage with her had taken a voyage to hell. Just like anyone's relationship had been when they were once in love with someone.

It's a tough hit to take in the last minute of your emotions. When their lives were no longer shared together. When the present becomes your past, and your past becomes your present, there are no prophets who will tell you, how to understand the regal of a woman.

Or show him how her love may lead him to a closed door, and never show him away through it either.

He thought if she continued to wait for time, it's what she did now. She couldn't see it, nor will she be able to touch it. The patience of time can be unpleasant as a result for her. Perhaps there were times when she didn't give a damn.

She had already been through enough. She failed to accept that time was passing her by for keeping secrets, which she didn't need to do, but did anyway.

So he guessed the skeletons in her closet were unholy. Or hanging onto a shoestring to try and change the world. In her eyes it wasn't good enough for her. The problem started from all the stuff, which was piling up in her. It became her against time.

She knew she didn't have a chance in hell, but she was there for the good on-going flight in life, except when it came to their relationship? Maybe it was her intention to play it out this way?

But someone else should have told her, what no one else didn't tell him. That time would be the reason for everything as philosophical, as her moonlighting as a typical ass for a mistake she made with him, her man, her husband.

What did this mean for them? Other than one of them will be the first to act against each other? This happens all the time. Now that the situation has changed between them, and the way they see each other.

Perhaps for him, an anonymous child won't hurt his mother anymore, after everything she has gone through in life for him. Or as a tribute for his respect to show more love for her.

Or perhaps for Jade, a smart-minded woman of celibacy will no longer be dishonest between her legs, while releasing on a man for the sake of it. But if you were to ask her now, is there really a cure for the heart when it has a whole in it?

Does she feel a loss of time? Is she alone without him in her heart too? No matter how much someone loves you, or how much you love someone. Neither one of you truly knows, how each other feels about each other, until time accumulates and then you are surprised, how you feel about each other.

But at some point and time, or from some event you will see what sets you apart from each other? This is coming as a real surprise to you. Or you already knew in advance by the sound of the day.

Does she feel her pain deeper inside than the hurt she caused? Is she feeling a premature conception of something which had abandoned her? Or is she lost without a forbidden taste, which is left in your mouth?

When she is assisting her need to continue biting on something, which doesn't exist between you and her anymore.

7

MARSHALL DECIDED THAT SINCE HE was in the neighborhood. He would stop by and see a friend of his, who lives in Parkchester. He couldn't help but think about how Linda, and Jason met. They met online from their social media contacts. Since this is the new wave of the future in relationships, quick, fast, and ready.

They managed to get together and hook-up with one another. But it was difficult for him to understand why they would be together. Marshall met Linda through some people he hung out with, and they introduced them.

Linda and him kept in contact and became close friends. They were there for each other. She was attracted to Marshall, but he was involved with someone at the time. She moved on to pursue other possibilities.

Eventually she met and hooked up with Jason, after their online confrontation like coffee and donuts. As always the beginning is the thriving thrust to each other's excitement. Like suddenly she was Miss Baby Ruth, and he was Mr. Good-bar.

But after two years, the good, bad and the ugly had surfaced. Like everyone was becoming an American runner. It's time to get away from all of this. Now that they saw each other for who they really were, and no one is perpetrating to be someone else anymore.

When Marshall approached the front door of Linda's apartment, you could hear a loud commotion, like an unorganized Rapp concert with uncontrollable noise. He tried ringing the bell first, and then he began knocking.

He didn't want to knock any harder, because he didn't want to add to the noise coming from the apartment. Then a noisy neighbor opened up their door and shook their head.

Suddenly the door opened, and Linda's young daughter came from behind the door, with tears in her eyes. He could hear the commotion loud and clear. Her daughter reached out, and said that mommy and Jason are at it again.

Marshall took her hand and escorted her to the kitchen, and asked her to stay there. He immediately ran to the bedroom where all the commotion was coming from.

He saw Jason on top of Linda, with one hand around her neck applying pressure, and the other hand was holding her other hand, with a large knife in it that was attempting to stab him. She was also swinging and attempting to punch him with her other hand. But he kept ducking and dodging to avoid the impact coming at him.

"What the hell is going on with you two? Do you realize that your daughter is in the kitchen afraid and crying, while you are in here trying to kill each other."

"Marshall, tell this son of a bitch to get up off of me. Or I will kick him so hard, where the sun doesn't shine?"

"You tell her to drop that knife first. Or I will knock the hell out of her."

Marshall couldn't believe what he was seeing or hearing. He approached them, and asked Linda to release the knife to him, she did. He asked Jason to removed his hand from around her neck, and he did. He leaned back and got up off of her, and backed up slowly.

Linda pulled her dress down, because she was exposed from wrestling and kicking at Jason. She was extremely cute, with an awesome body. She stood up, and looked directly at him.

"You get your stuff, and get the hell out of here now, before I called the police on your sorry ass."

"Go ahead and call the police. I am not going anywhere. And I will tell them, how you tried to stab me with a butcher knife. Let's not forget that your daughter is a witness to you attacking me. All I was trying to do was defend myself."

Linda immediately charged at him, but not before Marshall stepped in between her and Jason before she could get to him. Jason backed away.

"You, low life. You slapped me first. Don't you ever put your hands on me again!" she yelled.

"Jason, will you leave the room, so I can talk to Linda."

He left and Marshall closed the door to the bedroom. She rushed into his arms and began crying. He never saw her in this type of condition. He basically thought of Linda as mature, strong, and a responsible person.

He was surprised to see her in this vulnerable and angry state. He recalled how correct she was when they needed each other to talk to at times. This is why they were there for one another, because of their reliability and comfort toward each other.

He sat her on the edge of the bed. He got her to stop crying, so she could explain all of this craziness he witnessed.

"Linda, what happened?"

"What do you want me to tell you? That I made a mistake getting together with this asshole. That I let him into my house whole and introduced him to my kids, and tried to share my life with him. Then I let him move in, and began playing house with this knucklehead?

"All that I tried to do for him, and help him better himself as a man? That I tried to put up with his bullshit for two years. Oh, Marshall, please slap me silly. So I can wake up from this nightmare?

"I tried to care for him, even with all of his excess baggage, and he wants to act like he knows everything, but without no meaning.

"His attitude about a lot of things is really a shame. I didn't do anything to him, before I met him. But I seem to be part of some worldwide conspiracy put together by all women."

"Well, what the hell does that mean?"

"Why don't you take him out of here, and go someplace, and talk to him. I think you will see what I am talking about? I need to be by myself. I need to cool off, and attend to my daughter, before she becomes afraid anymore for her mother."

Marshall decided that he would do this for Linda. He really cared about her and what happens to her. She was a good person to him and in his life. She assured him that she would be okay, if he returned with Jason from their break.

After this long and drawn-out conversation that Marshall had with Linda, and Jason separately. She revealed that she loved him, and wanted to be with him.

Jason wanted to know, why do women always have to be a bitch about things? He said, that it was hard to meet a woman in New York, who doesn't have children. This is one of the reasons he wanted to relocate somewhere else. In his travels to other states and cities, the percentage of women who have children is not the same, like it is here in New York.

"But what does that have to do with anything? That's life, so what else is new," asked Marshall.

"Women are more into their careers, or well into supporting themselves, and are more independent than the women here." He continued to air out his frustration about always having to contribute to, or supporting some woman and her children.

Marshall became highly aggravated with Jason, as his points of views were beyond logical. As if he knew what the hell he was talking about? Where was he coming from with all of this stuff—again—as if it were that simple to determine about woman. If it was, then why were we having a conversation to determine the rationality of his behavior for losing it over a woman?

Because all women wanted to do was use him for his money?

"Wow, I didn't know that Jason had all of this kind of money? Considering the fact, that he was unemployed a year ago, and didn't have a pot to piss in. And not to mention, where was all the gold diggers coming from? I guess out of nowhere, or out of thin air?"

Right, they didn't care about him or love him, but they always wanted him to be there for them and their children. He did admit that he didn't understand women anyway.

"Who the hell does, if you're a man?"

But they have a kid with some guy, and then they break up. She moves on with someone else, and if the kid or her needs something. She expects him to provide it for them, since he is with her. Now that she is giving him all of her sex.

But in reality, she doesn't do a damn thing for him, or give him anything except for her sex. Marshall continued to shake his head because he knew that Jason's mother or sister had to school him better than a coconut without the oil?

But in the meantime, the child's father gets away with murder, because he abandons her and his child, and offers the child no moral support or financial support. But does she take him to court so he can support his child. No, she doesn't. Whether he wants to be in the child's life or not? Marshall wondered at this point, did this man ever have children in his life?

Then she moves on to the next guy, hoping that he will pick up the slack for her and her children. Like the last woman he claimed to be involved with. She told him flat out, that she wouldn't be involved with someone, who wasn't going to help support her and her children.

Because so many women he met had this mentality, but what about his mentality?

"If I was a woman I would walk the other way, than ride a moment alone with him in hell. And after all of this, he still gets involved with her anyway, and it eventually turned out to be a disaster. All he got out of it was some sex, and it wasn't that good or that much."

She was always tired from dealing with her children. So he put the brakes on and decided to move on. But he had to do the same thing with this other woman he met, because she had too many issues with him.

8

But with Linda, she was different. He really loves her. However, she can be a little too controlling for him. He said, that he is a man, and doesn't need a woman to tell him what to do? She needs to stay in her place, and let him call the shots. This had nothing to do with her children, but as far as him and her were concerned. He thinks he knows whats best for them.

And this is why they got into big disagreements, and then it escalated into fights. Then he wanted her to shut up, and she continued with her mouth. Then one thing lead to another, because she always had an opinion. He got tired of her mouth and opinions.

Marshall could see that Jason was a very complicated person, with a ton of personal issues of his own. And refused to acknowledge this at all. Don't you just love people like this? He had a way of not clearly seeing things for the way they really were, while the content in his demeanor was exactly what so many other people did, and he blames everyone else for their short comings in his life.

Marshall realized that if he wasn't involved with someone at the time. He probably would have gotten involved with Linda. Regardless of the fact she had two children. He considered her to be a fascinating person.

He knew for a fact when they first met, she was real. He hadn't met anyone like her in a long time. She was the type of woman who did for her man, and was there for him by sticking by him. She also didn't tolerate any bullshit being served.

She worked hard. She put herself through college and was married before her husband devoiced her with two children, a boy and a girl. She got a job with an advertising company and moved up. She made good money, and put her children through private school. She had a beautiful son and daughter. They were good kids.

This is why Marshall couldn't understand Jason and his issues. It's your choice, whether you want to get involved with a woman who has children or not. But you don't blame her or criticize her because she has children, without asking yourself? Why is the father always doing a disappearing act, when she didn't create those children by herself.

Linda didn't want any man she was involved with to have anything to do with her children. She exclusively made it clear to them, that this was between her and their father. They only thing that you had to be concerned about was your relationship with her.

When Jason first became involved with Linda. He was in between jobs, but she didn't hold that against him. She was there for him in any way that she could be. She gave him money for transportation to seek employment. She took him out to various places and provided for him. She knew it would be a struggle for him at the time, but she didn't complain.

She felt he appeared to be a nice guy, and was down on his luck. It was just a matter of time before he would experience a big changed. So for a while they were all doing well together. They became closer, and more involved. Then it happened, he got a job and everything changed. He was a Retail Mortage Banker, which was his back ground. He was a different person with a different view point. He was working and making money. Obviously, Linda had a difficult time trying to understand this now.

He thought it was his position to tell her, and her children what they were going to do. He thought that he was calling the shots. But not in this lifetime, especially where Linda was concern. She instructed him to take that crap someplace else, because his money wasn't dictating or doing anything here.

And over a period of time, he continued to persist with his superior attitude and such—which continued with repeated disagreements and arguments about their relationship and life style together. Now it had gone even further with fighting in the relationship. This was the first physical confrontation they had together. Prior to this it was simply emotional and verbal.

If there was one thing Jason failed to realized about Linda, she didn't need him. She already made more money than he did. She owned her own co-op. She had her own transportation. She was putting two kids through private school.

So she didn't need him for anything except companionship in a relationship, if he could handle this. And apparently he couldn't. Why would he think this way about women, because of his past with certain women, which was his choice.

When you think of all the women out there, that are single parents and raising children by themselves. But who are dealing with all of these issues by themselves and working to provide for them and their children. When they continue to face tremendous challenges on their own.

What is it that Jason was thinking they are asking for? You find that a lot of women out here, are women who are in these situations. They can be some of the best woman to get involved with, because they are caring, loving, strong, and giving women.

Who are doing their best with no help from anyone else, and really don't ask or want very much from you except for you to be real with them. It may vary though depending on who you are dealing with. But many of these women have more character than single woman do. Who can be quite lazy in a relationship, because they feel they deserve everything.

It would be nice, if they could find a man who would give them the moral support, and be there for them in their relationship so they can grow, and make something out of nothing, while helping many innocence children to grown, and become productive people in society.

Rather than have some man come along and use them for sex, or whatever he doesn't want to offer in a relationship. Because he feels he is the shit in her life, while he is not offering anything in the process to be the real shit.

Marshall felt that there had to be something else going on with Jason, and his point of views. He had some valid points, but not enough to provide about where he was coming from. Or what he was doing in his relationship with Linda and her children.

After Marshall took Jason to a restaurant, where they could have something to eat, and talk about what transpired. He was confident that he was going to behave himself with Linda, and see if they could resolve their immediate issues and move on with their relationship.

But this would be a big if, since he didn't know how she felt, after this last fight that they had. Or would she forgive him, and let him stay in her life.

Marshall and Jason returned to Linda's apartment. Where everything appeared to be fine. Her son was home and her daughter was in their room with each other. They came out to give Marshall a hug, and to say hello. They also spoke to Jason.

Marshall went into the bedroom to see Linda, and speak with her before he left. He closed the door. Jason remained in the living room with the children talking. She looked revived and breathtaking.

"Are you okay?"

"I'll be fine, Marshall. I was just doing some thinking about everything. After I sort somethings out. There will be some changes made for me and the children."

"I don't know what to say?"

"There is nothing to say. I just wanted to thank you for being there for me, like always."

Linda approached Marshall and pressed her body up against his, while she hugged him. He embraced her too. She looked up and kissed him passionately.

After they kissed, he looked directly into Linda's eyes, and knew that something was about to happen between Jason and her he couldn't explain.

"Marshall, go home, and get some rest. You no longer have to be my agent of shield. Me and the children are good. If I need anything I know where to reach you."

"Okay, Linda. I'll say goodbye to everyone. Call me, if anything arises."

"I will."

Marshall left. He wondered what would happen now. He recalled that distinctive look in her eyes, where she said nothing, but it means everything.

He was surprised after a few months went by, and he didn't hear anything from her. He didn't know what to really think. But he thought they were still together, since a mutual friend saw them with each other recently.

Then the following week, Marshall received a call from someone he knew, that also knew Linda and Jason to tell him about a story in the newspaper that involved Jason.

It turns out that he was involved with this woman, and her man was following them to a Hotel. He located them and knocked on the door pretending to be room service, and she open the door in her bra and panties.

She was shocked and he pushed his way in, and removed a gun from his coat. Jason was in the bed when he shot him twice, and then he shoot the woman. After he finished, he sat down in a chair and chilled, with their bodies in the room until the police arrived.

Marshall decided to give Linda a call, but she was rather busy at the moment, and explained that if he had some free time. They could get together tomorrow and talk. He agreed.

Wednesday evening came, and he arrived at her apartment at 7:30 p.m. She greeted him with a big smile and hug, as he replied with the same. Her children were hanging out with their friends and were supposed to be going to the movies. So they were alone with each other's company.

9

LINDA HAD PREPARED A LIGHT dinner for them to munch on, with a nice bottle of wine in the kitchen. She also enjoyed classical music as much as Marshall did, which was being generated throughout the apartment.

She joked about how her children always got on her about upgrading her taste in music. But like she told them, that whatever they listened to wasn't real music, and that they had no idea? She smiled, and he smiled back at her because he agreed.

After a present update about themselves and their week. They completed their meal. It was light, good, and tasty. The wine was excellent.

Linda escorted them to the living room, where they could relax and be more comfortable, while they had more wine and began their conversation.

"The reason I called you is because I guess you heard about Jason?"

"Marshall at this point, I am sure everybody in the world has heard about Jason."

"So how do you feel?"

"I'm glad I ended our relationship when I did, and for some reason I'm not surprised, and nor are my children. We always had this underlining feeling about him, and where he was coming from.

"But what I want to tell you is, the article in the newspaper wasn't the entire story behind his situation.

"Jason was deceiving and lying to everyone. I don't know what kind of game he was playing with himself. But he was also trying to mess up other people's life in the process. If you ask me, he needed some therapy for himself and his problems.

"I know that you thought that I was still seeing him. When he returned with you that night we had the fight. I had a talk with him, and asked him to leave.

"I could no longer continue our relationship under the circumstances, and thought that it would be best if he left within the week. Thank god, he left at the end of the week. He didn't give me any problems.

"Although if he had, I was prepared with a backup plan. An associate of mine I work with has a friend, who is a lawyer and I met with him. He drew up some papers for me to sign.

"So if Jason wanted to act stupid or be dumb about the whole situation, and give me a problem. Then I would have put his ass in a sling. I had my daughter take pictures of me and the results of the fight that night, which I submitted to the lawyer."

Apparently, Linda hadn't seen Jason for months, since their break up. But a month ago, she was coming out of the supermarket when this woman approached her, and introduced herself. She recalled seeing her and Jason together a few times, and with her children, and thought that he had a new family.

She didn't quite understand where the woman was coming from. So the woman offered her cell phone number, and asked her to call her when she had a chance. She would explain a lot to her about Jason, that she thought that she would like to know. Whether she was still seeing him or not. It would be worth her while.

Linda decided to take the woman up on her offer and give her a call one evening. She had nothing to lose. But after the woman told her, that she was an ex-girlfriend of Jason. Linda didn't understand what this had to do with her?

She decided to permit her to continue, and suddenly it all became clear. The woman had been seeing him for a few years and he was living with her. Then he began giving her a lot of excuses, and wasn't coming home on a regular basis anymore. Then she hardly ever saw him.

Finally she discovered that he had got married to some other woman, while he was supposed to be living with her. But never decided to tell her about his new marriage. There was very little she could do. Since he was married to this other woman. Now that all of her ties with him had been broken a while ago. But she still wanted to kill the prick till this day.

The real issue for Linda was when she told her, that he was still married to his wife when he was seeing her, and he has another family with her. They have three children together. So this is why she was surprised to see Jason and Linda together.

Jason and his wife were separated because she cheated on him with a married man. He went through some changes and lost his job over it. Then he began seeing Linda, and was living in a rooming house, and was paying rent every week with money he still had.

But that was a lie according to the woman. She knew Jason's sister. He was living in his sister's house and paying no rent. His mother past away and left the house to his sister, along with an insurance policy.

She left the house to his sister, because she was smarter, and more responsible with affairs and money. She also left Jason twenty-five thousand dollars from her insurance policy.

Now this is what she really wanted Linda to know about good old Jason, and the story from the newspaper that didn't have the full story about him. The woman he was shot with was his wife. After they were separated, they decided to get back together a year ago. When he got a job and started working again.

He had been with her ever since. But she was still seeing the other man who was married, that she cheated on him with. She never told the married man, that she was still seeing, that she and her husband decided to get back together. Apparently, for whatever reason he became suspicious of her, and began spying on her.

This man continued to tell Jason's wife, that he was going to leave his wife and be with her, but she had other plans of her own where he was concerned. She obviously was working them both, and nothing worked out for anyone, except tragedy and despite everyone involved. He was the man who showed up at their hotel room and shot them both.

Linda considered herself fortunate to have ended it when she did for her and her children. She was more concerned for them, and if they had been caught in the cross fire of all of Jason mess. This would have driven her crazy.

Now certain things where beginning to make sense, and fall into place about Jason. How he was one person when he didn't have a job, and when he got a job how different he became. He was trying to control them. So he could keep control of the situation, before it all exploded in his face, or he couldn't do anything about it.

And how things really only began to change within the last six months of their relationship, with his new demands and character assassination for his new life. *Wow*, she thought. What a real flake and SOB he was.

All the time Linda was seeing and trying to make sense of something with him. He was married and living with his wife and family, while he was seeing her. When his wife was cheating on him, and now, him and his wife are dead for cheating on each other.

"I knew when I looked in your eyes that night, that something was going to change in your relationship with him. I am happy to see that no harm had come to you or the children."

"Again, I just want to thank you for being there, Marshall."

"No, problem." They embraced each other and said their goodbyes.

When Marshall left to enter his car, he couldn't believe what Linda had told him about Jason and his escapades.

"Wow, what was he doing in another life?" He recalled when he was dating this older woman, when he was much younger. He made some mistakes in their relationship, which he had admitted to her openly. That he had faults just like anyone else did, and that he wasn't perfect.

She was more than polite and respectful to explain that he shouldn't worry about it too much because there were two kinds of faults that people basically suffering from. The faults that he had were faults that she, or anyone else could dealing with, handle, and work with.

But the other types of faults are called fucked-up faults that people have. These are the type that she, or other people can't deal with, handle, or work with. Because they have a serious problem within themselves. The kind of problem they need to get professional help with.

Marshall saw that Jason was seriously one of those people who had fucked-up faults, after what happened to him and his wife being shot like that? He thought about their three children being left along without a mother or a father.

Linda couldn't help but think about him with desire in her heart after he left. She realized that the situation was ideal for them to make love, before they departed from each other. But also realizing that she didn't want to take advantage of the situation or Marshall.

She understood how brokenhearted he was about what happened to him and Jade, and what his marriage meant to him. But she wasn't going to deny how much she wanted him. Although she wanted him to be happy more, and if there was a chance that Jade and him could resolved their issues in their relationship. Then so be it, he deserved that opportunity. She didn't want to come between this.

Marshall thought about how beautiful Linda really was to him, and also realized that he just dodge a bullet. He could see that Linda wanted him, and a part of him may have wanted her. He was relieved that nothing happened, because he knew that neither one of them didn't want to complicate anything for each other right now, with the changes that they were going through separately.

He wished that he could understand why is it, that everyone who wants to be in love, and wants to have a relationship with someone. But when they are in love with someone, and have a relationship with someone. Then they want to be in love with someone else, or have a relationship with someone else? It's enough to blow your own brain out over. When it comes to love, we should simply make more sense.

10

SHE IS STUNNING. SHE HAS a small nose with small lips. Rosy distinctive, but arrogant facial cheeks and large baby brown embellished eyes. Her hair is thick, loose at the top. It is styled in curl layers all the way passed her shoulders, as a brunette. But cute as a button.

She is five-ten, and weighs 130 pounds. She has a gorgeous body with a cute walk. She walks pigeon-toed, slightly bow-legged, and stands back on her hind legs being double jointed and all.

She speaks with flair and flavor. People like the way she talks. She has a southern accent. If you see her, you just say to yourself, if you're a man. Damn! She is hot with heat.

A lot of men don't seem to care much for a woman with a lot of behind, but when it has its place in other women—then it's appealing. But either way, Olivia has a fabulous behind like that? It is all round and curvaceous, firm, but solid, not sponged. Not overwhelming, like this wasn't the only thing she had going for herself, but just nice.

She is a beautiful woman with an awesome personality he discovered. Surprisingly, she is in bed with him this morning.

His mind drifted briefly, as he thought about how he used to run his fingers through Jade's full thick hair. He would kiss on her, and she would wake up with a smile on her face.

She would tickle him in return, and jump on top of him with affection. There was no better day than to wake up to her, and her playful self in the morning. When he missed her like this? It's like being out of control all the time.

It was one of those things that happened between Olivia and him. They began sleeping with each other. It was the first real step he took outside of the box.

Olivia was the first woman he had seen, and had been with since he separated from Jade. Olivia and him were also in the mix concerning their situations. She was married.

It was over a year ago, Jade began her rampage. But he was celibate for all this time. Desperately trying to do anything he could to handle or maintain their marriage. Especially when he didn't know what was going on with her.

While noticing she was desperately trying to do everything she could to throw their marriage away. She went off into another direction without him. Why do all of this, if she didn't want to ask for a divorce?

It is the third time Olivia and him have been together, and it continues to get better without hidden boundaries.

She is bright, open, direct, and straight up. You know the type, put up or shut up? There is no doubt, she could tactfully handle anything. She is clever with her emotions. She doesn't seem to waste them on trivia.

"Good morning, sleepyhead?"

"Hey there yourself, you early morn' in, rooster," said Olivia.

He laughed because of her accent. Olivia can be a funny person, because of the way she says things. He leaned over to kiss her, the woman can kiss. Something he enjoyed.

It was difficult to control his temptation of lust for Olivia. It was obvious she was well secured within her own sexuality as a woman. This is why the love making was so good on both their parts, and with natural effort.

With Jade it was something the two of them developed between each other over a period of time, and from there it became awesome. Like a physical connection made after between them.

Olivia had this alluring way about her, after being around her enough. He wanted her in the worse way. When he first met her, he was horny as a Jaybird, with a Broke-Dick-Dog for a friend.

But in spite of Olivia's attraction and physical presences. She is a woman with good qualities of interest in her as a person. Whether it mattered to anyone else or not, it made a difference to him? It didn't change anything, because of her involvement with him and her infidelity toward her husband.

It was a separate issue concerning him. He asked Olivia to excuse him. He wanted to prepare breakfast for her. She tried to modify her excitement. She didn't believe someone was getting up in the morning to really serve her breakfast.

The last person who did this for her was her mother. When she was commuting back and forth to college. Her mother brought her first car, which was a used one. She passed away several years ago. Her mother was someone special to her.

Olivia believed her personal growth as a woman was her mother's attained influence on her, and not from life's marginal inappropriate experiences. She missed her mother more than Candy-Peppers, which no one would try?

11

SINCE THEN, SHE HAD SETTLED for a cup of coffee for breakfast. She wasn't a big eater, but she enjoyed a good home cooked meal and would eat plenty. She wasn't accustomed to dinning out a lot, or going out to restaurants, and there were many to choose from in New York, she thought.

There was no comparison if you were a person from the South, and she was a person from the South. She was more than delighted Marshall was willing to make this kind of effort for her.

Olivia followed him. He entered the kitchen. He turned around to face her in his face. She was standing there nude looking cute and tantalizing, with all of her feminine beauty exposed to him. Their eyes were gazed at each other, as she approached him and loosened his robe.

Slowly she entered his space. She placed both of her arms around his waist. He did the same to her. His arms and robe covered up her body. They pressed themselves tightly against each other.

Olivia raised her head up from off of his chest, and looked at him. She kissed him hard, while standing on her tip-toes. She offered to assist him prepare breakfast. He suggested she take a shower first. She agreed.

He led her out of the kitchen, and into a large walk-in closet in the middle of the hallway, which was between the bathroom and the kitchen area. She expressed how much she liked his place. It was a beautiful Condo.

He gave her another robe of his for her to wear, while she occupied herself with her choice of towels, soap, lotions, and fragrances. She asked him to take a shower with her. Nothing would have pleased him more than to take a shower with her, but he took a shower earlier when she was sleeping.

It was his intention to make sure everything was prepared for her, when she stepped out of the shower. They started kissing again. He escorted her to the bathroom.

Twenty-five minutes later. Olivia appeared looking fresh, delicate, and hot. Her large brown eyes and curly hair asked for attention. When her small nose and lips were compulsively calling out for him?

He took her hand and led her further into the kitchen. Her face generously lit up, when she saw the food he had prepared.

“Marshall, I can’t believe you went through this much trouble to fix breakfast for me—like this!? I don’t know what to say!?”

He pulled out a chair for her. She sat down smiling. He seated himself at the opposite end of the table.

"When did you have time to do all of this? You have coffee, tea, juice, toast, eggs, fruit salad, bacon, waffles, cereal, wheat muffins, and strawberries."

"I didn't know what you liked? I thought a combination would be best."

There were two large rectangular windows, where the Sun was consciously blending onto the various plants that occupied the view from the windows.

Olivia resembled a little girl, who challenged her anticipation to choose the right item in a candy store. He asked her about the return of her husband?

"He should be coming home some time later this evening."

Her husband was away on a personal family matter. His parents needed to see him in North Carolina. Olivia didn't need to go. So she didn't go.

"I had a great time with you yesterday. When we met, and you took me for a ride out to Montauk.

"We held hands and walked across the beach sand. We smelled the ocean air, as the Seagulls were scrutinizing us from above when we talked and walked and laughed.

"I received a tan from soaking up some of the Sun's rays." Olivia had him laughing, when she started talking about how B-L-A-C-K she was.

"Look! Look at me, Marshall! I'm B-L-A-C-K!" with her smile and accent.

"Then on our way back. You took me to City Island for a Seafood dinner.

"Afterward, you brought me here to your lovely place. Where you served us drinks and we talked for hours.

"You are also quite the lover too. I wondered? Will you ever get enough of me?"

Olivia chewed on a slice of bacon, while she took a sip of coffee. She turned another page of The New York Times. She didn't want to admit, how Marshall gave her two orgasms in one night. She recalled only having one orgasm once in her entire life, which was too long and far in between, and it wasn't with her husband.

"I spend the night with you and I wake up to all of this? Am I being spoiled?

"After yesterday and this morning, am I going to ever see you again?"

Olivia looked at him curiously and seriously. It wasn't that she was looking for a one night stands. But he turned out to be a unique surprise to her.

"Yes, yes, and yes! Like you said, we made some real fireworks go off last night. I have to take care of my lovely one."

"You remind me of Michael J, when you refer to me as your lovely one.

"I love that song by him. Thank you for being incredibly sweet, Marshall.

"I can't imagine when I had a much better time by being with you, and doing the simple things in life and having so much fun."

"I don't mean to frighten you, but every time I am with you, I have a great time, Olivia. You make me feel good."

12

HE DROPPED OLIVIA OFF IN midtown Manhattan, near her job site. Where she parked her car overnight at Parking Systems. They were careful when they arrived at her destination. He looked around to observe, while she entered her Blue Lexus, and drove away smiling at him going back to her home in Long Island.

He was eager to know whether everything would be okay between Olivia and her husband. He made an illegal turn in traffic, and headed back uptown to Riverdale where he resided.

He thought about Olivia, she was thirty-three. She had been married four years. She married her college sweetheart, a few years after they graduated from the University of North Carolina at Charlotte.

They have been together for nine years. No children as of yet? Surprisingly, her situation sounded very similar to his, but the circumstances were far different.

Olivia and her husband were seeking greener pastures elsewhere. They were seeking new horizons, and wanted to abandon North Carolina—to pursue something different beyond what was expected of them there.

Her husband had relatives residing in New York, who agreed to accommodate him and her.

According to her, the husband wanted to establish their financial security first, before they decided to enter into a family. It was sound advice given to him by his parents, and judging by the way they felt about Olivia. They felt she was different.

They didn't want him to marry her, but his parents didn't know he needed her more than she needed him. She knew he wanted to make money and enjoy doing it first, and having his fun at the same time.

He was too influenced by his parents in this way, which she disliked about him. He showed no initiative in their own marriage to do what was best for them. Taking advice from someone else about how to handle your relationship is a bad mistake you can make in a marriage, she felt.

Marshall couldn't help but think, whether or not he would be involved with her, if she had children? The answer to this question is, he would have to decline. The situation is already complicated enough by being involved with another person's spouse, than to throw children into the mix as well, but it doesn't always turn out like this?

No one is going to take this lying down lightly. As he looked at himself. He was a perfect example. He wasn't going to go out and kill someone, because someone else is sleeping with his wife. Especially, when she chooses to sleep with them. Hell, they can have each other.

He had no idea what she was telling this other man, or told him about their situation and relationship. But if she told someone the real truth, then they may call her stupid, or tell her to go back to her husband, because no one else wants her like this?

People will lie about their situation at home when they don't handle things well, and when they are having problems with each other. In order to get a better perspective from the other person they are cheating with, but not every case is the same in relationships.

You honestly don't receive more information than you want to? It's not like the man was taking my wife's sex away from her. In situations like this, it's always going to be about her voluntarily offered the man her scathing sex.

Unfortunately, people always look at the situation the opposite of the way it really is? Rather than deal with the person and why they cheated on you. It's always about confronting and attacking the other person who cheated with your other half.

When they didn't know they were cheating with this person, until the truth comes out later after the intimacy. But this is not always the case, because other people know exactly what they are doing before the truth comes out.

Then there is nothing you, or anyone else can say or do, unless it makes no difference to you. Or maybe you prefer getting violent with someone, and then the choice comes down to-each-his-own?

When his wife cheated on him, did Marshall wish that the both of them were pushed in front of a moving car, at that precise moment…hell yeah!

But she moved out before she hooked-up with some-one else for the second time. He wasn't going to deny this by pretending it didn't happened. He didn't want to lose her this way.

He thought they would separate just like anyone else did, but without the constant screwing over and what for? He knew there was nothing else for him to do, but let her go fast. He realized he still loved her, but he wasn't in love with her anymore.

The feelings he had wasn't the problem, it was her. Also he didn't feel this was a consolation prize either. But if it was her desire to be with someone else rather than with him. He wasn't going to stand in her way or try and stop her.

This was completely on her. She knew better, they both did. It was a difficult challenge for him every day to try and forgive and forget, or try to forget about the fact that she not only got involved with someone, but contin-ued her involvement with someone else—when the first situation didn't work out for her—with someone else?

Where was she going with all of this? There were simpler ways to destroy something, if you no longer wanted it to be necessary for you.

She had one situation with someone, and then she had another situation with someone else after that ended. He thought that this wasn't love? How was he supposed to acknowledge anything good, or positive about this as love?

There was no need for either one of them to think about anything else. There was no way in hell. He believed, he gave her a reason to go out and be with someone else, please! He also knew that someone doesn't need for you to give them a reason, when it comes to this kind of a situation. People do what they want, when they want, when they feel it. And then in return, will gladly tell you that they don't give a f…?

Nor had she ever given him a reason to go out and be with another woman? Since they are still married in spite of their separation, and nothing has changed, except for the fact that she had walked out, and abandoned everything which concerns them.

He did miss her, but realized he was missing the memories more. It's hard to miss someone as much, when they are tearing up your insides, and forty-two of your best emotions concerning your life—because they are in a position to—whether they realize it or not?

He recalled her not being with him in his car on a beautiful summer day, after leaving Olivia. When they would be on each other the way that they use to do.

Jade and him would seek a secluded private area, park the car and have sex with each other. It's what they would do, they didn't care. Or talking and laughing about whatever comes to mine, and watching her project her smile, which wouldn't avoid interrupting them.

But now, any personal business of theirs wasn't being resolved. She was off somewhere, too busy playing mission impossible with herself? It was his complete responsibility to pan everything out, while she was with someone else. He guessed he was supposed to accept this?

But that was it! He couldn't deal with this anymore. If she wanted to keep the crazies going on with herself. He was no longer sorry. Enough was enough. If she didn't want to at least communicate with him, then it is what it is?

He was tired of her and the fighting. Where was her regard for anything? Again, he was supposed to accept everything without a reason, or an explanation for her nonsense, and be a dedicated fool without a conscious?

13

WHAT THE HELL DID SHE think was going on? He doubted seriously if there was a party going on up in here. While he continued to relive his life without her, and night after night try to understand the least of what he could. Why would she take them through this, without a substantial reason or explanation given?

Tell him something he thought? She and him could have been financially wealthy, provided that they stayed together as a couple. They had accomplished a great deal together in their relationship in a short time.

She was aware of this, also. He thought after being together with someone for this long? He didn't deserve an explanation or a reason. It was too complicated for him, or he couldn't see the handwriting on what wall that wasn't painted?

Why would she? Who he thought desired this more than he did, and allowed it to simply come a part? The life they had and build together with each other. It's never a problem until something like this happens, and it's over between the two of you before you know it.

He could hardly imagine this would be an experience he would hardly get over, or recover from anytime soon, after thinking about all of this crap. It's amazing sometimes how women seem to conveniently forget.

And don't care how badly or deeply they can break a man's spirit, as long as they have to prove a point to themselves or to him? And men not realizing that women go through much worse for their abandonment to become a single parent.

But…all men are not idiots, dump, or stupid. No matter what race they are from. They know what time of day it is. Or the moment when it will bring them completed despair to their hearts and lives. When you have loved and lost.

It's the same for everyone. It doesn't prevent your emotions from uninterrupted pain that is coming back to you, and what true loneliness feels like, because pain kills whatever you are inside.

He recalled how much of a struggle it was in his juvenile years. The painful issues in his home life he dealt with, and was cursed with, as well as his own fears of what life would bring to his future.

Some day's suicide was a thought, or an option to alleviate some of the continuous pain that was being accumulated within him and growing up. He couldn't imagine the impact it would have on his family, which he vowed to protect. He was the man of the house with no father around.

He had to help his mother, and there was never a father present—only a man around from time to time who he thought of as a father, and then he died. He didn't know his father from child birth.

Only a name he discovered later, which was listed on his birth certificate when he became older. What more could she do at this point, which was short of being a genie in a bottle, who could grant him three wises.

So she could erase everything that had occurred during his first wish? So he could use the next two wishes for emergency services, as a back-up plan to deal with her now. Whether she believed him or not, he knew what she was feeling to a degree.

He had made mistakes in his life before her. And after she tried apologizing to him for the two-hundredth time, and still having to accept all of the unpleasant stuff that came with it.

And having to put up with always being reminded of the mistakes she made, and the guilt that was backing up inside of her if there was any?

Then there was her family, which she tried her best to deal with by avoiding. They drove her crazy, and made her more difficult than she had to be.

The Department of Social Services couldn't qualify her family's application, until their case file received additional poverty. It was like dealing with a bunch of lunatics for her. Who she described as a band of gypsies unleashed upon her.

It wasn't because of who they were, or where she originated from? It was because of where her family had been in their travels with her. Jade's family was like a reality show, and frequently passing gas at the dinner table, and not saying excuse me, was in proper form for them.

Then they would scratch their behinds, and then reach for anything that was on the table, without excusing themselves for anything they did? It's a wild scene to see, if you are there. Nobody should be this unfortunate when it comes to someone's family.

He had all the sympathy and empathy in the world for her. The moment her family entered into your life. You couldn't help but run the other way. There were times when she felt a shamed of how she felt about her family, but she couldn't help it.

She couldn't help them as much as she tried. Figuring there couldn't be a time to come for her. Where dysfunctional families wouldn't require assistance to overcome their problems as a family?

Obviously it was wishful thinking on her part. It is something that will be about human nature, or the magnitude of their character in relationships.

But the personal back ground of her family is a bitch. As if, obscene myths and realities, with maladjustment offered in by society? Her family unwittingly preferred being cruel with a resistance to frustrate, and rape her struggle when her family accepted her help. For her, however, it kept falling off of the table.

We all know what families can do to us at times. How they can interfere into your life and make you crazy. Turn your world all upside down. Get all involved into your personal business, with no regard as to what they are truly doing within their own lives.

He felt sorry for her at times. Her personality would change when her family did a job on her, and worked her over afterward, to get her reacquainted with her real family. She couldn't deal with it. Her family was a real piece of work in these changing times.

They will suck you dry, until you don't bleed. You really didn't know whether to laugh or cry for them at times. This is how bad the situation was concerning them.

14

SUNDAY, 11:39 A.M., ALL WAS quiet on the home front. He hesitated before he proceeded any further. He saw how peaceful the place was, but also how empty and lonely it continued to feel without her.

He exhaled a deep breath. He recalled how much enjoyment she and him had together, and taking their time to furnish the Condo elegantly. The fun it brought to them making love in every room, closet, kitchen, bathroom, and the floor after they completed furnishing the place.

This is why it was difficult to make love to anyone else in here at first. But it was something he got over, and moved on with concerning the nonsense about their situation.

His cell phone rang, which broke his chain of thought. He went to the nearest wall to switch on the overhead light in the living room, while he comfortably lied back on the sofa.

"Hello. How are you, Sarah?"

"I'm fine, Marshall. And how are you?"

"As well as can be expected, I am taking one day at a time."

"I was sorry to hear about you and Jade. When you invited Lawrence and me over for dinner a few months ago, without her being present? We were baffled at first. Then sadly enough, you explained as much as you could without going into detail about the separation.

"We were shocked? We didn't know what to say. I mean, you and her had a lot going on.

"I think some people were envious of you'll. I wish I could say more to make you feel better."

"Thank you, Sarah. So how is, Lawrence? I can hear him in the background yapping about something?"

"Lawrence is upstairs trying to find something to wear. But other than that, he is just fine."

"Please tell him I said hello."

"Not a problem. As a matter of fact, I am calling you because…?

"I was doing some house cleaning yesterday, and I came across a piece of jewelry. I believe it belongs to Jade. It's inscribed on the back from you.

"It's a diamond gold bracelet. It's really a nice piece, and it's really pretty?"

"Yes, she and I couldn't figure out whatever happened to it. I brought another one to replace it. She liked it so much. It's different of course, but the thought was exactly the same."

"That's sweet of you."

"Thank you."

"Are you busy this evening?" Sarah asked.

"No."

"Then why don't you stop by, and you can pick up the bracelet. Say between Five and Six?"

"That sounds good."

"I'll see you then."

"Bye, Sarah."

He thought that was interesting. He wasn't sure whether to tell her about the bracelet discovered by Sarah. Since he brought her a replacement. He didn't want to use this as an excuse to talk to her or see her. It was still painful to deal with her, because they were only too close at one point.

He placed his cell phone on the long rectangular Gray Formica Table located in front of the sofa. He walked down the hallway to enter the bedroom, and changed the sheets to make up the bed. He brought a new bed after she left.

His cell ringed again. It was Olivia.

"Hello, Marshall?"

"Hello yourself, my lovely one," she laughed immediately.

"I didn't expect to hear from you so soon."

"I know, but since I knew a few short cuts home that my husband doesn't know? I made good time and plus traffic was light this morning after I left you.

"I am here well before he returns. I wanted to hear your voice and talk to you a little.

"To tell you really, how much I enjoyed myself being with you this weekend again. How can I explain to you how much you excite me, just by referring to me as your lovely one?

"You have sexy in your voice every time you say it to me."

"It's because you are a lovely woman, and this is the only appropriate description I have for you."

"Well, I am more than flattered you feel this way. Take care. I will talk to you soon."

"And you do the same, Olivia."

He walked over toward the bedroom window with a pillow in his hand. He brought it up to his chest and hugged it with both arms, while looking outside of the window. He smelled the pillow to inhale the provocative scent of Olivia's perfume, which was still strong and relevant in his bedroom.

Wishing Olivia was still here? Now that Jade is absent from his life. He thought about how strange it was that he was involved with a married woman.

He wondered what it was like for this other guy to be involved with Jade, knowing she was married. But he didn't feel like he was the other guy, because he was beginning to feel Olivia.

Was he doing the same thing that Jade was doing in a different way, because she hurt him by being involved with another person's wife? He returned to his chore of making up the bed and disposed of the linen.

He is a compulsively neat person. He made sure everything was in order before he left to visit Sarah and Lawrence.

At 5:45 p.m. He arrived at the house of Sarah and Lawrence in Yonkers. He drove the car further to the back of the house where there is parking. She has a big yard. The house sits on three acres of land. Sarah's mother left the house to her and her two brothers when she passed away.

Her brothers insisted Sarah take full procession of the house. They left New York after their mother died. Sarah met Marshall at the back door to escort him in, and greeted him warmly with a hug and kissed him on his cheek.

"You smell good, Marshall. You always do."

"Thanks, Sarah. You smell rather nice yourself?"

"I try."

She took his hand, and led him through the downstairs living area of the three story house. Sarah has a beautiful house she takes care of well, and there was classical music playing on WQXR FM 105.9. He enjoyed her taste in music. He positioned himself next to her, and sat on her cool beige couch. The air conditioning made everything feel more relaxing. Sarah crossed her legs as she sat there looking radiant, warm, and ravishing, simply wearing a light blue robe with slippers. Her hands were claimed together, as she massaged her hands with lotion she was using. She had taken a shower.

She looked good. The curves and swivels of her body could no longer hide from underneath her robe. Her hair was left free, but in a neat fall. She is tall. She is pretty. And her body is developed and defined. She is just an attractive woman.

He was surprised to hear that Lawrence wasn't home when she told him. He had an engagement to attend to this evening with friends of his.

"He will be in later tonight sometime I guess. He relayed his regards, and will catch up with you later."

Sarah and him had an opportunity to talk, and spend time together for the first time with each other, since they have become acquainted with one another. Several months ago, Sarah threw a nice party, and this is when he met her as the host. She was hot and everyone said it.

The time was used wisely. They took advantage of the privilege to get to know more about one another, as they continued to click instantly. He didn't expect something like this to happen with her.

15

When you have been with someone else for so long. You can be out of touch with a lot regarding yourself. In spite of the fact, you have a good relationship or marriage with someone else?

Surprisingly, he was trying to explain his sudden relationship with Olivia to himself. Since he had never been involved with a married woman before.

But their conversation began with self-reliance between them. They excelled with much in common. He couldn't help but make her feel sexy. Little that he knew, Sarah was consuming the intimate talk between them, and thinking before she speaks.

They made each other feel important, like a long term investment with their conversation. They laughed by being detailed orientated. There was a movement of romance happening between them, with an attraction being succumbed from mutual respect.

It was a courtesy that allowed them to be straight forward and honest with each other. They were sharing something that didn't over think it-self. After three and a half hours of talking to one another passionately. They had a lot of unexpected fun together.

He didn't want to over extend himself by staying any longer when he realized it was 10:40 p.m. They stood up from the couch after sharing a bottle of wine together. Sarah directed him through the living room to the kitchen, where the back door entrance was located and locked.

She forgot Jade's bracelet. She yelled out loud. She turned around, walked past him to re-enter the living room. He waited patiently in the kitchen, and in the dark for her to return. There was a night light off to the right, which generated a glimmer of light.

Sarah returned with the bracelet in her left hand facing him. Suddenly it felt like hypnosis drawing them together. Their eyes were intimidated by the attention. They stared at each other. They started walking toward each other and body bumped.

Her arms extended open. She placed them around his waist, raised her head, and inserted her tongue deep into his mouth. He placed both of his hands on her face, covering her soft smooth skin, and did the same thing she did. He connected with her tongue like a warrior.

He realized he had lost control of himself after all these years with Jade. Why was he like this with Olivia, and now with Sarah?

All of a sudden their desire for one another was out of control. They wanted to play up what made them different to each other. She felt him right threw her robe.

She expressed his endowment well before separating herself from him. They looked hard into each other's eyes for a few seconds. As if to say, is this really going to happen? Yes, it is going to happen.

Not a word was spoken between them, while they stared curiously at each other breathing heavily. Sarah anxiously grabbed his hand, and guided him straight threw the darkness over to the sink, where a long counter was adjacent and bare.

It was so intense, and lead up to the end game between them. He interrupted his hug of her. He started descending slowly, kissing her closely on both sides of her neck. He produced moisture from his mouth. He generously started sucking on her uncovered breast. She placed herself up against the counter.

Sarah opened her robe all the way. She had no bra on or underwear on. She invited him into her. They hugged softly and aggressively together. Their kissing was putting in the overtime for a make-out session first.

He descended further to maneuver his hands down her back, and between the counter to separate her. She helpfully provided more space to clear a path between the counter and her. So he could cuddle her.

His mouth and tongue sucked firmly on both of her breast. Her nipples were moist and hard. He descended even more, until he was stationed on his knees. He positioned his hands underneath her to guide her closer. He pulled her into him.

He kissed her all over her stomach. Inside her navel he stuck his tongue, and twirling it gently around. She felt more air than tongue, which made her smile with her eyes closed. Then kissed her pubic hair on both sides, and slowly working his way down. He kissed her inner thighs.

Sarah was wet. She was beginning to drip. Something she couldn't control and didn't want to. He rose up off of his knees to trace her lips with his tongue, and alternating stolen kisses while sucking on her lips.

He removed her robe and let it fall quietly to the floor. He secured her by holding her waist. He elevated Sarah up from the floor, and placed her on the bare counter. She leaned back and was positioned on her elbows, with the back of her head pressed up against the wall for support.

She lifted her legs. They were opened, as if she was beginning to give child birth. He placed his hands on the inside of her thighs to hold them back further.

Sarah cried out with relevant moans and groans, as he easily thrust deep inside of her. The foreplay was over, and she wanted to give him all of her, and all she could take of him.

He had no idea she fantasized about him and her together? Now her fantasy was real. She was feeling her lust severely when she climaxed and kept gyrating. He didn't stop. He continued to drive deep inside her, but softly. Shortly after, he stopped.

Her body trembled. He had no idea Sarah hadn't experienced an orgasm in years? It was about the same length of time she and Lawrence have been married. He immediately bent over to pull her up off the counter toward him and embraced her firmly.

She employed her arms around his neck, while he kissed her long and passionately. He was still inside her. She began rapping her legs around him, as far as she could. She felt him more.

They finally came up for air, and no words were spoken, but this captivating tenderness being displayed between the both of them. Oddly enough, Sarah didn't release the bracelet of Jade's from her hand while they made love. She offered it to him and they smiled. He removed himself from her slowly and with ease.

She lifted herself from off of the counter, and picked up her robe from the floor to place it on. He was fortunate to get another look at Sarah's body. He pulled his pants up and adjusted his clothes.

"It's getting late, Sarah. I think I should be leaving."

"Okay, but please be careful and get home safe, Marshall."

"I will." They kissed again, before he left to enter his car.

16

SHE WASN'T FEELING PROVOCATIVE ANYMORE about her imagination and her thoughts. She could easily see unreasonable doubts of jealous music playing in her mind. Suddenly attempting to victimize her new attitude into a universal concept for some sort of reasoning within herself?

Jade spend a lot of time alone in her new apartment. It was the second one she moved into within the last year after leaving Marshall.

Although he had no idea, he was unaware of the relationship between her, and the other men in her life. Who were predominantly there for her use now.

He didn't care. She wasn't his cup of pleasure anymore. She didn't discuss the changing circumstances concerning her new life style with him. They were at a substantial disadvantage in the discourse of their rhetoric.

They were no longer communicating with one another. It wasn't important to her. She realized in her heart, he was still the love of her life. He was still the man she cared for and loved. She wanted to redirect all of her anger by walking away into space.

Jade wished she could have introduced herself coherently into his life again, like a different spirit of autumn in local shades, and exquisitely combing the staying styles of falls riches dream. She wanted to smile again in the way that he made her smile. She wanted to laugh again with him. She wanted to live their life again.

Since it was exceptional, she wanted to love him again. She had seen too many walking dead movies in her life. She was feeling like an insolent ghost, who could see a revolution of tears emerging from within?

She thought she could no longer feel the reciprocal knowledge, which gave her another chance for hurting herself and him. Like she once said to a girlfriend of hers.

"A faceless expression from him, is like extracting the hairs off of her vagina one by one, and life has been cold backstage without him."

Her character really defined her negative behavior, especially without realizing it herself. Everything which had happened from within their relationship had been a flat out, and way out trip up until now.

It was sad that everyone else she knew as a friend, or an acquaintance took this opportunity to talk about her behind her back, and laugh about her before she could laugh about herself?

It is one thing to have business going on in your life, but it's another thing when other people know all about your business, because of the way she decided to handle her business.

Jade was really a nice person inside, a giving and caring person. She would do almost anything to help anyone. It's the way her nature is. It wasn't the easiest thing in the world to throw her life away with him, and lose one of the best things that had happened to her.

Being the person she is. She left him with stupid on her face. She was literally coming apart from inside. A unique feeling you don't get to feel every day. He wasn't a saint or a perfect person. But he was the best person she knew as a man, or as a woman she had met in her life.

No one had thought of her more. No one had done more for her. No one had ever loved her more. She didn't know what love was in a relationship until she met him. And no one had taken the time out to love her in bed the way anyone else had.

She recalled how he could bring the hunger out of her when it came to her sexuality. He was a sex machine to her. She cherished the fact, that Marshall and her were into each other—this was the real magic and tenderness between them.

She would go into work late, tired, and drained from the love making he gave her during the week. It was a good feeling. His love was unconditional. He never made her feel good one way, and then make her feel bad in another way.

He didn't tear her down, if she made a misfortune mistake. He wasn't the type to bring things up or throw them back in her face later, like many other men seem to do. His support was unbelievable.

It was guilt she felt about his love, his giving, and doing so much for her. She felt it strong from inside of her. How much of a better person he was, and for her to do the things she did to him and now to herself.

She was unable to explain it to herself. So how in the world could she explain it to him? It was as if she had awakened one morning, and everything felt different inside of her. She really didn't know what to make of it?

17

THERE WAS NO FEELING, OR life, or no course of reason for her to explain this—when she thought about it.

She felt this way once before in her life, which was motivated from a personal demon in her past. She was unable to make a connection, which didn't involve him or their relationship together.

He received the impression Jade might have been molested by her Father. Or maybe by one of her brothers when she was young? Without her coming out and saying it from the various conversations they had over the years. So, Marshall, wasn't sure what to think?

He suggested she see a therapist or someone she could talk to, if she couldn't talk to him. It was surely affecting her emotionally. Jade felt she was losing her mind. It was too painful for her to be seen around him. She made no attempt to try and even talk to him.

He felt nothing but complete betrayal from her. Perhaps when angry spirits run softly or something? Then there will be no more lights of red, blue, and green, without yellow as a warning sign for her.

If she continued to deal with men and her relationships this way. Then what good could she expect to become of it? When the light isn't going off in her head, or even at half-twilight? Or it can be a different kind of emotional survival, seeing the walking dead out at night in the nude.

She understood he was afraid to trust her again. Recalling, how life is just a journey through time with experiences?

She wished she could have found a way to compute her thoughts to him, like people being counted on unemployment lines. She was a woman who was better than most men on any given day at their job. She was employed by a business man who started a Technology company.

Two years later. He won the small business man award of the year, with his picture on the front cover of Business Entrepreneurs, and a picture of Jade with a half page article of her about being his right hand. He couldn't have achieved it without her, he stated.

Marshall was aware the man wanted his wife. She hasn't seen herself before within a business failure. In the intercourse of her nightmares, and from the mistakes she made. It was all hidden in her own morality.

The reality would surrogate her honor, and the caretaker of her consciousness was also invaded by her submission? Now she could see flowers growing from sarcastic dirt in her mind, and fire burning away from the truth in her heart without him.

Women have a lot of pride also, which is something men fail to realize and accept. When the script was flipped. She thought, if she could only wake up on the other side of tranquility.

So her thoughts could be invisible to him, and her beauty was only a deception for sadness now that he wanted to put it to death. When she wakes up in the morning and looks at herself. She can see from a mirror, or she can see chronic jumping smiles, with abbreviated pretty hopes of aim on her face.

That started her day off, with many unknown doors to open? What she didn't understand was that she was a mystery to herself, before anything else had a chance to reason with it.

And wondering will there ever be a day, if she will be able to ratify her loneliness into memories of comfort? Even though, she didn't see the light behind her door.

She continued to fight along with everyone else to survive. Her vanity is without mystery, and her warmness is substituted for coldness. It didn't make her smile any more peaceful. She could see her memories were in another place? She initially made the wrong move which cost her everything.

As if it was easy to love a man in return, the way she loved him? Or the bitch in her was beginning to go berserk to cover up the darkness, with a passion for her once brightness. She thought it was a good day in hell, when her love would grow from pain?

Or was she still kicking herself in the rear, when she felt her love was still lost? She wouldn't tell him how unhappy she had become. She didn't want to disappoint him any further in the joy of who she was now. The word hate began to surface. It was such a force in the ear on the head of another person.

She didn't have too many friends. The few she did have were trying to recall the composition of her life now.

Knowing it wouldn't concern anyone about the state of her mind. Her life without him would be primarily in the mix, also. Recalling how everything is temporary until it becomes permanent. So carrying the name of the perfect couple meant nothing.

The problem with this is that you are labeled with words. As if either one of them ever thought this about each other, or if they believed they did? She may have been perfect for him. He may have been perfect for her, but it still doesn't mean that they were a perfect couple?

He was her best friend before and after they became an item together. His ability to suffer with the truth was lower than an unethical lawyer, or he was trying to smile with tape across his mouth. But he was loyal to her. A quality she experienced to a fault in her life.

He introduced bad viewpoints from a dark place in his emotions also. Since many things have changed between them. She could see the identical pain in his personality. She saw he didn't like her new friends.

It's not like every day she wakes up in the morning, with a raw chicken kissing her for her divine knowledge. He felt she could have done a lot better without her new people. There was no better time than now, nor was there enough time to decide to be a realistic reality either?

Her new people were phony on top of phony, but being without him constantly was upsetting to her confused emotions. She would make it up along the way, and accept her reputation and life as a scandal. She was something for people to talk about, since she was on her way down.

Having to be better off from reading a Bible, a further insight into more relaxation and recreation into God, she thought. Maybe she could give life back something, in which, apprehension doesn't?

Which was now using her as a down payment for a final analysis of love? Sometimes life can run away with it-self, she thought.

18

"LAWRENCE, I AM SICK AND tired of this! Why don't you and I put an end to this marriage? Every time I turn around you have your piece, or whatever else you want to call it—in another person's whole?"

"That's not true, Sarah." Lawrence gazed back at her. He picked up his keys and walked out the front door. He drove away in his Infinity QX 50. At this moment, he saw the future and it wasn't working for him. And yet, Sarah saw the same vision in a dream the night before.

How she had sex with a married man on a peaceful evening in her imagination. Lawrence began thinking about the conversation they had before he left the house.

"It's all in your mind. I wouldn't cheat on you. You are my Love?"

"Please, don't insult my intelligence with that player stuff. This is Sarah you're talking to. I know you better than you know yourself. Like I said, you can leave the games at the door.

"I asked you before, not to bring that street mentality up in here to me?

"I am a real woman, even if you're not sure of what kind of a man you are? You seem to forget you are not the only person who has been around?"

There was a Jehovah Witness knocking at her door, with a separate message about saving Sarah's soul, according to the principals of a public dispute. Sarah stepped on a nail getting back into bed that night.

But it would be a step down prediction for her later. She tried to be sincere with Lawrence. It got her nowhere in their relationship, especially when the beauty of an idea was beyond his reach?

It's amazing how different you are from the person you think you are? He was a person who didn't look back on his mistakes. He was your typical bastard this way. When Lawrence became a Model, then no one could tell him anything. His ego was as big as Kim Kardashian's behind.

A young man who came from a nice upper class wealthy family. His parents were nice and humble. He had two sisters and one brother. They all graduated from college, and they were one and two years younger than, Lawrence.

They were all working with nice jobs. Their parents took a lot of pride and honor in their success and accomplishments, but they still held out for hope were Lawrence was concerned.

He decided to take a different path, and fortunately for him, there were many opportunities available to explore. So hopefully another one wouldn't bite the dust?

Whether you liked him or not, he deserved a lot of credit for his accomplishments. He wanted to be the best there was in Modeling, but let's not take this shit out of content either.

He wouldn't share space with anyone, and he still can't recall the dawn of a day. When another person's life is turned around in dismay?

When he first met Sarah, it smacked him right in the face, like raindrops coming down heavily.

She was the rhythm of people to him. The feeling of love was prevailing, as a feeling being given back in return by two people. Sarah was the shake in his quake. He married her to become closer to her as a saint.

Lawrence's family enjoyed Sarah, and was quite taken by her. Her race as an African-American was irrelevant to them. They all felt she was awesome, but everyone's concern was mutual. They didn't think that Lawrence was good enough for her plain and simple.

However, they could see how much she loved him. So they wanted to give her all the support they could, and wished Lawrence the very best.

Sarah came into a lot of money when her mother passed away. She and her two brothers were the recipients of 975,000 dollars after taxes, and divided three ways equally between them. Their mother's personal assets, property, and her term life insurance policy provided a nice nest egg for them.

Lawrence could work a room of people when it counted, and when it came to his career in Modeling, and keeping up with appearances. Or without the oddest essence of heaven's stolen spirits coming true for a person, with a plain day break for himself.

The first two years of their relationship was good not great. And after they were married his career began to blossom. This is when he began to perform, as if he was all of this and all of that?

This is when his marriage began to decline, far from a blue pear river they could see or imagine together. No more dreams of quality were left are since gone. The both of them took a fall and confronted one another to be opposing forces.

In order to pursue separate careers of their own they decided not to have kids. He became bored with his life with Sarah. He wanted more for himself, than to feel satisfied with a good woman and their future.

He wasn't feeling any one right now, and this included her. What about her? How does she begin to bring something a live by herself? How does she take something which is not hers, to declare positively a vow in his life?

There were no mysteries concerning a bad idea. It was Sarah just being Sarah. She realized she was taking a chance when it came to Lawrence. You luck out sometimes, and sometimes you lose out unfairly. Also, she knew she was a loser on this one.

It was as if he had become a feeble-minded politician, who's only desire was to campaign for the presidency of The United States. Who was unable to keep a hand puppet in his possession with very large breast, and witness the blind spots in his judgment?

Sarah was feeling Lawrence was a bad person inside. He had his priorities in the wrong place, and needed to improve upon his superficial feelings of showcase. He continued to be in his own mix. He didn't care whether they had much in common or not.

Of course a person he once loved and trusted before betrayed him, she guessed. Since he was intoxicated by his own insecurities, and some nightmares frequently appeared. So it was no surprise, when idiotic looks appeared on the faces of Sarah and Lawrence.

19

Since they were both horrified by the feelings they once imagined was there. But no one misunderstood better than they did what they knew about themselves, and their relationship wasn't working.

Their lives were about two people, who were driving down a flexible highway of hell and disarray, while carrying a book of lies being kept from one another. It was no longer available for them to go down this road again for reasons of no entertainment to enjoy each other?

There was no fighting without a break up for Sarah. A lot of couples like to fight, because someone doesn't want to do anything about anything. It was ironic for him to pay attention to her, while he was doing his thing and changing.

What the hell did he think she was doing, when she realized this was going on with him?

Sarah was no longer the same woman he was dealing with, like she wore long dresses until she changed her wardrobe. Now she wears her dresses above her knee caps, and her behind and legs are attention-getters.

But all she wanted to do was go to sleep, and stop waking up feeling dead in the morning lying next to him in bed. It was clearly a new order in the alphabet of a stink zone for her to be stuck in.

She realized sometimes, which can't always be explained by words. He is a person who hardly ever gets it? How her marriage had gone bad in the blink of an eye. You can't help but want to kick someone in the rear when this happens, because you figured you did the right thing.

It's a fact of life, Sarah thought. She was feeling she couldn't love him, and cherish the survival of a marriage to exist with him any longer. To her, it was his aim and target, which was spinning off course, and out of control with every other women.

The man positively needed help, but you couldn't tell him that? And he wouldn't listen to her whether she was right or wrong? She was a woman who didn't make sense to him. This is why he became a true diagram of a bastard to her.

His eyes seem to always want what was in the bigger bag, only to see other eyes bigger than his. She couldn't tolerate it anymore, before he became handsome to her in another way of serving hell?

Sarah imagined with his jazz being lose all over the place. It was time for her to start kicking the situation, and him to the curb. She was disappointed she tried to help him polish up his act. For his lack of knowledge on how to treat her better. She continued to compromise on her direct confrontation with him—only to avoid the obvious.

It was her desire to try and understand. Why do men have to act like dogs? Like there will no longer be enough women or sex to go around. Women are born more every day, or maybe their desperate because of their lack of ability to get sex?

She asked herself, if it was a competition? About who could be the lowest dog of variety, when she directed her question to Lawrence? It's the same old story, when it comes to men. Do you ever change?

"It just doesn't matter to a lot of men if a woman is pretty, ugly, big, skinny, a shank, a slut, a hoe, old, young, smart, stupid, Black, White, Hispanic, Asian, or Indian?

"As long as she has a vagina then she is good to go. He will always try and find a way to put it in right, Lawrence?

"It's what I mean about a man being a dog like you," said Sarah.

Lawrence asked Sarah, "Then what is it that you do?"

"I use to do you, a long time ago and treated you special, but not anymore—since you can't seem to handle the love of a good woman?"

He listened and showed his disappointment on his face, while wishing he could still receive some of that special treatment and attention of hers.

Sarah was a much better lover than he was. He received much more out of it than she did. His ego again was larger than his effort was, as she continued with patience not to hurt his pride and feelings as a man in their relationship.

It made no difference with him apparently. Since he continued to behave like a fool always in question to her?

20

It was a hot and humid August day. Raining on and off during the day. Also late night thunder showers where forecasted. He was accelerating to get home. It was a lackluster day at work. He sucked it in for the remainder of the day.

The day was long because of the rain, which made the day seem slower and dreary. Home sweet home, as he walked through the front door trying to capture the rain water on his suit jacket and umbrella?

A white long shaped mental cylinder can, with intimate design hasting on it. Where Jade and he kept their umbrella collection off to the left, but on the right side next to the closet door. He placed the umbrella into the cylinder can. He gave his jacket one last shake, before he placed it into the closet.

He sat down on the sofa and viewed the mail concerning anything which had to do with him and her. She was no longer living with him, but she still received mail here. It was nothing important or pressing.

He thought about something to eat. He realized it was the wrong notion to start thinking about her. He decided to play some music. Some of the music reminded him of memories when they would dance and play to this music, and open up a bottle of red wine with candles burning with intrepid spirits, which was followed by playful intimacy, and exciting sex erecting him to do her like a desperate man.

He didn't want to admit it to himself or to anyone else. How much he still cared about her and missed her like a tooth ache sometimes.

He knew it was over for him, when she began sleeping with someone else, and after his first encounter with Olivia.

When you lose a woman who is a twelve, and then she is replaced by another twelve, you are in trouble? Your hands are filled with more than you can handle. You really didn't lose anything in a woman, but you have gain more because you don't often meet women back to back who are twelves or more?

There always seem to be a vacancy in between the woman you had and the woman you meet next, unless faith is kinder than you hitting the lottery.

He felt a sense of emptiness, and loneliness before he met Olivia. Amazingly, she had fulfilled so much about the void he felt in record time. Also the unexpected fulfillment he had received from Sarah was incredible. So far he couldn't believe it. His phone ringed. It was Jade.

"Hello Marshall. How are you?"

"I'm good. I'm still standing. The real issue is how are you doing, Jade?"

"I could be better, but I won't get into all of that? I called to say, hello, and to see how you were doing?"

"I thought you had too much on your plate to be concerned about me?"

"I can't do this, Marshall. Every time I think about you, every time I speak with you, every time I see you and I am with you. It breaks my heart.

"I still love you, but I can't make you realized or understand this anymore? And a larger part of me still wants to be there with you, in your arms, but it is not the same between us after what I did.

"This is why it is so hard to visit you, because we will sleep with each other. It only confuses the situation for the both of us.

"I wouldn't call it sex that is wrong, but it is mad sex between us, like we are trying to hurt each other, or attacking each other, and doing it aggressively to one another.

"And like the last time when I was there and it happened, I tore your shirt off, and you tore my dress and underwear off. We kissed hard. You turned me around, and rammed me from behind forcefully.

"There were moments when you were hurting me. This was something you never did to me before, but I took all of your anger and pain.

"I felt I deserved it momentarily and more. I understand you weren't giving me love, when you did me like this? Never have you touched me like this?

"It is obvious we are still hot-wired to each other, like the current we have in bed, nothing has changed this?

"You know how crazy we get with one another. It's like we are obsessed with one another in bed.

"Marshall, I didn't want you to think because we continue to sleep with each other on and off, that something was going to change between us after we separated.

"It was a booty call. I wanted you. I always want you, and you apparently still wanted me.

"The person I am now will only hurt you more, if I try to do the right thing? It will still hurt you more, either way. How screwed can a woman be, if she still wanted to fight for her man?"

"So instead, you refused to deal with any of this? You just leave me hanging with everything. You won't even try to work anything out, as far as our personal business is concerned?

"So I guess you just wanted to get the hell out of Dodge, as soon as you could?"

"Marshall, work what out? I know I have hurt you deeply, and with much disappointment.

"This is not all about you. Why would you even want to work anything out with me?"

"So you think we shouldn't have tried to resolve any differences we may have had, before all of this happened?

"Or come to some conclusion about our personal business affairs before you moved on? You don't have to tell me this is over between us."

"Marshall, if you did this to me or us, I wouldn't want you back either. I would be so afraid to open myself up to you again.

"I am sorry. I didn't mean to lie to you. I probably would have allowed you to walk all over me, and just use me some more before I came to my senses. Isn't that what usually happens when you are still in love, with someone after they break your heart and you lose them?

"And to be honest, I couldn't tell you how long I would have allowed something like this to go on?

"And before I was able to kiss you off completely, I don't know? I just know it wouldn't have been easy with you, which I guess is the same in your case?

"And with a man like you, after everything we have shared together is not easy to get over. It takes real time. I am embarrassed by my past behavior.

"Sometimes I wish I could be a fly on the wall in the apartment. So I could hear how you really feel about me?

"I wish I could make you realize, I am not the woman you fell in love with or loved anymore.

"Hell, I don't know who I am half the time anymore. And you still need to know why we couldn't work this out?"

"I am sorry you keep on misunderstanding me, Jade. This is not about us, personally. It's about closing out our business affairs and property with each other. Why would you want to drag this out any further?"

"Why I did what I did? If I knew I would honestly tell you. I just don't have any answers for you or myself at this point and time. When I am regretting everything I have done to you, Marshall.

"It hasn't come together all in my mind or heart as of yet?"

"And how long are you going to continue down this self-destructive path of yours, Jade?"

"I really don't know? It's no longer your concern anymore. I lost something more than good. I don't know if I can ever go back to. It always hurts me to be reminded of how much I hurt you, and then myself."

"Do you have any idea how much this hurts? Why don't you move on with your life?"

"Well, I didn't know I needed your permission to do something I have done a while ago, and it's really good now."

"You deserve to be happy with someone who can love you the way that you need to be loved. God knows, you have made me happy, Marshall. This is why I am so unhappy now.

"You know everybody deserves to be happy in this life, but unfortunately it doesn't always work out for everybody, does it?"

Then the conversation with her was ended, which turned into much turmoil for him. She didn't understand a damn thing he was trying to say to her. What happened to her? Why does she think all he wants is her back?

He realized how unfair it is. Every time they talked to each other. How she has to be reminded of how much she hurt them? She was tired of it. He was tired of it. He didn't receive any satisfaction from it. No reason. No explanation. Only her choice of action toward him and them. It continued to be what it is to her—unfair. He didn't care.

He thought that stepping into shit made more sense than this? His phone ringed again. He was hoping it wasn't her calling him back. He was frustrated enough with her. They felt twisted together.

"Hello."

"Hi, Marshall, this is Abby Delaware."

"Hi, Abby, is everything okay?"

"I didn't want to disturb you at home, but I have a report to forward to you. I wanted to make sure you were aware of the report and received it before I leave."

"Where are you going, Abby?"

"I am relocating to Memphis with my husband and family. Friday is my last day."

"I can't believe it. I don't know what to say? I don't want you to leave, Abby. I am going to miss you a lot."

"I am going to miss you more, Marshall." There was a five-second moment of silence between Abby and him on the phone.

"You can expect the report on your desk by tomorrow morning. If you have any problem with it, please don't hesitate to contact me."

"Thank you, so much Abby. I'll see you tomorrow, good night."

"Good night, Marshall."

He was surprised and disappointed to hear what Abby had told him. He already felt the void in his thoughts. She is the Computer Support Specialist and System Administrator of her department.

Abby has been with the company for eighteen years. When he was first hired by the company, and introduced to her. They discovered immediately there was a mutual attraction for one another, but they were married.

Abby was a mature beauty, and intelligent woman. She was forty-two, and really had it going on. She was the best dressed woman in the company with a full-figured body. She was well liked and respected by her peers.

When they talked to each other, they made each other laugh with a lot of harmless flirtation. He didn't think about it consciously before until now. They couldn't afford to be alone together. It was too dangerous, like fourth of July fireworks.

She was the first woman who raised his eyebrows, since he has been married to Jade. But when he first met, Abby. It was a bitch. When you connect with someone else, and you are with someone else that you love, and you have done nothing to establish this between you and this other person.

21

HIS INTERCOM SPEAKER WAS BUZZING. He heard the rain coming down heavy outside on the Terrace. It was Security announcing a guest to see him. All visitors are announced in before being permitted to enter the building by Security twenty-four-seven.

It was Sarah. He gave his permission to allow her in. His first reaction was a pleasant surprise on his face. He had no idea. His eyes were moving like a crocodile, with sharp thoughts of excitement by patiently waiting for his prey to appear.

The doorbell ringed. He was anxious, pleased, and curious about her unexpected visit. He could hardly contain himself.

Sarah, walked through the door looking hot and smelling great, with her hair up in a ponytail. It was nice to see her facial features exposed again. It shows how pretty she is.

A plain pastel colored body blouse, with a pair of breast that could suffocate you, jeans, and open hills with a carrying bag. He closed and secured the door. She dropped her carrying bag on the floor. There was much excitement accelerating inside of them—which drew them into each other's arms as they affectionately kissed.

She had a certain quiet innocence in her personality when you got to know her. Her eyes will follow you as she gazed right through you. She had bedroom eyes in his opinion. She could also determine your deception easily, and well before you know it.

He found Sarah to be quite an interesting person. It's always something that you don't know about someone that makes the difference at times.

She didn't talk a lot like a lot of other women do? Who love to run their mouths on an on, like something important is being said. She is a person you need to observe more of and communicate with. This in it-self told him a lot about her.

She didn't discuss her personal business with other people. She handled her own concerns. She was specific about her topic of conversation or reply to things in general. You have to listen and pay attention, and think about what you say to her.

She was different and with a daring quality about her he liked. He was drawn to her affectionate manner. It went without saying for him. He enjoyed affectionate women because he was an affectionate man.

He prefer showing his feelings to a woman rather than putting up a front about them, which men and women don't do much of anymore by showing their feelings for one another. It's all about going through the process first?

Sarah and he were blushing foolishly with smiles. He moved her bag out of his path. He took her hand and walked her to the sofa where they sat down together closely.

"It's good to see you like this, Sarah?

"It's even better to see you, Marshall."

They smiled as she leaned forward to kiss him. He kissed her back.

"I hope you don't mine me stopping by like this to see you unexpectedly.

"I thought a lot about it before doing it. It was something which was inside of me, that said just go and see him," as she looked at him with mystery on her face.

"After the first time we were together at my house, I didn't know what to think? But they knew and realized—how excited and turned on from the love making—that was more than good between them.

"I wanted to see you before I leave tomorrow. I have a flight out to California.

"I will be gone for four days?" Sarah, is a Flight Attendant for Delta Air out of La Guardia Airport.

"I am glad you decided to be impulsive and come and see me. I think you got here just in time, before the thunder showers arrived.

"It's really okay. I didn't have any plans. I was going to relax for the rest of the evening. Now it's something we can do together."

A loud interruption of thunder, lighting, and rain suddenly hitting up against the window pane. It was a feeling of excitement and wonder inside. He excused himself to change the CDs.

He walked into the kitchen. He returned with a large platter filled with four large scented candles encased in glass. He lit the candles and positioned two of them on the Gray Formica Table in front of them. The other two were placed on top of the entertainment unit against the wall.

The living room was illuminated by the candle light when he turned off the lamps. He walked to the hallway closet to return with a pair of slippers. He elevated her legs, and placed them on top of his thighs. He removed her shoes and replaced them with slippers.

She was feeling relaxed, comfortable, and good being alone with him for the first time, without having to anticipate anyone interrupting them.

"Would you like something to eat?"

"No, I'm good, but what about you?"

"I'm good too, how about something to drink instead?"

"That sounds good."

She was impressed how he had control of everything at a moment's notice. He made her feel warm and secure within herself, and about everything they were doing together. Sarah couldn't get enough of the attention he displayed on her. He was really nice and sweet.

He return with a tray containing two cocktails and a mixture of delicious almonds, pistachios, pecans, walnuts, and hazelnuts in a serving bowl. She began joking with him about, how his cocktails and nuts were much better than the ones she served to the passengers on the planes. She stated the airlines could take a cue from him. He thanked her.

"What is this? It's really good."

"It's a frozen Mai Tai."

"I never had one before. You made this?"

"Yes, I dabble a little as a bartender."

"Well, you are good."

"Thanks. Would you like some nuts?" They laughed.

"How does one make a frozen Mai Tai?"

"Well, you can start off with some white rum, pineapple juice, fresh lime, cherry herring, simple syrup, and apricot bandy.

"Chill everything first. Add a dash of almond syrup, and then blend. Then serve it in a tall glass filled with ice."

"Maybe when you have some time and it's a good time for us, you can teach me how to make drinks. I would like to be able to do something nice for you too."

"No problem."

He took her hand and directed her to the center of the floor, as the music played on the CD. She kicked off her slippers and walked on the carpet. They haven't danced together before tonight, but they were obviously good together on the floor.

He was surprised Sarah was a better dancer than, Jade. She was real smooth with an undercurrent of funk in her gyrating hips. Also he was surprised to see a different side of her, which was more open, more assured, and more fun. She stopped after she had taken another taste of her drink.

She removed the straw from her mouth. Since she was drinking fast and taking large sips. She experienced a brain freeze from drinking to fast with the drink being cold. He sat her down.

"I'm okay. The drink is really good."

"I can see that you're okay. Would you like to go in the back and lie down for a while?"

"No. I'm fine. I want to stay here with you."

He excused himself momentarily to return with two huge shams, pillows, and a handcrafted quilt comforter set and sheets. He laid them down quickly on the floor on top of the carpet to provide support and comfort for her.

She went to the bath room only to return in a two piece under garment, with her hair let out, as her hair covered her shoulders. She walked directly up to him and kissed him gently pressing her body up against his.

He leaned all the way back to lie on the floor and felt the comfort of the fresh linen under him. The thick quilt that made the floor feel soft on top of the carpet. He positioned her body on top of his. She was absolutely hotter this time and brilliant to be exact.

He was right about, Sarah. You could see and feel the difference in her exposing herself. The openness, and confidence in her attitude. She said he brought the best out in her, as a woman, and she was able to be herself around him.

This is why she was different around him. He made her happy. Sarah and him made love. No rush. No hurry. No being hasty with it at all. Time was on their side this time and night. She was like fresh warm smooth butter, you simply couldn't get enough of. When you put it on something you like and want real bad, and know that you are not supposed to have.

Sarah had a gorgeous body without her close on. You couldn't help but keep your mind in the gutter. When you saw and thought about her like this?

Her body carried a fresh strawberry scent of mush oil—luring enough for him to kiss her all over her body. He turned her over to continue kissing her on her back, and down to her behind.

He was pleased she didn't mine making love on the floor. It gave them an opportunity to explore each other's body. Since they had much more room to move about, unlike being in a bed. Where you didn't want to fall off if you became too active.

Her legs parted slightly when she moaned. It was like the bottom had fallen out between them. They were owning the act of love making tonight. They climaxed together which gave them power. It was strong and it was easy when they emerged together.

They knew it was more than just sex they were experiencing. There was too much compatibility in the way they connected physically and otherwise.

She didn't realize she could feel this good within herself, while still being married to someone else. With him, she felt no comparison. He thought it would be an unnatural feeling being involved with someone so soon, after over a year of being without, Jade?

He was beginning to realize he was wrong about a lot of things, after Jade and his separation. It's amazing when you are together and in love.

There is much more that is there that you can't seem to see, but after you have separated from someone. You can see all of this stuff you thought that wasn't there. It makes you wonder sometimes about yourself, and the judgment you have about being with someone.

The rain was still wicked outside, and hitting intricately up against the window pane. It sounded good to him. He liked the rain up to a certain point.

The day it brings with it, especially if it rains for the majority of the day and into the night—the candles burned low inside the glass encased, which was now acting as a dimmer for the light.

Sarah's concentration was strong on him after they made love. He held her closely into his arms. She kissed him with affection. They cuddled up closer together under the sheets.

They kissed more, while listening to the last CD play out. They started to make love again, before they fell asleep in each other's arms.

22

THE NEXT MORNING AT WORK, he was aware people with abstract minds will play irrational games with each other? Like he realized that part of his heart still belonged to Jade, but he wouldn't let her know this?

It doesn't stop until someone wakes up in the middle of the night to go to the bathroom. Then the morning comes to light, and your life begins to change but for secondary reasons.

He didn't want to mention anything behind this epic in his life, or to himself.

He thought about Sarah. She wanted to prevent him from walking into her legend of problems with Lawrence. She was an acquaintance who became a friend, and now he was her lover. She tried wisely to relieve herself of the conclusion belonging to all of this, because deception will never take a break, or see her beauty as someone else for Lawrence.

She knew and understood that the problem with betrayal and cheating is, that there is never a logical or appropriate excuse for doing it. And if there is one, then it hasn't been given yet, as everyone else knows? Who has been cheated on before.

Except when you make a decision, and she had made a decision that her marriage was over. When she decided to have sex with Marshall at her house that night, and then again, when she came to see him at his place. She spend the night with him. It was magical for her. It was just incredible. Her memories weren't passed on like some wrinkled flower for being with him.

Once you reach a certain age, then every relationship you encounter comes with baggage, which includes you too. When you bring your baggage in addition to what you have gone through—or where you are coming from?

There is no way around it, and no way for you to avoid it. It's the fatality of relationships. He could see happy tears transparent and being retrieved from the light of a candle. When Sarah and he were romantically together the previous night.

Wondering, if love would ever hurt him again this deeply? When he can see it in someone else. He turned around to observe the report Abby forwarded to him. He decided to review it later. He needed to see Abby to say goodbye, and to wish her well in her new endeavor.

Upon arriving at her office, he saw people in pairs. A small group coming and leaving Abby's office. She is very popular among her peers. The word is? The company is throwing an after hour party for her at one of the popular restaurants in the area. She will be greatly missed.

He entered her office to see people circling around her. They were obviously competing for her attention, it was okay for her. He didn't want to get in the way of things. Because any way you looked at it, it was her day. She earned it plain and simple.

Without warning, Abby captured his attention instantly. It was eye to eye, then away from each other, then back at each other, then a smile. He walked away to avoid her at first, but Abby wasn't having any of this?

She rubbed her body up against his intentionally, which no one was paying attention to? Thank God. He was surprised by what just happened. They looked up and down at each other. They were interrupted by her assistant, Rachel Joyce.

"Hello, Marshall. Mrs. Delaware and I are hoping you make a guest appearance at the company party in her honor, before she leaves. Are you coming to the party," asked Rachel.

"No. I won't be able to. I have too much to attend to after work."

"Even, on a Friday?"

"Yes, even on a Friday? Rachel."

Abby intervened to say, "I am sorry you won't be able to come to my party."

Rachel continued to stand between Abby and him to redirect any attention away from them, while they talked to each other back and forth. He was surprised at how devious and good they were together.

"What does your weekend look like?"

"I will be home all weekend."

"I guess at some point you will probably have a little hot-tie coming over, later?"

"No. I will be home alone. Why do you ask?"

"Then I am coming over to visit you tomorrow."

He raised his head and eyebrows, and stretched his eyes in disbelief.

"Oh really," he said. Abby asked him, "Is this going to be a problem for you?"

"Yes, it's going to be a problem, if you say you are coming and you don't come?"

They smiled at each other loosely. Rachel continued to behave, as if she was part of the entire conversation.

"Then I expect you to call me tomorrow, and confirm it one way or another, Abby?"

He went along with the game to call her bluff. He knew they were attracted to one another. He didn't think this would go any further than it did with her. He smiled at both of them as he said goodbye.

Abby and him exchanged hugs, while she bit his earlobe when no one was watching. Then there was an unexpected adrenaline rush when he separated from Abby's body. She felt a rise from between his legs, and looked into his eyes because of her mischievous behavior.

He walked away calmly, nervously, and puzzled. He returned to his office to review and evaluate her final report for Monday's meeting. She does excellent work. This is what made her who she is. She was a woman who sincerely knew how to work, resolve issues, and complete project reports.

This is why the company will miss her, and have a hard time trying to replace her, if they decide to. Sometimes one person can make a tremendous difference in your life and in the life of others. When it comes to a job that needs to be done?

Also, he thought about how clever Rachel was at times. He wasn't unaware of how much she wanted to lie down in bed with him, like she was wet water dying of thirst. He could see how horny she was when she looked at him. She had a way of looking at him like he was cheap, because she felt he was someone easy to get.

Given the right situation, Rachel felt she could have him, if she could only be alone with him. Even though she wasn't his type. He knew she would take him down, like a bad boy who would take her down, and think nothing of it.

Rachel was bad. She wouldn't hold anything back, but she wouldn't say anything to you, either. He recalled when she discovered his separation from, Jade.

It was one afternoon. He walked off the elevator and realized, he had forgotten a folder he left in someone's office. So rather than wait for another elevator to come. He decided to use the staircase to go back down stairs. It was only two floors down.

While in the event of walking down the stairs, someone was coming up the staircase. It was Rachel. When they approached each other his attention was focused on her as she came closer to him. He turned his head left to speak to her, while she slowly walked by.

Suddenly he couldn't catch his breath. She had a hand full of him in her hand squeezing him gently, while she pulled him closer into her and forced her tongue into his mouth.

And before he reacted it was over, and she continued to walk away from him, while she began running upstairs. He was surprised, but not once, did she stop to turn around to see if she had his attention.

He stood there watching her run away, as her behind provide all the attention he needed. Ever since then, she had always acted like it didn't happen, until she would undress him with her eyes again.

She was waiting for him to make the first move, or work him like the way she wanted to, in order to get whatever it is she wanted.

Rachel had looks galore, and a figure that would put any Model to shame. Honestly, she scared him. She is also a handful to deal with. He wouldn't describe Rachel as a lady of the night, but one thing is for sure.

Rachel, can roll a man over in the blink of a wink. She's that good. He understood he couldn't be with her, without using her first before she used him. There was too much uncertainty about her personality for him.

You could see she was no body's property, whether she had a man or not. But she was good people, and could be a lot of fun to hang out with. She would do what she wanted to do when she wanted to do it, and with whom ever? Regardless of the fact she kept her personal business discreet.

He answered his cell phone. It was Lawrence of all people calling him at work? He wanted to know if he could stop by after work and see him. He was the last person in the world he wanted to see. He didn't want to provide him with a reason to get suspicious about Sarah and him.

People are not as stupid as you would like them to be. Don't underestimate a person's need to see what's right there in front of them. They may not want to believe it at first or accept it. You can always deny something as long as you want to, but it doesn't mean that someone doesn't know something?

He reluctantly agreed to see him. He wasn't looking forward to seeing him. He was unfortunately sleeping with his wife. He couldn't believe how much she and he were enjoying each other, and it was so much fun. He told him he would be available any time after eight.

He thought about his relationship with Sarah, which brought back past memories of when he sat into a large chair eating delicious red bone chocolates, and thought about teasing a woman. She was on a diet. Although she didn't need to be on a diet.

He recalled a second box of white chocolates. When he left one woman to meet another woman at her apartment. Who he hardly knew? He touched her in the light of day, before he witnessed her nude. And she touched him again following the day of night.

Perhaps, they didn't feel each other, like shinning as illuminators until they were parted life feathered claims.

He didn't mean to deceive her with utmost images, but he did. It wasn't one of his better days with a woman.

He didn't forget about what Jade told him, that Lawrence tried to make a pass at her at their place one day. He claimed he was passing through the neighborhood, and wanted to stop by to say hello. Marshall was at a job function for the evening.

She adamantly didn't want him to say or do anything about it. She assured him. She was able to take care of him and his advances, and put him in check without any problems. He was a sleaze-bag to her.

She thought he was attractive in his own way. He dressed well, but that was it. There was nothing else to consider? He had no real personality except his fake charm. She also told Marshall, how she felt Sarah was attracted to him and liked him.

Naturally he didn't listen to her at the time. He thought she was just being selfish because she had him. He was wrong. She was correct.

23

Jade and Sarah didn't seem to like each other, but they were civil to one another in public. He wondered what it was they saw in each other he didn't see in them. It was Jade's belief that Sarah was crazy, if she thought she was going to lure him away from her. This was before their problems and separation began.

He wished it wasn't him, who first became a part of Sarah's life like this? He didn't want to cause any more problems for her with Lawrence. But after their involvement, things changed between them.

He knew Sarah and him were connecting with each other. It didn't matter what happened in the future between Jade and him or Sarah and Lawrence. There was something that seemed to be predetermined with Sarah and him that he couldn't explain.

It was something Jade saw long before it became a thought to him, but there was nothing he could do about it now. They do have feelings for one another, and whatever they are doing is real. The situation has changed for everyone else involved. Whether they knew what was going down or not.

This was happening to Lawrence as well. It was like the perfect crime gone wrong for him, and his marriage is coming to an abrupt end.

Sarah is attractive, beautiful, and an intelligent woman. The same is true of Jade and they are consistently being approached by other men. The type who had money, and can promise them anything their hearts desire. They are women who can write their own tickets?

The world Lawrence was living in was changing to being a joke, and as a sign of reply to people around him. The reality of it was difficult for him to distinguish about being sincere, with himself and anyone else.

Just because someone becomes a model, and has a bit of marginal success, and thinks he knows more than he thinks he does.

Then let's take love for example, or the emotion of love. He often tried to avoid the question. He is unable to answer the question with any true visibility from his thoughts about it?

Whether or not he really cares about the woman he married. He is trying to come off of it, like it was a flashback of something he shouldn't see or do, which was only known to him and Sarah as a mistake. He remembered the secrets they didn't share together.

But only a profound scenario to him for why he would want to ruin, or run their marriage into the ground? Women are not the only ones who will confuse the issue.

Men can be as much of a pain as women can be. When they don't know what they really want, either.

Sometimes it's a man who needs to find validation in his life more than a woman does.

He continued to imply he is a real man, but can't take control of anything to redirect him and his wife to a better future. He expected her to continue to be with him, and keep up appearances for his professional image.

Sarah came to the conclusion about his behavior in their relationship, which should have been placed into a created fairy tale. Where no one wants to read about it in heaven or in hell? Marshall had no idea they were having problems in their marriage so soon after.

It was too silly for him to think about what he should see, feel, or do and wish for. This is his problem, and not Marshall's.

She did everything she could of falling short of dispersing with him. He was always trying to roll over into another person's thoughts, which also belonged to another person's imagination? He didn't have any. This is why Lawrence couldn't take the answers out of his pockets fast enough to satisfy, Sarah.

She realized he was pretending to be someone else he wasn't. Marshall knew that two wrongs don't make a right. Nor was he passing further judgment on him without being a hypocrite himself. When he is the one who is serving his wife. It wasn't his intention to do the same to him. Since he made a pass at Jade first.

If Marshall wasn't naive about what Jade tried to tell him about Sarah, and paid more attention to what she was saying. Maybe he could have avoided the whole situation with Sarah. If he knew what was going to happen between them.

But they didn't know what was going too happened. This is why it happened. You don't always stop what you suspect is going too happened in your heart, but this is what he was saying about Sarah and him earlier. It's hard to say, before they arrived at this point, and getting caught with his pants down because he didn't suspect it coming.

24

Now, Sarah had his pants all the way down. He had to admit. He really enjoyed it, and he definitely wanted her to keep his pants down. He hoped she continues to at all cost, because she does turn him on. She has energy, passion, and satisfaction when she loves. He had no idea where this was going with him and her?

He interrupted his thoughts to complete his evaluation of Abby's report, before signing off on it. He was the last one to authorize it before the report is scent upstairs. He returned the report to Abby in her office.

She was alone and packing up a few items, which she accumulated from her years of employment. He briefly assisted her, until Abby was too busy being bad. She was rubbing her body up against his every opportunity she could get. It was at this point he knew he had to make a U-turn, and rush straight for the door.

He was curious as to where this was coming from and leading to? First, there is no one in his life for the longest? He didn't try to change this at the time. Then out of nowhere comes Olivia. Then Sarah happened.

And now, Abby? Nobody could be this damn lucky, he thought. She watched him walk away toward the door without drawing any attention.

"You won't be able to get away from me so easily tomorrow," as she gazed at him with a larger smile.

"Right, good-bye, Abby. I am going to really miss you."

He walked out of her office thinking that it wasn't going to happen between them? She was being a tease, he figured, but a good one. Because of the excitement being generated around her last day? It appeared no one was working or getting anything done today.

It was apparent everyone was excited and looking forward to the party after work, free food, free drinks, and ample time to seek out the latest gossip on anyone. He figured he would walk around, and touch base with several people in the department.

His calendar was clear for the day. He was going to leave early. He needed a distraction before he confronted Lawrence for this evening. He circulated around the department. He got involved with coordinating a few computer details which came upon the job.

He couldn't resist the challenge to assist someone since he was still there. He liked his work and his job at the company. He changed his mind and stayed for a while longer to say one last good-bye to, Abby. It was hard not to deny she enticed him when they first met.

She was a secret for him to keep to himself. Since he knew nothing would become of it. Abby saw him appear at the party given in her honor. She lit up like a quiet

Christmas tree. Abby couldn't have looked any hotter than she did.

Several of the Executives in the company were in attendance for the party. He heard through some gossip that two of them were attracted to her, and liked her for a while. He had one dance with Abby before he left to meet with Lawrence.

She kissed him. Again no one saw it. He wished at that moment she did come by, and see him tomorrow before she left. He would give her some outrageous passion of his own, so she could take with her to Memphis—as a thought to remember him by.

Abby is like a fascinating question mark, in which, you hold firmly into your hands, with very large thorns on it, that you don't care about? She is wicked in a playful manner. It's hard to feel less motivated with her around you. She had a unique way of making you aware of the obvious, without embarrassing you and insulting you.

He arrived home a little late. Lawrence, was there at the security desk waiting for him. They exchanged greetings, as he apologized for being late. They went directly to his place. They relaxed for a moment, and he served them beer.

He was starting to get bored and tired of his conversation and company. Everything was about him. He wasn't concerned about anyone else, nor did he ask about anyone else. The man was trying to establish his case for the ego-maniac of the year award.

He was going to discuss Sarah's sexuality with him, and the fact he hasn't slept with her in over eight months.

Marshall refused to listen to anything concerning her. He told Lawrence that was his business. It was something he didn't need to know.

He walked around a corner in his mind with this, and left it two blocks over, as he passed it by in his mind.

Sarah was now his concern. He cut the evening short and politely shuffled Lawrence's ass out of his place, with an excuse for being tired, and he had a long week… stuff, before he could continue his conversation about his new women, which he met recently.

While Sarah was away out of town doing her job. He didn't want to hear any more about it, or about her from him. He was surprised how little respect he had for himself or Sarah, and their marriage. The only thing he talked about was how she locked him out, and how she locked it down.

He was beginning to see what she told him about Lawrence, and he could also see the man was way out of control, and thinking he was all of this? Marshall was tried. He went directly to his bedroom and went to sleep. Hoping, this guy would get his act together alone, without involving other people?

25

Saturday, 8:30 a.m. He was on the highway taking a drive on the New England thru way, which is something he liked doing on the weekends. He thought about Lawrence's visit last night concerning Sarah. He had to know she was an excellent lover in his opinion. She gave a lot of herself, and does a lot in bed, where other women are lazy in bed.

They will give you all the sex you want, but they won't perform with you in bed. Or open themselves up to satisfy you without being satisfied in return. It had to be one of the real reasons why he was staying with her.

They could have had a reasonable chance together, if Lawrence didn't allow his ego to get in the way of something nice with her. Of course everything had to be centered around him.

Like if Jade was still there, but she wasn't there. And out of all the women in his life, he asked himself? Was he following a pattern by being involved with only married women? Why was this the case lately, when he never was before? He wanted to know, if he was acting out of some hidden frustration involving his separation with Jade? He hoped it wasn't anything but this?

He didn't need to react to her anymore after separating from her. It was time for a change. It was time to accept the new differences in his life, which were taking place, and basically deal with it.

When he returned home from his morning drive. He attended to a few things in hopes of the unexpected, before he attended a matinee movie. He knew it would be crazy on Saturday, with kids and family.

He was going to see a suspense thriller. After he returned from seeing the movie, he took a short nap and woke up at 3:30 p.m. His phone was ringing. "Hello!"

"Hello, Marshall. How are you?"

"I am fine, Abby. How are you doing?"

"I'm better now that I am talking to you."

"So I guess you call to say one last goodbye?"

"No, I called to see what time you would like me to come by?"

"Are you serious, Abby?"

"Yes, I am. I am not playing games. I gave you my word. I am coming to visit you today."

"Then how long can you stay?"

"As long as you want me to stay with you, Marshall."

"Then enough said. How soon can you be here?"

"You tell me?"

"How is Five?" Abby started laughing.

"Did I say something wrong?"

"No. It's an hour and a half from now. I didn't think you wanted to see me so soon? Most men would prefer to cut down on the time they have to spend with a woman.

"So they can get right to the point. They don't like entertaining a woman. It's either too much effort, or trouble to deal with. Instead they prefer being entertained by a woman. I can see you are quite the opposite. I had a feeling about you. I can't wait to see you, Marshall."

"Abby, seeing you today would make my whole weekend. This is why I won't believe it until you walk threw my front door. Your presence is expected more than you know. Then I won't have to fulfill myself with fantasies about you?

"I hope this doesn't put you in a compromising position with your other half?"

"No more than you are in with your wife, Marshall. I appreciate your concern, but tonight will be about you and me."

"Have you had anything to eat?"

"Not since this morning."

"Good, we can have dinner together. I will see you at five."

Abby laughed again. Marshall was direct and serious. She was beginning to see how much he wanted to see her. Abby said, "Goodbye."

He anticipated the remote possibility she may show up. He was prepared in advance just in case. You never know when it comes to women? They have a tendency to change their minds, whenever they care to and if you're wrong? Then you have to fight with them to show them where they are coming from. Telling you one thing and doing another.

He didn't have much time left. She would be here in under an hour. It was hot outside. The temperature was 97 degrees and humid. He was more than pleased he had centralized air conditioning. He changed into a light polo shirt, beige shorts with sandals.

He returned to the kitchen. He completed a dinner of Angel Hair Pasta with Smoked Salmon. Lemon Garlic Jumbo Shrimp, with a bottle of White Wine, and picked up desert from the bakery if she desired.

The door speaker buzzed. It was security announcing he had a visitor. "Ms. Abby?"

He was thrilled she arrived promptly standing in front of him. Smelling like honeydew suckled with another scent of coco immanent, and being released from her body.

She had a beautiful tan, and her auburn hair was full and neat, with highlights throughout. She wore a unique white cotton linen handcrafted stitched dress, with open toe wedged shoes. She had a hand bag.

Abby looked hot. She sizzled with desire even in the heat. Her breast protruded from her bra, and from her low cut dress with spaghetti straps.

Her lips were like red gapes, you just wanted to suck on and swallow. He came up for air after kissing her for the first time. He tried to make it count of course. He didn't want to be one of those guys, who is dumped based on his first kiss with her?

He could see she was thrilled by the kiss too. He brought her into the kitchen were they sat at the table.

"Wow! You really have a nice place."

"Well, I can't take all the credit."

"Your wife helped?"

"Yes."

"You and her did a great job. Did you order this food?"

"No, I didn't order it. And yes, I cooked it in honor of you being here. Would you like some wine?"

"Yes. Your dinner looks great. It tastes really good. I can't believe you are a cook, and a good one at that?"

"Is it because I am a man?"

"No, not at all, everyone knows that men are good cooks if they can cook. It's because you are Marshall, and you don't seem like a cook that's why?"

"Okay, point well taken. How did you get here?"

"Rachel brought me, since she is my partner in crime tonight. She is going to pick me up tomorrow. She is my alibi for this evening.

"It's a girl's night out, but obviously I have other plans with you." Abby pointed to her cell phone. "Rachel can reach me whenever she needs to."

"Are you sure everything will be okay? We can cut the evening short. I certainly don't want to create any problems for you."

"You and I are good to go Marshall. This is all you need to know."

Abby smiled when she finished her pasta with Smoked Salmon. She looked forward to eating her

Lemon Garlic Shrimp as well. He refilled her glass with more wine. She gazed at him directly, while she maneuvered the wine bottle away from his hand. She pushed her chair back.

She stood up and proceeded toward him, and poured him another glass of wine. She kissed him repeatedly, and then returned to her chair. He tried to imagine Abby in the nude accidentally?

26

You could see all of her blueberries were blessed with a true confession. He stood up and took a morsel of shrimp, and easily placed it into her mouth. She stood up to approach him. They hugged each other while they began caressing each other's body, before they started to kiss again.

He handed her the wine glasses. He took another bottle of wine with him. He reached out for her hand. Abby placed her hand into his.

He thought about how scary it can be, when you are first with someone. How compatible you seem to be together because of a natural flow. This is the way it was with Olivia, Sarah, and now the same connection with Abby.

He escorted her out onto the Terrace where a lounge table with reclining chairs where positioned. They sat comfortably gazing at each other. They were seven floors up. The design of the building was different.

Your terrace was private, because the terrace was on two sides of the building, but on every other floor. It was only a Terrace above you and one below you, but not on the same side of you. They were relaxed and holding hands. They enjoyed the view as they took it in together.

"How much do you still think about your wife?"

"Excuse me?"

"If you don't mine me asking…?"

"It's been a year and a half of unnecessary changes, with no positive results in sight. I don't understand anymore now, than I did before."

"Do you still want her back?"

"When the problem first began, I believed I did. I thought I was fighting for something.

"But it was like another day of hell in our relationship. When the hell and suffering lasted for this long. I didn't know what I knew now. It didn't enhance or motivate any positive emotions, and the need I thought I had for her anymore.

"I couldn't recognize her or her emotions, because trust was non-existed as far as she was concerned. She didn't feel good about herself anymore. There was no way I honestly expected her to relate to me, or in a sincere or compassionate manner anymore.

"No. I don't want her back in any sense of the word."

"Then why does the drama continue to exist in you?"

"Abby, I was hoping by now. I would be able to say to myself? Oh yeah, this is what happened besides the obvious. But it still doesn't make any sense, and this is what had been a thorn in my side. Because nobody had to put anybody through all of this, either?

"I think that is the problem right there," Abby replied.
"What do you mean?"

"I understand how deeply and disappointed you have been hurt, and what you have been going through. Have you ever stopped to reconsider what she had been going through?"

"Yes. I have tried, and she hasn't made it easy. It continues to pursue the fear in our hearts. It was like an overflow of unfamiliar reasons being misused and confused.

"Like I said, I tried more than you could imagine and came to the conclusion, that this was a big mistake on my part?"

"Then you should have looked at it from a different view point. They say most experts agree? People who cheat feel less appreciated. This is why they are out there trying to make another connection with someone else?"

"But do you believe in all of that, Abby?"

"Well, no. But sometimes it's true and other times it's not.

People make things more difficult than they have to be. When they are motivated by their own selfishness. I can't imagine being with you, Marshall, and not being appreciated or loved.

"You are a very romantic man who respects and appreciates women. It speaks in volumes about you.

"I have seen you and your wife in action. I use to say to myself she is a very fortunate woman."

He was pleased to hear about Abby's assessment of him.

"It was transparent how much you cared and loved your wife. I knew how much you enjoyed being married, which is something most men don't.

"I doubt very seriously a lack of appreciation was her problem. She was more than lightly very spoiled too? It was probably something far more personal with her. A woman goes through so much more in her life, than a man could ever imagine, or consider sometimes. Because they see what they only want to see.

When it comes to a woman, and her past life. Sometimes things from her past could have resurfaced and frighten her, which she felt she couldn't discuss with you. It happens all the time, and not for the best of reasons.

"You don't see things from a woman's point of view. How could you? And for a lot of men, they wouldn't get it, even if you laid it all out for them on a silver platter.

"You can believe in what I am saying. She was probably as surprised as you were, after considering what was happening to her. A person doesn't change their nature overnight.

"More than likely she wanted to talk to you about it. Until she got caught up in her own mix, and couldn't explain the turmoil in her emotions to you or herself?

"You don't want to hear this, but this is when shit happens, and you can't explain it. How can you expect her to explain it to you rationally? She is reminded every day of the horrible mistake she made, which cost her everything with the man she loves.

"People are still imperfect human beings, remember? We all fail in one way or another.

"She might have hurt you really bad, and Marshall you may have lost a wife. But she lost you and herself in the process, and trust me it is not something you can change, or make her feel better about concerning what had happened to her?

"This is something a man fails to realize about women, or what they go through. Would you like to trade places with her, since you loved her so much, and she had hurt you so much?" Abby asked.

"I am not saying I agree with her, but I can understand what she may be going through."

He took another sip of his wine. He stood up to take along look at the sky on a warm, beautiful night from the view on the Terrace. He considered a number of things Jade had said to him and compared them too, with the point of views that Abby mentioned to him.

He realized and discovered several connections he didn't make with his mind before. He felt slightly embarrassed he didn't see it, or make the connections before then. He asked himself, how could she feel unappreciated?

She was more than spoiled. He knew that for a fact, he was the one who spoiled her. It had to be something else she didn't want to talk to him about, or felt a sense of shame to talk about.

Abby approached him from behind to interrupt his thoughts, and turned his attention back to her. She hugged him with her body pressed into his.

"I really think it is time for you to back off, and give the both of you a break. You need to stop dealing with it. You need to stop punishing her or yourself so much. You need to see the good you and her brought to each other's life and let the rest go.

"One of your biggest problems is, that you were to close to the situation. I'm sure someone had to mention this to you before, who cared about you at least?

"So something went wrong. It happens every day to people you don't know. So no matter whatever you do, and how hard you try. You can't fix it, or put things back together again.

"But you are left with the pain and memory to live with. So stop and ask yourself? Do you want to really continue this verbal, emotional war of words between the both of you'll, which absolutely leads nowhere?

"She made a mistake and didn't tell you, or explain it to you. Why in the world would this happen? When you and she had all the togetherness in the world come to an abrupt end?

"The both of you really need to put this puppy to sleep for good now. It's a dead issue. So you can begin a healing process for yourself, and begin to forgive the things you don't want to forget.

"Marshall, things like this happens to people every day. There are no explanations the way you would like them to be, the way that this should be with right or wrong answers.

"I am sorry for your lost. I know how much your marriage to her meant to you.

"Since I am sharing this evening with you tonight. I can only imagine the lost and the pain she must be feeling to give you up, and not be here with you—herself.

“Whatever she is doing, or you think she is doing, you have to be crazy not to know how much she continues to miss you.

“No woman loves a man like you, and shared the things you’ll have shared together and loses everything, without knowing something had gone wrong within herself, as well as everyone else does?

“But this is her problem now. It is something which you cannot help her with. Also, you can believe a lot of the problems she is having, or what she is going through isn’t because of you?

“Do you really believe she wants someone else to have you and be with you intimately, while not having you and being with you herself?

27

"ANYONE COULD SEE HOW MUCH that woman loved you, when you and she were together. I have seen you and her on occasion. You can see there was something uniquely different between the two of you.

"Don't let bitterness, negativity, hate, and selfishness consume you. It wasn't just your relationship and marriage, Marshall.

"Stop acting like you are the only one, who is a victim of circumstance and lost something here. Just try your best to deal with her lost, and cherish as many good things as you can about the way you were.

"Suppose she died tomorrow, and you were unable to see and speak to her ever again. How would you feel? Probably a lot more lost than you feel now?"

"Thank you, Abby."

"What for?"

"Up until now, I only looked at things from my point of view. She failed to make any effort to communicate with me, or help me understand anything from her point of view.

"This is why a person will come to their own conclusion. Or make a judgment call when they don't talk to the other person."

"No one has tried to help me understand where I was coming from, and what I was putting her through because of the way she hurt me, and what we lost together.

"I am not saying it has changed much, but it has given me a different perspective on things. I admit I can be a bit of a hard ass at times."

"I know. I have seen you in action at work. You fight the good fight for the underdog. That's rare these days. This is why they appreciate you so much at work."

"Even though we aren't together anymore, I still want to see her happy and safe. She made me happy before all of this happened to her, and she was a great friend."

"But there will be times when a woman will check out on you. When she feels her feelings are more than what she saw? Sometimes we as people, no matter how much we love someone, don't live-up to love? Abby said.

"Just because you and her had a great relationship, and marriage for the last several years. Doesn't mean that she wasn't dealing with something personal in her past, and it resurfaced within her. Or she didn't feel she was the right person for you. This is probably where all the changes in her came from.

"But since we all keep secrets within ourselves about things, that happens to us we don't want anyone else to know. I am not going to say that she was right or wrong, but she had a problem dealing with it, and a problem dealing with you which caused you and her to separate."

For the first time in along while. He was feeling a true sense of relief thanks to Olivia, Sarah, and now Abby for different reasons. Their presence and personalities removed much of the negativity from within him.

He took her hand to lead her off the Terrace and inside. He guided her through the living room and down the hallway to the first bedroom, which was a guest room. He started kissing on her. He started undressing her. He kissed her scented body until she was completely nude.

Abby, surrendered herself to him without the slightest hesitation. Her breast were firm and up right. Her eyes were fixated on him. He licked on her nipples. He wanted to send her a recent wavelength as a new sign of chivalry.

He tickled her on her neck with kisses and his tongue, like unfamiliar people giving away dreams without secrets.

Abby, became more and more excited to see him focused on what was important to him. He diligently searched her body for a reason to precipitate the flow between them? She felt her legs weakening. He elated her, picked her up, and held her in his arms.

He needed her to know how impressed he was with her and her body. It came back to him like a diamond shining with more horizons. It was better than a dark secret being kept in the house. She wore a small Teddy Bear tattooed on the left side of and above her pubic area. Her hair was shaved.

Gently placing her down on a Queen sized bed, and removing his arms from under her. He stepped back to remove all of his clothes. She was equally as impressed to witness how defined and developed his body was for his age.

Abby, was pleased about pursuing something she felt passionate about with him. Everything was beginning to burn inside of her, like a borrowed drink which didn't say what play back wouldn't say?

He excused himself briefly to return from the bathroom, with a warm towel and lotion. At that moment, he felt he was born to run solely for the thrill with a sensuality to do this with her? She peacefully relaxed and quietly observed him. She searched for the same guidance.

He took both of her feet, and positioned them into the wet warm towel to begin massaging her feet. She closed her eyes, but the effect caused her to moan. After he finished, he applied the lotion to her feet and continued massaging them.

He began massaging her body. He turned her over with her eyes closed. She felt a sense of his generosity, and how much he cared about her to do this.

She said that he was rubbing her feet were neglected spots were. So he varied his strokes evenly for her.

"This feels so good. What can I do for you?"

"You are the one who is leaving. Just let me served you. I want you to remember this and more. Our time together is special, and for the right reason in my opinion."

Her eyes opened, as she rose up to pull him closer to her. Abby kissed him. She placed her left hand around his waist, and with her right hand she held him. She stared into his eyes and began kissing him across his face.

She continued by tracing along the outside of his lips. He gathered both pillows from behind her to position them under her. Slowly, he lowered her backward onto the pillows and slightly bending her knees.

He stroked her clitoris several times feeling her wetness reprieve before the ultimate concession came. There was much foreplay, which excited her before he entered her. Abby was longing for his touch as he was for hers.

At first, she didn't believe how relaxed, and open she was when he began to touch her. She wanted it to be different because she desired it to be, and it was different for her. He positioned his aim to thrust high up in her for their intercourse to come.

He didn't come as of yet, while she raised her legs higher. She could no longer maintain the size of her imagination from the climax she received. It was like a touch of evil, or he was a thief in the night to her.

Abby, was flowing like a stream which didn't care where it came from. He continued to thrust evenly, while she climaxed again losing control. She yelled out his name uncontrollably over and over. He had reached and hit her spot more than once.

Finally, she felt him releasing into her as her body vibrated. He relaxed his body gently up on top of her. He kissed Abby between his breathing. He kissed her on her neck a few times before he lifted himself up off of her.

He went to the bathroom to wash himself off. He returned with a warm cloth to do the same for her. It was soothing to her. She rolled over and placed herself into his arms after they finished.

He openly welcomed her in. Her head rested comfortably upon his chest. He held her closer to him. They joked with each other enthusiastically, before falling off to sleep stimulated.

28

LIKE A SIGN OF SHATTERED glass in her mind. She woke up. The dream she was having continued to give her smart pain for days. She wanted to know what it was about. A message which had to do with the past politics of her relationship?

She was still having trouble with the legitimacy of her feelings for losing him. Hoping after this length of time, they would have subsided by now, and she could see things from a different perspective.

She began crying. It was difficult for her to be immune to the agony. She carried in her heart for him all this time. She recalled one day. When Marshall and her were riding the Bus, after they purchased Love Toys from this store of Erotica.

He didn't want them to be viewed out in public, but she didn't mine. She was being bad that day. It didn't matter to her who saw them, while she laughed about it.

Although, he was trying to keep the items inside the bag. She continued to be bad and kept taking the items out of the bag for anyone to see. This woman and man smiled at her when she continued to misbehave.

Upon departing from the Bus, her New York magnificent behind was conveniently exposed to the Bus Driver. Who seconds later, was involved in an accident. Something you rarely see with a Bus? But Jade had taken away the Bus Driver's sanity temporally. When he extensively looked at her behind.

Marshall, joked about how she had put their lives in jeopardy with her body? They shared much fun between them on this day, just like they would do on any given day with each other. She thought about how he was able to get her to do things she hadn't done before?

She went to the kitchen to fix herself some coffee and toast. She wasn't hungry. She concentrated on trying not to cry anymore, because misery was enough in it-self.

Her phone rang. It was her new friend, Ryan Parker. "Hello."

"What's up, Jade?"

"Hi Ryan, how are you?"

"I am fine, but you don't sound too good."

"I didn't get much sleep last night."

"I hope it didn't have anything to do with your husband."

"Why would you say that?"

"I don't think you are being honest with yourself or me, when it comes to him. Why don't you let me help you deal with this?"

"Thank you, Ryan. It's something I prefer handling by myself. I created this mess. However, if I need your help I will ask you."

"Okay, Jade. Since you feel this way about it?"

"So what are you doing today? Would you like to get together later on?"

"I would, but I have some things to take care of, and if I change my mind about something I'll call you."

"Okay. I'll talk with you some other time."

"Bye."

She initially didn't mean to lie to Ryan, as she went to get her coffee and toast from the kitchen. She relaxed on her sofa while sipping on her coffee. She took a bite of her toast. She didn't have any plans for today. It was Sunday. She would be attending church services this morning, but since she had a lack of sleep. She declined to attend morning services today.

She discovered a neighborhood church after moving and separating from Marshall, hoping to find some guidance again in herself and in her life. She felt she was there to gain support and forgiveness for her piggyback sins.

She didn't want to be selfish in the way of her sins also. She believed she was a better person than what she had become lately. She decided not to take a shower, and reconsidered what she would do today?

****

With both her legs pinned back, and he rapidly thrusting deeper inside of her. Abby climaxed again. Her entire body trembled which caused her toes to curl.

"Wow, Marshall. What are you doing to me?"

"I am trying my best to please you, satisfy you, and fulfill you."

"Well, if I allow you to please me, satisfy me, and fulfill me anymore.

"Then I am a shame to say it, but I will have to go home and tear up my marriage license, and leave my husband for good. What happened last night and again this morning? I hope this hasn't been all one sided for you?"

"From the moment you arrived, Abby. I was too self-absorbed into you and being with you last night, and this morning has extended how good it has been with you.

"You have no idea, what it has been like to make love to you before you leave.

"It's sad in a way, it's exciting, and it's mysterious. But it's all good."

"I had no idea you thought of me this way, Marshall?"

"Trust me, it has been everything and more I have imagined it to be. You're no lame duck in bed either.

"Between last night and this morning, we have really given ourselves to each other. There were no games, pretense, or manipulation. It was desire and pleasure to feel for each other."

"I know what you mean. It has been an adventure with you. I would hate to imagine what this would be like, if we did this on a regular basis," said Abby.

"I wish I didn't have to let you go, but it's not my decision to make."

"You say the most interesting things, Marshall. If I wasn't married and you weren't married, or if one of us wasn't married, I wouldn't leave."

Abby gazed heavily into his eyes, like the responsibility bear no one's name. She kissed him like her affection was a weapon, as they hugged each other to claim each other's heart for the moment. They took a shower together. She explained to him, how her husband and she didn't take showers together.

"He didn't see the point in it. But with us, it is like we have a common admiration for each other's body."

29

HE WAS GLAD HE WASN'T one of those men, who had too much water on his stomach, and not enough knowledge on his penis to feel more secure about himself. When it comes to a woman, you don't know what you are really making her feel, or doing to her in bed.

Only she knows. She will say anything sometimes to pamper your ego, or unless she doesn't give a damn. And you are a fool if you think you do know. They were having fun exploring each other's body, while they applied more soap, lathering each other down as the soap disappeared from their bodies slower than honey. They were tempted to take it further again.

Abby, became concerned about her emotions and what this made her feel. When they dried each other off, he purposely touched and rubbed her pronounced and sensitive spot with his towel.

He couldn't tell how hard it was for her. When he gazed back into her eyes. She resisted politely and courageously. He took her back into the bedroom, and laid her across the bed. He applied a fragrant lotion onto her entire body. He kissed her on her vagina afterward. She asked him to stop.

Abby couldn't take it anymore, so he did. He saw tears quietly fall from her eyes. He held her for a moment. He apologized. He put his robe around her.

She enjoyed helping him prepare breakfast. They sat at the table eating, talking, and reading the Sunday News. They had an amazing conversation about relationships and marriage before Rachel called to pick her up.

She explained to him. Why they were able to spend the evening together, and experience the intimacy between them. It was a night breaker with a naked rhythm for her. Abby told him, that her husband provided her with a free dick-card.

A card she figured she wouldn't use, but when the circumstances leading up to her relocation provided her with a opportunity to pursue a feeling she had for him. She elaborated further. How she was aware of a one night stands, which took place between her husband and someone else recently.

It didn't change anything between them; a few feelings were hurt before and after it happened. She understood why he did it, not that she agreed with his course of action. She realized that Marshall and her couldn't be an item, but she knew because of her husband. She was now entitled to the same, if this was her choice?

She had no reason to take advantage of the possibility until now. If there was anyone she ever consider cheating with, Marshall was her man. She felt heat in her blood when she thought about him. Abby further explained, how she had been married for more than fifteen years. It can be the best thing in your life, or it can be an unexplained thing in your life.

"But this was a good thing to have, as an outlet to experience something different with someone else sometimes, if that's possible? Without you causing any problems, or destroying everything you have worked so hard to obtain with someone?"

"Sometimes people know how to come together and do something, with each other and move on without any problems. And then sometimes people come together for whatever reason, and get all caught up in the moment and the situation, which causes all kinds of problems for themselves and others."

Not that she was condoning adultery. It was about the intricate aspects of their relationship and marriage. Abby and her husband had a unique understanding in away. They loved each other. They were extremely committed to one another.

She is looking forward to starting a new life with her husband and her family in Memphis. It was her children who came up with the idea for them to join them. Her son and daughter have a thriving business there with a huge home. They wanted their parents to be a part of their good fortune and success, since they were a close family.

She realized her husband was aware of his one night affair. He was hoping she would take this opportunity and time to go, and do whatever she had to do about it?

So she could clear his conscious about the mistake he made.

So she could forgive him and get it off of her mind, because women have a tendency to never let a man forget anything that he does. No matter how long ago it happened? He wanted them to be able to put it behind them, and start out fresh when they relocated.

It was the way in which, they communicated with each other through out their relationship and marriage. With or without words: after all this time of being together. Her husband knew Abby was an experience woman—and more than likely—she was going to do the most experience thing.

He knew that she was a smart, particular, and rational woman. If she wanted to hurt you, Abby would just hurt you. She wouldn't waste her time with a lot of emotion tandem, or take you through a lot of unnecessary changes. She reminded him a lot of his mother. When he made a bad mistake, she would just burn the back of his behind.

He had no choice except to deal with whatever she dropped. There wasn't a damn thing he could do about it. He wasn't going to lose Abby over this, or anything else, he felt.

To him, nothing had changed between them, except the inconvenient mistake he made regarding this. He wasn't leaving, he wasn't going anywhere.

They were both smart enough not to bring anything back home, which would hurt them or their family. It was a mutual understanding between them, and really not about cheating on one another, if something like this happened.

Marshall was going to miss her more than he thought he would. What he enjoyed about her more than anything was no pretense in her—this was it with her—all the way. After being with Abby, he was left with a strong desire to be with her more.

Some people know how to love and give love to a person. Then there are many people who don't know how to love or give love to someone else. This is the connection we try to make in life with someone else—who knows how to love and give love to you, like you know how to love, and give love to someone else?

He had learned from experience that people have all kinds of relationships, which you think you couldn't have or even consider. The success of it is not what you thought it was about or should be between you.

It isn't because of the intimacy that you shared together. It was because of the way you talked, the way you communicated, or the insight Abby brought to him, or he let her bring to him. It was something he could understand, and relate to concerning her and her husband's situation.

He recalled trying graciously to do something similar with Jade, as much as it tore him up inside. He detected she was approaching a cross road in her life, and in their relationship. It had everything to do with her as a woman. He didn't want to lose her or their marriage because of it.

He also knew she could be at a fork in the road at this point in her life. He didn't know whether or not it was a seven year inch for her either. Or she was going through a mid-life crises. Or something completely different which involved them or didn't involve them?

Women hide under the fact that it is complicated, which usually involves a lot of issues. So he didn't know?

When she was searching for more than just a reason of being in love with him, or being his wife. He offered her an opportunity to seek out whatever she wanted to do without him.

He talked about it. He offered her the chance to pursue whatever it was which made her happy out there. Their marriage would be put on hold. The only obligation they had is to each other. They didn't have any children yet.

He assured her they could continue to be friends. Since they were friends before and throughout their relationship and marriage. In spite of everything, he would still be there for her, and she could still be there for him.

It was strange how they endured all of the changes which ended their life together. But it didn't matter whether she was with someone, or sleeping with someone else. She was still there for him, if he needed her. Her life was hers to live as she pleased without him. It was a break up, a separation, and not a divorce as of yet.

Also, a possibility they could get back together. Or the journey could lead them down a different path and into the arms of someone else. It was a serious point of no return lingering between them.

It brought a lot of sadness and uncertainty to his emotions to consider and do this. He could see something different in her. He just wanted to do what was best for her, if this was the case. Up until this point, the ride in their relationship had been many great thrills.

Neither one of them may not experience this again with someone else throughout their life.

In the beginning, she appeared to be intrigued about the whole idea of being on her own again without him. It could be a solution to her problems possibly or whatever she was going through? She would have the time and space to search herself throughout? Or if the whole idea didn't appeal to her. Then they should find a way to sort out whatever problems they could be having, without being aware of them?

He would begin to divide their accounts. Her money will be separated as well as her credit cards. She had her own car. So to insure this would happen, all she had to do was make a decision one way or the other. Then he would begin to implement the plan or not?

30

He didn't want her to feel like she was being pressured, whether she wanted to do something or not? He gave her as much time as she needed to decide. It was more than ample. They dealt with their lives for the next month differently.

Still, she hasn't made a decision about their talk. Or the proposal he made to her about venturing out on her own.

He was surprised after a while. She didn't show any interest in the fact he made this offer to her. Like he might be stepping out on her, or wanted to get rid of her. Or maybe what he was doing was irrelevant to her at the time?

If it was something she needed to do for herself. He was surprised and curious when there was no follow up on her behalf at all. Jade knew how to take care of business. But during this time, he noticed there were several changes in her attitude, like shadows standing next to each other, who now opposed each other.

It was the first time they had ever experienced serious tension between them, and he didn't understand why it was even present. There was some kind of underlying behavior between them he wasn't recognizing on her part.

Don't get him wrong, it's not like Jade and him didn't get into serious heated discussions, but they didn't fight with each other. She pissed him off, just like he pissed her off. There are times when they would find their separate corners, and space and leave each other alone.

Then at some point they were back in each other's arms, and loving it all the way. After they thought about making up to one another. It didn't matter who made the mistakes between them.

It was about them trying to be on the same page with each other. He know it had nothing to do with being this time of the month for her either? He could see something was bothering her, which she didn't want to share with him, which was affecting their relationship in a real negative way.

He came home one day after work before she arrived. Usually she gets home before he does. Later, he received a call from her. She tells him she wasn't coming home, and she was staying at a friend's place. She wouldn't tell him what was going on about this, and decided to be vague and emotionally confusing.

This wasn't some sort of joke, he thought. He flipped. He felt she was lying to him. He realized something else was also wrong. He thought it was something they were supposed to be dealing with together. It was their personal business they were talking about or attending to?

Why the sudden change in her, he thought? What is wrong with her all of a sudden after ten years, and now she can't speak her mind? Any other time you can't get her to shut up. When she has a point to make?

How could everything about her change like this? He searched through the apartment, and discovered certain belongings of hers were gone but not everything.

She planned the whole thing in advance, while being intimately involved with someone else he figured. This is one of the reasons why she was unable to talk to him about what was happening, or explain anything to him, or make a decision for herself.

He was furious with her. Why all the deception? He tried to offer her a perfect out for her if there was one? So she could deal with whatever she was going through. But she blindsided him instead, like an anonymous day in life. Why?

What the hell was going on with her? She had to know this was a trip. She was taking with uncertain fun for the both of them. He was more than disturbed by it. She made him feel like he was supposed to hurt her back in return. Whether he wanted to or not, or knew about this or not.

He thought at the moment, if he could request she split an apple in half, or located a seed from within, which could have an orgasm in the spirit of life? Then he couldn't love her any more than a fat woman, who couldn't elevate her stomach to see her feet.

Why would she do something like this? Here comes the fun part. She was no longer a dedicate Fallen Angel at a Comedy Festival.

He blamed himself for not seeing something like this coming. We act like we are geniuses, and can immediately recognize deception in any form, or manner when it is displayed to you. Then how come the discovery only takes place after the deception comes, and not before the deception comes?

He knew he was being unreasonable within himself. When someone else close to you is deceiving you. He understood what it was, before it became what it is now, after speaking about the devil in her. But that was then, and this is now he recalled.

He received a call from Jade, shortly after Abby's departure. She wanted to stop by and see him. Since other women like Olivia, Sarah, and Abby are here, he agreed. He is a much stronger person, and different now, because of his involvement with them.

He really didn't have a lot of time to contemplate about the B/S that Jade continued to generate anyway, because of the other women in his life—they simply took away all the garbage he had to deal with. He discovered a wisdom received in the process from dealing with each of them.

Jade's appearance could hardly be threatening to him anymore. He was enjoying himself immensely. Even though, all the new women in his life were someones wife. It was an odd situation to be in, but like the moment of silence and apprehension when she arrived at first.

Jade made an attempt to hug him, which he wasn't prepared for. She reminded him still of a large Jigsaw Puzzle, too difficult to figure out, or too difficult to put together in terms of seeing the big picture. He reconsidered and hugged her back.

She held him for several seconds before she released him, like she always hugged him—when they were once together.

"Please, make yourself comfortable."

She briefly scanned the place to see if there were any new changes. To her delight there were none. He had a suspicion why she came over to see him.

31

He wasn't going to mention it, but they were cautious in the beginning. It was a feeling out process because there were differences in both of them now. They offered each other a different kind of customer service.

Jade is a pretty woman with a medium complexion, and short hair, she cut it. Brown eyes with a smile that can seduce your heart, and her body is built like the Bravo of Bitches.

Whereas other women try hard to show off everything they have or don't have, it made Jade feel self-conscious. The attention she receives from men about her body. She stands tall with a medium built, and large parts. She implied she was hungry.

He asked her would she like to go out for dinner. She didn't want to. They ordered in. They agreed to have Chinese Food. It was one of her favorites. They were having a good time. When stolen fantasies were in a borrowed life.

They talked more in the kitchen. They laughed a lot at the table. They shared another bottle of wine together with their dinner, like a virgin is seeking her turn at fate. She was coming in with a clean wave of passion.

They were having fun together being themselves again. Something which had become a problem for them? They would clean up together after they would eat. This evening was no different.

She made him laugh during this time with her antics. She could always make him laugh. He was walking on a hesitation line with her. He didn't know what this was really about with her. She walked out on the Terrace with her glass of wine.

He followed her moments later, after he put away the kitchen utensils. She was crying. He asked her, what was wrong? She didn't know he wanted to get a divorce. She received the divorce papers from Jacoby & Meyers Law Offices.

"Jade, you gave me no other choice. I am sorry. You should have realized I was the last person whoever wanted a divorce.

"You could have brought back the allurement of excitement in our lives, if you wanted to. You didn't have to sleep with other men to do this, but this is where you went with it.

"Apparently you had an ulterior motive unknown to me. I don't want to fight with you anymore. I don't want to hurt you, or want you to hurt me anymore.

"I can't be with you, and you can't be with me now. I had no other alternative I felt, but to file for divorce. It was something I didn't understand about you.

"I didn't believe in divorce either, but when you cheated twice, before and after our separation since we have been marriage. Then I believe in divorce.

"It isn't about how many times you cheated. It was about the first time you cheated, and all the deception, and the lies you were telling me, just before it happened.

"You know Jade, it seems when our people get married to one another, and then serious problems occur which causes us to separate or break up, there is hardly ever a divorce.

"My mother had been married for the majority of her life, and for the majority of her life she had been alone.

"And yet, there isn't a divorce from a man I have never seen or met in my life.

"So we move on with our lives with other people, while we are still married to someone else, and deceiving this person until you can come up with something else better? Or like I still believe in Frankenstein?

"I believed this ship has sailed a long time ago. Maybe there is some kind of wisdom in living free this way, but I don't want this for myself.

"I can't. How can I begin my life over, if I am still married to you, Jade? When we are not together?"

"Well, have you met someone else, Marshall?"

"Yes and no. Right now, it's complicated and too soon to tell, but that's not the point I am trying to make."

She stood up to wipe her face, but cried like her tears had a license to appear before him. He held her in his arms and recalled, you can't buy luck back like this?

Her pain was real, and he knew why? He felt the same pain she did for different reasons. He didn't want to say anymore to destroy her pleasantness, or her pain in a strange way. It didn't stop being his pain also, which was something she didn't understand either. He couldn't stand to see her hurting in the worse way.

She cried more. He guessed they were living a breed apart in a different life? Many of their emotions were like the air they breathe. She made an effort to seize with the crying, and it was time for her to leave.

She released herself from his arms still sobbing. She was in no condition emotionally or physically to drive home, after all the wine they shared together. He suggested she spend the night. He couldn't allow her to leave this way.

"After you get a good night sleep, you will feel better in the morning. Everything is still where it used to be. I guess it never stopped being your home."

She looked at him without feeling suppressed. She went to her closet and then to the bathroom to freshen up. He went to the bedroom to do the same after her. She appeared in front of him in her pajamas.

He wondered how much pressure she felt about feeling like The Black Sheep, who couldn't come home anymore as he looked at her? She didn't want to sleep alone. She wanted to sleep with him. He thought about it and then he said, okay. When they were in bed he was feeling like a man of no importance to her.

She rolled over into his arms, and asked him to make love to her. He asked her why? She replied, it might be the last time she may know of love between them?

They began to indulge in each other. She tried to be a passage of pleasure between them, but it was more like a midnight public tease to him.

She was still a charming and erotic young woman, who he always tried to serenade from down under?

Jade and him realized this was sex. It was a good and meaningful attempt, but they couldn't make their dreams a harvest for the world again. Or like a fear that didn't exist in two fugitives on the run. Who wouldn't be taken down easily by the law?

Something was missing, like a natural born thriller of excitement was gone between them. Vigorously, after dark and for the last time they did it. They kissed each other good night.

32

HE WAS SURPRISED JADE WAS gone when he woke up. He was relieved. Since they didn't have to discuss what happened between them. There was a note left on her pillow. He thought about it before he picked it up. It wasn't necessary for him to read it, but he did.

"Marshall, you will never know, how sorry I am for hurting you the way I have. If I ever wondered, what it would be like to be lost. I know now being without you.

"Some mistakes you make in life, are so difficult to understand that you made them, and explain to yourself, why at the time you made them.

"You ask yourself over and over. What would possess you to do something so out of character, or stupid like this? When things don't make any sense to you. Well after you have done it?

"A mistake you wish from the bottom of your heart, you could take back, but you can't. So you are merely left with the misery to live with it, and everything you have lost with it.

"In my heart, I will love you always, and probably will never stop loving you, Marshall.

"Whether you believe me or not, or can ever accept me back. Please believe me.

"Can you give me some time to process the divorce, before I sign the papers? I love you, said Jade. I wish you well."

Marshall thought about the contents of Jade's note briefly. He was feeling indifferent, as if he was selfishly sticking it to her. It's strange how circumstances prevail in love? When you watch other people's dreams die—trying to survive in your life—before you become their nemesis.

And how other people forget to tell you, that life walks with a limp some times, which disappoints you more than you care to admit. He was trying not to feel anything, about what he was asking from her with the divorce.

When he arrived at work, he realized that Abby was no longer there. He was fascinated by the events, which took place between them on the weekend. It was simply great. Damn! It was outrageous he recalled, and that he had a meeting to attend.

He is the computer and information systems manager. Abby's position had to be replaced soon, and until that is accomplished. A decision had to be made about who will assume the responsibility of her department.

Will there be any rearranging at this juncture? He will be tied up in meetings with various people until this is resolved. The play by play conversations at work: when he spend his unresolved time thinking about Abby and her sophisticated adult variety of romance.

She was a wealth of knowledge to him. She was older and definitely wiser. He could also see, that she was his Cougar. Like a man who wants to learn, and a woman who wants to believe, but the child is still a Nickelodeon?

He realized he wouldn't have been able to deal with the confrontation, between Jade and him at the apartment yesterday. Without it turning into World War Three, if it wasn't for Abby. She took something out of him, and replaced it with something else inside of him.

He felt that was unique of her. The fact that he didn't want to hurt Jade yesterday, and punish her for continuing to hurt him was a change up. He tried to bring her a message of friendship and forgiveness, and to also save her from herself.

After recalling, when he first met Jade, and eventually became involved with her and married her. He knew then, he genuinely loved her, and knew he would always care for her. This is why it was difficult to continued being her friend.

When he didn't want to recall her affairs. When he had to step on his pride and continue to care for her, as a person that his pride wouldn't allow him to care for. Since a part of him knew that Jade and he, may love each other for a timeless obsession. They just couldn't be together anymore.

It was good to see her smile and laugh at dinner to enjoy herself, as if she had many wet dreams without him. When she cried after bringing the divorce to his attention.

First, it was his desire to comfort her. She was now a wilted rose. Never thinking he would agree to sleep with her again, but he did.

Secondly, as a result, he remembered when they were once the ideal couple in love. Who didn't spend a shrewd night together yesterday, but may have kept love a live in a mystery of silence?

Now that the meetings were over he was relieved. He returned to his office to see, he had several messages. One was from Marcus, his friend. It was 4:15 p.m. He returned Marcus's call before he left work.

"Hey! How you doing?"

"I' m doing great? I just got in from California. I was hoping if you weren't too busy this evening. Maybe you could stop by, and we can catch up on some things."

"Sounds good, Marcus. Let me take care of a few details here and I will see you later."

"Okay Marshall, I'll see you when you get here."

He completed putting the final touches on a few business matters on the job, and closed up shop for the day. He briefly spoke to a few people also, before leaving the building to enter his car. He mapped out what directions he would take to White Plains on his GPS. He will be going in a different direction. He had another stop to make before he arrived to meet Marcus.

He was looking forward to seeing him, as he began driving. It's been a month since he last saw him. He thought about how long they have been friends, and the first time they met each other at a New York Knicks game at the Garden.

Marcus graduated from Columbia University with a bachelor's degree in business administration. He worked for a company as an Insurance Underwriter, and specializes in Property and Casualty. He has done well for himself. After eleven years with his company. He makes a nice salary, and he owns his own home.

Marshall graduated from New York University with an MBA in Computer Science. He had worked at two different companies within the last twelve years. So he could obtain the experience he required to be promoted, as a Computer and Information Systems Manager with his company.

****

It was over nine years ago when he met Jade. He was invited to a Halloween Party by an acquaintance he knew. Who was a friend of the person who was giving the party at their home in Long Island? They had a beautiful home.

The party was active with a lot of people, and with women all over the place, which made it a good party because they had everything else. But nothing makes a real good party, unless you have a lot of woman there. He was pleased that he attended.

The first time he saw her was at that party. He couldn't believe how gorgeous she was. It didn't matter at the moment, what she looked like underneath her cape. She was dressed in a Vampire custom with a great make-up job. A nice window's peak, with her hair pressed back and slick as it could be.

She wore Blue Contact Lens, a Black Tuxedo with a Blood Red Bow Tie, and a Blood Red Cummerbund. A Black Silk Cape, with pike hill Hooker Boots? He loved Hooker Boots.

She was hot. She was a pretty vampire, and a hot one at that. She walked through the crowd of people just observing. He swiftly moved through the crowd of people to meet with her, and introduced himself to her wearing his costume.

She was nice and polite when he approached her. He kissed the back of her hand. When he introduced himself in his Jack Sparrow costume, as a low life, scoundrel, no good thief, cheat, lover, and fighter? Because he was hoping in this case, she took advantage of him?

"Would you like to take a bite, or would you prefer to make a significant withdrawal later?" He asked her.

Her face lit up with laughter, before he asked her to dance. They began dancing. He removed the mask from his face, so she could see what he looked like. She was pleased by the results. Before the evening came to an end, she and he exchanged numbers. Later, they talked and started seeing each other.

Four years later, they were married and invested into a Condo. The first nine years of their relationship was damn near perfect and unbelievable, until a year and a half ago when something went wrong with her. She and him were no longer themselves anymore, but had become a lost love.

Marcus was sitting out on the porch when he drove up. They greeted each other with a solid hand shake and hugged.

"Long time no see, Marcus?"

"Tell me about it, Marshall? Have a seat. I ordered Pizza. It's too hot to cook, unless you prefer something else?"

"Pizza is just fine. I haven't had it in a while."

"I can only imagine, with all the healthy eating you are doing."

33

JUST BEFORE THEY SAT DOWN to get comfortable on the porch, the Pizza delivery had arrived. Afterward, they entered the house. They walked a head. They came to an open door way. It led them to a narrow long room, and to the left at the end of the hallway.

The furniture was arranged differently with two distinct zones. There was a table and two chairs in front of a fireplace. On the other side of the room was a sofa, two arm chairs, upholstered Ottoman's clustered off to the side, they sat there.

Marcus placed everything on a medium sized table in front of them. He entered the kitchen and returned with Lemon Ice Tea. They sat on the sofa apart from each other. He reiterated about his company trip further.

Marcus was five-ten, and slim. He is an attractive white man, with an outgoing personality and a pleasant demeanor, and very easy to talk to.

"The company is down sizing again, and several of our positions are being relocated to their branch in California. My position is also being considered strongly.

"What can I tell you, the economy has been a slow process, but you still have to discover a way to generate income or you lose your business?"

"So how do you feel about it?"

"I am not liking this at all, but I like my job. Strangely enough, a lot of companies are still going out of business. I have worked hard to get where I am, and I have learned a lot. Also, there is a big raise upon the table to sweeten the pot.

"If I give up everything here, and accept the position to relocate there. After doing a system analysis and range insurance application, the company is losing more money here in New York.

"While business numbers continue to escalate at their California branches, and the International markets. It is also about the future of the company

"This is where the revenue is coming from. For the time being until something else changes. If I want to stay with them, which I do, then I'll relocate."

"I would hate to see you go. But then again, you have to do what you have to do. So how was the trip overall?"

"It was different but it was good. I felt like I fit in out there. I met a few women and received a few numbers also.

"So how is Jade doing? How are things between you and her now?"

"Well, more has happened since you have been gone." They took large bites of their veggie pizza, followed by a long swallow of lemon iced tea.

"Olivia Isaac and I got together."

"Are you for real, Marshall?"

"And before I had a chance to come down from on this cloud with her? Sarah and I jumped on top of each other, also?"

"No shit! Get out of the basement, you and hot Sarah!? It's a shame how she got stuck with that fake-ass guy, Lawrence."

"Oh, and I can't forget about, Abby?"

"Marshall, how could you touch all of this from the Devils Gate?"

"I have no idea. It just happened. Trust me, it wasn't something I did to encourage or jump start? Who knows, maybe I was in the right place at the wrong time?"

"Yeah right, and I wouldn't believe that even if you paid me a million dollars?"

"But to top it all off with, a complete unexpected blessing. Jade and I had dinner together at our place, and we slept together, but it wasn't all of that anymore.

"She spend the night and left in the morning. Since all of this happened. I feel like a madman out of control. Who doesn't know he is a madman out of control?"

"Yeah, but what's up with all the married women? I thought that you told me, Olivia was married with no family. We know that Sarah is married. You also said that Abby was married, also.

"The only person who isn't a problem is Jade, because she is still married to you? Who is the problem in the first place? Damn!" They laughed about it together out loud.

"I can tell you one thing."

"What?"

"You won't be getting married anytime soon, with all of the wives you have in your life?"

"So how are things between Brenda and you?"

"Why do you ask? Marcus smiled. "I guess we are doing fine, as long as we stick to our arrangement.

"I don't want anything serious with her. She is good in bed when she puts out. Or brings out the freak in her, but on the real side. She's a real head case at times. She loves drama more than drama loves it-self.

"You know the type always bitch'in and complaining about everything and everyone else, never happy, satisfied, or pleased about a damn thing.

"She wanted to try and whip me in my own house. Do you believe this? She was serious too! So that she could prove to me, that a woman can physically put a man in his place too?

"I tried to tell her, that woman need to stop acting so much like men, and should go back to being themselves, which was the better part of the deal?

"I don't know why her last name is Gentle, as far as I am concerned, there is nothing gentle about, Brenda. She was here the night, before I left for California on my trip. Apparently, I made her jealous about something I was unaware of.

"Are you ready for this? She reacted by grabbing me by the collar. She threw me up against the door in my own house, as if I was her little bitch or somebody. I couldn't help but laugh at her.

"She was serious. You know, that Brenda is a fine looking woman, with a hell of a figure. But for a woman she is a ruff neck, not a red neck. And would you believe that she is heavy handed.

"I kept trying to tell her, keep her hands to herself. Can you believe, I am telling a woman this? I was going to knock her out. She kept putting her hands on me.

"I know, she had a rough time with her childhood, and growing up and all. I understand she was sexually abused by her father. However, you can't try and compensate for your heartaches by mistreating other people for it? When you are out of your comfort zone?

"She didn't have to threaten me, so that I would be her man, and go out with her, either?

"I choose who I want to be with. I thought about it long and hard. I gave her a chance, which is why we only have an understanding between us. No strings attached under no circumstances.

"All I need is for her too flip out on me, and take my life for her own selfish reasons, which is for no apparent reason, other than one, that I don't understand.

"She could probably be a good woman to some man someday, but she needs some counseling first.

****

Marcus had a very unique moment with Brenda once, in which, she swore him to secrecy. At first, he couldn't believe this was the same person he was with.

She was absolutely different. She decided to open up to him, and share a personal part of herself.

This was after the third or fourth time they made love, and it was different that time with a sense of vulnerability for her. She cried in his arms. He was touched, and he held her firmly. She said, she felt safe for the first time in years with him. Although he had no idea what she was talking about, because he didn't think that she had a real intimate side to her. You know, where civility and compassion were concerned.

He agreed with her at the time, that he wouldn't tell anyone else about it, but Marshall was the only person he cared to trust with this. Since he knew he wouldn't betray his confidence.

Brenda began saying, that he was the first man that she had real feelings for and cared for. Since she realized, how much of a joke the other men in her life were. She knew that they wanted what she had between her legs, and nothing to do with her.

This is why she was so comfortable with him sexually, because he treated her much differently after he received the sex. He still treated her with respect, and not like an asshole would. This was also why, she never gave herself to anyone like him before. He didn't understand what she was talking about concerning him and her.

She explained that when she was little, she had a sister who was a year older.

Unfortunately, her mother was an alcoholic. She was always drinking, drunk, and passed out. But her father would beat them severally, and take one of them into his room, and have sex with them, while the other sister had time to think about it, before her beating.

So she wouldn't put up much resistance toward her father's sexual advances. Their father was a huge and over bearing man. So there was a lot to be afraid of.

When he would finish with the oldest sister. Then all the youngest sister would have to do is just comply. When he brought her into the room for her turn.

34

BRENDA DIDN'T WANT TO GO into, or talk about all the things he had did to them. But she remembered—how careful he always was—by using his protection of condoms. He obviously wasn't going to make the mistake of getting either one of them pregnant, which would crucify him in the name of the law.

Sadly enough, this went on for years, with the beatings and threats for them to continue with their sexual compliance to him. She said, that her mother was a basket case from all the drinking, and beatings she absorbed from their father, and eventually she was committed to a mental institution.

It became a big problem for them, because they loved their mother, and they could never talk to her about anything. She seemed to always be entangled into her own pain and suffering. So there was no one her sister, or her could go to and explain this problem to.

But as they got older, they did good in school and kept their grades well above average, and worked hard after school. So they could avoid being in the presences of their father, because he was still looking forward to his benefits with his two beautiful and developed daughters, as they became older and more mature.

But after they graduated from high school, they moved out and got an apartment together, without their father's knowledge. There was nothing he could do, they were of age and employed, and committed to their own responsibilities.

So he was at a lost emotionally and physically, because the mother and the girls were gone. But the girls didn't care anymore. They were finally free from him, and all his abuse which they had to tolerate all that time.

Naturally, because it started so young in their lives. They had no idea what kind of emotional, and mental effects it would have on them afterward.

When Brenda and her sister had their first sexual experience. It turned out to be with each other, this was just the first of their after effects, which caused two sister to share physical intimacy with each other. They felt such hatred toward men, and couldn't allow a man to touch them, after everything they experienced with their father through the years. They thought that all men would be the same.

They were simply afraid of what they would do to a man, if he ever attempted to touch them sexually for whatever reason. They just wasn't feeling it with men. She and her sister stuck together and were very close.

Although they didn't indulge into their sexual activities too much, unless they were overcome by their loneliness and despair, which caused them to reach out to each other. It was a secret they felt comfortable with keeping between them.

Unfortunately, another misfortune took place. Brenda shared some pictures once of her, and her sister when they lived together and continued to grow into adulthood. He was surprised to see two beautiful sister as they were.

Her sister was pretty, just as Brenda is. It was sad, that their mother never got the chance to see her two daughters grow up, to be two beautiful and intelligent women, before she passed away in a mental institution.

Brenda and her sister made every attempt to go and see their mother. Officially they were declined the visit by the people at the institution. They claimed that the mother was never in the proper condition to receive them for a proper visit.

After suffering this big disappointment, Brenda and Robin continued to grow. They began interacting with men more, because of the constant contact and communication through their jobs.

It was still very difficult, but they began to realize that they couldn't judge every man based on the behavior of their father. They came to the conclusion, that their father was simply a bad man, and had his own source of problems with women that he failed to resolve.

Then eventually, they individually moved into their own apartments, and conducted their own lives apart from each other. But they remained close, and kept in contact with each other.

Then Robin, met a man. She fell in love with him. Brenda was confused and disappointed to hear this. When it was brought to her attention. But she felt she had no choice, except to support her sister, and her new feelings for a man.

However, Brenda continued to feel and remain confident toward her negativity, and still couldn't tolerate men in her life yet. Her sister appeared to be happy, as the years went by for them.

She was surprised, how long their relationship continued to last. Then she met him, and he was different. She saw the feelings he truly had for Robin, and it affected her differently. She was able to develop a friendship with him as well.

Then she began to see men in a different light from the way she saw her father, and other men. But she still didn't allow herself to have a relationship with a man for the time being. She was pleased for Robin, but she wasn't quite there yet.

And a lot of it had to do with the sex in a relationship between the man and the woman, which she wanted to know more about in reference to? So she began to open up, and talk to Robin about it, and her relationship with her man.

Although, there were two strange events that happened after this. Her father was discovered in his apartment dead. A neighbor next door to him, began smelling a peculiar smell coming from his apartment and told the Super. After he checked it out, he agreed and called 911.

When the police arrived, the Super opened the door, but it was unlocked and the police ushered him behind them, before they entered the apartment.

The smell became increasingly stronger when they entered further into the living room. There in the middle of the floor was a man lying on his back, and covered in blood which was splatter all over the floor, walls, and furniture.

The damage to the man's body was gross to witness. The Super identified the man as the apartment tenant. Her father was intoxicated heavily, and his alcohol level was .35 when they performed a autopsy on the body, and he was struck in the head with a hammer twenty-one times.

His eye was hanging out of his socket, and his nose and teeth, along with his gums were crushed. Then his torso was stabbed throughout with a butcher knife twenty times. Interestingly enough, Robin was twenty-one, and Brenda was twenty at the time when this happened.

But after the police informed them and investigated their whereabouts. They had a solid alibi for their whereabouts according to their fathers time of death. The hammer and the butcher knife, and any other evidence with DNA were removed form the scene. The person who murdered their father was let in the apartment, or they had a key to the apartment.

The second thing that occurred was the two suicides of Brenda's sister, Robin, and her boyfriend, Kincade Charles. After the detectives investigation into their deaths. They came to the conclusion, that due to a misunderstanding and a lack of communication. There was a problem that caused a problem for them.

When the detectives talked to family, which Robin didn't have much of except for Brenda. But with her boyfriend, his family, friends, and business associates expressed the same results. They were the couple of the century, and all that good stuff, and madly in love. They were also looking forward to their wedding.

Then all of a sudden, something strange happened which coursed them to distrust each other. When the detectives came across evidence, which suggested that they thought each other was cheating, and betraying each other.

They were sending each other incriminating texts messenges, and accusing each other of things which they had no prove that took place. This however, continued to escalate into further problems for their relationship, and coursed them to behavior differently toward each other.

Then there was a lack of communication between them that took matters to another level, and went to the extreme for the love they had, and shared with each other. They felt lost and empty without each other.

When they stopped seeing each other. When they were discovered dead in their apartments. There were two completely different suicide letters from him and her located at their apartments.

The detectives thought it was odd, that they would resort to this kind of action. Considering the magnitude of their relationship and feelings for each other. The both of them poisoned themselves, and left a letter of confession of love to each other, before talking their lives.

The letters were confusing to say the least. When their feelings were supposed to be so compatible. One of the letters were like the person just met the other person, and didn't know much about the other person they were about to marry, but they were so much in love. This letter seemed as though it was written by someone else, who was outside the relationship the detectives thought.

35

When the detectives questioned Brenda about this and more. They discovered she had a solid alibi at the time of all of this, and didn't appear to be an essential part in this. But still the detectives had a bad feeling about the circumstances of this case.

They couldn't release their own suspicions, that this could have been all manipulated by a third party. The suicide letters were hard copies from a computer and printer, but they were unable to discover whose equipment it belonged to. Since Robin and Kincade didn't own computers or printers, but they did have lap tops.

Then there were the cell phone messages, which could have come from their cell phones. Or didn't necessarily have to have been sent buy them. If someone else was present at the time. But that was a long shot, and who was that other person as a third party.

Or what would be their motive, which continued to confuse the detectives about who this would be? Brenda said, that she was always curious as to why? One of the detectives still calls her on occasion, after all this time to inquire about her, and the case was closed years ago. But they never found the person who committed the crime, or the person who committed the murders.

"Wow, Marcus, that is an earful to hear about someone you are involved with. What's your initial feeling about all of this? Do you think that Brenda had anything to do with her father, or Robin or Kincade's death?"

"To be honest with you, I didn't know her back then. So I don't want to act like a true hypocrite about it, and place my judgment on her concerning something I honestly don't know anything about.

"But I am going to say, that I can surely see where a lot of her problems stemmed from. She had a rough past, just like many other people have. There is just no way, anyone can ever know about what someone had been through in their past. "Especially when we do our damnest to conceal all the misfortunes, and painful experiences we have encountered with people and within life. I can honestly say, there is a lot of stuff in my past, I definitely wouldn't won't anyone else to know."

"I agree, Marcus. I feel exactly the same way. There are things that you will never be proud of that had happened to you in your past."

"Now getting back to what I was saying. You know me, why should I settle down and live with a woman, or get married to one? When I am having so much fun being alone and doing my thing?

"You suggested that I be open, honest, and up front, as much as I can be with a woman, and don't keep the important things a secret to her."

“They may not like were you are coming from with your politics, Marcus. But hopefully, they will respect you for being open, honest, and up front with them.

“And if they don’t, then that’s on them. If not, then that’s their problem.

“You want to give them an opportunity to decide, how they want to deal with you. Since they know everything in advance about where you are coming from.”

“I agree. It worked out successfully for me, until I decided to get involved with this psycho like, Brenda?”

“Come on, Marcus. You know you are crazy about her?”

“When was the last time you seen a Dog and a Bull get together for some hang out time, Marshall? Especially when they don’t have anything in common to hang out for? They laughed again at each other.

“I mean seriously she is good up until a point. Then it becomes about her releasing the crazies on you. I have had better sex, but Brenda just gives you more of it, and however you want it.

“And you know that this is something that would turn any man on. A woman who is uninhibited completely in bed? How soon can I book my appointment?

“You have to be crazy to turn that down with all of her looks and body, and she rocks you in bed.”

“I didn’t know you were so superficial, Marcus?”

“Don’t get me wrong. She is intelligent, but if it wasn’t for her attitude, and a bash of liaisons delivered by her. I would give her a better opportunity?”

"I am glade that you are being honest with yourself, Marcus. I like Brenda."

"And Brenda is attracted to you and likes you, but she isn't ready to go Black."

"I know that you would be good for her, Marcus. But not everybody wants to deal with another person's baggage?"

"You're right. Like I said, I am not ready to accept Brenda like this?"

"So if you accept this offer from your company to relocate. How long before the actual move takes place?"

"It will be fifteen months from now. Everything is being put into place. So they will need a decision within the next eight months?

"So you mean I am going to be stuck with your ugly face for another year or so?"

"If I do decide to leave, you are going to be lost without me. Then again, I could be wrong with all the women you have in your life now?"

"All joking aside, I am glad that it will be a while before you check out. If this is the case, if you decide to leave?

"It won't be the same without you, but I am happy for you, Marcus.

"I am sure we will continue our friendship regardless. I haven't been to California. I would be interested in going to visit. So we will have to wait and see what really happens?" They looked at one another with compassion for their friendship.

"Oh, I forgot to tell you. I served Jade with divorce papers."

"Wow. I have been away much too long. How did she react to it?"

"She was surprised, caught completely off guard. I guess I stuck a pin into her Voodoo Doll's heart. Like I explained to her. She left me with no choice. Living my life in limbo for nearly over a year isn't me.

"Just as I was trying to understand what the hell was going on with her, and making an effort to see if we can resolved something and find a solution to our problems.

"During this time, I didn't know what was going on with her? She continued to lie to me. I could have strangled her for this, that's how mad I was after I discovered this? You can't help but wonder? If this was the way that she really felt about me?

"After the way that she handled things poorly concerning me and our relationship? Jade was better than this, and I expected much more from her.

"But I didn't get it. When I should have gotten it? It's not like I was someone she was afraid of? Trying to understand and deal with what she was going through, and to find out about her cheating in addition to this.

"The other men in her life. It wouldn't have occurred to me in a million years, that it could have turned out like this?

"I know in my heart the love is still there, but the feeling isn't the same. We will more than likely cross paths again down the road, but not now, it may not happen between us again.

"It wouldn't work as much as I loved her. I don't trust her anymore. I don't know her anymore. It's a feeling she took away for us. We needed to get away from each other."

"I was sorry to hear, she would begin her indifference off like this, but I am concerned about you of course.

"You know, how much this is still affecting you. Also the things I don't know about? Will this bring a change about in you?

"Or will you go back to dealing with women differently?

Or will you jump right back into the same frying pan? After she broke your heart. You still stood by her. You continued to walk a straight line by doing the right thing.

"I admired you for that. Knowing that if you wanted to be with other women, you could have been with them. Like you have them now. Since they have come your way with it?

"You didn't have to tolerate any of this. You were a much better man than I could have been about this?

"They would have had to call the Cookie-Truck to come and get me. I definitely would have lost it. Or went off on her for this and more.

"H-e-l-l-o! I doubt I would have handled this so well. And now, you are being blessed from all sides with one catch?

It has to be a lot of excitement and fun to experience, Olivia, Sarah, Abby, and still Jade.

"I wish I had a fairy Godmother like you do, Marshall."

"I know, Marcus. All I am trying to do is enjoy myself. Without having to hurt someone's feelings, which is damn near impossible. When I could be the one who will be taken down again by surprise and disappointment?"

"I know that too Marshall, but knowing you. I am sure you will figure this out, before someone else initially gets hurt. I am going to keep an eye on you for the time being. Until I know, that you are out of harm's way from yourself or everyone else."

"I appreciate that coming from you, Marcus. I do understand where you are going with this?

"I wouldn't want to slip off into oblivion without anyone else knowing about it. I think it's time for me to go. Now, that you're back. We can catch up on more later? I am going home to get some sleep."

"Okay. I'll talk to you soon," as they embraced. Marcus led Marshall out and watched him drive away.

36

SARAH WAS HOME PONDERING AROUND the house. Lawrence was at work, which gave her the privacy she needed. But she thought about Marshall. She wanted to call and tell him that she was home, safe, and missing him.

She discovered cell phone numbers with name's on papers, which was carelessly left around the house—the numbers belonging to other women. She could no longer take playing house with Lawrence.

Her marriage was a farce for both of them. Being away and traveling for the last four days was great. Her preoccupation with Marshall generated moments of intense heat between her legs, just thinking about him.

She missed him so much, but didn't want to overwhelm him, with all her negative issues concerning Lawrence. Whatever she had to do? She would do by protecting Marshall and her from the nonsense, which is likely to follow when it comes to Lawrence.

She thought about how some people don't like each other. Even though, they can be attracted to one another. She was trying to work to a place within herself. Where she could feel good about herself, and about her mistake with Lawrence. Like children were beginning to smile large, but the smile is beautiful and warm and without true deception.

She understood from day one of her involvement with Marshall, that he wasn't going to have anything to do with Lawrence—that was her problem. She was going to be the buffer. Right or wrong? She knew that if she couldn't handle this, then she shouldn't be doing this with Marshall?

Something Lawrence failed to realize about himself. She had a particular plan in mind to deal with him. The process had already begun for her.

Sarah didn't feel comfortable or safe being back home, and not speaking to Marshall. Instead, she changed her mind and called him.

"Hello, Marshall."

"Hey, it's good to hear your voice."

"I hope I didn't disturb you at work."

"It's okay. I am glad to hear from you. How is everything?"

"I am fine. I really miss you."

"Well, I miss you too, Sarah."

"Unfortunately, Lawrence has been showing his natural born ass again, while I have been away. I discovered three cell phone numbers of his playmates throughout the house.

"You know what, Marshall? My mother use to say, if you are going out to get into some dirt?

"Then have enough common sense not to bring the dirt back home with you, because dirt always leaves a trail. Or make sure you keep your dirt to yourself, but this is not why I called you. I have been dealing with some personal issue about him for a while.

"I wanted to call you sooner, but I have another trip out tomorrow night.

"So there are a few things I want to do before I leave. The first is to arrange an appointment with a Divorce Lawyer. I should be gone for about five days. When I get back, I would like to call you. So I can see you. Is that okay?"

"Please let me be the first thing you do, when you get back from your trip. Take care. Have a safe trip. I look forward to your safe return."

"I can't wait until I get back too, Marshall. Bye."

"Bye, Sarah."

She made sure everything she needed was prepared for her flight tomorrow, after she spoke with Marshall. She had to get up early in the morning to begin taking care of her business. So she could arrive at work ahead of schedule.

She was going to turn in early. She didn't care whether she saw him before she went to bed. Also, he knew not to put his hands on her body. There is no sex life here. The head was cut off a long time ago by her.

Lawrence wasn't going to sleep with someone else, and come back home, and then do her too.

Sarah didn't think so, not on her watch. She told Marshall. She wouldn't sleep with Lawrence, and him at the same time to keep up appearances, or whatever?

It would be either her husband or him, if this was the case, or no one, but this wasn't the case.

She hasn't slept with Lawrence in over eighteen months, before she began sleeping with Marshall. Lawrence lied to Marshall.

He told him the time was much less. He didn't want another man to know, that his wife wasn't giving him any sex for this long period of time.

Marshall knew that Sarah was telling him the truth. She had been without sex for a while herself, which no one likes to admit to.

Her sex life is being provided by Marshall now, with adventure, excitement, interest, pleasure, satisfaction, and fulfillment for the first time. She is getting something out of it in return.

****

Lawrence went to visit a good friend of his, Johnny McRay. He is a wheeler and dealer. He is a big time music producer and had connections up the rear.

At one time Johnny dated Lawrence's sister for a few years. Lawrence liked him very much and was always impressed with who he was, along with Johnny's life style and the people who surrounded him.

When Johnny separated from his sister he didn't care. He felt that was his sister's problem. If she couldn't hang on to a man like Johnny. It was his desire to continue his association and friendship with Johnny well beyond his sister's break-up with him.

He introduced Lawrence to many well-known celebrities, and set him up with a connection in the Modeling industry to see if he had anything going. This is how their friendship continued over the years. He was always there to do anything he could for Johnny, if he needed it.

Lawrence realized that Sarah was departing tomorrow for several days. He didn't care if he saw her or not. It wasn't like she was going to give him some attention, love, or sex?

But he felt he didn't have to think about going out, or spending his hard earned cash on another woman? When he had a women like her twenty-four seven, since they were married.

But when she refused to sleep with him. He decided it was time to reconsider. When it affect his love life with her. He called her to tell her not to wait up. He would be conducting business with an associate of his.

Whatever, it meant nothing to Sarah. She didn't care. Lawrence was feeling a sense of attitude and power. When he was in the company of Johnny, and the people around him, who would take a bullet for him. He looked around the living room he entered.

He acknowledged Johnny immediately. When he looked further. He saw an attractive woman who had awakened his attention. She was coming down the spiral staircase to his right.

Johnny introduced the two to each other. Her name was Zoë, but right from the start his judgment fell into place. He couldn't understand why a woman would ever name her daughter, Zoë.

He thought that it was an odd name for a woman to have, but Zoë didn't see any Lawrence of Arabian in him either.

After investigating her further, Lawrence accepted that Zoë Pamela Ames was no joke. A serious piece of nature she was.

37

IF YOU LOOK AS GOOD as she did. You can name your own price, and call yourself anything you want to. Zoë, had looks she could surrender, and then take back. This is why Lawrence wanted her like a personal loan.

You can't run away from almost heaven. In a glory of hope, that is like dominion. Or with your need to be with her. He thought about Sarah. The possibility of her sleeping with someone else behind his back.

He dismissed the idea. He doubted it seriously. She would only put up with his garbage to a point? She would end her relationship with him first, before she began another relationship with someone else. He was convinced he knew that much about Sarah? Her morals and principals were better than his.

Whenever someone's feelings change for you. Then they no longer revere you with the same respect and consideration. Especially after, you have shown no respect for their feelings over a period of time.

Sarah no longer gave him this kind of consideration as her husband. Their relationship was over a long time ago. They shared little in their marriage, and shared a bed with no involvement. She decided she wasn't going to continue being miss faithful, simply because they were still officially married.

When he continued to do whatever the hell he wanted to, with whom ever he wanted to do it with. She just didn't see the point in being morally correct for him. When he decided to be morally incorrect for her.

She felt it was time to put a little hot sauce on his menue. So when the time comes. He can witness a difference in her behavior, that would cause his insides to burn. When there was very little he could do about it, but absorb the heat and feel the pain.

His only recourse was to cheat on her behind her back throughout the course of their relationship, in order, to satisfy his own self physically. She is filing for divorce. She just didn't tell him about it. It would be to his surprise. She is seeing someone else.

Sarah has been straight laced and correct all her life. Up until now, she hasn't been cheated on. Or has ever cheated on someone else in her relationships.

Lawrence proved to be the exception. She didn't appreciate his sleeping around behind her back, especially after they were married. She didn't know any woman who would appreciate it for whatever reason it was done?

She was feeling the true dog in him. A man who did everything to play her from the beginning?

She knew it was a gamble for the most part, but she took a chance to see what it would amount to. So he could be with someone of quality. Or who had character in their personality to further themselves.

She saw right through him after they were married. He was an opportunist and a so-called, "Player."

She also knew that a real "Player" had more game than this? He didn't deserve the privilege of being with her, or to share what she had to offer.

When you have a woman like Sarah who can bring it. Then you have to step up to the plate and serve it. So you can stay in the game. So you can give her what you have to offer. Or what she requires and needs. But Lawrence didn't stop to think, with his own rationality or to question it?

For example, if you continue to take a woman through a variety of sad changes. Then you really don't know what she will do behind your back? He returned his undivided attention back to Johnny.

Zoë was well aware that a bitch is a bitch, and a lady is a lady. So you are either one or the other, or you could be something else in between this. For her, it was more than another man coming up from his hidden darkness, who wanted her?

Recalling, how you can want anybody in this life. As long as nobody else knows about it. Secrets are more than truth. Or any man can cherish the thought of coming up from between her legs? But in reality, it doesn't really put him there for his hope or desire.

But a smart woman can basically see right through most men, she felt. Or try to walk like a serious devil to frighten her. Or give her an aura of excitement from it. Since she was misused and hurt by a man once. She didn't care about men or her feelings for them.

She didn't trust woman either. No man could hold on to her now. It wasn't going to make her a better person either. She would only sleep with a man on her own terms. Depending on how she felt about it. She had only slept with one man in her life since.

She thought of men as Under Water Pessimist? Then again, she was trying to imitate the ideal person also living above water?

Zoë was no Mammoth Red Leaf either. Who was left swaying in another person's mind that would claim love, without music to her ears? It was time for her to leave. Johnny was conducting business with his associates, and the other people who were there with him.

"So I will talk to you later, Zoë? Give me a call and we can talk," replied Johnny.

He tried to give her a kiss to impress everyone, but she didn't respond to it by turning her head. She left and caught a cab home. She thought about another day when the moment will be forgotten.

Speaking to Johnny Mc Ray, was like trying to communicating with the elements, when there were none. He only hears himself. She didn't care for people too much. While other people she knew had to be validated by someone else.

Zoë simply was using people to get from one point to the next. After her relationship went bad with someone, she loved hurt her.

From a promissory of such? She often spoke about how she didn't invent numb-nuts, and stick-people also wanted to enjoy movement. Making her move into the night, like a charmer who was in another person's way.

There were no hidden stars on her body, which may have highlighted a wet candle in her thoughts. Or watch the sky smile on the surface of water from desiring her.

Johnny Mc Ray wanted to sleep with Zoe, but she wasn't going there. It was a time for her to be hot, but not with him. She needed a favor, a personal loan. So she could help children who were less fortunate than she was. Who needed her help, because she couldn't walk away from them?

Their survival was important to her. Her destiny was lost at the moment. There would be assassins already out on the street trying to kill her reputation. From the talk of her feelings she kept to herself. It didn't stop anyone from wanting to know about her business. She was always an exciting young woman to most.

Zoë could have died that night for the deal she made with Johnny, because she hate owing him anything in return. But by the next morning? There would be birds that once dropped their vital disclosure, as a new criteria for her life?

Or maybe without little running shoes in the picture? And using their feet to negotiate the crumbling of a relationship she didn't care about? There were many questions she thought about concerning this topic.

Johnny had to realize, Zoë didn't really give a damn about a confrontation with Whitney Cook. Who is Johnny's girlfriend? It was like a certain shadow covering a new born babies ass, with beautiful anatomy lessons for this man to learn.

Zoë arrived home. She gave the cab driver something extra. He drove her to lower Manhattan from uptown.

38

A BURNING CELEBRATION FOR A mentor he wouldn't be to her. He thought about it in a wise way. He could see that the memory was still painful to her, and traveled with her. Like many things that come from a Sesame Place? Or like Emily Water was moving forward to a dear sound? She didn't hear in her life.

Johnny could see his need to hear her heart again, after her heart was dead to him, without any time after?

He didn't want to hurt Whitney. No one starts out wanting to hurt someone in a relationship. It will happen, or you will let it happen. And all the damn excuses in the world won't change that?

Since he wanted his emotions to come from high in the light of a distant sky, and hoping that someone would admit that he was smart. Zoë was the woman he knew, he couldn't have, but desired anyway.

This is what men do when they desire what they first see. Or what women do when they first see what they first desire. He was blessed because of all the misfortune in her life, and she wanted to do good for other people.

Nor was it for the benefit of a challenge in a triumph. He felt he could at least dream about it? He was fortunate to be familiar with near-by things about her. She would see better, unlike sleeping causes, who didn't know.

His imagination allowed him to see immortal slaves up in the sky with no references, when he was around her. She was there as a tease. Like it complimented the color of her large almond shaped eyes. It made him feel like a raindrop with no sense of direction, after you keep falling.

Or hidden in a shower where you hide your disobedience from others. Or walking away from shit, when pigeons are gazing down up on you, before they decide to drop their disclosure on you.

In his mind, he felt he had to have her for himself. Regardless of the fact, he had to give her money to do it. It wasn't as if he was grotesque. He just wasn't her type. It was all about Zoë, or the challenge he couldn't have.

Where else would she be in the essence of a Lady Bug in Africa, but who really gives a damn about this?

There was more meaning in that statement, than in his purpose. He realized by having sex with Zoë for any reason was wrong. It would be like two people having to be exactly what they are not to each other, larger in someones life.

One week later, Zoë picked up her cell phone and Johnny Mc Ray answered.

"I' de like to know when we can get together?"

"What is this about?" She asked.

"Why are you up in my life? Just because we conducted a piece of business together, doesn't give you the right to invade my personal privacy.

"It doesn't mean that we are in synch with each other, either?"

"Well, I thought that because of your situation, maybe you would like to conduct some business on the side?"

"If I do, then I'll call you. Don't call me, or sweat me for anything!"

"What's the problem, Zoë?"

"My problem is this? The first time we laid eyes up on each other was at the Funeral of Whitney Cook's brother. Who I believe you were with and comforting her. Who I am sure had given you, her version of me, and about her brother.

"Then one day you appear in the night club I work at in Brooklyn, while watching me move and dance for most of the night. Then you left, leaving me a large tip."

"So I found out who you were. I have a cash flow problem at this time, just like anyone else does. I want to help some people out, which I can't afford to do on my own at this time.

"When you showed up again, I approached you on my break to see if you were interested. I automatically knew, what you wanted from me. It didn't take an expert to figure that out.

"If you want to conduct something else private away from the club. Or if you are looking for a pro, I can arrange an appointment for you.

"Someone I know who does that kind of thing exclusively. I am definitely not on your list of hoe's as a retainer. And I know who your woman is, and I believe she hates the guts I have. So what are you trying to get me mixed up into?"

"Can we just slow things down a bit, okay? I'll be honest with you. I heard a lot about you, not all good of course. Yes, Whitney doesn't care for you much.

"I was curious about you, who you were? Then I saw you at the Funeral. I just had to see you again, and then when you stopped by my place to inquire about a personal loan. I became even more curious about you.

"Did you tell Whitney this?"

"Believe it or not, Zoë. I thought that you were the hottest woman. I have seen in a long time, and I have traveled a lot."

"And you expect me to drop my pants because of this? And what do I look like to you, now that you have seen me?"

"You look like someone who stops my heart every time I see her. You don't know how attractive you are? I just thought that we could see each other again under different circumstances. So we can talk and get to know each other better?"

"What about Whitney?"

"I am not worried about her, I can handle her. The question is? Can you handle it?"

"Maybe I can, or maybe I can't. If and when I decide, I have your number. I will call you. Don't call me." Zoë ended the call.

Johnny knew that very few dreams will fall without help, but with her? He could lose his civility over. Whereas with Whitney, she didn't make him feel that way, but she was hot to have around and she was a good woman.

Even though it was a long way down from being high in a distant sky, he thought. It was much better for him to think, but not so high of himself? Or not realize how many times, Whitney should have changed her mind about him.

Or why she would stand by him during his days of extensive traveling due to his business. He had to know that her sex life was inching real bad without him being present. After placing herself on lock down off and on for four years, or she couldn't tell him how dark and vulnerable it was for her.

It goes way beyond horny; when you are doing it intentionally for whatever reason and sacrificing yourself like this? She wanted someone to love, like an affair with a stranger.

She was under a lot of pressure when he was on the road for long periods of time, and she having to see pictures and read articles about him in the tableau's.

Not to be the person who gives it up first? While men and women were constantly talking to her. They knew what she was going through after being acquainted with her. They were trying to deliver a blue note of bad news about Johnny Mc Ray, they didn't like him.

He was constantly in the press with other women around him, or the gossip that circulated as rumored. He wasn't good enough. Or worthy of her patience to minimize her own self-worth by sticking with him—love or no love.

It was as if her unforgettable anger, and frequent changes were getting harder for him to deal with. He became aware of it in the back of his mind. Several other people had a stronger desire to be with her, and touch her, and do Whitney in their own destiny of faith.

So they can say, it is coming from a safe heart without a stitch up. It's not easy when you want someone that bad. You can only paint a picture of walking tall in your life. Now, that her sex had been locked up in a manner of speaking?

Whitney could have grown a multitude of cobwebs. If she desired to down there, and she still would have been a very hot old maid. The woman had a lot of sex appeal going on. She wasn't going to give anyone any parts of her sex, not just yet?

She watched her edible smile pretend to be a purpose for madness, or not knowing about her grace of revenge toward her man. She was strong and too focused for Johnny Mc Ray. The man didn't know how to appreciate the value of her. She saved her sex for him. The one thing she valued about herself.

It was her way of saying he had something good to come home to, which was always there for him. Which no one, until this day can understand. Her sacrifice in a semi-private open conversation about nothing?

As sweet as Whitney was. The danger was in Johnny Mc Ray's purple tongue of lies kept coming from his mouth—by serving a safe passage to look at her in a false way. The unusual statement's off of the top of his head comes out.

She will eventually see right through Johnny, right after she looks into his eyes every time. She will not be on the man's thrill ride forever, no one is. Or if forever is just another moment of lust to speak of?

It won't bring back the sunlight of her hold on him, if there isn't any anger under her siege.

Johnny should get down on his knees to ask for her forgiveness. While Whitney removes her hands from around his neck. When she beats the hell out of a different kind of bastard in her life.

Zoë will bring Johnny seasons of trouble to his life, which he thinks he can handle. Where there is laughter in exchange for six sliver lies when she speaks to him, and if the lies were golden. She wouldn't mine escorting him to nowhere.

Now he can try and tell her, or anyone else for that matter, just how many more future lives. He thinks he has left, before he is released from another woman's jail house?

39

HE ARRIVED AT WORK AN hour earlier. He wanted to remain on top of the work load until someone is officially hired to take over the position Abby Delaware left vacated. The people in the company aren't real keen on promoting someone from within, because of Abby's experience and knowledge.

It was their ambition to have someone who was close or equal to Abby. Who could provide immediate leadership, and make the transition easier, which would cut down on the training process for the productivity not to decline and effect profits.

He thought about Abby, and the fact that she is permanently gone. He thought about what she was doing at this moment. It would be nice to see her, and witness her smile again in the environment of the job. He missed her a lot, and she wasn't gone that long?

He had to oversee the Internet Operations to direct Network Security. Also coordinate the work of Systems Analysts, and Computer Programmers.

Long-range perspectives of Operational Strategies needed to be determined. It was for the personnel and equipment latest technology to stay abreast of.

He continued to work out of his office for the majority of the day. His work progress was interrupted briefly when he received a call from, Olivia.

"How is my lovely one doing?" She laughed softly when he said that to her.

"How's my, baby boy? I miss you much, Marshall. I wish that you were here, right inside of me.

"Wow, Olivia, you need to be more careful. Uncle Sam could be monitoring our call on the other end, or surveying our actions as we speak. They may send the man to pick us up soon?"

Olivia laughed, "I don't care Marshall, as long as they lock us up together. So I can be with you."

"You know that you are crazy?"

"Just crazy about you, this is why I miss you so much. I am sorry we haven't been able to see each other lately. It's been a while for me.

"I wanted you to know that it isn't because of him, but because of the job. A lot of stuff is going on."

"You don't have to explain or apologize, Olivia. It was our decision to take this chance with each other, and so far it has been all good.

"Maybe I should, but I don't feel any regrets about ever meeting you, or seeing you because you are married.

"It's not like we plan this or went out of our way to make this happen? Somehow, someway, or for some reason we connected. And that is the thing that truly concerns me most about you.

"I don't want you to think that I am saying this, because of what happened between me and my wife. Remember, I am still married too, but I filed for divorce."

"I didn't know that. Are you sure that's what you really want to do? You know, when you are in this kind of a situation? You are supposed to back away from the mistakes and give yourself some time, but that doesn't always work either."

"I agree. So let's just say, when she signs the papers. I will be a free man."

Olivia was surprised to hear what he had said to her. She was unaware of all the particulars involved in his marriage. He didn't talk about her or their lives together in her presence. She respected that and she liked him for this, but she also knew he was sincere about his emotion for her. He was more than honest, or sometimes too blunt, she thought.

However that was Marshall. He didn't play games with you or your emotions. She couldn't believe he was at this point so soon, after seeing him for only a brief time.

Men have a tendency to let these things drag on, but not Marshall, she saw. Soon he will be a free man, and she will still be married, she thought.

"I don't know what to say about your divorce. I can't deny I am a little concerned. It makes me wonder, how much longer will I be able to see you?"

"Olivia, I am not going to let anything or anyone change our situation, unless this is what you want. I miss you more than I care to admit.

"I think about you like a man who is earnestly out for some justice. But I will not complicate your life any more than we have. I will walk away, before I hurt you or let things get out of control.

"I realize it is easier to say than to do at times, but we all have to accept some responsibility.

"I am your friend first. There is a strong, confident, feeling that is revealed to me from you, Olivia. I do understand the details about our situations, or how this could all end up?

"I am not the type of person who is going to make problems, no matter how much I feel for you or how much I want to be with you."

"And how do I tell you, Marshall? How good I feel about you without scaring you away. You are an amazing man to me."

"I received your card that you sent to me recently. It was more than thoughtful, but really sweet. I laughed and smiled at the same time. It touched me more than my thoughts about you. I have to go, Olivia. You will hear from me soon."

Olivia's husband is a Financial Analysts and Personal Financial Advisor on Wall Street. She is a Forensics, licensed CPA for a large insurance company. Her company was a victim of the Ponzi scam by Bernie Madoff at one time years ago.

She also worked with law enforcement during their investigations. Or with lawyer's to appear during trails as an expert witness for white-collar crime. She is a forensics accountant for criminal financial transactions.

He met Olivia at a job fair, which was hosted at The Jacob Javits Convention Center. They had lunch together, and exchanged business cards afterward. The event was very pleasant for them.

On another occasion, they walked right into one another at The Manhattan Mall. He had no way of knowing in advance, that her marriage was getting progressively worse. The distance between her husband and her was huge.

They purchased a few items individually from shopping together. Their conversation was like rolling out the red carpet for one another.

They started calling each other on the job. Eventually it happened, they slept together after six months of conversation. Their communication level was on a high and intimate level.

She suspected that her husband went from covering up his prejudice, and became more sophisticated here in New York. She could see how he had learned a lot from his new acquaintances. He had a problem with African-American people—they were black.

He didn't appreciate black men offering their attention, kindness, or affections to Olivia. He did everything he could to assure her. He was just insecure and jealous. She fell for that in the beginning, but not since their arrival in New York.

He didn't want to lose her. Olivia was not convinced about his emotions.

When she was a child. She grew up not too far from Charlotte. Her best friend was a black girl, and her brother was Olivia's boyfriend. She was called many things throughout her juvenile years, which were lies that were fabricated about her.

Her knowledge and experience with African-American people elevated her intellect, and about what she really knew and didn't know? Olivia and people of color just clicked. Just like people of color and Olivia clicked.

Her open and sincerity as a person was exactly what people of color related to and accepted her for. She had no fear in her. She stood tall on her principals. What other way was there to put it or say it about her?

40

MARSHALL ENJOYED HEARING FROM OLIVIA. She was turning out to be a complete breath of fresh air. She was funny and sweet, but serious with her aim. It was something else about her besides being another person's wife. She appeared to be the type of person, who would put herself out on the line for you. If she feels that way about you.

He returned to his work to research Computer Programmers and Support Specialists current assignments to relate other computers after two hours of consolidating, with top management for business and technical skills. He received another phone call. It was, Sarah.

"It's good to hear from you."

"How are things going?"

"I am okay."

"I'm glad to hear you are safe and sound."

"I am only going to be here for tonight. It's a short stay over. I'll be gone in the morning for a week. I would love to see you. Is it possible for us to see each other today?"

"No problem, Sarah. What do you have in mind?"

"I am staying at The Crowne Plaza Hotel—Resorts across from La Guardia Airport."

"My company had a meeting and Banquet there. I know where it's located."

"I reserved a room for us. We can have dinner downstairs or upstairs in the room when you arrive.

"Then after dinner, we can do anything that you would like to do to me?" She laughed.

He told her. He would be leaving early. He completed his assignment and left. The traffic was bad. It was good that he left early. He took Grand Central Parkway out to exist off Ninety-Fourth Street to Ditmars Boulevard.

When he pulled up to the entrance. There was Sarah. He could see the reflection of his emotions getting personal, with her standing tall and smiling with him on her mind.

He summoned her to enter the car. He called a head to have her meet him downstairs. He recalled how much she loved German Chocolate Cake. She kissed him after she entered the car. He hugged her, and then took her for a ride.

"It seems like forever since I have seen you last. I have to stop traveling so much. It's not like I need the money."

"You smell good, Sarah."

"Thank you. Let's just say, I have picked up a few tips from you."

"Then back at you, Lady."

They came to a stop as he parked the car off of Queens Boulevard. They walked a block smiling at each other and holding hands. They entered a small Bakery. The smell inside of the Bakery was making him hungry.

The fresh baked items were intimidating, as Sarah smiled and licked her lips. They were assisted by a very kind middle age woman. Sarah was surprised when they approached the counter.

He ordered her a freshly baked German Chocolate Cake, earlier before he left work. She giggled like a little girl when he gave the cake to her. She smiled at him directly, and thanked him with a kiss. The lady behind the counter smiled too. She was surprised to see someone get that excited over a cake.

She related that no one has ever done this for her before. Her mother would make German Chocolate Cakes for her and her brother's. That's why she loved them so much. It was a touching thing that reminded her of her mother.

Now he understood her reaction to the cake. They entered his car. He returned to the Hotel. She was surprised he remembered about the cake. He could see how much she appreciated his gift to her.

Sarah removed one of her hands from under the cake box to hold his free hand. He didn't know it before, but he knew it now. She is at her happiest when she is with him. He parked the car in the garage. They used the walk way entrance to the main entrance and lobby.

She took his hand like she was proud to show him off as her man. She led him into the lobby. They made a sharp turn and walked passed the bar, and into the

Pavilion Restaurant. It was warm, relaxing, and elegant. They were served immediately.

"Marshall, may I?"

"Yes, you may."

"May we have scrimp cocktail as an appetizer, followed with a Caesar salad, with surf and turf—petit filet mignon and lobster tail?"

The waiter offered to accommodate her cake for her, but Sarah politely refused. She joked about not letting the cake out of her sight. He was pleased and enjoyed how happy she continued to be about the cake. He couldn't help but wonder, what it would be like, if he gave her something different of significant value?

The dinner was great. He told her about filing for divorce, and he was considering moving into a new place. He was looking to make a fresh start. She feed him a morsel of her Lobster Tail. She leaned over and moved closer to kissed him.

Sarah wanted him to know she filed for divorce also from Lawrence. She said being married to him was like having a fire on Thursday, and being an orphan child on Friday. Where do you begin? He understood what she was saying given his current situation.

He respected her abundantly as he did women in general. She wasn't a person of procrastination. She took care of her own business quite well. She wasn't the type of person to sit around and use this as an excuse, or use that as an excuse. Or let time pass her by without taking advantage of it.

It was one of the things that made Sarah unique and intriguing, she had it all. Without question, a man would consider himself the lucky one by having her.

Dinner was over. She tipped the waiter before he proceeded to do the same. The entire event and everything else was charged to her room on her account. As a man, it's kind of nice when a woman makes you feel special too. He was impressed by the way she planned, arranged, and took care of every little detail about their evening together.

He couldn't have planned it any better. He was definitely enjoying himself with her. They left the restaurant to the main lobby. They entered the elevator where she directed them to the room. It was a nice deluxe guest room for two, with a pleasant environment. She put her cake away and kissed him again for it. She excused herself to go into the bathroom. She changed into a sexy revealing piece from Victoria Secret.

Sarah took his hand and sat him down on the sofa chair. She sat down on top of his lap. She felt his sudden erection. It was warm to her, but she was hot to him. It was in the right position where it needed to be. She smiled at him and crossed one leg over the other.

Showing off her money green out-fit with spike hills against her youthful complexion, and her smile grabbing his attention. She and him talked for hours. They joked about how different things were now in relationships, and when you went out with someone in the past.

"I recall when you had to go through a lot before you could sleep with a woman."

"That's right! You had to be with her first, before you could think about having any kind of sex with her," said Sarah.

"You know that a man wasn't going anywhere without making his play to sleep with her first."

It was something they laughed about. Sarah continued to talk in a deep low voice, which made her sound odd and funny.

"And that is why women meant more to men back then, than they do today.

"Everything is about now and having easy access to, and much more about money. Too much has changed about men and women.

"But Marshall, it is sad how young beautiful girls and women are different now. Too many pretty young intelligent women have decided to imitate too many things that men are doing out there."

41

"YEAH I KNOW. WHEN YOU meet a woman now. You can roll her over depending on who she is? The first time you meet her, or before the evening is over, you can be in her pants? And if you wake up in the morning side by side in bed." Sarah interrupted to sigh.

"Then she is expecting to have a relationship. Since she didn't give herself to this man for nothing?" Marshall tickled Sarah to watch her laugh.

"Unfortunately, neither one of them know anything more about one another—than they did before they had sex with each other. It's a hell of a way to start out in a relationship, and you want to know why most relationships are over before they even begin?" Marshall replied.

"Do you still love her?" Sarah asked Marshall. She sat up further into his body while looking into his eyes.

"Yes, a part of me does, but it's not the same kind of feeling anymore.

"Just because you separate from someone doesn't mean you don't carry feelings for them anymore, which is the toughest part of the situation after it's over.

"Trying to deal with those feelings you still have, but are changing inside of you. When you are no longer with that person.

"And the next answer to your question is no. I don't want her back. I don't think so. I know so. I have filed for divorce.

"A friend recently helped me understand a few things about myself, rather than my focus on her. Or the outcome of the situation between us."

"Do I know this female friend of yours?"

"How do you know it is a female? I didn't say anything to this effect."

"Because of your eyes, there is a warmness you have when you speak of them."

"No. You don't know her. She is a special person." He was referring to Abby.

"I haven't loved anyone the way I loved her. So I will carry love in my heart for her until it disappears. Or until I love someone else. I simply wish her well, and the best.

"Never give someone advice that you wouldn't take or use yourself, and always take your own advice.

"Sometimes we try to work things out, and try to give things another chance. Thinking that we are doing the right thing. Even when we know that the curb is still there, and we are running all over the same side walk.

"So there is no need to go down this street again. Once you have been down this street before, and having accident after accident on it. While you both continue to suffer from the injuries of this event.

"I knew I was too emotionally focused on her, which definitely put me in the mix. The problems we were having in the relationship. More than one person told me. They felt I was too close to the situation to see things clearly.

"You see, I thought she was taking me around the world. Then she wanted to get bazaar with it, and take me for another trip around the world.

"Once was enough for me. The answers were right there. Whether she wanted to give them to me or not.

"Not in a million years. I would have realized it was marriage I enjoyed more. We were having a ball together until that ball dropped, and the lights went out for us.

"I realized I wanted what we had more in our marriage, than I wanted to be back with her.

"I loved her. Or I convinced myself otherwise. After the way she came across with her behavior and the things she did. It took the seeds right out of the soil in the pot for us to grow anymore. I couldn't believe how selfish she became in all of this?

"I couldn't continue with the changes she took us through, when we once connected like parts of a machine.

"We had an unbelievably situation in our relationship together, I thought. The future continued to be bright for us to grow, with or without each other.

"She made some tough choices. Not every mistake can be forgiven within yourself. It was irrelevant if I wanted to find a solution to her madness.

"It was obvious that she didn't care about resolving anything through her changes or her pain.

"I overlooked something she was supposed to be suffering from. Another part of her I couldn't see, impaired my judgment to deal with the situation better.

"In spite of everything, she still deserved some peace of mind in her life too, I feel."

However for Sarah, when it was good it was okay. When it went bad it stunk. Now she is at the point of divorcing Lawrence too?

"I am tired of the nonsense with him. If he didn't want to be married, then why get married in the first place?

"I am not going to be married to someone, and be miserable for the rest of my life. He is a jerk and doesn't care what he is doing?

"If you don't want to make anything better, then what's the point of being together?

"Lawrence wants to have sex whenever he wants to. Or whoever he wants to have it with and damn everyone else. Do I look like a fool who was remade into another fool?"

"This is old. The man wants to continue playing games in the relationship. I under estimated how immature he was. One time he had the nerve to raise his hands up at me. I went into the kitchen and returned with a knife.

"Whenever you are ready, I told him. I didn't know how fond he was of Swiss cheese?

"One of my brothers is a Navy Seal. He taught me how to defend myself, and I have a permit to carry a gun.

"He doesn't know this? I am not going to give away my secrets to someone like him. He started laughing at me.

"He thought I was joking. He saw it wasn't a kitchen knife, but a military blade."

Sarah got up from having the pleasure of sitting on him so long. She stood there with anger on her face. She took a seat on the edge of the bed, with her defined body looking better than any unconditional death. When you are asking to die because of it?

"I will not let any man put his hands on me, and not to mention my brothers." Sarah's attitude changed without warning or provocation.

"God bless my father, but he was a bit of a bastard at times to my mother. He had heavy hands. My brother's on separate occasions, would fight with my father when he was drunk, and he would tee-off on my mother.

"My brothers and I didn't play this, we didn't allow it. Don't mess with Mom. So like you said, Marshall? I wish him well in another person's life."

He approached Sarah, and sat down beside her on the edge of the bed. He hugged and kissed her. They lied back on the bed, rapping their legs around and in between each other's.

Sarah asked him to stay with her for the night. She was aware it could be an inconvenience for him, not having a fresh change of clothes for work in the morning. He reassured her that it wasn't a problem, and he could work something out.

She was happy and pleased that he showed no hesitation or thought about being with her. When she asked him. Even though, it was a big inconvenience for him concerning work in the morning. It's just like a woman coming into work the next day with the same clothes on, and you begin to wonder?

She was delighted again. He excused himself to change into a white terry cloth robe, and returned to the bed to reposition himself comfortably next to her.

She hibernated into his arms. She wanted to know if there was anything else that he needed or wanted. He told her everything he needed was being here with her. She dimmed the lights with the remote control, and she smiled at him.

Sarah and him continued talking about relationships, until they finally became tired of fighting inkwells of hostility not to go to sleep—but they did.

42

It was 5:15 a.m. Sarah woke up comfortably in his arms. She was pleased and enjoyed sleeping in bed with him again. She recalled how much it annoyed her to be in the same room with Lawrence. She refused to allow him to put his hands on her body.

She smiled, while she observed him lying peacefully next to her. It was a lot different for her. How he would comfort her when she'd go to sleep. The things he would do when they were together, and not make her feel like a sex object—by following her around with his tongue hanging out?

She felt he had a way of always thinking about her. When she would fall asleep and feel safe and comfortable. He was taking care of her. And not trying to always screw her, because she was someone he was seeing or wanted.

He was the only man who made her feel, like if she didn't have sex with him all the time? Then he was going to disappear out the back door, before he had to wait indefinitely for it?

Or she was going to drag it out with time. Or make it like, he wouldn't be able to generate a walk in the sunset again. If she didn't do it with him.

Or continued to separate herself from men who were blessed with dead air in between their ears?

Sarah easily withdrew herself from his arms and kissed him. She talked about how good he was. How he always made her feel good. She went into the bathroom to take a shower.

Moments later, he surprised her and entered the shower behind her. She hugged him. They kissed. Their bodies rubbed up against each other playfully. She separated her legs. They kissed more, but they didn't do anything.

They enjoyed the warm water running intentionally over them. Afterward, she ordered room service for their breakfast. They continued to get dressed. Everything from that point was sweet and short.

Sarah and he arrived in the lobby. Where she approached the registration desk to pay her bill and check out. He proceeded to the walkway entry to the garage to retrieve his car. He picked her up at the main entrance, and escorted her to the Delta Shuttle Marine Air Terminal.

She didn't want to detain him any longer. She expressed her excitement about them being together again. There wasn't enough time to convey the exhilaration in her heart about them departing from each other.

She was feeling like a cat in heat. She didn't want him to leave her under any circumstances, and she definitely didn't want to leave him. However, she didn't want to give him the wrong impression about herself either, but he understood where she was coming from.

One moment she is a strong, smart, and independent woman, rather than being a helpless, needy woman in despair—because she could be falling in love.

Now that her marriage had been coming apart for the last two years? From the look in her eyes it was apparent to him, that her feelings were growing stronger for him, like his were for her.

"I really wish I could fold you up and place you in my travel bad. So I can take you across the county with me. When you and I are apart from one another.

"Then I could be there for you. If you need me like you have been there for me. She continued to kiss him.

"It's an interesting concept, but totally unrealistic. Although I do get your point?"

He kept kissing Sarah on her neck. "Oh not there," she said. It was getting her hot and bothered.

Sarah was a sensuous and sexy woman. It was hard not to get enough of her. It was time for her to leave. She exited the car to look back at him, and waved as she blew a kiss while watching him drive away.

He could see her holding onto her cake tightly. He couldn't help but smile. He saw how she became more and more attracted to him. It was like watching someone fall in love with you.

He realized how attractive she was before he became involved with her. Now it was like watching someone change, grow, and captivate you with their own personality and sensuality.

He felt indifferent about Lawrence, but surprisingly not guilty. He was unsure of how this happened between Sarah and him when it happened.

When something happens, it just happens, and then you have to deal with the circumstances, or consequences afterward. There is nothing you can do to change it. When it begins unless you can stop it before it begins.

No matter what the outcome is. Once you sleep with someone you can't take it back. You are either glad it happened, or you wished that it never happened, because the feeling in between doesn't change anything.

Lawrence was okay up to a point as a person. Since there was a side of him Marshall didn't like. This is why he didn't consider him to be a friend, but someone he was acquainted with.

He wished it would have been someone else that he didn't know. Since there was a remote possibility, he could discover the relationship between him and Sarah. Consciously it wasn't his desire to be involved with someone's wife, like someone else is involved with his wife.

It happens to the best of us, more than anyone knows. He realize it doesn't change anything or make it right. In spite of the fact, he had been relentlessly cheating on Sarah for some time now.

And all because he doesn't want to step up, and be a man to her in their relationship. She is still his wife. You can only disrespect a person but for so long. He considered there could be a confrontation between them eventually?

Sarah had to be disappointed in him. When he decided to drop out of St. Johns University. It happened just before they met, but she didn't know.

He lied to her about it along with several other matters, which had come to the surface with him. He was supposed to be majoring in psychology after three years in school, and after their marriage he became a Model.

43

SARAH FELT THAT IF HE ever received a degree. It would have to be in Psychology 101, as a Bull-shit-artist. He lied to her. He never had a degree in anything. It was her mistake with him, after three years of dating and two years of marriage. He knew that the fall-out from this situation was going to be rough.

You can't fool yourself for a minute. About a lot of things which are going to happen. And everything you didn't expect to happen will happen—but it's not the worst thing that can happen.

If you are not paying enough attention to your situation or the woman in your life, then you can be sure someone else is paying a lot more attention to your situation and your woman.

Like when you take a dangerous walk on the opposite side of the street, and to say nothing about the event that embarrassed you and all.

Marshall decided he would take another day off from work. He was reminded by Human Resources he had four more days he had to use or lose them without pay he had accumulated.

He called the job on his way in from the airport after leaving, Sarah. He was home listening to classical music on WQXR, 105.9 FM, and sitting at the kitchen table doing finances, with a remote thought about Jade and how healthy their financial portfolio was.

Each of them would alternate, and perform the chore of handling their finances for six months. He set-up and organized everything for her to know, and have access to.

They were working like alcoholics, when it came to making money. From the moment they became friends, and into their relationship and marriage. They didn't have a single problem with money and their investments.

She was like a squirrel, always putting something away for a rainy day. And along with his saving habits he learned from his mother—their money kept growing.

It felt strange to cancel her name, and existence from their financial folder. He listened over the phone at the automated recording waiting for a selection to end the process. She and him taught each other a lot about finances in different ways, after the task of canceling their joint accounts. He began packing up the remainder of her belongings.

He stopped by CubeSmart Storage to purchase several boxes earlier in the week. After everything they have been through the last two years. She continued to put money into their joint accounts. He also continued to do so.

They still had a feeling of pride in the things they accomplished and continued to do. Oddly they had established together in their relationship and marriage. In spite of their long separation. He may not have been able to trust her with his heart, but he was able to trust her with money. How odd this had become?

It was hard to explain. But if he needed her in any way. She would be there for him. She was still a friend until the end. It was difficult to touch and look at her belongings. Or the personal momentum he gave her. The many items she gave him, also. It brought a certain kind of sadness to his eyes and face. He continued to look at her stuff.

It brought back memories of how many ways they had fun together. Just like he knew whenever the sale of the Condo took place. It will be divided equally in half with her. She was paying for her own BMW X5.

So there wasn't much more to divide up. He took a break to check the entertainment online. He saw a dance performance by Alvin Alley American Dance Theater at Lincoln Center tonight.

Good seats were still available he could pick them up at the box office. The performance was great as usual by Alvin Alley. He like the performing arts. He admired dancers for their ability to move gracefully, and with a creative dance style.

He allowed this extremely attractive woman to pass by him in the aisle so she could exit first. She accidentally stepped on his foot and began falling. He caught her to prevent her from falling any further.

She thanked him, and apologized for stepping on him. When she cleared the aisle her ankle gave way and she stumbled. He was able to catch her again.

"Thank you, again."

"Are you okay?"

"My ankle seems to be a little sore. I might have twisted it when I stepped on you.

"Hi, my name is Marshall."

"My name is Zoë." She offered her hand to shake.

He offered to assist her further. She leaned on him for support. She limped slowly on her ankle out of the center. By this time her ankle was slightly swollen. It wasn't bad. It was just sore from the weight she was putting on it.

She didn't have a car. She took public transportation from West Houston Street where she resides next to. He offered to take her home.

She gazed at him with concern, asking herself whether he is a serial killer. Or a crazy person with a dark side. Or just a regular human being. She thought he was attractive, and dressed too well to be any of the first two from above, that she thought about.

Looking into his eyes with her approval. She shook her head that he was okay. He made sure she was safe before he left her momentarily to get his car. When he returned to her. She smile and waved so he could notice her. He smiled back at her like he knew her.

They arrived at her building address. He left her alone and safe in front of her building—in order to find parking. There were people outside the building who knew her.

Her ankle was considerably swollen. She removed her keys from her coat pocket. He carried her to the elevator and then to her apartment door. She continued to curiously looked at him. She opened her apartment while he carried her. She was able to turn on the lights. He carried her further into the apartment.

He saw a couch in front of him. He put her down gently. It was a small one bedroom apartment, but nice. It wasn't too tidy at present. She apologized for the condition of the place.

She didn't have any dishes piled up in the sink. Or garbage piled up in the corner. Or unmentionables lying all around the place. It was just unorganized, like a person who was in a hurry to leave. They will take care of it upon their return.

He asked her, did she have a first aide-kit? She did and with her permission. He took a plastic zip-lock bag filled with ice from her kitchen. He helped to remove her coat, and couldn't help but see how incredibly built she was physically.

Exactly like a dancer, he thought. Powerfully build with tremendous legs. He rubbed her ankle with alcohol. He applied the ice pack on it with adhesive tape. She was surprised and delighted by his kindness in her moment of need.

He tried to make her comfortable so she could relax more. He assured her that she would be fine in a day or so. If she stayed off of it for a day and attended to it. She thanked him.

He offered her his cell phone number in the event that something else happened, and she needed help with something? He waited until she securely locked her door before he left her.

Zoë hopped back to her couch as she thought about him. This interesting man. She whispered to herself. She was relieved to see there was nothing wrong with him. She allowed him to bring her home and come into her apartment.

If there was something seriously wrong with him? He was just going to have to take it out on her, and do her all over the place. Or put her out of her misery. She was really attracted to him. This is why she had the small accident with her ankle. She was too busy staring at him. She smiled.

She thought about how good he smelled and better than she did. She couldn't believe how much she desired to kiss him. When he carried her in his arms to her apartment. Then she felt a moment of horniness just thinking about him more.

44

TWO WEEKS LATER, MARSHALL RECEIVES a call from her. He was surprised and wondered whether she was okay.

"Hello Marshall. I am not sure if you remember me. We met at Lincoln Center. I was the clumsy person who stepped on your foot and twisted my ankle."

"Yes, I remember you. How can I forget a woman who is as pretty as you are? Hello, are you still there?"

After the comment he made, there was a pause in their conversation. "I'm sorry. I was surprised by your comment."

"Why would you be surprised by something absolutely true?" She made a slight effort to laugh, and thanked him for the compliment.

"How is your ankle?"

"It's fine, thanks to you and your kindness. It was much better the next day. I took your advice. I rested my ankle and took care of it. Something I haven't done in a long time."

"What's that?"

"Take care of myself. I can't tell you how much I appreciate everything you did for me. You are a kind person. Would it be possible to call you again?"

"Why not, anytime, you take care of yourself, and please take care of your ankle, bye."

"Bye, Marshall."

She didn't know what to make of her conversation with him, except that she was interested in a curious way. She couldn't explain the attraction to him other than the obvious. The man is hot, sweet, and thoughtful. And he is a hell of a catch, if you can get him, she thought.

She couldn't recall ever thinking like this? Or feeling like she did. Or how this didn't present itself with her ex-Randall. A certain kind of mystery and excitement fulfilled her when she thought of him.

She began her stretching exercises and performed in her living room. What he didn't know about Zoë P. Ames is, she is a professional dancer, and was briefly acquainted with a music producer.

The problem for the producer was that he couldn't leave well enough along. He had to have her. He was getting greedy over something which wasn't his to be greedy over. She was no man's whore or property, but she could be the ultimate fiction in his dreams, however?

Also, she didn't care about him or his girlfriend, Whitney P. Cook either. She needed the money for something more important to her. Fifteen thousand dollars was the amount she desired.

The money was for kids she wanted to help. This is why she needed money. Johnny was the only man she knew, who had that amount of money in cash and wouldn't miss it?

For her, it was strictly a business proposition and transaction. But Johnny's desire for her sexually, after he had seen her for the first time. He felt she was teasing him about what she had to offer.

Even though, she had no personal interest in him what so ever. It was more about what he was thinking she couldn't control.

It was his hang up and problem, and knowing she wouldn't sleep with him for money or under any circumstances? He hoped she would need more money. In his mind. He could see himself saying yes to any of her demands.

She didn't tell him about the hard fall. He would take in the event of being involved with her. He wouldn't feel her inside lying down, or standing up, but merely in the vacancy of his mind.

She wouldn't wear animal clothing either. So he could offer her anything he desired to with money and power. The results will still be what they are—nothing to her. She had to open his eyes, so his first seduction would come to an end.

Johnny, felt Zoë was like intensive care. She was in a position to satisfy him religiously, but all he had to offer was more money promises to be with her. She thought it was funny enough to laugh with her enjoyment of a joke, while she watched his illusions soar.

He wouldn't understand, that the sun doesn't shine on a woman's leg against the fountain head of sanctuary.

Or was this over his head come to think of it? He was like another man on the streets, with another hustle to her.

While she would dump on him, and he wouldn't mean anything to her. This is why men were so dump. When you are generous enough to give them away out of their dilemma. So as to avoid any drama between him and his woman. He turns it down, like a fool with a hopeless heart. It didn't say anything, unless someone else was interested in her sex.

So regardless, he still made the wrong decision to choose Zoë over his own woman. She didn't understand him, but wasn't surprised when she told him a hundred times. She didn't want him or his money.

"That's the whole point?" She said. When you walk away after speaking with this person, and they don't understand anything—but then they continue to talk garbage to you. When you don't want to hear it.

It appears Johnny has failed to remember now, that guilt arriving from him was like a Chameleon bug, which didn't do him any good on the surface of Tea-top sandpaper.

She made Johnny feel cheap, and low about his consistent offers. Like all the children in the world who weren't going to cry again? Zoë wouldn't joke about her body without her soul.

Johnny could see there were disbelievers moving around him, but also against him. He saw something besides sugar-honey-ice-tea flying in his thoughts about her. There was nothing but broken lies, and there wasn't anything that was forthcoming from her. She was a hard nut to crack.

How could he think she wasn't going to play this out without her using him?

There was no way he was going to avoid this, since she had men coming back to her for another play, while she continued to turn them all down to be with her. You had to be used by her first. She discovered it was her play away from bondage that made it possible.

The more you try to talk to her, the more she will rap you up into the situation. Where it will become your problem, and you can't get over her in your mind. Also, Johnny didn't recall what she discussed with him about run away bitches, either?

She expressed her damnation about not caring about Whitney Cook. Or if she discovered what happened between Johnny and her. It was all on Johnny anyhow. She was just going to let him slide right up into a tight hole, that he came up out of.

She felt either way, the man was lost and didn't realize what he was doing? Johnny Mc Dope, she thought.

45

JADE RECEIVED THE DIVORCE PAPERS from Marshall a month ago. How messed up the situation had become for her. She continued to punish herself for the things she did and the mistakes she made.

The thing about mistakes, the worse the mistake is, then it's not leaving on its own. Since the mistake is still there, you can't continue to harp on it. You have to find a way to live up to your responsibility for the mistake you made. This can be difficult, if you can't refrain from kicking yourself in the rear over it.

"I can't believe you haven't signed the papers yet? I thought you wanted to get on with your life?" Ryan asked.

"I do, but we still have financial matters to close out, pertaining to the Condo? He may not be ready to sell. We have to come up with some kind of agreement or arrangement."

Jade was feeling slightly uncomfortable about telling Ryan what she did. She was lying to him. Nothing was standing in the way of her signing the divorce papers except her.

"I just want to make sure our agreement stays in affect, before I give him everything he wants."

She continued to lie to him, while they were spending the evening at his apartment. She spoke with Marshall a few days ago to confirm their meeting. It was her decision not to involve Ryan into her personal business. This was something that was between her and Marshall.

No one was going to tell her what she should, or shouldn't do when it comes to her husband and her marriage. All decisions were between them. She didn't care what Ryan thought.

Jade and Marshall planned this in advance a week ago. They took a day off from work, and met at their place. Her emotions and personality was different. Her emotions were calm, and settled more like herself, but with more curiosity.

She had a desire to talk with him. He could see she was bothered about what to say to him.

It worked out to their advantage. The plan was to have lunch together, and then they would take it from there. He explained about the financial adjustments he made to their accounts. He prepared her personal belongings for her to pick up, when it was convenient for her, also.

He didn't have to be there for this. She could contact him in advance if she wanted to stop by for any reason. So when she arrived there was nothing to be surprised about. Which had to make her feel at ease with herself, because it was well over do.

Feeling confident he wouldn't screw her over concerning anything about their business? He would do the right thing, even if she didn't do the right thing. It was one of the things he didn't understand about her now.

So far, she kept their agreement about not dropping by unannounced and possibly getting her feelings hurt, if he had company.

It was the first time since they separated, they had an opportunity to lay low from each other's anger. She contacted him to touch base again. She was acting civil and sensible with him. He was her best friend, and her husband, and the person she still loved. She didn't want the warmth between them to change into absurd coldness. He had no idea at this point.

She explained it was incredible to have a man like him. He was different to her, but he was still a man. He thought about telling her, how she was as a magnificent woman. But he didn't want to give her any ideas to reclaim, with a different kind of concern this time.

She and him were in a comfort zone again, but with one foot in hell and the other foot in limbo? For the first time since it happened, they were beginning to communicate. They forgot about their lost illusions of who they weren't to each other.

She laughed freely from inside, like anyone could appreciate stealing a million dollars on any given day. Then there was the affection expressed with their bodies. They watched a DVD movie together, while they continued to drink wine.

She laid back into his arms. He hugged her on the sofa. They made love on the sofa. It was different, and it was better this time. She felt all of him and he felt all of her. There was no need to know how this was going to be, they were in synch.

Like they made a life-less bird sing in the air for no reason. Her eyes rolled back when she closed them. He came right behind her, as he released to be subdued blissfully.

Afterward they showered together. They played with each other. They had a lot of fun as a way of further temptation. They dried each other off. They gazed at each other seriously. They felt their private parts gently and tried to recall better days. Something returned in its nature between them for the moment.

They lounged around briefly in their robes, while talking more and laughing. They reminisced about their relationship before their dreams came to an end. It was sweet, but harmless. They were seated in the bedroom. He showed her the open boxes he prepared for her to examine. She smiled at him, laughed, and was sad when she observed the many items which were largely given to her by him.

The material items meant very little to her. It was the memories she associated them with him, and when he retrieved them for her. She began to cry.

"What's the matter?"

"I'm sorry, Marshall. I said I wasn't going to spoil our time together."

She placed her hands up to her face, and began wiping away her tears. She appeared helpless at the moment. He removed her hands from her face and began kissing her tears away by nibbling on her facial cheeks. She smiled and laughed. They hugged each other. She began crying again. He held her tightly in his arms. He told her things will be okay.

"No it won't." She made an effort to stop from sobbing.

"Why?" he asked.

"Because the mistakes I made will haunt me for the rest of my life. I don't want to get a divorce from you. I can't imagine you not being in my life, or you with someone else?"

He told her it wasn't as bad as that. The divorce was a process they had to go through. He assured her that he would be there for her. She was still his friend. He was pleased she accepted his explanation about the divorce.

46

IT WAS HIS DESIRE FOR her to step back and take time from this. So she could give herself some space. She needed an opportunity to deal with herself, and reflect on why something like this happened to her.

It wasn't easy going back and forth with one another, and over a year's period. They didn't live together any-more. He wanted her to know he was still hurt and affected by it. But was able to resolve a lot of his anger issues and pain toward her.

He advised her to take a few more days to process her reality, before she signed the papers. If it bothered her that much, but their marriage to one another was over. She realized he was right without expressing any malice toward him. Her understanding of everything was good, after admitting that he was presenting a valid point.

They required healing and time away from each other. Getting back together wasn't the answer, or the solution for them. She understood and accepted, how important it was for her to reflect on her own self and life—and begin to confront her own personal problems.

She continued to admit it wasn't anything that he did to her. She struggled with this internally, which he wasn't aware of? Her crying and tears subsided, and it felt good to be able to talk to him again.

It took them along time to get to this point. After rationalizing about surviving without him, as her strong source of support. It would prove to be painful for her, but it would make her independently stronger.

She said she couldn't lose him as a friend, in spite of everything that happened. Also, he was unaware of how much she still relied on him, which was something she kept to herself.

****

After a heated conversation took place with Jade and Ryan about the same subject. He told her that he wasn't going to be taken for granted, or be taken for a ride. He didn't understand what she was doing?

How Marshall still meant so much to her, after she claimed she destroyed their marriage and life together. She further revealed, how relevant her past actions involving Marshall was, and why he still meant so much to her.

He was the only man she ever knew, who liked her and appreciated her for herself, and cared enough about her feelings. He loved her, and took care of her.

There are man who know how to provide for a woman, but not a lot of men know how to really take care of a woman, and deal with their emotions

It's no secret that everyone likes to be taking care of. Whether it's a woman, or a man, or a child? It has nothing to do with money. This is why Marshall was special to her. She clarified this to Ryan about what he didn't know?

He was the only person she could trust and talk to about anything. He didn't judge her which is something everyone does. It wouldn't matter if she killed someone; she knew Marshall would be there front and center for her as a person. When she was younger, she took care of herself. She didn't like depending on her family for anything or anyone else. She had a good job. She had a degree in Business Administration. She makes good money. She could more than provide for herself, but it didn't stop Marshall, she expressed.

He not only provided for her, he took care of her. She didn't want for anything. What made it great was that she was the same way with him. She would spoil Marshall any way that she could.

Everything in their relationship was accessible to her. So she wouldn't get caught out there without anything. Or left in a compromising position with no way out. When they were together. He took good care of her needs because he adored her.

The thing that she loved about him more than anything was, he didn't spend his time trying to always impress her. But he was always honest with her. When their lives and their relationship were at its peak, which was automatic with them, she claimed.

He took care of her needs and wants better than she did. He was a unique person to her. She wasn't this close to anyone else in her life, and it was something they both were aware of. She didn't want to embarrass Ryan, by discussing her sex life with him concerning Marshall.

There was no comparison, Marshall was a great lover and a legit sex machine, she felt.

He constantly desired her, and constantly had her. But in a way that he always made her feel wanted. He satisfied her any day of the week and anytime of the day. It was difficult to cut his switch off, because he didn't have one.

He would do her twice in one day, and on other days she couldn't keep up with his energy. He often wore her out even on her good day.

Usually she thought a person would get horny from a lack of sex, but not with Marshall. She became horny from having too much sex with him. She knew he was going to service her and always good.

It was one of the qualities she loved and appreciated about him. He amazingly was never off his game. She didn't know a moment when he wouldn't hit her off, and when she leased expected it. Or when she would expected it. He would or he wouldn't, even after all these years.

Then he wouldn't touch her all week and it would drive her crazy, and then she would begin hitting him off surprisingly when he arrived home, or try and catch him off guard. He was still spontaneous. He kept it fresh, fun, and exciting with her.

She felt wrong about what she let happened to her. It was more than a fall from grace. She believed Marshall was the only man for her, and truly cared about her and her life.

Her recent affair with other men didn't excite her, or satisfy her in or out of bed, which she discovered about herself. This was the bottom line where she was concerned. She was open and sincere with him. She wanted to stay for the entire evening, but she had an appointment with Ryan.

Marshall and Jade had no idea so much would happen between then on this day. So they purposely went with the flow and left everything else alone. It was good, great, natural, and appealing.

Whatever caused the changes in her, and the excitement which occurred that wrecked their lives. And she still couldn't give him an explanation or reason for this happening. He wasn't fooled, or side track by any of it. Jade knew why she did what she did, and when she did it. So everything had changed and matters have settled down.

Now she can recall, why she did what she did by being open and real with herself. Although they didn't go over this, but they hugged and kissed each other with hard passion to say good-bye. They said, take care to each other, as something unexpectedly had happened between them.

47

AFTER SHE LEFT HIM WITH felicity on the same day and evening. He received another visitor, Marcus.

"You just missed, Jade."

"So how is she?"

"I was surprised, but she seems to be doing better. It is still a lot for us to deal with and accept. Finally after all this time, we are beginning to talk to each other.

"It isn't going to change anything for me. Perhaps some of the issues we will connect with each other. Or should offer an explanation for her odd behavior which destroyed everything we had.

"She did tell me. Some of the things that happened to her, and what went wrong with her. But this is stuff I already knew, which didn't offer me anymore enlightenment.

"But everything had to do with her as a woman, which is what I already suspected, and had nothing to do with our marriage. So it continued to be a mystery for me. She sounded more insecure than anything else, which was surprising.

"So far we covered a lot. The tragedy is that our feelings have changed toward each other, after all the negativity we have endured together. It doesn't leave you with much of a positive feeling concerning much."

"So did she sign the divorce paper?"

"No, but she will in a few days. The point is that we were able to talk. Something we haven't been able to do, since the situation changed between us. It seems to have meant a lot to us."

"Now that you and her have made some progress. Are you going to reconsider anything? I always liked, Jade. I thought you and her were great together."

"I know, Marcus. I appreciate hearing this, but no. I am not going to reconsider anything. It's over between us. Perhaps we can be friends, but that depends on her. I realize that that in it-self won't be easy for either one of us. But it's a start to savage whatever? I can't promise anything more than this.

"I told her. She could take a few more days, before she signs the papers. She is having a hard time struggling with it now, but it won't change anything between us."

"So what happens now? Where do you go from here with two new women in your life, and they are married."

"Well, I am trying to keep a level head about all of this? Since the women aren't available to me like you said."

"It seems like cheating is really getting out of hand for a lot of people, Marshall?"

"Yeah, I know. It seems like people aren't satisfied unless they are cheating on one another now. One way or another everyone has an excuse for it, I guess."

"Let me ask you a question? I realize you loved, Jade, like hearts are never lonely. Your marriage was everything to you with her. I remember when you were quite the lady's man, before you met her and did a 360. You abandon all of that and became very serious with her."

"I know, Marcus. I was praying everything would be different and work out. You have your ups and downs, but this is not the same when you get into a marriage.

"It becomes a whole new type of thrill ride, that you never would have expected. There is a lot to be gained, but there is also a lot to be lost.

"Either way, someone always goes down with the ship. I was hoping to avoid this. The stakes are considerably higher, and now being involved with other people's wives is not my thing.

"I feel uncomfortable at times about it, but it's nothing I can't handle. It's just not the same as being able to claim, and deal with someone who is yours.

"It allows you all the freedom you need to do anything you want to do with them—when you want to do it. It doesn't matter how much you receive from her, or the situation. It all belongs to someone else anyhow. I was never involved in this kind of situation before.

"I dealt with free women, and women who were available. I don't like dealing with another person's woman, and they are offering you more than you imagine they would. You should know from experience, that there is always some kind of situation that follows."

"I can relate to that. Here is my question? If you had met Olivia when you and Jade were still together, or if Sarah had approached you sooner, before Jade left. Would you have gotten involved with either Olivia or Sarah?"

"Hypothetically speaking, it's a damn good question. I have considered the same thing, when this first happened between us. But it's not a difficult one to answer. You also forgot to include someone else in the mix."

"I know, Abby? She is a lot of woman for any man."

"You're right about that. I discovered this the hard way, but it was a pleasant surprise. I feel it's because of her, which had made the difference in me, and in my rationality, and in my relationship with Jade at present.

"Abby helped me to overcome many of my issues. I had a serious conflict with Jade about? She released so much anger in me, which I kept denying and hiding from myself, and other people.

"Getting back to your question? Realizing, what I know about Olivia, Sarah, and Abby now. I won't lie to you, Marcus. It would be as if, I admired trouble with hostile intentions.

"It would be extremely difficult not to cheat on Jade, with women like Olivia, Sarah, and Abby. Or not want to sample any of this?

"The answer is no, as much as I would like to try, and justify it to myself. I couldn't use that as an excuse. Or anything else if something happened as a result in our relationship. When all I have to do is leave her. If I don't have a reason in the first place to cheat on her, nor did she offer me a reason to.

"Don't misunderstand me, it's not always that simple. I'm just saying this is what I would have done. Sometimes when it comes to your feelings and another person. You never know what you will do sometimes.

"Now Marcus, here is the flip side to your question? When I first started working at the company, and I met Abby. I became very attracted to her personality, and had no idea what attracted her to me.

"It wasn't until we became better acquainted through our working relationship on the job, that I began checking her out physically, and she was absolutely gorgeous. Then every time we confronted each other on the job. We were connecting on all cylinders, no matter what it was pertaining to.

"I was alarm by this, and was so much aware of this, that it frightened me. It was like dealing with Jade, but it was completely with someone else. Who I had this compatibility or chemistry with, if you want to call it that?

"This is why, I always kept my distance from Abby. I didn't want to ever be put in the position of exploring this with her. I think she was aware of this as well as I was. This is why we respected each other's marriage status and remained professional, until her departure from the company.

"Abby could have been the one. I could have had an affair with back then. When everything was great between Jade and I. But I just didn't have a legitimate reason, or necessarily feel motivated to cheat on Jade with Abby, because of the attraction and connection we were having for each other. Olivia and Sarah were not present in my life at the time.

"Then again, If any of these women had caught me when this first happened between Jade and I? When I was vulnerable during that time. It would have been the right time, and a weak time for me.

"My ass would have been in trouble. When all three women were coming with a full package. There was no skipping and missing a beat with them. This is why I felt a small void, and emptiness in my life with them. The time we were together was all the time we were supposed to be together.

"Life has its own way of deciding how things work out for you sometimes. Doing it on my own wouldn't have been enough reason. There would have to be something else to push me that far over the edge, and then I am open to suggestions?

"Oddly enough, I believe if I had cheated on Jade, with anyone of these women in my life. The circumstance would have been a lot more devastating for her than they were for me.

"Marcus, I am not saying I haven't cheated on someone in the past as a first mistake. It was obvious I didn't know what the hell I was doing back then? And what I have learned from it, has helped me to do things a lot differently. When you are dealing with people and matters of the heart."

48

He thought about things concerning infidelity. Or simple cheating for that matter. It wasn't as simple as black and white. Anyone who has ever been in a relationship, knows that it's the complication that gives you that intrigue? Some people prefer making things more complicated, when they don't have to be?

When things begin to happen and based on your experience. You can understand why something like this would happen in a situation with people. Just look at who you are talking about besides yourself?

But in another situation or circumstance, you can't understand why in the hell something like this would happen? When there is no forgetting. It takes time to even begin forgiving, and that's when the real problem begins. It doesn't make sense regardless of whatever you want to call it.

"Somethings I can understand, which makes sense for some people and their situation.

"But if everything you do is based on fear, then you shouldn't be doing it at all. It doesn't matter, what the hell you are feeling for someone else inside. And then there are things, which makes no sense about cheating on someone at all."

"Yeah, I know what you mean, Marshall."

"I am saying if it isn't working, then cut it loose and be on your way. But I guess women have a different idea about that it seems. They prefer getting together with someone else first, before separating from someone. Or consider being alone without someone?

"The one thing I have learned about this whole situation with Jade, is sometimes trying to work things out in your relationship isn't always the best thing to do for you, either.

"Sometimes you can cause more harm to one another by trying to work things out? Why would you start up another relationship with another person. When you haven't resolved anything with the person you are still involved with?

"This is the kind of stuff that gets people hurt and killed, while everything continues to escalate. The law of averages hasn't changed recently either?

"You can't expect someone to accept that you are screwing them. And then you are screwing another person as well, without them feeling like you are just screwing them completely over? It's like being a guest on the Jerry Springer show."

Marcus began laughing. He took another drink from his beer. He stood up and began impersonating a guest on the show.

"Well Baby. You know how much I love you, and I love you more than anything in this world, and there is nothing I wouldn't do for you.

"But I have something to tell you. I have a secret I have been keeping from you. I had sex with your mother a couple of times.

"Then all hell breaks loose. You know what I am saying? You brought me here on national wide TV to tell me. You have been sleeping with my mother? What the hell is wrong with you?

"Did you get paid to say this? How long have you been sleeping with my mother, after we have been together all this time? Now she wants to kill the SOB or commit a crime for everyone else to see.

"Come on, what did you expect was going to happen? It becomes utterly ridiculous," as the both of them started laughing.

"This is one of the reasons why I was so disturbed by Jade's betrayal. Before this happened, I even offered her a solution to whatever was going on with her, and she still refused to take advantage of it.

"So instead, she screwed us both and allowed us to go through this unnecessary drama in our lives. It was hard to comprehend. She is an intelligent and bright person."

"I agree, Marshall. Sometimes you never know what's going on inside of another person's mind and heart? I would have never seen it coming."

"Jade on top of her game. It was another reason that made her more attractive to me. For example Marcus, I didn't know how much I would care, or love someone as much as I loved her.

"You know after all these years, my emotions continued to grow and grow for her. I loved her more every day than I did yesterday. I was surprise and afraid of my emotions when it came to myself. I couldn't believe the enjoyment, the pleasure, and the satisfaction I received by being married to her.

"I learned a lot about myself as well as her, and this is why I married her. I mean with Jade, I realized I was able to spend my life with one woman. Something I thought I wasn't sure about at the time?".

He didn't want to tell Marcus, when it came to making love and having sex with Jade? It was about his own weakness. She wasn't only pleasing in bed, but she was good. She was always there with it, and giving it to him. He discovered that when a woman is like this, she had a way of always keeping you in check.

No matter what her emotional and physical disposition was. She wasn't the type of woman. Who would say she is tired and had a long day with a headache, because she obviously didn't want to be bothered.

However, if you still wanted, then knock yourself out, while she just lay's there. Dead to the world. It's all on you. She didn't have the desire or energy to put out.

But Jade could walk right through the door, with tire irons on. And if she knows that you wanted her. She would flip the script and become Wonder Woman, and rock your world. She was different like this? Never complained about anything including her day.

Sometimes when they would stay in on the weekend for whatever reason? Jade would get up in the morning and take a shower, and put lotion and fragrance on her body. She walked around the apartment nude, and doing whatever. Or she would sit at the breakfast table talking, and eating with her legs open. Driving Marshall crazy. The longer she walked around, the more he would lose his objectivity when it came to her. And after they completed making love for the second time?

She would just take another shower, and begin walking around in the nude again. Looking sexy and smelling good, and then they would start making love over again. If they didn't foreplay themselves with each other first, then it wasn't going to happen. If they didn't hit their connection switch. Or they would change up, which didn't happen too often. She is an incredible lover. This is one of the reasons why he was celibate for so long, after they separated.

49

THERE WAS NO DOUBT TO him, she was a hard act to follow. And yet, she would credit him for being the better lover. It takes a certain kind of woman to make you feel this way. All he wanted was her when he got her. When they became a couple. Also when he lost her. He still wanted her in the worse way.

He didn't care about other women, and didn't feel stupid for not realizing? There is another world of women out there. Who was as equally as good as she was—but that's like looking for a needle in a haystack. When it comes to all the women out there.

Physically you will be able to replace another woman with looks and body, but whatever makes her different inside won't be an easy task to replace. Its what's inside that motivates her as a different woman.

She was it for him, plain and simple. People can say whatever they wanted to say. It was a hell of a discovery about himself. He valued himself more. He knew now, he was cable of being more than just a male whore. Because of what he shared with her, and who he was, and what he did before he became involved with her.

"I saw how much you changed when you met her, Marshall. Love does strange things to you, that's why it doesn't make any sense.

"It was obvious she was a good influence on you and you on her. But it wasn't like you haven't had a serious one on one before? You had quite a few than most have.

"Also, I hated to see the changes you've been going through, back and forth for the past year. I felt like you were being destroyed by a woman who we both admired."

"I know, Marcus. Jade would often say, how she was attracted to you, because she liked you a lot,"

"It was difficult because I didn't know what to do. I cared about the both of you. I tried to stay objective, and just be there for you anyway that I could.

"I know you would have done the same for me."

"Yeah, you're right, Marcus."

"I hope you don't have to repeat the same experience with someone else? Trust me, this is something which is absolutely not pretty," as they laughed at each other.

"Enough about me. How are things between you and Brenda? Anything new on the home front?"

"Well, if she keeps messing with my head. I am going to have to clock her. She is a beautiful woman, and her body is definitely worth the effort. But why is she so physically aggressive?

"Let me tell you what she did. She purchased love toys one day and freaked me out. Of course, it was a surprise I wasn't expecting. So I said I would give anything a try within reason.

"I had to admit she looked like something I couldn't afford, with her maid out-fit on and all of her behind being exposed. You know the type, too much behind for the wardrobe? When she is conveniently bending over for my attention?

"Then she offers me a pair of Leopard briefs, which were edible that she wanted me to wear."

Marshall began shaking his head and smiling. "I am trying to imagine you looking like George of The Jungle?"

"Yeah you're right, tell me about it. Then she pulls out a pair of handcuffs from her goody-bag, as she referred to.

"Then she wanted me to get on the floor and prowl like an animal. So she could whip me and dominate me. I wasn't into S&M, or anything else for that matter. Where I was going to allow her to inflict bodily pain up on me." Marshall began laughing.

"I told her I don't think so. I asked her, what was wrong with her? I suggested we could get in the bed together and we can take it from there?

"Or she could handcuff me to the bed post, and get on top of me and dominate me this way. She was disappointed apparently and was mad at me. Since I was telling her, how I didn't mine being dominated, and she agreed.

"After we did this? She stopped and removed herself from off of me, and said I was a bad man. I needed to be punished. I asked her, what did she mean by this? She removed a small whip from her bag of goodies.

"Brenda demanded I turn on my side. I said no. Are you crazy? She began whipping me."

Marshall laughed and couldn't control himself. "So what did you do?"

"I couldn't do anything. I was the dummy who told her, remember, she could handcuff me to the bed post and dominate me this way?"

"Did the whip hurt?"

"You damn right it did!"

"So what happened next?"

"Brenda whipped me like she owned me, and instructed me to shut up or else? Take it like a man for being bad and disobedient. Finally she stopped. She changed into her clothes, and then threw the keys to the handcuffs on the floor.

"I started yelling at her. She walked out of my house undisturbed by the profanity I used at her. I was mad as hell at her for abandoning me like this?

"Fortunately, I was able to maneuver my body over enough on one side, like I was a contortionist. Who didn't know what the hell he was doing, and retrieved the keys in order to free myself.

"I couldn't believe what she did. I had to apply rubbing alcohol to my legs and behind to alleviate the sting from the whipping. You can believe. I wanted to shake some sense into her after this?

"So for the last two weeks. I was calling her at home and at her job. I wanted her to know that it was over between us. I didn't want to see her face again.

"I didn't want to have anything else to do with her. I haven't been able to reach her. All of a sudden she is unavailable. So I left her messages on her voice mail.

"She is aware I am mad as a man who is naked without any mercy for her. But she doesn't care. It doesn't matter if I ever see Brenda Gentle again. Her sex is not worth the aggravation of her personality."

"I apologize, Marcus. I didn't mean to laugh. I just didn't think she would do you like this, and take things this far? I thought you were kidding at first, but I can see how upset you are."

"It's okay. I probably would laugh at you if the situation was reversed. It's over for me with her now. It's time for me to move on.

"There is this other person I have been trying to get together with. But I let Brenda interrupt an opportunity for this to happened. I gave her a shot first, what a big mistake.

"But I am going to pursue this other woman, Dominique. Wait until you see her, she is outrageous."

"Marcus, I have no doubt she is?"

"Oh by the way, before I forget. I stopped by Lawrence's last week to pick up some money he borrowed from me. And all I can tell you, is that Sarah won't be happy. If she finds out what is going on in her house, while she is away."

"And what is that?"

"Lawrence had another woman there. She was cute, but she looks a little too young for my taste. You know the type, immature with a big body. It looked like they were playing house in another person's house. I don't know what lies he was telling the young woman.

"I am not saying that this situation between you and Sarah is right or wrong? I know you wouldn't intentionally pursue another man's wife or woman, unless you have changed?

"I knew she had to initially make the first impression, which would open the door for you to come in, and she did. This is why you were caught off guard.

"I am glad Sarah had you for an outlet, because Lawrence is a real snake and he is way out of control. How could anyone screw up an ideal situation like that, and not appreciate a hot woman of Sarah's caliber? It just doesn't make any sense where he's concerned."

"I agree with you. Sarah is quite a woman. I can see why Jade probable didn't like her, Marcus. Perhaps in her own way, she felt threatened by Sarah, and my involvement with her now probably confirms this?

"You know as well as I do, woman don't trust other women when it comes to their man. If she does, then she's a fool."

Marcus decided to call it a night, and expressed his pleasure in seeing Marshall after his visit. He assured him they would talk to each other soon. He had one more stop to make, before he called it a night.

50

IT WAS A MONTH SINCE she last spoke with him. Time had been different for her. Since he became an important but intriguing mystery to her. Something tangible inside of her, like she would get it right this time?

Zoë distrusted men. She had no purpose but to use them for her benefit, and never trust a man again? She felt they would try and use her first, like other people who were preoccupied with minding her business.

She couldn't forget the image she saw from a picture in her mind. When she walked into her apartment one day. She witnessed her fiancé and her best friend having sex in their bed room.

He was doing her from the back in the A-order. A place where she didn't like or wasn't ready to explore, and wouldn't take it in the anal if you paid her to.

But her best friend didn't have a problem with it. Zoë was still bothered by the images re-emerging in her mind. When she thought about it, and considered romance and relationships—along with men?

It was ugly for her to watch it in shock. Her girlfriend got really low-down and vulgar. She demanded that Randall do her harder from the rear, but when they discovered Zoe was standing there. They didn't stop to interrupt their pleasure zone, but continued until they got their pleasure off—like her presence excited them more.

She could still hear their voices of ecstasy, as they climaxed, and did whatever they did together. The images where horrifying to recall of Randall and her best friend. She remembered running as fast as she could to get out of the apartment with nowhere to go.

Zoë really loved Randall, and meeting him in college when they were sophomores. Four years later, they were living together and engaged. Then the event of his sexual conquest with Molly Shaw began. He was doing her on a regular basis, and she didn't know about it.

It did more than break her heart it broke her spirit, and caused her to distrust all men. She couldn't believe that this is what love was for her very first time. She didn't care. Her disposition wasn't going to change anytime soon about men.

She was afraid that if Randall did it, then any man would find another reason to do it, and hurt her. The mystery surrounding Marshall was interesting and different to her about his demeanor. Why was there a silent and hidden feeling of hope, motivation, and an inspiration to her? She didn't know what to imagine or think of it, but Marshall stayed on her mind.

Zoë went to see a teacher. Who was a consultant, and dance instructor that was associated off campus with Columbia University. She received a degree in Liberal Arts, performing arts, dance.

Ms. Peters believed Zoë was one of the best young dancers, she had seen come out of nowhere in the last decade. She is athletic and powerful. A talented dancer with physical stature. She was a perfect fit for dancing and performing.

Zoë was her favorite and most gifted student by far. Ms. Peters was able to arrange an appointment for an audition with Alvin Alley American Dance Theater, because of her personal contacts throughout the dance community.

That was the day that Zoë went home to prepare herself, and to tell the man she loved about her excitement for the audition. She didn't get the chance, only to discover the nightmare of her life. When random sex was being displayed to her by Molly and Randall, and with no definite regard for her feelings what so ever.

Zoë went MIA. She missed her audition. Ms. Peters was surprised and disappointed in her heart for her with concern. Her first instinct was something had happened to her for her not to attend her audition, or something went terribly wrong.

She didn't buy the fact that Zoë panicked. Or it was too much pressure for her to handle. The woman strive on pressure. The more pressure the better Zoë was, but it was still a mystery how she disappeared. Or imagined that her child was getting her heart broken and torn out by some man.

But she couldn't believe her eyes, after all this time. It made her happy to see who was standing in front of her; immediately they hugged one another and cried.

"Hello, my child. I thought I would never see you again. How have you been? You look great. Where have you been all this time?"

Ms. Peters was this strong, vibrate, caring, and neutering white woman. Who conducted her own dance studio off campus? Who was Zoë's mentor, and like a second mother to her when she attended Columbia University. Zoë lost her mother years earlier, and her brother was killed in Afghanistan.

"It's been crazy the last year, but I missed you so much." Zoë revealed to Ms. Peters with tears in her eyes. How she regretted leaving the way she did, without talking to her first. She was unable to hide the fact she was an emotional wreck. Who was blow away by what happened to her, and didn't do a good job of dealing with it.

She discovered that a lot of people don't deal with break-ups too well in relationships, and when you are together you don't see the end. So you don't know what it will feel like when you are separating, which is difficult to walk away from and feeling anything positive. When there is something there that kicks you in the rear.

Ms. Peters suggested they go to lunch and catch up on things. Zoë began to explain to her about the events which led up to her disappearance, and the up's and down's of her life since then. When she suffered from her past humiliation of this event, and the loss of her brother?

But she found ways to help kids who were less fortunate than she was. Who were from all walks of life, and from all around the city. Something she learned from Ms. Peters about how to give back when you are fortunate than most.

She shared with her what she did for the kids, and what she did to get the money to make it happen. Ms. Peters looked at her with love, and explained how proud she was of her. She was sad to hear how Zoë's heart was broken, and the difficulties she had encountered for the past year.

She remembered the last time a man broke her heart, which motivated her to become a dance instructor, which changed her views and feelings about men, love, and relationships. She wouldn't consent to marriage in her life.

She was too pleased at calling the shots completely in her life. A man's companionship is secondary to her now. As far as she was concerned, she could take them or leave them. Men were not a priority in her life.

In a way, she was pleased that Zoë experienced this negative set back in her life. She still had a bright future ahead of her as a dancer. She needs to grow and get stronger from this experience. It will give her what she needs to develop from here on.

"So what turned you around back to me?" Ms. Peters asked. She wiped the tears away from her face with a tissue.

"It was you, Ann."

She was embarrassed because of all the pain, hurt, and disappointment she failed to confront. Or deal with for the past year in her life, which dominated who she was as a person since she was alone with no family. Somehow she was able to maintain her focus concerning some objectives in her life

"Girl, I am your family and I will always be, don't you know this by now?"

"I didn't want to burden you with my personal problems. You have done so much for me, even though you worked me like a hard trained dog," as they both smile at one another."

Ms. Peters sat closer to her in the restaurant and held her tightly in her arms. They were approached by a young woman. Who waited on them to see if they needed any further assistance?

"No thanks honey, were okay," said Ms. Peters. The woman took their order and then walked away.

"Girl, you are going to be fine.

"You are going to put the past behind you, and regain your self-esteem and confidence to be the remarkable woman you are."

51

SHE HELD HER BEAUTIFUL FACE in both hands, while looking directly into her precious large light brown eyes.

"You are a dancer with unlimited ability and potential to accomplish so much, but honey, potential is something that doesn't hang around for very long. Have you been keeping up with your exercises and training?" She asked.

She smiled at her. It brought back memories of a time when she was happy and hearing Ms. Peter's voice. When they were together working hard toward a common goal, in spite of all the changes she had endured.

The one thing she hasn't forsaken was her dancing skills, and everything that she had learned from Ms. Peters. She kept her skills as polished as she could, and ready to dance with passion and fire in her heart again.

The way Ms. Peters encouraged her to. She was consistently putting herself through a grueling training regimen. She recalled the Ballet lessons her mother and father paid for her to have. It was something she definitely wanted to do with her time at a young age.

She wanted to forget the pain that Randall caused her that day, and losing her brother in the war. She was amazing and determined in this way. Ms. Peters decided that Zoë and her would come together again, and continue with her dancing.

She thought wow, as talented as Zoë is. She didn't need to train for anything. She wanted to assure herself that her discipline was still there as a dancer.

She had no idea at first, then thought of a director she knew. He was searching for a lead dancer to perform in his new Musical, "Wishing For It To Happen?"

She needed Zoë to be this person. She convinced her to compete for the part. She agreed to do so, and welcomed the challenge. They knew the opportunity could be great for her future and career. She was teaching kids to dance at a school in Harlem and in Manhattan.

She could begin her dancing again with Ms. Peters at night. She was truly excited about something for the first time in a long while. It felt like Déjà Vu all over again. This time there was no man in her life to derail her or was there? She thought remotely in the back of her mind.

Her progress was quick and reassuring, after a week of reacquainting themselves with each other. Again Ms. Peters said to herself. She didn't need any training. She was happy to know she was correct.

She was ready to take the world by storm. She was also excited to see Zoë introduce new developments in her dance routine, which wholeheartedly impressed Ms.

Peters equally. Zoe revealed a lot of new and different movements for her to see.

Curiously looking to see, if there were any bad habits she picked up. There were only new routines she added to her repertoire. She was proud of her and happy to confirm her belief in Zoë's ability as a dancer.

She remembered everything she taught her and more. She was amazed by the growth and development, and what she respectfully learned on her own from her teachings. This time she will dance like it was for her to arrive in someone's heart.

Zoe took the butterfly out of Madam Butterfly; she graced the director and everyone else with her energy and ability to dance on stage. The spectators and potential dancers who were competing for the position also, watched her in silence and amazement.

She took the floor apart and the music down, like she had heard the music before and did the dance before. Quickly, Mr. Cohen turned around to witness his old friend of many years, Ms. Peters.

"Where did you find her? She is unbelievable."

"That's my Baby," as she responded with a huge smile of excitement on her face.

He stopped the audition without warning. He wanted to meet her, and offer her the part because there wasn't any need to continue. She brought out the excitement of a little boy in the director, as he approached her on stage.

At this moment, he realized that the critics were going to love her. Now, they will have something to write about which is joyful and positive for a change—than to enhance their ability to judge and criticize.

She will increase the shows ratings and revenue with her performance. She is good and she is unknown. The other potential dancers knew at this point they were doomed, after a performance of this nature.

So they were thanked and instructed to leave by the side exit door of the theater from his production crew.

****

He received a call from her again. She invited him to a show off Broadway. She told him that a ticket would be at the box office under her name for him.

He was curious, he didn't have any other plans. He accepted her invitation. She appeared to be excited.

"Please don't panic, Marshall, if you don't see me there when you arrive. I might be late. I will be there, okay."

"No problem, Zoë. I'll take you at your word."

She was pleased. He assumed she had something to take care of before she arrived.

When he arrived at the theater everything was in order concerning his ticket, and his seat was up front as he looked around to observe the theater. It was nice, small, and packed by the audience. Every seat in the place was taken. He was concerned there were no available seats on either side of him for her, whenever she arrived.

He wondered how this was going to play out if she didn't arrive soon.

The lights were dimming. The music sounded softly as it began to escalate. The curtains were drawn slowly. A man and a woman confronted each other on stage in dance. They were wearing a mask at first. Out of nowhere, a woman leaped high into the air—followed by two other women dancers performing to classical music.

He returned his attention back at the lead woman closer to examine her further. There was something familiar he could see through the wardrobe appearance. The audience was thrilled. She removed her mask.

He was enthusiastically excited to see it was her, watching her delightful spins and twirls. She leaped into the air with her magnificent body.

She received applause's from the audience when she began to sing. It was fun to see her perform on stage. She was athletic, graceful, and talented as a dancer, with a strong powerful voice to compliment her dancing.

Anyone could see she is obviously good. It was something which stood out about her. It was incredible to see her in this type of environment. Zoe had closed the show with a comedy dance routine which brought the house down. When the show concluded. She was introduced last. She received a standing ovation.

He patiently waited for her after the performance. She approached him finally. He greeted her with a warm kiss on her cheek. She turned in midstream, and kissed him on his lips with emotion. He couldn't help but express his surprise, and enlightenment about her ability to dance and how good she was.

Also, where did she get that voice from? He continued to offer his praise and compliment's about her talents. She didn't have to jump-start anything, she was the jump-start. He offered to take her to dinner in light of her surprise and current success.

He took her to a restaurant on the upper West side. She was impressed and was enjoying herself immensely.

Her conversation with him was like having to get ready for it all. Or sometimes what you see just looks that damn good to you. But it doesn't free you from the thought that it's still just a leap of fate. Afterward, he took Zoë home. He didn't stay with her.

As they walked away from each other, with thoughts of wonder and curiosity in the back of their minds. She kissed him good night without any mystery or curiosity in her. It was her way of letting him know she had a great time without over stating it.

52

It was done, Lawrence packed his bags to leave. Sarah rushed to the door to assist him out. He looked back at her strange. Like the dialogue of two people were belabored with each other. It was the third of three incidences, that escalated Sarah's stress level within the last month.

She hasn't contacted Marshall since she had returned. Or since their meeting with each other at the hotel. She had been away on three separate occasions, and on each return trip home. It was a reminder of how bad another day could be. Or having her gross anatomy go up in flames?

Since her emotions were left with no meaning in a dictionary. It wasn't her desire to tell someone. Or to talk about the feelings Lawrence and her didn't have for each other. Sarah stopped to think for a second, only if she could use magic as a determining factor.

Her magic would be for a real man. A man she could whip up just for herself? You can't beat the Devil on a consistent basis. Especially with a pure love for yourself when you want it?

It would be nice to have it this way. Considering all the wrong people you meet in your life or in a relationship. The percentage is always against you. But to Sarah, Lawrence was a genuine fool.

She could only ask herself at this point? What was she thinking when she first got involved with him? But nothing was going to change this for her. He was a fool regardless of whatever she felt for the person.

After the first time she returned home and saw Marshall.

She had Lawrence served with divorce papers. It turned into a battle zone, like an unknown thief who came to steal their weapons. So they could start another war between them with other means. They argued nonstop for an hour. He always had to have the last word, and didn't know how to just leave shit alone.

Not this time. Sarah took total control of the situation and put everything back into motion. He got caught with his pants down while over playing his hand, and not paying enough attention to someone. Who was blowing his peace up right in front of his face? She warned him about what she was going to do, as she told him again.

Lawrence thought that it was better not to listen to anything she had to say. He knew that women always have something to say, whether you want to hear it or not.

But sadly enough, he was caught in a Catch-22. They screamed on each other, like a web of pain, with no restrain to keep each other from attacking aggressively.

Sarah didn't care anymore. She wasn't backing down from him. But he wasn't going to accept the big picture. Even though his arrogance was looking forward to betraying him this time.

Taking Sarah for granted was no longer a luxury for him now. He didn't want to sign the divorce papers without riding on this train a little longer.

"I fail to understand why you don't want to sign the papers? I am no longer in denial about anything concerning us, Lawrence.

"I don't love you. I don't want to be with you. I simply don't care about you anymore, or as a person of interest. Just make your move and leave me with some dignity.

"We have nothing more to say to one another, but good-bye, or have a nice life."

"Why are you so cold, Sarah?"

"Is that supposed to be a trick question? You have inspired me to be nothing but? I have tried over and over to give so much of myself to this marriage. I believe in a real marriage. It was all a waste of time with you and for what?

"So I could come home and watch you shit on me? I have been too nice, too good to you, but no more Lawrence.

"If you want to run around with every woman in the city, then go ahead with my blessing and get your rocks off! Just not with me, while you make our marriage an even further mockery than it is?"

"Well, Sarah I have needs. I am a man."

"Don't make me laugh, Lawrence, a man of what? The hell with your needs. I don't care about you or them. All I care about is that you sign the divorce papers. So you can play your games full time, with someone who can appreciate what you can drop."

Sarah turned and walked away in anger. "So this is really it? You are telling me, there is nothing we can do to change things?"

"Is the Pope Black, Lawrence?"

"No!"

"Then I believe you have answered your own question? Please, don't make me laugh any more. You don't want me, and I don't need you. We don't have to go back and forth with this anymore."

Before he left, he was encouraged strongly by her to sign the divorce papers. After several other points of his behavior was revealed to him, which he couldn't deny or dispute which took place during their marriage.

Sarah was also in a position to blackmail him without any mercy. She kept all the proof on him from day one, which could have caused additional problems for him later. If he decided to contest the divorce. He wasn't smarter than her, but he convinced himself that he was.

He was obviously more devious than she was. He consented to her final demand as a last act of kindness, he felt.

She offered him ample time to find someplace else to stay before he left.

A week later, Sarah returned home and he wasn't home. She was relieved but saw several of his things still lying around. And on the following day, while she was cleaning her house, it pressed on her last nerve?

How he could live with her and not show any interest in the house. Or expressed no interest in maintaining the place, or clean up behind himself. Like he enjoyed having maid service, and someone clean up after him. She didn't have time to pick up after him, like she was his mother. Or like he was still a little kid.

Sarah lifted and moved the couch to the side in order to clean under it. Her eyes were shocked to see a woman's pair of underwear rolled up, as if they were removed quickly and tossed to the side, and a used condom lying next to them.

She shook her head and removed her latex gloves. She placed the two items into a large zip-lock bag to save for who else, when she confronts him. This is what she meant about additional proof concerning him.

She thought that if Lawrence had money. She would take him for all the alimony she could get. But she couldn't see herself taking advantage of a fool already.

53

It was going to be another war of the roses, or a lonely heart that is wishing for some attention. But would get none here—before the roses died. It was her desire to give him back a hard kick in all of this, and borrow another person's body to hurt him with.

It was her utmost desire to mess him up physically, because there was no more familiar excitement between them. The fact that he could continue to do the things he does, with nothing in common for a shared memory. Or a moment of consideration was nothing to him.

Sarah thought how sad it was, that his mother and his relatives didn't have more influence on him to be a better person. Or how to have respect for a woman and himself, but it was all on him now. He frustrated Sarah to the point of being, like her pleasure zone was consistently being neglected. He couldn't satisfy anyone more than himself in bed.

But the sex stopped a long time ago, and it wasn't worth the emotion or the effort to consider faking it. Why he wanted to hurt her, or come closer to escape in her? Like she was a woman to be used for that purposed only.

She hated feeling this way about her marriage, but caring enough about it to try and work on it was wishful thinking; upon deadly blessings when it came to Lawrence.

He is a man you don't want to fall down with, or cry with a dirty look on your face. She refused to be a neglected woman, who was walking in the rain lost. Just waiting for him to come by and drench her even more.

She needed her body to be in motion. To know where she is going before she can help him. Or be trapped in his problems. He didn't have much to testify to about concerning the panties and condom.

The woman was someone he was trying to get together with, long before he got married to Sarah. She wanted him now. He didn't refuse the opportunity to take advantage of it. There was no attempt on his part to try and pass the items off as Sarah's or his. Or as a past event that they forgot which happened between them.

He took the bad with the bad, and continued to deal with Sarah flying off the handle on him again. He would have been better off putting a foot up his own ass.

"Are you waiting for me to die first? So you can dance on my grave?

"Just what is it, that you are trying to prove to me or yourself, Lawrence? You have gone beyond the point of being a simpleton?"

"Okay, I don't see the point of rehashing all of this over again! So why don't you just trash this, Sarah? I will sign your divorce papers, because I have had enough."

"Well, it couldn't have come soon enough for me. I am tired of coming home to complain about your antics and behavior, Lawrence.

"You show no respect for your own business or me, but if I did what you did in our marriage. Then I would be the biggest slut this side of the city. Or another dumb and useless bitch to you, right Lawrence?"

"It's like I said, it won't be too much longer now. I don't want to be with you either."

"Great? That's the best news I have heard in a while coming from you. I thought we had something nice, but you are just like the rest of the women out there. Always bitching and complaining about one thing or another.

"You'll are never satisfied with anything a man does for you. Anything I do is never good enough to meet up to your standards. You think I don't have standards, either?

"Do you think I am going to sit around, like some obedient child? Waiting for you to give me sex? It may be good, but it's not the only sex that's out there. Especially, when I can get all the love I want whenever I want?

"Well, I wish you would do exactly that, and leave me alone. I didn't sign up to be some man's sex slave. How can you not understand a relationship is more than sex?"

"Maybe to you, Sarah, but half the time women don't know what the hell they want anyway?"

"Well not this woman. I know exactly what I want from a relationship, a marriage, and a man, and it's nothing attached to you, Lawrence."

"Then that's fine with me." He moved around Sarah to walk upstairs to enter their bedroom. He opened the closet and removed his clothes away from hers. He began folding certain items of his, and neatly placing several of them in a suit case.

He arranged and prepared additional stuff that was in the bedroom, which made him angry Sarah was kicking him out of their home. Even though, the house rightfully belongs to her.

She gave him sufficient time to find someplace else to live, but he took his time and procrastinated. He was still bothered by the chain of events. He knew he really had to go once he signed the divorce papers.

It was no way they could resolve anything. They were past the point of no return. He surely didn't want to leave now, after realizing how good his set up with Sarah was. He also knew he was tired of her rules, and conditions when it came to their relationship and marriage.

But to be honest, Sarah didn't treat him this way. She stayed with her good nature. He admitted that Sarah was a good person and a good woman, but he felt he was a better man. Or she didn't know what she was doing.

How and why he was able to come to this conclusion and dilute himself was anybody's guess?

He needed a different type of woman. A woman he could roll with and have fun with. Not a woman to come home to every night and play house with. Or live up to other people's expectations of one another.

It was time for him to pursue his own thing. Now that his modeling career was beginning to take off. When he becomes famous, he can piss on Sarah's parade any time he wanted to, he thought. Then she would be just another one of his ex-women.

After being away for five days, Sarah returned home for the third time to witnessed Lawrence and a younger woman leaving her house. She gets out of a cab in front of the house.

Sarah couldn't believe this low life conniving SOB. She yelled at the top of her lungs. Her emotions exploded into the air. The Asian cab driver was busy being nosy. He was attracted to Sarah, and was enjoying the entertainment.

He waited before he decided to pull off and witnessed the excitement between her, the man, and the other woman.

54

SARAH DROPPED HER CARRYING CASE and bag to the ground. She approached him, and began swinging it at him with all the strength she could generate. The second the other woman saw Sarah grabbed a top from the garbage can. She immediately jumped into the waiting cab and left Lawrence there.

Leaving him alone to deal with his on-going problem? He did his best to avoid getting hit with the garbage can top, and prevented most of the blows coming his way.

He knew that if she connected with him it's over for him. Sarah was athletic. She was very good in martial arts and gymnastics. Also in college she was a basketball player. She was a point guard on the starting five. She was the captain of the team. She was all conference in their division, but she wasn't interested in playing pro ball when she was approached.

Sarah was still a handful to maintain. She was mainly out of control at this point. He could have been seriously injured by her, if she connected with any part of his body. Sarah wasn't taken any prisoners.

He managed to take the can top from her, but it didn't stop her. She began punching him with her fist, and kicking him in the ankle. She provided a round house kicked to his face.

He saw an opening and began running from her. He got out of the way of her flurry of punches. She was tired at that point from the energy she had exerted, and was angry with the fire of hell in her.

He was afraid to retaliate at this moment, in hopes, that one of his nosey neighbors would call the police. Or report he was beating his wife out on the front lawn. When she turned to retrieve her carrying case and bag, she left the door open. He followed Sarah into the house.

"After everything we have talked about, you still go behind my back and bring another woman into my house!

"I mean where were you, Lawrence. When God was passing out brains? Did you miss out on your day? Or were you just late for your appointment to get one? Or did they run out of brains before you eventually got there? Or did you have to wait for the next shipment, which was more than likely damaged?"

"I do know, that if you put your hands on me again. I am going to knock you out." Sarah abruptly jumped in front of his face, and demanded he do just that. She advised him, it would be the last woman he ever raised his hands too.

"Get out of my face, Sarah, before I hurt you." She removed her coat rapidly, and stood her ground anxiously waiting for the confrontation to begin. She gazed upon him with contempt. In her heart he was no man to her—just an inflated ego.

"It's your play, Lawrence. I am not going anywhere." He was really surprised and taken by Sarah's heart, her courage. He didn't see this side of her coming. She was meaner and stronger than a lot of men he knew and hung out with.

He was undecided about what he was going to do at this moment. He could see Sarah wasn't going to back down from him any time soon, regardless of his words or threats. So he backed away from her.

"The party is over, Lawrence. You can definitely turn the lights off. I am tired of trying to be civil to you, or considerate of your feelings. When you just continue to screw me over. Like I am some kind of woman who is turned on by your abuse. I want you to get out now, today!

"You have the next three days to get your personal belongings out of my house. I will be here, and if you don't. Then I will have your stuff removed and put out on the street.

"And if you think I am joking about this, then you try me!? Also, I want your set of keys to the house now!"

He removed the keys from his pocket, and threw them at her. The keys hit her on her right shoulder and fell to the floor. He went upstairs to pick up the bags he prepared earlier. He came downstairs to walk past Sarah and out the door. She slammed the door behind him, and watched him angrily throw his bags into his car and drive away.

Sarah turned around and slowly seated herself on her couch. She started crying, but it wasn't because of him. It was because, she didn't want to bring this kind of madness out of her, or bring herself down to his level.

What could she do when someone else does everything they can to bring the worse out in you? Just constantly pushing your buttons. Like no one had every told them—what this button is for?

If she ever did something to him, she would regret it for defending herself emotionally and physically. She always judged her sense of fairness. It was like wearing a skull cap, with time to kill herself inside.

She was disappointed she had to get real nasty, and bitchy with him, in order for him to get the point. She couldn't allow him to disrespect her like this, or treat her like this. Her relationship and her marriage meant a great deal to her, even if it didn't to him.

A part of her felt something good with him in the beginning, it was real to her. She was happy it wasn't a case of love being blind, but after a period of time, she began to see right through him.

It was an unfortunate mistake on her part. Although she realized now it wasn't love, but the emotion of love. The real Lawrence came out, before she could get a chance to know the fake Lawrence.

He had an exceptional person in Sarah, as well as a real woman. Who knew what she wanted, and didn't play child's games to get want she wanted. Lawrence couldn't step up to the plate, and be the man she needed him to be for them.

His biggest motive was to screw around on her, when she wasn't present. So she could be emotionally under his thumb, or some needy person. Who couldn't think or depend on herself. Sarah couldn't see herself losing it over him, but Marshall, she thought, possibly

She would be home for the next three days, before she headed out to Atlanta on Sunday. She didn't trust him. He acted like he had a wrong man's burden. He didn't have to care, it was all about the money, she figured.

So for the next two days, he called Sarah, before he arrived at the house to remove his belongings with two of his friends. Then on the third day, he figured that Sarah would be gone by now on her flight.

He made a private attempt to get into her house without her knowledge—since she was away—with a second set of keys he had made for himself. But to his surprise, and from the look on his face, he was dumbfounded.

The keys didn't work. He couldn't believe she had the locks changed that quickly. He didn't want to take a chance, and try to force his way into the house without the keys. He was aware of the neighbors who were aware of his presence.

He didn't want to give them a reason to call the police on him. Sarah also made a stop at the police station to file a report on record, with the police department about a potential act of theft or vandalism committed by her husband to her house.

After she served the divorce papers he threatened to harm her as well. She provided as much information, or evidence as possible, since she would be out of town.

One of the police men remembered her as his flight attendant from a holiday trip he took to Jacksonville, Florida to visit his relatives. He was attracted to her, but he saw that she was married. He still made every effort to accommodate her in anyway, that she needed to be accommodated by his department.

The police thought it would be too obvious if her house was broken into. Or ransacked right after she had all the locks changed on the same day, and filed a report with the police. And her husband was served with divorce papers.

Whether he realized it or not. If anything happened, he would be the first suspect they would express interest in concerning any of her property damaged, or missing in relationship to her house. After she provided a recording of their argument that day to the police?

Lawrence knew that she knew, that one of the most undermining things about love is? When it comes to a relationship with someone else.

You can never tell what someone else really feels about you. You can feel one way, and think another way. You can be completely blown away. When you discover that someone doesn't really give a damn about you.

55

He was feeling great. First, he received his divorce papers from Jade, with a kind sympathy note from her attached. The papers validated by a Notary Republic at the court house. It brought a twinkle of sadness to his eyes, because losing Jade was like losing—a pretty rose of the first power.

Their love was a time to die for, when it was right. And for all he did, and for all he gave, and for all he wanted was mainly determined by what? When he looked at things the way they are now, he thought.

It was time to move on and confront the challenges that lie ahead for him, and the current unknown which awaits them.

Secondly, he spent the weekend with Olivia. Sometimes her job position required her to travel out of town, with multiple locations to perform different audits at different companies.

Olivia arranged for them to be together for the weekend. She fabricated a phony weekend trip to provide to her husband. She knew it meant taking a huge risk, but she didn't care anymore. She felt Marshall was worth the risk to her along with their development.

Olivia was taken by surprise. She thought they were going to spent more time in bed. Not that she was disappointed, but it was more than she expected being with him. When they began their weekend together.

He took her to his friend's house to visit in White Plains. So she could meet Marcus and his new girlfriend, Dominique.

Olivia was having a great time and enjoying herself. She and Dominique hit it off, but somehow they knew it was apparent. She thought Marcus was kind, nice, funny, and sweet.

It was a long time since she felt comfortable, and enjoyed herself around people she could also relate to. Everything about the evening was great to her. She was happy and enjoying herself. He was open with her about sharing aspects of his life with her.

She could see that he wasn't going to hide her away, because they had an interracial relationship. Or he was afraid of what people might say. Being seen with her or her being seen with him, or back down from anybody because she was married. It was too late for this. The cat was out of the bag on this one, as far as he was concerned.

But they weren't going to be foolish because they had special feelings for one another. They did a lot of things out of respect and consideration for others, as well as for themselves. She was amazed by his attitude toward her.

He seemed to have it all under control, but not really. She just made things easier for him. Now, she was beginning to feel more and more like his "lovely one."

The weekend didn't stop there. The next morning, they slept late together from the love they made the previous night.

He recalled Olivia had a thing for pancakes. He took her to I-Hop, so she could fulfill her desire. She loved being on the move with him, the adventure, the unknown, and the excitement was like a big thrill to her in their relationship. The simple things they did together.

It was a ten minute wait, before they could get a table. Finally, there was an unexpected departure from a couple with two kids. They were escorted to the table by a young and cute Hispanic woman. After they were seated. Olivia looked around and asked the attractive waitress.

"Was there something wrong?" When she realized the attention they were getting.

The waitress said, "No. That always happens when you see a fine ass Black man, with a beautiful looking White woman. They just look so damn hot together, when they are into each other."

They all began laughing. They thanked the sassy waitress, while she started to take their order. He looked at Olivia and replied to her, how hot she was. She smile and kissed him. No one has ever told her that she was hot before, or ever made her feel this way.

Not because she was white, but because Olivia was simply hot. She could have been born with a multitude of colors. It still wouldn't have changed the fact, that the results would have still been the same. She is hot.

After they finished their bunch. He whizzed her off on a drive up to Connecticut. He wanted to take her to this unique Flea Market. She was impressed and excited by the wonderful items, and how kind and friendly the people were.

Before they left, they purchased a hand full of items together, and they were offered a free one.

He then took her to The Museum of Natural History. They had dinner afterward. He took her to see a movie, she was interested in seeing. Her husband apparently was too busy to take her to see it.

Marshall took her to see the movie. It turned out to be a good choice. They enjoyed the movie together. She was thrilled, how they were able to do so much in a day. When they arrived at his place. He made Olivia comfortable, while he did the same. She lied on top of him.

A CD was playing when they talked, laughed, and joked, with each other about the fabulous day they had together. She relaxed her head on his chest peacefully. They fell asleep on the bed from today's events.

The next morning, Olivia decided she would go jogging with him. He was delighted but didn't insist. He knew she was a smoker, and didn't have any idea or knowledge she was an athlete. She pushed the notion of her smoking aside, and insisted going jogging with him.

He was surprised, she was prepared with her own gear. She said she never leaves home without it. He was more impressed, with how well she was in shape. She stayed with him all threw out, after jogging a mile and a half. He discover she was a runner, regardless of her smoking.

It didn't prevent her from keeping in excellent shape. She was competitive too. Her body was more than an apparent statement. He became more and more intrigued with elements about her.

They sat across from the breakfast table having a short meal. He prepared for them, while they read the newspaper together, and discussed current events of interest to them about their politics.

Batting eyes back and forth at each other, while smiling with a way to come at each other. This time they took a shower together. It was nice. They caressed each other with foreplay. They were soothing each other with body oil.

Olivia and him made love to each other, but the intensity of their love making affected them more than they thought. It becomes more difficult when you feel good about another person, and you are having great sex with them also. They continued to make love throughout the day. They stayed in bed for the remainder of the day. She was unbelievable, and he stayed on it like a machine.

Later that evening, he drove Olivia to La Guardia Airport, so she could meet her husband. He was picking her up from her weekend trip. Marshall watched her from a distance waiting for her husband. His car appeared in front of her. He drove away after this.

Before he went to bed, he received a call from her. She was falling in love with him. She didn't want to tell him, or put him in a position by saying he felt the same—so she didn't tell him. They have been involved with each other for over a year now.

She wanted him to know, and realize how much he has changed her. How good he makes her feel. She admitted to having so much fun, and feeling alive again whenever she is with him, than she has had in four years of marriage. Or at any other time in her relationship with her husband.

It wasn't a comparison, but just another thing that wasn't happening in her relationship or life. She literally thanked him for being the person he was.

Olivia was feeling she couldn't contain her emotions any longer. She had to be honest with herself, as well as with him. It wasn't that she was expecting him to run off, with her somewhere in order to be together.

But more or less, knew how much he had changed her perspective about a relationship. What she was really doing in her life with her husband. She wanted more out of life for herself, and also from a relationship and marriage.

She was prepared to make a significant change in her life. She was no longer this naïve person from the South concerning her new options in life.

56

NATALIE NORMAN WAS A HARD act to follow. To plainly put it, she was simply dangerous. She left Portland Oregon to restart her life by relocating to New York. She left a man who was her husband, but he agreed to divorce her in fear of his life.

At first he didn't want her to leave him. She broke his back, which left him paralyzed. Then she tortured him and physically abused him. He had no choice after this. He was a wealthy business man, with lots of money and possessions. She didn't care about him, except for his money.

When he wanted sex. She told him to get a prostitute or a call girl. The well wasn't working here, or everything was dried up and disappeared. She would rather masturbate than to have sex with him. Not that he was unappealing, but he just wasn't her type.

He couldn't take it anymore, after she hurt him the way that she did. He wanted to press charges against her, but had no way of proving his case. In spite of the fact, he was rich and powerful. She was smart, meaner, and wiser with her own source of power.

She was the type of woman who could get any man to do what she wanted for her. Like when she had two men assist her in a nasty fall, which caused him to break his back. Naturally she was out of town visiting her relatives.

But the two men mysteriously died before they could be question by the police. He decided to give her a divorce and all the money she needed to leave and get the hell out of his life. She contacted an old friend of hers, Katherine Johnson.

She lived in New York. They attended college in Portland Oregon, and were roommates in their Senior year before they graduated together. Katherine received a job offer in New York, because of a Professor who was a friend of her fathers, and kept in contact with some associates in New York.

And furthermore she really wanted to leave Portland. She felt it was an okay place to live, but she didn't want to spend the rest of her life there.

Natalie wanted to stay for the time being and explore her possibilities. Or see what Portland really had to offer her. Now that she could persuade job ventures, and see what the other half lived like. She wanted the good life, and she didn't care how she got it, or who she had to use to get it.

This is how she eventually met Derrick Lance. Who owned his construction business, and she did a brilliant number on him, after they were married. She became bored and restless with him, after she continued her life with him in Portland. Everything was increasingly limited for her motivation, and offered her little excitement to look forward to with a lack of fun to have.

She often thought of herself as an adrenaline junkie, but she wasn't sure. She didn't have the compatibility that she needed to experience with someone else. Who could confirm her actions for the behavior in her.

When her husband gave her everything that she wanted, and released her from any further obligations to him. She was cleared by the authorities for any miss doings.

She arranged to finally leave Portland for good to spread her wings, and enjoyed her life the way she wanted to. She had an enormous amount of money, and whatever power it brought her. Thanks to her ass-in-nine husband. Who she didn't have to worry about anymore.

A month later, Katherine was picking Natalie up at La Gaurdia Airport. Her boyfriend had accompanied her to greed Natalie. They exchanged hugs, and the boyfriend was introduced. He escorted her bags to the car. They got her settled and situation.

She was fascinated immediately with all the people, the confusion, and the lighting and various structures throughout the airport. She thought Portland would be so much different if they had an airport like this?

"So how was your trip?" asked Katherine.

"It was okay. I was tired because I stay up late last night. You know, excited to see you, and be here. I slept for most of the trip.

"So how was your day Curtis and Katherine?"

"Thank you for asking. It's been pretty good," said Curtis.

"I also had a pretty good day as well," said Katherine. "Natalie have you eaten or are you hungry?"

"Now that I am rested and wide awoke. I think I could go for something to eat. What did you have in mind?"

"We would like to take you to a restaurant, that we frequently eat at. It's a very nice place. You will like the atmosphere and food.

There was a parking facility near the restaurant. They walked to the location, while Curtis and Katherine held hands. Natalie was distracted by the people, the lights, the traffic, and the many different stores to shop and buy things at.

The doorman opened the door for them to enter the restaurant, while Natalie attracted the man, and returned a sudden smile. His eyes followed her behind into the restaurant. They were approached and escorted to a table.

Natalie was excited and was enjoying herself already, by all the attention and request they received for their food entertainment. Curtis and Katherine selected wine, but Natalie selected something stronger.

She tried her best to not be too obvious, but Curtis seemed like he couldn't take his eyes off of her, and her large beautiful breast which was exposed from the low cut blouse she wore. Natalie was strikingly pretty, with nice breast, and a desirable body.

She carried herself eloquently, with a pleasing personality.

They were all having a good time, and talking about everything that came to mind. There was no doubt everyone was feeling a little nice and heighten from the drinks. But the meal was also very enjoyable with everything else.

After a sizable tip and a trip to the restroom. They made their exit and Curtis proceed to drive them home. They were location on the lower west side in a luxury hi-rise co-op apartment, which was owned by Curtis, and Katherine moved in with him two years ago.

After he inherited it in a will from his father. Who pasted away and was a member on the New York Stock Exchange. His mother didn't want the apartment. She was living in Florida.

57

When they entered the apartment Natalie was impressed. She was given a grand tour of the place by them, and was escorted to her own room. The place was huge and gorgeous. She could see herself owning this. Hell, she had more than enough money to afford this and more.

Once everyone became relaxed and comfortable, they consumed a few more drinks and continued with various conversation. Curtis continued to observe her body when Katherine's attention was distracted. Natalie smile at him, rather than alarm him with any annoyance. His interest was well received.

Natalie wanted to know more about the city, with a multitude of questions. But was considerate enough not to keep them up long by imposing on their time. There would be more time for this later. Once she was properly settled in and was looking into matters of her own.

She began undressing in her room. Then she opened the door wide when she heard Katherine enter the bathroom to take a shower. She walked over to the window nude, and looked up into the dark sky.

She turned around to see Curtis at the door staring at her body. She stared at him when she bend down, and placed one of her fingers inside of her. Then withdrew her finger to place it in her mouth. He was mesmerized and didn't know what to say or do at the moment, but continue to watch.

Suddenly she walked over to Curtis. He thought that she was going to close the door. When she approached him. She did the same thing with her finger, but this time she placed her finger inside his mouth, and took it out. Then she turned around and closed the door without looking at him.

Curtis started breathing heavy, and turned around to lean against the door. He was more than aroused. He was terrified by what he had seen, and by what Natalie had did. He rushed to his bedroom and immediately changed into his pajamas, and entered the king size bed.

When Katherine finally entered the bedroom from taking her shower smelling good, and looking sexy. He jumped on her and made love to her like he never did before. She was surprised and wondered what had gotten into him. She wasn't complaining when he did it good to her, and it wasn't a rush job like after work.

The next morning, Curtis had already left for work. They had decided that Katherine would take the day off, and show Natalie around more. This way she could get a better idea of what it was like in the city, as her stay increased.

When Curtis arrived at worked at the World Trade Center on the seventieth floor. He greeted various people walking to his office. He entered and closed the door abruptly. He hung his coat up and sat in his swivel chair, and look distantly out his window.

He couldn't stop thinking about Natalie and her performance last night, which scared him to say the least. What if Katherine had saw this, and what her reaction to this would be? But the bigger question is, what was Natalie's motive for doing this? Did she think that he wanted her, or was she merely a trouble maker?

He didn't know what to make of it, because he didn't know her. He didn't want to give himself away by asking a million question about Natalie. Or give Katherine suspicious thoughts about them.

He thought he would come home later, and hopefully the two would be separated and prepared for bed. But when he walked into the apartment they were up talking, and laughing while drinking wine.

He was greeted by Katherine, and Natalie greeted him with a glass of wine. She looked him dead in his eyes. Like nothing had occur between them the night before. She showed no sign of guilt that he was concerned about.

She made him feel easy and comfortable. He felt like he had dodge a bullet, he hoped. Finally everyone said good night, and headed to their rooms. Curtis and Katherine's conversation was brief with each other, before they turned in for bed.

He continued to talk about his day when he realized that she was fast to sleep. He wanted to review a few proposals before he turned in. He relocated himself at the table in the living room.

Suddenly Natalie came out of the bathroom, and walked past him in her pajamas. She said good night without looking at him, and he replied the same. He didn't know what to think.

He woke up to the touch of Katherine's hand on him. She pulled herself closer to his back and behind. She felt him all up. She left nothing to the imagination. He began smiling, thinking that she was a little horny this morning.

It was very dark in the room and no light presenting itself from the window. She began moving forward, backward, and circling her motion.

She continued by lifting herself up and down. She reached to grab his pajama top. Now she imitated her efforts as if she was riding a bull. He was more than surprised how aggressive and wild Katherine had become.

He was excited by her new behavior. Curtis decided to grab and pull her into him. So he could penetrate her further, but she slapped him hard instead. Without hesitation he pushed her to the side and she fell off the bed and onto the floor. He switched the table lamp on.

"What in the hell has gotten into you, Katherine?" Suddenly he saw and realized that it wasn't her. It was Natalie smiling and summoned him with her finger to get on her, with her legs open. He stared at her and began breathing heavy. He elevated himself from the bed, and placed himself on top of her and in between her legs.

58

THE NEXT MORNING, MARSHALL TOOK another day off from work. He had two remaining days left. He thought about being a free man, no longer married. It felt good. It felt different. It felt strange to him. It felt like he was relieved, or a little sorry at the same time.

It was scary to see someone you loved and admired, changed right in front of your face? Then behave like they didn't know, what they were doing to someone else?

Being with Olivia this weekend was amazing. Now he knew why he always referred to her as his "lovely one." His cell ringed. It was Katherine, a close friend of Jade's.

"Hello, Katherine."

"Hello, Marshall. I tried to reach you at work, but they said you were off today.

"So I tried you at home. I hope I didn't interfere with anything."

"Katherine, it's no problem. What's up?"

"It's Jade."

"What about her?"

“She is in the hospital. No one is supposed to know about it, but I felt you had a right to know.”

“Is she okay, is she hurt? What happened to her?”

“She had an argument and a fight with her new friend?”

“Who is he!?”

“He is the guy she has been seeing lately. It isn’t anything serious going on between them, but however, he would like it to be.”

“So why is he hitting her?”

“I tried to tell Jade. I think it’s because he is jealous, and insecure about the feelings she still has for you. I also told her, that Ryan needs to wake up and smell the coffee?

“Her emotions weren’t going to change and go away for you overnight. Regardless of whatever changes you and her have been through.

“How could he not acknowledge the fact, you and her have been together for over ten years.

“And not to mention, the feelings that still exist between the two of you. Regardless of whatever happens, shit can always become complicated with this other person. You really don’t want this complication to be confused with love, pain, or suicide.

“Yes! I was jealous of Jade. What she had with you. Why would she mess up a good thing? But it didn’t stop me from being a true friend to her. That’s a fact of life.

“What did he expected her to do, just throw her emotions away for you? How unrealistic is that? He doesn’t know anything about her and her relationship with you. He only sees what he wants from Jade. I didn't trust him.

"Where is she going to put her emotions? I think he was trying to force himself on her. When she was vulnerable in the beginning of their relationship.

"He was trying to tell her, what she should be doing with her business concerning you.

"You know, Jade told him where he could go with that? She isn't going to let anyone tell her. What to do when it comes to her precious, Marshall. Whether you and her are together or not."

"I want to thank you for everything. I appreciate it. I owe you one, Katherine."

"Thank you, Marshall. Please, take care."

"You do the same. Good-bye, Katherine."

Katherine was a girlfriend of Jade's from work. She is very pretty, sweet, and with a tough personality. She had been a good friend to Jade. Marshall always liked her, and felt she was very attractive.

He had all the information he needed from Katherine. He decided to go to the hospital to visit Jade. He arrived just in time for visiting hours.

It was difficult to see her lying there helpless, injured, quiet, and looking out the window day dreaming. Because some man gave her a beating. Her face was swollen with black and blue bruises. Jade's arm was in a cast. He felt like his heart had stopped from seeing this dynamic woman lying there injured and hurt.

It was obvious she put up a fight, But that was Jade's character. She wasn't anybody's push over. She wasn't going down without fighting back. Or they would have lost everything that they had a long time ago.

She not only could be a pisser at times, but she could be damn tough. It was one of the things he admired most about her. It didn't matter how much the odds were against her. She would take a serious behind whipping, before she gave upon her believes. He always loved that about her too. It was apparent that something must have really gotten out of hand for this to happen to her.

He was angry that some guy thought he could man handle his wife, and hurt her. He had to be crazy stupid. When she turned around and saw him. She was embarrassed and hurt to see him standing there.

Her eyes were filled with tears. She began crying. He walked over toward her, and sat down on the bed next to her. He bend over to gently kiss her all over her injured face. Her eyes kept following his lips on her face. He made sure he did everything he could to avoid her arm.

"I love you, Marshall."

"I love you too, Jade." She cried more, while placing her free arm around his neck as he came closer to her.

"I didn't come here to argue with you, or talk about your business. I don't want anything to happen to you. I care about what happens to you."

"I have always known that, Marshall." She stopped crying? "I miss you so much."

"Well…when do I get one of those ridiculous smiles of yours? I miss you too." He was proud of her, after seeing the discomfort it caused her. He kissed her lips fully. He stayed with her for a while, until visiting hours were over.

She allowed him to feel her bruises. They laughed and talked about how hard her head was anyway, and everything else around the issues which brought her to the hospital.

A nurse came into the room to take her temperature, pulse, and examined her overall condition before he left. He excused himself briefly to place a call to, Marcus.

When he returned, she told him the nurse informed her, that she will be able to go home tomorrow. He was pleased to hear the good news. He wanted to know who will be there for her.

She explained how Katherine had agreed to be there to pick her up, and stay with her for a few days. The arrangements were made in advance between them. It was time for him to leave. He kissed and hugged her goodbye.

"Please take care of yourself until you get better. I will be in touch."

"I will, Marshall."

"I will call you soon, to see how things are progressing."

"Thank you."

He could see the pain in her face, and being unable to position her arm in a cast. She was feeling much better due to his visit. She didn't know what he would do, but she knew he was going to do something. She saw that look in his eyes too.

He could see she was beginning to feel concern for Ryan, once he confronts him. That's why she wouldn't listen to him about Marshall.

It doesn't matter if they are together or not. She is the one person without a doubt, who knows how much he loves and cares for her wellbeing. He wouldn't let anyone hurt her. He would do anything for her.

Jade knew this over and over. She expressed how she didn't want to bring charges against Ryan. Because of a false sense of guilt for him being there, when she couldn't come to Marshall.

Ryan was there for her. When she was going through a rough patch, and was having a problem dealing with her separation from Marshall.

59

He couldn't deal with certain aspects about their separation. Or the feelings she continued to have for him. She was hoping that Ryan would come out of this okay, after Marshall saw him. The relationship between Jade and Ryan is definitely over. If it isn't over, then Jade and Marshall have no need to continue their friendship.

Marcus met with him after work. He had to make a stop at his place and pick up something, that Marshall requested his help with. He filled him in on everything concerning the subject at hand, before they left his place.

They used his car to drive to Washington Heights toward the G W Bridge to confront Ryan, who physically abused Jade. Marshall asked Marcus to come and basically keep an eye on him. He didn't want Marcus to participate in what he was about to do. But wanted him to be there to stop him from losing control, and do something that he would regret later.

Marcus agreed specifically for that reason, and knew that he didn't really need him to deal with this guy. He also knew Marshall wasn't afraid of anybody.

Considering the extent of his anger sometimes. He could hurt you real bad without realizing it at first.

He didn't want Marshall to repeat this mistake with this guy. This is why he had to be there. So he wouldn't take it too far. They arrived at Fort Washington Avenue, and parked the car across the street to wait for this guy.

Katherine also provided him with a picture of Ryan from her cell phone. So he would have an accurate description of him. Fifteen minutes later, a man resembling his description was approaching the address Katherine provided.

He double checked the photo. It wasn't him. Shortly after another man showed up, walking closer to the building. Marcus and Marshall left the car to make sure if it was him or not. It was him this time. Marcus approached him from the front, while Marshall came up from behind.

"Excuse me, is your name Ryan Parker?" Marcus asked. "Who wants to know?"

"Me. Mr. Big Shot."

Ryan turned around immediately to see who, and where the other voice was coming from.

"What's going on?" Ryan asked. He saw he was at a disadvantage standing in between them, who he didn't know or recognized.

"Do you know who Jade Abbott is?" Marshall asked him. "Like I said, who wants to know?" Marshall walked up to him closer. A woman walked by, and witnessed him get slapped hard for being a smart ass.

"I wish you would." Ryan moved toward Marshall. He stared at him with disgust in his eyes. Ryan turned back around where Marcus stood in front of him.

"My friend is not your problem. I am. He is only here to make sure I don't go berserk on your ass. I think you need to come with us," said Marcus.

"I am not going anywhere with you," replied Ryan.

Marcus opened his coat jacket to show that he was wearing a Glock semi-automatic strapped to his side, and a badge worn on the other side strapped to his belt. One of his hobbies is a Marksman. When he was in college, he spent a lot of time on the firing range. He is remarkably good.

Marshall raves about him when he sees him compete. He is also a member of The Fire Arms Shooting Club. Where he met a lot of police men and became acquainted with various officers, which enabled him to come into possession of police wear and equipment.

The badge, the handcuffs, and the pistol he provided for the situation was a caliber semi-automatic, which shot pellets or BBs. Although he does have a real weapon with a permit. Ryan saw the gun being exposed from Marcus's Jacket. Since Marcus was white, tall, and clean cut. He assumed they were cops, and Jade gave him up to the police. He turned around as if he was confused at first.

He decided to comply. Marcus placed the handcuffs on him. Marshall directed him across the street to the car. He became alarm when he noticed there was no police car. He was asked to enter an Acura Infinity.

He hesitated before entering the car. Marshall gazed at him, and opened his coat to reveal another gun. It was also a fake, but he didn't know this.

"Get in the back," Marshall demanded. He entered the back seat of the car with him.

"Who are you?"

"Shut up! Shut up! I don't want to hear another word out of you," as he yelled at him. The car pulled away from the curb.

When they reached their destination at a 116th Street and Pleasant Ave. Where isolated parking was. They walked through the park further down the FDR Drive. There was an over path to walk to the other side of the highway. Where the river was located. Ryan began to question them. This time Marcus told him to shut up. He removed his gun to conceal it behind him.

Once they were on the other side of the over path walk ramp of the FDR Drive. Marshall wanted him to know what it was like, to take advantage of someone when they are at a disadvantage.

He positioned himself behind the wall. A dark area behind and under the walk way ramp. The cars continued to zoom by on the highway unaware of any presences, or immediate intentions toward him.

At this point, Ryan became concerned for his life. He had no idea who they were, except that they had guns, badges, handcuffs, and didn't drive in a cop car, unless they were different undercover detectives, he thought.

"So you like beating up on women, huh!?" Marshall asked him.

"I don't know what you are talking about?"

He slapped Ryan, like the little bitch he thought he was. "I told you to shut up." Marshall unloaded a powerful blow to his stomach. It took the air out of him. He fell to the ground as he gasped for air.

"Why are you doing this to me?" he asked.

"Get up! You can play dumb all you want, he told him."

He capped him on the side of his head on his way up, and immediately he fell back down on the ground.

"I am only going to tell you this one more time. Get up!" Ryan didn't want to get back up again. In fear of what he might do to him next, but he did.

"This time Marshall did nothing, when he got up off the ground. But he grabbed him, and dragged him over to the rail where the water was located.

"Can you swim?"

He took his time to catch his breath before he answered. "Yes," he replied.

"Then good for you?"

He asked Marcus to remove the handcuffs, while he pointed the gun at Ryan. He told him to jump over the rail and into the river. He looked at him like he was crazy. He was afraid at this point that he may shoot him. So he jumped into the Harlem River.

"I guess you will think twice before you put your hands on another woman, you son-of-a-bitch."

Marcus and Marshall walked away from him with no concern. He was screaming for someone to help him.

But no one could hear his cries. They continued walking away to return to the car.

They began their conversation like nothing had ever happened on their way back home. Marcus dropped him off at his place. Marshall thanked him from the bottom of his heart for his support concerning this matter.

"You know how we do, Marshall. No problem. I will always be there for you."

"The same goes for me, Marcus." After he arrived home, they hugged, and said later. Then they went their separate ways.

They didn't care about Ryan going to the law about what they did to him. They welcomed it, because he would have to explain to the police about his motives. Or reveal what he did to Jade. He could be wrong. He doubted seriously that Ryan wanted this kind of attention on him.

When you physically assault someone and injure them, and you have no legitimate reason for your actions in a court of law. Then trouble is your new best friend, with no attention span.

60

IT WOULDN'T BE A SURPRISE to anyone or even to those who have an imagination? Whitney couldn't forget. She couldn't talk to anyone else about her problems concerning, Zoë. She felt the one thing in her life, that wasn't touched or tainted by her was Johnny Mc Ray. Although he was used by Zoë in a way she couldn't imagine.

Lawrence made an attempt unsuccessfully to try and sleep with Zoë behind Johnny's back. He figured that she didn't mean anything to him, but she turned him down gladly.

Out of some misguided sense of revenge. Lawrence thought that Whitney should know about her sleeping with Johnny. Since the three of them had become pretty good friends, with each other over the past few years.

He didn't know for a fact, but merely assumed she did. He viewed her as one of these high-maintenance women, that was all show and tell, with nothing else really to display. Whitney was feeling disrespected with an extreme prejudice toward Zoë.

She told Johnny over and over, about how she couldn't stand this woman. Who he claimed he never met. She wanted to know when and if this really happened? Did he sleep with her?

If there was any truth to this? How could he consider having anything to do with her. When he knows how she feels about her? She wasn't aware that Zoë had knowledge of who Johnny Mc Ray was?

After everything they have been through. He couldn't be that much of a fool, she thought. Yes, Whitney and she were friends when they attended Columbia University together. But after they graduated, she heard that Zoë experienced a lot of misfortune and was down on her luck.

Also, she had stopped dancing. Or there were rumors that she might be using, which meant she could have been sacrificing her body for this stuff. She had no way of really knowing if this was true or not. It was an assumption being made about her, being a street-hoe for her habit, she hoped?

Now in the back of her mind, Whitney really didn't want to believe this of her. Because all kinds of stories are created by people who are out on the streets. But for Zoë, that's exactly what it was. Your typical rumor started by someone in the streets. Who was jealous of her, and in addition to her looks and her talent?

Randall Cook was Whitney's brother. She loved him because they were close. Somehow, somewhere, and without her assistance he met her. Whitney discovered that her brother was involved with Zoë. She was delighted at first, because they were good friends.

She never led on that she knew about their relationship. She was waiting for them to tell her. What they all had in common, but they never did. It was something that surfaced inconveniently which annoyed her.

Randall was really taken, or love struck with her. She began to resent their relationship. It was never enough time for her anymore.

Whitney and Randall's relationship changed drastically because of Zoë. There were more than a few people, who was aware of the fact. She wanted to push Zoë off into another view point, which would be lost in this city where no one could find her?

Zoë on the other hand, had no idea she was running around with Whitney Cook's brother. Until afterward, she and Randall shared a conversation and it came out. She suggested that they tell Whitney about their relationship, but Randall refused. He didn't need her approval concerning the women in his life. He wasn't having it. He loved and respected his sister's feelings, but Whitney was not going to dictate to him. Who he was going to see and be with.

Randall and Whitney argued over and over about his involvement with Zoë, and her sudden disapproval of her. And yet, he tried to help her realize. How hypercritical she was by being involved with Johnny Mc Ray. The man who is always traveling on the road with his groups and other women, and leaving her alone with nothing to do. But wait for him when he returns.

Not once in all of these years, had he ever taken her with him on tour. So he could let everyone else see that he already had a woman, and it was her, but that didn't happened.

He asked her often, why would she spend her time, or life waiting around for him to come home to her? He told her. There wasn't that much love in the world, for him to wait for some woman under those circumstances. He would have to be blind, deaf, and dumb, and he knew his sister wasn't either.

So what was the deal with her and her feelings for this man? The dark and ugly truth is, there were many other men around, and in her company who enticed her. Who wanted to do Whitney's brains out? When Johnny Mc Ray wasn't around, while she waited for him to come home every day?

She simply forget about the men and moved on. Why would she want to dry herself up like a raisin? Her father insisted she close the door in his face. As if mistakes are forgiven in Fahrenheit? He wanted the man to continuously burn in hell.

He didn't raise his daughter to graduate from college, and systematically ruin her life by waiting around for some man traveling around the world without her—job or no job?

61

He was always on the front cover of a gossip magazine, with some woman he is supposed to be doing something with, and this is what Whitney calls love. He felt that Johnny was trying to sell his daughter a forbidden climax, like she was some kind of slut in heat. Who didn't know there was a limit she had to deal with.

He also felt that his dear wife and her mother who passed away. Would be turning over in her grave with disbelief about now? If she knew her baby girl was misbehaving like this? After everything she had tried to teach her about men, and then the person says something dumb like—I didn't ask you to help me?

It still doesn't change the fact, that the person made a dumb mistake from bad judgment. They don't want to admit that you were the only person, who reached out to help them when no one else would. But everything is your fault because you help them, and they didn't do the right thing anyway.

Whitney couldn't get over her petty jealousy toward Zoë. She believed she was using her brother too, because of the men who wanted her. So her dislike and anger grew more out of hand concerning her.

It was like she left behind interviews of fiction from a bad story line. Whitney's emotions were generally nude with agony toward her. Or she didn't care about the sum of all races, that could have improved her compassion for life and people, but not where her brother was concerned.

She forever blamed her, and didn't forgive her for their break up. It was all Zoe's fault. She was the problem in their lives, but he couldn't see it. She broke her brother's heart, and wrecked his life.

Randall died of AIDS a year later. She also tried to blame that on her as well. But people who really knew him, and associated with him wasn't buying this? Whitney was the only one who was unaware of the reality concerning her brother.

Randall was a legitimate undercover dog. He would screw anyone over for sex. He loved women more than he did money. He lied to Whitney and reversed the story about what happened between Zoë and him. It was his idea to take the attention off of himself, and place it on her. This way he could move on as the injured party in all of this. Since she was no longer around to deny it or not.

Whitney had no idea how many women Randall had dogged behind her back, by screwing over them and getting what he wanted. He always lied to her about his feeling about these women. He used women by the dozen's. She would believe anything he told her, since they were close.

Allegedly, he raped this young, pretty, and developed Intern. She was to frighten to confess to anyone about it, or testify to it in court. Also in fear of losing her job. After the raped occurred, several of his friends reached out to her with threats, and on occasion followed her home.

It became a secret that they all lived with. The young woman eventually left, and was able to obtain a transfer at another Medical Center to continue her Internship to become a doctor. But she never forgot the violation committed by Randall. She was a virgin when it happened. She had no sexual experience, and thought that it would happen completely different.

She was receiving therapy, because of her continued nightmares of possibly contracting some STD. She also heard about the sexual rumors about Randall. There was nothing she could do about it since her attacker was now dead.

Zoë hasn't slept with anyone before she met and began seeing Randall. She was wise enough to practice safe sex. When she decided to take the next step. Even though Randall didn't like it, and tried to convince her otherwise.

Zoë wouldn't have it. She wasn't going to forfeit her future just yet, by having an unexpected pregnancy before she began her life. She still had herself tested on several occasions to see if she had AIDS, after she heard about Randall's death.

She didn't want there to be any unsuspected surprises in her life like this. She didn't care whether or not,

Whitney knew the whole truth about her brother now. Or continued to blame her for what happened to him. All she knew was that he was lower than a "Junk Yard Dog." It was well over for Zoë.

Whitney cried like a new born infant for exactly a week when Randall died. She missed him terribly with no time to die for herself inside. He was a great brother to her with a promising career as a doctor, but no more.

Now he was gone. Maybe it was for the best that she didn't know. How he played more than doctor at the hospital he worked at. There wasn't a woman he didn't touch on any floor in the hospital. Doctor's, interns, medical assistants, employees, and paramedics, and he took down a couple of patients as well.

It made no sense, and was utterly ridiculous since it was all Zoë's fault. She needed someone else to blame for Randall's behavior and his demise. He never met anyone quite like Zoë. Whether Whitney knew it or not, she was a truly exceptional person to her brother, but it was something that he wouldn't admit to a woman.

It is sad and disappointing, but everyone is capable of losing themselves at one time or another in life. It wasn't her fault, if she continued to lose people in her life, like her father, and her mother, or her brother all to death unexpectedly.

Then the person she believed she loved broke her heart, but that was different for her. No one is immune to this kind of tragedy in their lives. Or can survive it without feeling confused from within?

62

HE CALLED JADE FOR THE last two weeks, in order to see how she was recovering. Katherine was still with her, but one of Jade's sisters had joined the mix to help out with her recuperation, after she was assaulted by Ryan.

"Thank you for everything, Marshall."

"I really didn't do that much. You seem to have everything covered.

"Yeah, but Katherine told me. How you covered her back by contacting one of my sisters. Who couldn't keep her mouth shut, without involving the rest of the family? You seem to have everything under control like always.

"Now, Katherine can receive a break after looking after me. I appreciate you arranging all of this for me.

"Even though we are officially divorced. You still find a way to take care of me, huh, Marshall?"

"Well, whether we are divorced or not, I guess some habits are hard to break. I simply wanted to make sure you have everything you needed. So how are you really doing?"

"So much better. Thanks to Katherine and my sister. I was able to get a lot of rest. The soreness in my body is gone. The bruises and swollen area's on my face are gone.

"Initially, we thought my arm was broken, but the X-rays showed a hair line fracture. So I have a soft case, which means I will be able to return to work next week, before I go stare crazy from boredom."

"Well, I am happy to see you are recovering so well."

"Are you happy enough to come by and see me soon?"

"Yes, but I will give you a little more time. I will call you and we can set something up, okay?"

"Thank you, Marshall."

"I'll talk to you later. Bye, Jade."

He took the last day off from work. So he could finish his cycle of days remaining. Sarah and him had been together for the last two days.

"How is Jade?" Sarah asked.

"She is feeling much better and healing nicely."

"I am sorry to hear about her misfortune with her friend. I came pretty close to going through the same thing with Lawrence believe it or not?

"I realize how frightened she must have been to experience something like this? Domestic Violence is no joke, if you allow yourself to become a victim.

"It's different when you get into a confrontation with a man than with a woman. Because with another woman you know how to defend yourself.

"But you don't know how far a man will go to prove a point and hurt you."

"I agree, Sarah. I think Jade would be surprised to hear about the concern you are expressing for her. Since the word is that you and her don't like each other."

"Excuse me, but where did you hear or get that from?" She gazed at Marshall curiously.

"I didn't imply that I didn't like her, but to be honest with you. I believe Jade and I didn't trust each other. There was something we read about each other on one another?"

"And what was that?"

"I had a feeling something was going on with Jade before you did. I am not saying I knew she was cheating. But I knew it had something to do with another man.

"I simply read her, like she read me. Women do that quite well with each other and are good at it.

"Just like she was reading me. She realized after a while I was attracted to you, and I liked you. Or a part of me thought about what it would be like to be with you.

"This is why we didn't trust each other. It had nothing to do with disliking one another. I peeked into her script, and she read my story.

"I hear you, my beautiful. So that's what it was about?" He kissed Sarah vigorously. He took her breathe away, and then he stopped.

"He suffocated her air, when he kissed her again. If for no other reason, so she could become a frantic heart. Who was overwhelmed and consumed at the moment.

"I want you to understand Sarah, if Jade was right about you or not. I am really glad I am getting the opportunity to experience this with you.

"I consider you to be a good person on the inside, as well as on the outside. Nothing will change this for me, and I am really happy to be seeing you.

"I am not implying that we should get together with each other right away. Or consider getting married again, but since we are free.

"Let's just keep things open for now. Have some fun, and enjoy each other's company. Or find out what we want while getting to know each other better.

"I like that, Marshall. I realized there are other people in your life. I don't want to rush anything either between us. I am enjoying myself much more, than I ever thought I would be in a long time.

"There are things I would like to work out for myself too right now in my life."

There is no doubt Lawrence messed up a good thing by losing a woman like, Sarah. He had nobody to blame but himself. Do Bee's Love Honey? A woman like Sarah is all that heaven will allow you to misinterpret her gifts to you.

He was basically a cock-hound, who couldn't see his raging happiness also missing in action. How long did he think someone was going to continue to accept his crap? Since he wasn't about to grow up and seize with the games on top of losing?

"Marshall I don't believe in coincidences. I find it interesting how your relationship and mine were dissolving at the same time, and we got a divorce at the same period in our lives.

"I was attracted to you the first time I saw you at the party I gave, and then I discovered from Lawrence that you were married to, Jade.

"I was surprised I met her, before I met you at the party we had. I wasn't trying to get into your pants then." She made him smile.

"Lawrence and I were just married. Then I started taking these long journeys with him down hell's gateway to disaster.

"I couldn't understand how this man was behaving after we were married. Like it was his first priority and only mission was to walk all over me.

"I am sorry. My mother didn't bring me up to be like this? Or to be like some excuse for some man's burden.

"He had to be kidding? Since he wanted to do this idiotic thing, and destroy everything that we had. I don't understand people sometimes.

"They know when they are in a situation they don't want to be in with someone else.

"Or instead of doing something or anything about it. They would rather take you through a whole lot of unnecessary drama, rather than find a solution to their problem or want you to believe how complicated it is?

"When all you have to do is make a decision and be on your way.

"I realize things are not always black and white. But when they are—you need to do something about it than just sit around. Or bore everyone else with your drama.

"The main avenue with people is always complicated concerning life now, but it still doesn't make any sense either, Marshall."

"You are right, Sarah."

63

"SO MARSHALL, WHEN YOU CAME over that Sunday for Jade's bracelet and Lawrence wasn't there. It wasn't my intention to approach to you like I did.

"It happened like unexpected things happen sometimes. When you don't want it to happen, it still happens. So there is very little you can blame anyone else for?

"I am not going to apologize for expressing myself to you like I did.

"I'm not surprised, when we made love together. I received so much pleasure from someone that I didn't know. Or couldn't receive any pleasure at all from a man, I have been married to for two years?

"He was too unreal to believe. He had women calling the house three months after we were married, and that is when we really stopped being physical. I wasn't taking any chances with him anymore after I discovered this?

"When you and I sat there for over three hours, talking, laughing, smiling, agreeing, and introducing happiness for every hour you were there.

"I felt something about you, Marshall. I guess it was just deep down inside of me. I really didn't want you to leave that evening.

'Something inside of me took over instinctively. I was drawn to you more like a pulley. I know I shouldn't have put you or myself in that position, but I did. And I am really happy I did it.

"What does that tell you, when you do something which is wrong, but it feels so damn good and it turns out right?

"Remember, it was well after you and Jade separated, before anything happened between us. And my marriage was a dead issue at that point also.

"So we didn't hurt anyone, but we were hurt deeply before, and in return for whatever reasons ourselves.

"When we made love to each other that evening in my kitchen. I realized I had to put an end to my marriage. I wasn't going to be married to one man and sleeping with another man. It just wasn't me. I had to change this situation.

"It was really over between him and I, and this is when I prepared myself to divorce him.

"I think if I am right, you had already filed for divorce from, Jade.

"So you see it was hardship which followed us at the same time. I know it sounds strange, but this is why we are together. It is our Karma which brought us together."

He looked at Sarah with conviction and fulfillment. He liked to hear Sarah when she talks, because of her voice. It disturbs him in a romantic way, and then she stops, while his hunger is begging for her to speak some more. It's a turn on for him. The way that she talks and to hear her voice.

"Getting involved with you, Marshall, is one of the best decisions I have made in alone time, and being with you has been good for me. It has changed me.

"I wouldn't do anything to jeopardize our relationship after the wonderful year I have had with you.

"It has been very special to me. That doesn't mean we are a couple as of yet. I haven't been with anyone like you. Now, that my marriage is over with Lawrence.

"A lot had been happening. I received a promotion to advance from my reserve status, and more than likely I will have to relocate.

"Are you going to accept it?"

"I have some time to think about it before I give them a final answer.

"In some cities, it can take up to five to ten years longer for a Flight Attendant to advance from her reserve status. Since I was with Lawrence, I elected to live here. So I made this my home base.

"And the routes worked for are bid for on a seniority basis. I wouldn't be on reserve statue or on call anymore. The only thing which really concerns me is you. I really don't want to leave you.

"I also don't want to put any pressure on you about our relationship. Or give you the impression that I am expecting more from you.

"You have been the perfect remedy for me. I cherish all the time we have spent together. All the conversations we have had, and all the things we do together.

"And let's not forget about all the fabulous sex we have been having together. I always look forward to making love with you.

"If only I could have met and married you. I would be the happiest woman in the world. I would be one happy-bitch with no complaints, if you know what I mean, Marshall?" He smiled back at her, and hugged her firmly.

"You make me feel very good inside too, Sarah. I don't know what to say about you possibly leaving and relocating, but I am happy about your promotion regardless. I am glad you are moving up, but at the price of you residing someplace else is disappointing to hear."

He recalled when Abby first mentioned about her leaving the company, and the unexpected was an exciting first encounter for them. It was a surprising shock to see her go. Sarah had presented him with another surprising shock. She could also be exiting from his life. It was beginning to feel strange. He thought about the absence of Jade in his life, and the loss of their marriage.

Then Abby's departure was no fun to hear about. Now Sarah may be departing soon. Also, Marcus had to make a decision about relocation to California.

Sarah looked at him indifferently and asked, "Was he okay?"

She was contemplating whether her conversation with him was affecting him more than he cared to reveal. She had no idea it was much more than this. It was a combination of a series of things, which was happening to him that he couldn't explain now.

64

A FEW DAYS LATER, HE received a call from her. She was doing great. They talked about her last performance from her off Broadway Show. The reviews the show received from the newspapers the following day were good. Especially the paragraph about an unknown beautiful and talented, but upcoming dancer name, Zoë Pamela Ames.

He expressed his happiness and excitement for her, along with his encouragement. He had only been acquainted with her for a brief while. He wanted her to know how proud he was of her. He felt it was only the beginning for her.

You could see there was much success in her immediate future, or like a star is born.

She was extremely touched by his plateaus of her. No one else other than Ms. Peters had expressed more confidence in her. She explained how it brought tears to her eyes, wishing her mother, her father, and her brother could be here to see her.

Recalling, how much her brother enjoyed watching her dance when they were growing up. He believed she would be a great dancer one day. Her mother and father just wanted her to get a degree from college and be happy. Something she did do after they passed away.

It was something difficult to do, because of the emptiness she continued to carry inside of her without them. She thought about God and Ms. Peters, and all she had become to her. She thanked him most emphatically in her prayers, and conveyed to him how interesting, she thought it was.

How her life had changed these few months, ever since they have met? Marshall told her, that her life would have changed anyway, and it had nothing to do with him.

He thought that she was failing to realize, she made a mistake along the way earlier in her life. But considering she is still young, and is gifted with all the potential in the world, to take this anywhere she desired too, with the right people behind her.

If she was a person with desire; then time will turn everything around to make it right for her again—because she had the determination and the talent to succeed.

He had nothing to do with the type of person she is, and the gift she possessed to dance. Ms. Peters would definitely tell her the same thing about herself.

She was feeling like a different person. She wanted him to know this? It was her contention, that he had a lot to do with her feelings. She felt trust in him, which was a big issue for her concerning men.

He thanked her for the thought, but he reassured her she deserved all the credit for her efforts. He told her that he thought of a lot of things, which were occurring in her life now was because of timing. She was being approached by different things and people because her life is different.

So it's natural that you're going to feel like a different person. It was over a year ago, she obtained the money she needed to finance a business proposition for a kids dance program she created. So the kids could compete throughout the city for better opportunities.

She claimed that she met him afterward, which was something that was good, positive, real, special, and different that attracted her very much.

It's like she said, "You see the same shit every day when it comes to people and relationships."

She felt fresh inside she claimed, ever since she met him.

She restored her reunion with Ms. Peters, and because of the bond that they have with each other. Ms. Peters changed Zoë's life over night because of her talent to dance, and the strong will she was made of.

Now she is becoming famous. Just picking up from where she left off at, because of a rough set back in her life.

"I couldn't in a million years, forget the most important person in the world to her, and that is Mr. Peters. It was her who made my dream come true. Without her, I am not sure where I would really be?"

Zoë was working on something new, but didn't want to spoil it by telling him about it. She wanted it to be a complete surprise. Now that he had become someone special to her. She would talk with him soon.

****

Whitney went to see Johnny about Zoë. It was her desire to know whether it was true or not. If he was dealing with her in any form, fashion, or manner. Since there would be serious repercussions in it for them both.

"Johnny I heard that you are associating with her?"

"Where did you hear this from?"

"Never mind, where I heard it from. I simply want to know whether it's true or not?"

"I don't know what you are talking about, Whitney, or where you are getting your information from, but no!"

Whitney wasn't sure whether or not she believed Johnny. He would tell her anything, and expected her to believe him because of who he is. Although she didn't care to tell Johnny, that it was his own friend who told her about Zoë and him.

She tried to play it out. When unexplained things were difficult to explain, and without a given reason which was no problem for Johnny Mc Ray. It was the kind of day that he was having?

He was left with the feeling, nothing was making any sense, given to reason for him to conclude. A part of him realized that if he told Whitney he did have something to do with her. Then their relationship would turn out to be a disaster for them.

And the other part of him realized, that he didn't need to appear as a fool to her. If she became aware that Zoë wouldn't sleep with him for money, when he offered it to her when she was in a bind, and didn't want to have anything else to do with him. The way that you are on a collision course with someone on a day of fury. So he lied to her to keep the peace between them.

He didn't want people around them to take Whitney, and him to another planet with all the nonsense of what was going on in their lives. So that they could be separated from this happening?

"I really hope you are not lying to me, Johnny. One way or another I will find out. I will not be played by you, after everything I have been through to be there for you. When everyone around me has warned me, to leave you alone.

"Since you are known internationally and are considered to be a man of women, but I love you and you treat me good."

"I know, and I hear you, Whitney. You know I have much love for you, and I am going to make some changes regarding my work load and being on the road so much.

"So I can settle down with you and we can raise a family together.

"I know you don't like her, but what does this have to do with me? Remember, I don't know her. I know you blame her for your brothers down fall. So why would I want to be involved with your arch enemy?"

****

Katherine didn't know when she left Curtis that morning to go into work early. So she could catch up on her work load. When she took a day off from work to show Natalie around the city.

That Natalie and Curtis were back at their place having sex with each other. She had no idea that anything was taking place with them like this. Then she wanted to be there for her friend Jade, because of the injuries she sustained from her relationship with her friend Ryan.

After she discussed it with Curtis, who had no problem with her being there for Jade. But when she returned she notice some irregularities, which she didn't pay much attention to at first. She figured Natalie was doing everything she could to adjust to being in a new city, and the choice she had to make about changing her life.

In the meantime, she was still going back and forth to check in on Jade. They talked a great deal and confirmed their friendship. Within the months that past, she became broken hearted.

It turns out that Curtis and Natalie were having an affairs.

When she wasn't there. Apparently there was another person involved with Natalie, and Curtis was being blind sided by her lies.

Natalie was picked up by this man. He was an ex-con and was released from prison a year ago for an assortment of crimes, which involved big time scams of stolen money. She was taken with the gentlemen, until he worked her over a few times and forced himself on her physically.

But she was in tune with it for a while. She was excited by the adventure and mystery, and finally meeting a man who she thought was smarter than she was.

When he discovered that she had money. She became a real person of interest to him, and began inviting her to meet his business associates. She was thrilled by the attention, and the various business angles to increase their cash flow.

Naturally Mr. Lenny Hayes was using her and her money to finance his venture with his associate, and deceiving Natalie about the percentage of her investment return. She was completely in.

But they needed one more person to set up a phony business paper profile for them. This is where she came up with the idea of including Curtis. After she presented her idea to Lenny and his associate. They began hyping her up that if was a great idea, it she could lure him in for a cut of the profits.

She was convinced that she could, but she needed a week to arrange it. She explained the situation she was in with him. It was just a matter of talking to Curtis, and showing him how they were going to make some extra cash for him and her.

She was already meeting him at his place of business twice a week. Where she was keeping phony appointments they had set up. So she could see him and have sex with him in his office, during working hours with no interruptions.

This is why her friend, Katherine couldn't see anything going on in the apartment. They were doing it at his job in the office two and three times a week. This was Natalie's way of distracting Curtis whenever she wanted to, and to keep him off guard about her business.

Unfortunately the scam turned out to be a total bust, because the police were conducting an undercover sting of their own. It was a setup, with everyone taken into custody by the authorities for their participation in the shake down of their scam, which included Natalie and Curtis on surveillance tapes.

Katherine was shock and please at the same time. She didn't have to face their deception along with the affair Natalie and Curtis were having behind her back. She had to find another place to resided at.

Jade told her that she was welcome to stay with her as long as she needed to, and she would enjoy her friends company. Now they both had stories to share of lost and pain and humiliation to bear.

65

WHITNEY WAS CONVINCED BY JOHNNY'S reasoning and logic for now. It sounded good to her. She calmed down without any frustration. Johnny and she became affectionate with one another before she left.

Johnny was pissed off. Who would put his business out there like this? Or who would drop a dime on him. He knew that it wasn't damn well, Zoë.

She didn't like Whitney no more than Whitney could stand her. She just wouldn't deal with her like this. She was much too smart and sophisticated for this kind of drama. Whether you knew her or not, Zoe is a person of her word.

So it had to be someone in his circle that became stupid, he figured. Since there was no contact between Zoë and him for months, and now this happens. When Whitney arrived home. She called Lawrence, asked him to come and see her.

Three hours later he appeared. She told him that she confronted Johnny about Zoë, and he denied everything. She didn't tell him how she knew. She wasn't going to betray Lawrence at present.

Johnny had no idea when he was away on, and off for the last three years. It was his friend who was there for Whitney. If ever she needed anything. He provided her with attention and a shoulder to lean on, until Johnny returned from after being away for six months at a time, but she didn't sleep with him.

But sometimes Lawrence and her would get drunk together or high, but she didn't do drugs. It was something he concealed from his ex-wife, Sarah.

She had no idea or knowledge that Lawrence did coke behind her back. When she wasn't around in their marriage. It was something he enjoyed. He didn't have to pay for it with all of the connections he had established.

Johnny was into all sorts of things when it comes to business and money. He was good at supporting people's needs. When he wanted people to do whatever he wanted them to do for him.

Whitney was devastated and felt betrayed when he tried to persuade her it did happened. When Lawrence wasn't sure himself about whether Johnny and Zoë slept together. He wanted to convince himself. So he could give Whitney the impression without uncertainty it happened.

He made a slight miscalculation in his scheme of things.

He was hoping that Whitney would have approached Zoë, and not Johnny about it. She did just the opposite, because he didn't know anything at all about their relationship.

What he knew was from talk that he heard from someone else. Now that it was a known fact, he didn't care. He would try to cover it up with something else.

He figured, he would be able to mend any broken fences between them, and since they were okay with each other like this. They wouldn't allow any woman to come between them, it didn't matter who she was?

Johnny always had too many women around him, and a lot of them he slept with or would be sleeping with? Lawrence felt either way, that Zoë would get what she deserved. His ego wouldn't allow him to be defeated in his mind since she rejected him. And according to him, she was just playing hard to get. She was going to want him eventually?

Who was she, but another woman? Believing that everything was all about her. She had no idea who she was dealing with?"

After Lawrence was able to convince Whitney to think differently about Johnny and Zoë. She began crying. She was surprised how insecure she was feeling. She couldn't accept that Johnny was lying to her like this? She tried to understand. Why she felt vulnerable to Lawrence's influence concerning Johnny?

In her heart, she realized the power Zoë had over men, but not on Lawrence. He was siding with Whitney to come closer to his motives.

Why would Johnny be any different, but he was her man. She didn't want to believe the worse about him. So why would his friend lie about this? When she thought about how Lawrence had been there for her.

There had to be some truth to it, she felt. He of course came to her aid once again. Whitney let him comfort her. She is very attractive and sexy. She is all looks, hips, breast, and behind. That's why men in the neighborhood would give up more than money to sleep with her.

Lawrence prepared a drink of Gray Goose for Whitney and him, while he pulled out some nose candy from his pocket. She was already on her third shot straight-up, while he indulged himself with his powder.

They decided they would get high together using their own choice of pleasure. She was angry now, and she was hurting, while being truly disappointed in Johnny.

Lawrence knew she wouldn't believe this about anyone else accept, Zoë. So for whatever reason she didn't want to feel anything inside. Finally after all this time, he couldn't believe she was dropping her guard. She took him into her bedroom, and then they removed their clothes.

Whitney did Lawrence like another elephant walk, hard and heavy with no emotions. Like she couldn't, and didn't want to remember who she was doing it to. She wanted to give someone else pleasure. Who always desired her and couldn't have her. Now she was going to make their dreams come true, she felt.

It was sinful how she made him cry out. He knew she could only narrate her sex for him once. It was turning out to be the best he had in a long time. Since Sarah and him weren't physical, he thought.

Whitney pinned him to the bed, while she rotated on top of him, and causing him to call out. Like he just lost his mind over someone who didn't care about him.

He was going out of his mind. When she continued to go on with her erotic friction. His insides were burning with a wonderful tale of passion, as he felt.

When Lawrence was upstairs with Whitney getting his freak on. There was an unidentified man sitting in a parked car downstairs across the street from her building.

He had been stationed there since Lawrence arrived. He is one of several men, who Johnny Mc Ray employed for five hundred dollars a day to watch his woman, and cover her back.

In case anyone ever tried to get to him through her, he would know about it. The man stayed there until 12:00 a.m. He figured, Whitney was in for the night. So he left the premises.

Upon his return in the morning at 6:00 a.m. A half hour later, he was surprised to see Lawrence leaving, which meant that he spent the night at Whitney's.

Lawrence was feeling on top of the world, after the night he spent with Whitney, and believed that Johnny would never know anything. Who was going to tell him. He smiled to himself?

The man outside the building, who witnessed this, asked himself, "What's wrong with this picture?"

He figured, this was also going to bring him a nice hefty bonus, with a big smile on his face. When he returned to tell Johnny McRay.

66

THINGS WERE JUST CONTINUING TO get more and more intense between Olivia and him. It was a good thing that none of the women he was involved with had children, but a bad thing that Olivia was still married.

You often wonder how long you can keep up a secret like this, before you are eventually discovered—or exposed! Since you are caught up in it. He knows no one really wants to get caught with another person's wife or husband for that matter. When it happens it becomes a moral issue.

Then you can't help but feel like you have committed a crime. So thank God, you don't have to go to jail for sleeping with someone else's spouse. It is still considered a sin, depending on whose point of view you look at it from.

Or there is always the repercussion of things getting violent with someone. When the situation finally comes to a head. He was thinking the only reason why he would cheat on someone is…?

He met someone else he really wanted to be with. Even though it doesn't always work out this way. It's not because he was having a problem, or he wanted to sleep with someone else. It's not enough. It's like the old saying. "I can get sex, when I can't get money."

Going out and cheating on someone is always difficult. But going out and doing it without understanding, what you are doing in regard to the consequences is even more irresponsible?

When you don't care, or love, or don't really want to be with the person you are with and cheating on. It makes it that much more meaningless to you, the person, and your relationship with each other.

It just seems like something good should come out of it. If you think you are in love with someone else?

If you are going to risk everything you have, and putting yourself on the line, by cheating on someone else. In other words—there should be some kind of method to your madness.

But when it comes to human beings, it's the madness and not the method that's more relevant? Maybe that's why so many people can never get it right?

He could see Olivia was falling in love with him, just as he saw the same thing in Sarah's eyes. He admired how difficult it was for them to restrain themselves from telling him. Because now a day's—people are basically thinking about themselves first of all.

Also it was obvious to him. They were trying to be considerate of his feelings and the situation, rather than thinking about themselves completely. This is why, he felt they felt the way they were feeling. There was no selfishness displayed by them.

It wasn't something he could take for granted and use for himself later. It showed him a lot about how unselfish they were about their own emotions. It made him feel good about them, and his involvement with them. They didn't make him feel like he was trapped, and taken hostage by the situation with them.

He could see how difficult it became to deal with his honesty. Now that he had taken that uncertain chance with them, or if there were expectations expected. He felt he was very fortunate with Abby, Olivia, and Sarah coming into his life.

After his marriage with Jade was over, and it wasn't him who was generating the dirt in their relationship. But it didn't make him feel any better. When he felt he lost the love of his life, and a marriage they had enjoyed. Just ask yourself, how often can you enjoy yourself with someone else being married to? That's what he thought at least.

Zoë, on the other hand was a friend. It was too early to see past this? It seemed like to him. She had been going through some changes in her life, and was now getting her life back on track. She required a positive influence in her life, and no more confusion or uncertainty in it.

Olivia and Sarah haven't met each other, but they knew about each another. He made absolutely sure of this. He knew all women don't have the same sex. Or don't kiss the same way on any day, either.

Especially when you meet a woman, who doesn't need you as a man to validate herself as a woman?

If she cares about you and her feelings are deep for you, then you have a real woman who is there for you—which means—you don't have to—or need to play games with her. You have to be sincere with someone that you are with. Even if the honesty is about two quarters of your relationship?

People are screwed up enough already, and they know it. Olivia and Sarah didn't care much about someone else being in his life. They are married and didn't have any claim to him, while his ex-wife was still in his life as a friend.

Either way you looked at it, it didn't matter whether they were able to be together or not. The outcome was the same for all of them. They would either gain or lose a lot. All it took was the next decision to be made by any of them regarding each other.

Olivia and Sarah on occasion, openly expressed their appreciation to him for keeping them in the loop, by being honest with them in their relationship. It was another reason why Olivia and Sarah decided to move forward with him. He could be trusted and was honest with them—no matter what was involved.

They were aware in advance about what, if anything, they were up against. It is your responsibility to secure the best possible decision concerning yourself. He had become apprehensive about women and relationships at this point in his life.

It was hard sometimes to accept Jade, or their relationship as a remote memory when things happen and it happens. Then this is the reality of it. He didn't know whether it was possible for him or Olivia to be together.

She is lovely. Or look forward to a future with Sarah now that she is divorced. She is a gem. Or will his future be with someone else, or without someone else?

A question he couldn't answer, or was prepared to answer for himself now. He couldn't suggest to Olivia to leave her husband, or consider the fact, she could be undeniably confused about something.

What she is going through in her mind. Maybe this is why she is presently involved with him. Then there is Sarah. Who watched her marriage melt away, like a box of salt when you added water? She had suffered a lot of heartache and despair with Lawrence, and why he would treat her like this?

He is naturally a character. Sarah needed some peace of mind from him. She needed to regain a sense of herself after enduring a really bad marriage. And now, she had a chance to do this with the opportunities that lie ahead for her, rather than return to another relationship so soon.

He had no idea. How this would play out, or end up for all of them. He realized, he would have to make a serious decision about Olivia, and Sarah, and himself soon.

67

MARSHALL AND MARCUS MET EACH other after work. They were going to attend a Knick game. They were season ticket holders. It was a good game. The Knicks pulled off an upset and defeated The Lakers.

Marcus and him were remarkably surprised and excited about the win, as well as many other people were. They went to a restaurant bar in the area of Madison Square Garden to get a bite to eat. The house special was steak, which is what they ordered, with all the trimmings and brew's to wash it down with.

"The steak is good."

"I agree Marcus, and thick."

"Just like the game was?"

"I hear that! The Knicks were on point tonight." There were several people reacting to the win, who now entered the restaurant also.

"So what's been going on lately, Marcus?"

"Well I didn't say anything earlier because…? I knew, we would be getting together to check out the game tonight. This way, we could have some extra time to talk to one another after the game.

"Are you ready for this? Dominique and I had to have Brenda Gentle arrested."

"What! Are you serious?"

"Yes. I'm dead serious, Marshall. It turned out to be real scary that night."

"When did this happen?"

"Today is Tuesday. It happened Friday."

Marcus and Dominique were enjoying a pleasant evening together at his place. She wanted to cook dinner for him. He didn't know she could cook. She stepped on some food, and it was exceptionally good. He was beginning to realize, that Dominique had many hidden skills he liked.

Marshall was surprised to hear that coming from him. He thought Marcus was more interested in doing his own thing. It appeared he not only liked her, but cared about her more than he wanted to admit.

It doesn't take a genius to see he could be falling for her. He took another bite of his steak, before he answered him back about Brenda.

Marcus began to explain. Why would Brenda show up unannounced and without any warning, after all that time went by confused the hell out of him? He was in the bathroom when his door bell ringed, but Dominique answered the door for him since he was unavailable.

It sounded like two people were arguing. When he came out of the bathroom to witness the commotion. Who did he see in Dominique's face exchanging words back and forth with her, Brenda?

He immediately stepped in between the both of them. He asked Brenda, what was she doing here? She came over to apologize to him, and wanted to know why Dominique was there? He told her that she was his guest and his lady.

Brenda said, tell the bitch to take a hike. So he told her, why don't you take a hike?

Any business they had together was concluded a long time ago. She had no business being here. She pushed him out of the way. He stumbled, lost his balance, and fell to the floor.

Then she rushed toward Dominique, and they began fighting. It was like trying to break up two professional fighters from two different weight classes, and nobody held anything back. You didn't want to get in between this, by this time they were rolling over the floor.

Dominique had the upper hand at first. She was positioned on top of Brenda, and was trying to bang her head into the floor. When Marcus was able to separate them. He asked her to call 911. He didn't care anymore.

Brenda was way out of control, coming into his house, attacking Dominique and him like this. He was sitting on top of Brenda trying to subdue her and calm her down. She wouldn't stop, but continued to wrestle with him. She may have been a woman, but she was strong like a bull. He recalled that's why the sex was so good with her.

She managed to throw Marcus off of her. Dominique jumped back and threw her hands up for more. She was ready for round two of the confrontation.

Brenda relaxed suddenly. She decided that she wasn't going anywhere until this was resolved.

Then the police arrived. Marcus opened the door to let them in. The police witness Brenda sucker punch Dominique in the face. When they were standing in the door way to enter the house. They immediately grabbed and handcuffed her, while she was cursing the police officers out.

One officer removed her from the house and escorted her to the police car, while the other officer inquired further about the incident. He asked Dominique did she want to press charges against Brenda. After the officer was informed about what happened. Dominique said, "Yes, she wanted to file charges."

So they followed the police in Marcus's car to the precinct, and filed charges against Brenda for assaulting Dominique the way she did.

At first, she wasn't going to press charges against her, in spite of everything that happened. Dominique is basically a sweet person, but when Brenda sucker punched her like this, while being sneaky. Then she felt that was just too low and dirty of Brenda. So this is why she changed her mind.

"I am sorry to her this. I guess you were right. Brenda does need someone's anger management course. So how is Dominique doing?"

"She has been great through all of it. I will be seeing her later, after I leave you."

Marshall also expressed his appreciation, how grateful he was for his help with the situation concerning Jade and Ryan. Up until now, there had been no word on the guy from Jade or Katherine. Since he forced him to jump into the Harlem River.

He wanted Marcus to know and realize, that Jade was doing much better. It was his intention to visit her soon, and see how she was doing for himself. He gave Marcus an update about the ongoing situation, with all the women in his life.

He explained how much he still cared about Jade, and a large part of him will never forget his first wife. He didn't know if time would be a friend, or an enemy in the healing process for him and her. It is extremely difficult to try and trust someone you loved with your heart again, after they have stepped on it and caused it to brake.

When all the trust you had in the world was characterized by her betrayal. He needed Marcus to understand. So much had happened which he didn't understand, or couldn't imagine. If it wasn't for Abby at the time, who helped him with the error of his ways.

It would have taken him longer, before he was able to stop punishing himself, and Jade for their marriage coming to an end the way it had.

When Olivia entered into his life. It was more like shock therapy, a fresh breath of air. It helped him take the first real steps. He wasn't interested in getting involved then. But now, the relationship has blossomed into something more than they expected.

In spite of the fact she is married. How much more can this be complicated? And now, Sarah is a free woman, and he is a free man. However, it scared him. How close he had become with Sarah, in a short period of time. This was the difference between the other relationships, everything developed according to time, but not when it came to the compatibility of Sarah and him.

One moment, they were acquaintances who were married to other people. Then the next moment, they were making love to one another in her house, in her kitchen, and then again at his place.

Since then, they have been seeing each other without anyone's knowledge of their relationship. If it wasn't for a matter of selfishness, then he wouldn't care. He would be with Sarah, he thought? Because of her unselfishness which had brought them closer together.

When she carried her loneliness across the sky, and he is walking with suicide steps, and it was time to replace them. Sarah was beginning to mean a lot to him. And yet, he forgot to mention Zoe to Marcus.

Even though, there was nothing much to tell him about. Since they were just acquaintances, but it was hard not to rave about her either. He believed there was something unique about her. Someone he was curious about, but had no reason to explore?

"I hope this doesn't get any more complicated for you, Marshall. I don't know how much more of this you, or I can take. If it were me? I would be hiding in a closet, and hope that no one would be able to find me.

"I would be going crazy trying to deal with all of these beautiful, intelligent, talented, and independent women in your life, that you are having a relationship with."

Marshall and Marcus finished drinking their second beer. Marshall picked up the tab, before they left the restaurant to pick up their cars from the parking garage.

"Get home safe."

"You do the same, Marshall."

They hugged and fist bumped, and drove off in opposite directions.

Marshall drove through Time Square. He saw a nice Billboard of a female dancer in motion, followed by two male dancers above him.

He wasn't sure at first, he thought there was something familiar about the female dancer. After he turned the corner to the side of the street, and parked the car illegally for a second to observe the Billboard closer.

"Well I'll be damn. It's Zoë on the Billboard," he said. He returned to his car feeling outrageous, as he drove away. He realizes what she meant about her new surprise. There was a Billboard of her around the city appearing in another performance at Avery Fish Hall.

68

It was shocking and embarrassing to say the least. He did everything he could in order to maintain his cool. He didn't want to fly off the handle in front of his people, who worked for him about a woman. But if looks could kill. The people around him knew someone was in trouble. He was mad and boiling when he gets like this?

Then take a look over your shoulder. You need to watch your back. The information he received from Carl about Whitney, and Lawrence was more than disturbing to him. It was a deep focus of deadly charades, with three naïve hearts to digest, he felt.

A connection was formulating in his mind. Zoë called him a while back. She told him about his sleazy friend. Who made a pitch to sleep with her, and offered her money and drugs. It was Lawrence.

Zoë wasn't interested in him, his money, or his drugs. She didn't do them. It was something she expressed emphatically to Johnny Mc Ray, also. Now the pieces were beginning to fall into place for him. It was Lawrence, who stabbed him in the back and was out for himself.

Selling him out to Whitney behind his back and sleeping with her, and spending the night at her place. It was time he received a huge reward for his double betrayal.

Johnny Mc Ray couldn't understand him. He was given every opportunity to do good for himself. He thought of him as a younger friend, with a lot of talent and potential.

Johnny wasn't blessed this way. His parents made him sacrifice things in his life. So he could learn to do better, which forced him to break away from the family and pursue his own ideas about life.

The fact that he was a big music producer and business entrepreneur wasn't their dream for him. But the one thing his parents couldn't deny, or dispute was how wealthy Johnny had become financially and famous.

Lawrence seemed to always take the easy way out, if he could. He choose to play games, lie, hurt, and used people for his own selfish benefit. He had taken too much for granted.

Johnny called Whitney. He asked to see her. She replied, "She'd be there."

She wasn't thrilled about going to see him, but felt it was important to go along with the program. Since she knew more about Zoë and Johnny from Lawrence, and to conceal the fact they shared a secret. They welcomed each other with a new dilemma.

Yet Whitney was waiting and wishing Johnny would walk right into a brick wall, with a plastic suit on for safe wear.

Then explode on impact, because he lied and cheated on her with Zoë.

She thought about how much she loved him. How much she now distrusted him. She tried so hard to stand by him through everything. Merely to discover, she was a fool, she felt. Somehow she was going to lead him to believe. He was kissing the wrong person's ass, when he was right about something.

Ironically, they were in the same identical situation. But Whitney wasn't buying it. Unexplained things are better served when they were filtered through Johnny Mc Ray's intelligence. She continued to search for left over ingredients from his mind—but wished now—that Johnny was the center of gravity. So she could release this shit forever, while clearing out her mind, and moving on with her life.

"Thanks for stopping by, Babe. I want to talk to you." Johnny decided he was going to nip this all in the bud, and take care of business to make everything right between Whitney and him.

But most of all, teach Lawrence a thing or two in the process about? Who he was dealing with. He took Whitney's hand and directed her to sit down with him on the couch. He positioned her comfortably on his lap.

"Look Babe. I was at the club in Brooklyn. The one I was going to buy, the one you liked. When I walked in and your friend was dancing and singing there. I concluded my business with Raymond, the owner and I left.

"When I saw her there, I turned down the offer to buy the place. Since she was working there. I saw a conflict of interest. We never spoke to one another."

Whitney gazed at Johnny, and rolled her eyes at him. She didn't know what to believe. Since he had turned down a business deal because of her? She was aware how much he loves to make money from business.

"When I came home Lawrence was here. I asked him, did he ever meet your friend the dancer? He said, no.

"I told him she was dancing at the club in Brooklyn. The place I was considering buying.

"Then one of my people told me. They saw him hanging out there trying to pick her up, but nothing developed for him with her.

"And you know how much he likes you. So I was trying to figure out? Where all of this stuff about your friend was coming from? I hope Lawrence isn't jealous, and trying to play out some fantasy of his that he has about you?

"This is why I am surprised someone would tell you differently. My people were all around me, and he was here. So I would like to know? When did all of this take place between Zoë and me?"

Whitney became confused and started to wonder about it herself. She didn't know who to believe. She didn't ask Lawrence to supple any of the details. She jumped to conclusions, and over reacted to the situation since it involved Zoë.

She did ask herself why she believed him over Johnny. It didn't make any sense to her now. Even if Johnny was lying to her. She had no proof to believe Lawrence over him.

It made her feel ignorant and foolish at the moment for giving away, that kind of power and her sex to him. Did she really over react and do something she shouldn't have? Or did Lawrence play her, and do something he always wanted to do, which was sleep with her?

"Is there something going on between you and him, that I should know about? Or do you want to tell me something, Whitney?"

"No, Johnny! Why would you think something like this about Lawrence and me?"

"I was just curious." Johnny went into his pocket and handed Whitney a small velvet box.

"What is this?"

"Open it and see." He began kneeling down on one knee. She couldn't believe it was an engagement ring.

"Will you marry me, Whitney Louise Cook?" She erupted with excitement and happiness, after seeing all those carats in the ring. She hugged Johnny for dear life.

"Yes! Yes! Yes! I will marry you, Johnny!" They kissed each other passionately, as if they had finally made up by forgiving one another. He didn't care anymore whether Whitney had slept with him or not. He knew how much he meant to her, and how much she meant to him.

Because he slept with many women behind Whitney's back, which he was confident they would kept their mouths shut. If they wanted to continue their association with him and his business. There was no way he wanted to lose her over something Lawrence had engineered and was behind.

Johnny accepted that Whitney might have done something out of character by being hurt, or disappointed in him. He had no proof to substantial someone else's conclusion about what happened between them. It was still no reason for Lawrence to open his mouth, or spill his business about Zoë. Or take advantage of the situation with Whitney.

69

HE COULDN'T GET IT TOGETHER with what he had? Johnny questioned Lawrence's true character as a man, and didn't appreciate what he thought he was doing. After trying to cut his throat behind his back. Especially were a woman and sex were concerned. Friends don't do stuff like this to one another.

Yes, he fabricated the whole story about Zoë and him to Whitney. Everyone else knew it wasn't true. So this is why everyone else knew to keep their mouths shut, but Lawrence didn't. It was his way of resolving the problem between them, which was created by him, but it was still his business to handle.

He considered what he did with Zoë, was an unsatisfied quickie which never happened. He gave her the money she needed for a business transaction. He returned downstairs, before Lawrence showed his face in the place. Then Zoë came down after.

Why he would use this against him to play on Whitney's insecure ness upset him. So much so, it was time for him to teach Lawrence a lesson, and show him how it's really done.

A week later, Johnny called Lawrence and offered him a business proposition. If he was interested in making some money. One of his connections needed a favor from him. Lawrence immediately jumped at the offer, and wanted to know what was in it for him?

Johnny explained the job to him. He didn't have anyone else available to handle it at the time. He needed a package dropped off to someone in Queens. His compensation would be twenty-five hundred, if he wanted to make the trip.

The errand was simple. Give the person the item and wait for a package in return. Then return home with the package. He was all smiles and hyped. He took the package and the envelope filled with cash.

Johnny gave him the name of the person, the address, and the best way to get there. Thirty-five minutes later. He was on the Van Wyck Pkwy in route to Queens.

Upon his arrival, he saw a woman entering the house of the address he had. He pulled into the drive way. Everything was quiet. He walked up to the front door and ringed the bell. The door opened. It was the woman he saw moments earlier. She was nice looking but short. Part of her was concealed behind the door.

"Can I help you?"

"I' m looking for Bobby. I have something for him, and he is supposed to give me something in return.

"I am Bobby. Come in." He thought Bobby was a man. He stepped into the doorway.

Then a man jumped out from behind the door with a gun in his hands, grabbed and turned him around. The man instructed him to get against the wall and spread them, with his hands up. The woman quickly shut the door. She removed the item from his hand and opened it.

The package contained a substance of white powder, a significant quantity. Also the man removed the envelope filled with cash from him. The man was satisfied there was no weapon on him after patting him down.

Handcuffs were placed on him. The man turned him around to face them, while the woman he thought was Bobby had a gun drawn on him. Now, he could see that another man was tied up in a chair to his left, which he assumed was the real Bobby. The person he came to see. It was obvious the man and woman were undercover cops.

He was escorted to an SUV around the corner from the house. The female cop asked Lawrence for his car keys. She followed them to the precinct, while she drove his car. After Lawrence entered the precinct. He was questioned further about the item and money in his possession.

He answered the elementary questions pertaining to his identity, and that was it. The officer continued processing his report. He was taken to a holding cell where other men were being held. Later he was permitted to make a phone call. He was being arrested.

"Johnny, I am in jail."

"What happened?"

"I think something was going down before I got there. I think your man, Bobby, was being busted by two undercover cops. I think Bobby was tied to a chair, that's how they got me. They left him behind for someone else to pick up. So what happens now?"

"I don't know, Lawrence. I need to find out for you. There is nothing I can do for you at this late hour. Just sit tight. Keep your mouth shut.

"I will have my people there for you in the morning. So you can make bail. Okay?"

70

JADE ENJOYED HER RECENT VISIT with Marshall. Recalling, how things use to be between them. When you are in love with the right man in your life. It is a great time in your life, before you see another reality of what people can be.

And thinking about what she had become to her ex-husband, and accepting the responsibility for ruining a good man's love for her. And a good marriage which was the corner stone of a cherished life together with him. It was the border line between her mornings and her nights.

There was a look in her eyes that was more open, and demonstrated how she disliked that part of herself.

A magic she felt suddenly disappeared between Marshall and her. A magic that comes along once in a life time with someone. The compatibility with another person you love for the fire of burning reasons.

The search for coherency? She was now another person with another mystery, and another way to fall and fear things in her life without Marshall. It was still a guide to hurt her. Love shouldn't destroy who you are, but it does for some reason.

Would Marshall ever see her any differently, than the person she has become to him? Realizing, that someone who still loves you is really not enough?

Jade wanted to know whether he could ever trust her again with his feelings. From the changes to a chance with hell and undue influences. She wished he could have stayed with her when he came to visit her.

A sweet, kind, and gentle giant he is, but she wanted to imagine him as she once did, before she changed him and brought out the rage. A side she didn't want to see in him again.

In spite of his gentleness, you didn't want to make him mad. She thought about when he would rip off her clothes and take her, when she lease expected it. She always believed she was a good woman, and didn't do those things which excited men, until Marshall turned her into a different woman.

She couldn't get enough of him. If she didn't know any better she believed he planned it this way?

It didn't matter, being anything he wanted her to be was worth it to her. He was what she wanted him to be to her, and he always had her best interest at heart. Something she knew you couldn't always say about someone.

The wonderful things he consistently did for her. How he basically took care of her, and didn't make her feel like a sex object. How he would think of her first, before he considered himself.

Jade was not trying to convince herself or anyone else, that Marshall was a saint or was perfect. He was far from it, but he was unique. And for her, he was the perfect man to have. She realized how attractive and desirable he was to other women. The things that made Marshall different.

Even though, he could play the field successfully anytime he wanted to. He has a knack of knowing how to sincerely treat a woman. He is truly yours. You definitely don't have to worry about any other woman.

Once he makes a commitment to be with you. You are his life line. It isn't about what any other woman can do for him, or he would have left you, or cheated on you a long time ago.

Regardless of how much he loved, Jade. There was nothing left to fight over. They didn't have any children together. It wasn't the right time for them, they felt. She recalled how thoughtful and caring he was when she was in the hospital.

Afterward, she knew in her heart. How desperately Marshall wanted to go after Ryan, until he confronts him one way or another.

She asked herself, "What man do you know who would do something like this, after you dismantled his whole world?" This is why she granted him a divorce, and he continued to be there for her like a guardian angel.

She also wondered how unusual it had been not to hear from, Ryan. She only hoped that Marshall didn't do anything too hoarse to him, which would get him into serious trouble. Marshall wasn't a violent person by nature, but he is someone you didn't want to get angry either, as Jade referred to earlier.

It was great to still be able to talk to him, and see him now, without all the dirty looks he gave her before.

It was difficult now, that things have settled down, and the dust has cleared. It still hurts her to see them separated from each other. Living apart like it was the last kiss of love from another person's pain, Jade thought.

Her emotions jiggled from the thought of breaking her own heart. When it was jumping all over the place.

If she could kill the regret of her bad judgment and pain, she would shoot it to death. She wished God could answer her prayers, by showing her the magic once more in her life with him. Forgiving her for her past transgression and her mistakes, but her tears flowed heavily from her eyes.

She covered her face from the guilt, and pain she continued to feel and serve, as medicine for her own illness.

The changes she experienced wasn't because, she hasn't been in a relationships before? This relationship was so damn good and different to her. She missed him this much. She wasn't sure about what she would do about it anymore. She didn't want to make a fool of herself, just because she still loved him, and didn't want to put him through this?

Jade is a competitive person when it comes to something she needs or wants. She didn't want to give up the thought, but she didn't want to sweat Marshall, with the prospect of them reuniting so soon after they were divorced. The choice was hard for her.

She knew not everyone deserves a second chance. She believed she was one of those people. Who didn't serve one, no matter how much she wanted it.

It still wasn't enough to convince her to give up on herself, with him in the back of her mind.

71

HE THOUGHT IT WAS ODD that he missed her after visiting her, and communicating with her brought back many memories. When they were a couple, and functioning as a unit together. He was curious, as to why there were let downs in his armor. A moment of emptiness, and he was alone in his solitude searching for answers to what?

A resolution to convey about what it was he wanted now. As much as he continued to care, and feel for her, he couldn't see them getting back together.

But stranger things have happened, when it comes to love. He was glad and confident she would be getting back on her feet, and on with her life again. He was feeling good about her needing to be strong for herself now.

And not let what happened between them take her down, or allow her focus to be lost again. He didn't want her to live her life without forgiveness. She had too many good qualities in her to lose sight of this. Mistakes will frequently be a part of everyone's life, along with the growing process we fail to realize and want to accept.

Living without mistakes would be great, but what would we learn about ourselves or something else—

nothing? Sometimes we act like mistakes are never supposed to happen to us. It is for this very reason they do happen, and to show us, that all we do is commit more mistakes, and the same mistakes for other reasons.

Hopefully she is on her way back to healing—just as he hoped for himself. He was tired. He decided to relax now that he was home, but not before he called Zoë to see how she was doing, lately.

"Hello, Marshall. How are you?"

"It seems like I haven't talked to you in a while."

"Well, I guess I don't have to ask you. How you are doing? You must be on top of the world, with your latest performance at Avery Fish Hall?"

"How did you know? I have been so unbelievably busy. I have been meaning to call you. I would like you to come and see my performance."

He began to explain to her that her request was much too late. He witnessed her performance a week ago. She didn't understand at first, why he didn't tell her he was in the audience. Or why he didn't wait for her after the show?"

"It was amazing to see a large crowd waiting anxiously outside to interact with you.

"How could I interfere with your moment of fame and glory? You really deserved every moment of it. Your performance was great.

"You have this gift, this ability to leap, and move with such grace. Your movement and style is like harmony. You are a really good dancer, Zoë."

"Thank you, for the compliments. I appreciate them so much coming from you. It still doesn't change the fact that I missed you, Marshall.

"Whether you realized it or not, I could have shared all of this with you. I can't explain it now, but I find myself needing to be with you in away. I wish I could explain it. I wish I could see you more. Then I think that my feelings would explain my actions."

He wasn't sure what to say to her, but she didn't expect him to say anything. She just wanted him to know this, and hoped he wasn't uncomfortable about what she said to him. He was a big inspiration to her whether he knew it or not.

She told him, that she would be booked for the next eight weeks, and that the show will be leaving to go on the road in another three months. She made it perfectly clear how much she would miss him, and wanted to see him upon her return. Anticipating, he would be able to share some time together.

He was surprised and curious about her feelings. He wished her well on a safe trip, and a successful performance when it happens. He looked forward to seeing her when she returned. It was a quiet Friday evening. He figured he would turn in after talking to her. She continued to be a fascination person to him.

There was something else there also, that he couldn't read about her. When you see every indication of her life changing for her?

Saturday 6:30 a.m. His cell phone began ringing. “Hello, Marshall.”

“Yes?”

“My name is Ben Robinson. I am one of Sarah’s brothers. Sarah was killed in a plane crash.”

“Oh no, I just spoke with her on Wednesday!”

“It happened Thursday. We were informed that there was a malfunction to one of the engines and landing gear, upon landing at the airport at the last minute. The investigation is still on going.”

“I am sorry. I don’t know what to say. I am really hurt and disturbed by hearing this?

“I am truly sorry for your lost. Please give my condolences to your brother as well.”

“Thank you, Marshall. Sarah was extremely fond of you, and spoke very highly of you. My brother and I were very pleased that you cared so much for our sister, and made her very happy before this happened. She talked about you non-stop all the time.

“We never got an opportunity to meet you. You seem to be a better match for our sister than her ex-husband was. We think she was falling in love with you. I am sorry I have to bring you such bad news about her.”

“Once again, thank you for calling me to let me know, Ben. If I can do anything for you or your brother. Please don’t hesitate to call me.

“I hope that you will keep me informed of any further developments. I would definitely like to be included in the services of any kind, which you may have for her. I will be there. Take care of yourself, Ben.”

"You do the same, Marshall."

He was filled with sadness, and pain to hear about Sarah. What a shock? He will never see her again. He will never talk to her again just like that. Or enjoy her company every again, because death is always final and forever.

He could feel the emptiness and lost generating throughout his entire body, without his permission to do that to him. But at the moment, and for some unexplained reason. He no longer felt like taking on the world anymore.

He was feeling like a Firecracker-Baby. Just waiting for his insides to explode. Just waiting for someone to light him up? So he wouldn't feel his own body coming apart, while someone else is picking up the pieces?

Now, he felt dead inside and didn't want to bring it? There was no way to understand this. Or explain it to himself, how he felt. Death is just another fact of life, which he didn't care for, and no one else liked either. He read somewhere, "That dead is more universal."

But the magnitude of Sarah's lost shattered the image of appropriate love between her and him. The last time he talked to her. He received the impression she was trying to say something to him without really saying it.

She was in love with him, before they could run off into an unknown togetherness. He was surprised and concerned about how intimate, and personal they became in the short time they were enjoying together.

Sarah had a way of making their time too special. This is why he missed her more than he wanted to say.

He enjoyed being in another world with the likes of her on his mind. He didn't wash up or take a shower. He threw whatever clothes on that were in plain sight, and put a cap on his head.

He picked up the car keys on the table and left the place, and took his Saturday morning drive much earlier.

His eyes were filled with tears, as they rolled rapidly down his face. Giving the grievance, he would begin to feel without her being around anymore, and to the selective meaning to all of this?

Sarah was as easy, as a date with an angel. She gave him her enormous body of love. The pain in his heart ignited a smile for her when he thought of her. In the gathering of a possible lost love in his life, because of her ability to handle things in the manner in the way she did.

Just like someone, he saw in a dream down the road, before she was taken away from him.

72

MATTERS OF CONCERN DIDN'T GO well for Lawrence at his court arraignment. He is out on bail which was posted by Johnny Mc Ray. It was the DA's intention to serve him up with the maximum for his offense of possession of a control substance and a large quantity of money.

Lawrence was stunned beyond words. He could be facing serious prison time. All because he did his friend a favor, and got paid. He was reminded by Johnny, it was a business transaction which he was handsomely paid up front for.

Someone inquired about a favor from Johnny, and he agreed—but developed and idea to establish a plan to compromise Lawrence's situation. Sometimes matters don't always go down the way you want them to. These are the breaks in this business that comes with the territory.

He advised Lawrence that his people were doing everything they could to work out a deal. He wasn't God. He was going to have to serve some time. It was only a question of how much time.

Lawrence wasn't too thrilled about this. He couldn't imagine himself confined or locked away in jail somewhere.

Especially for an indefinite period of time, without the pleasures he enjoyed so much with his freedom.

Johnny also told the arresting officers to reduce the gravity of his criminal offenses to the DA. Because of Johnny's power, he was able to change the scenario up considerably.

The arresting officers doubled as body guards, and worked security at his concerts and various other events. The money was large. So they continued to remain on Johnny Mc Ray's payroll.

The meeting with the DA was introduced differently this time, after confirming the facts of the case for a second time. They had been waiting for Johnny Mc Ray's orders on how he wanted them to proceed on the bust of his acquaintance. So Lawrence went from being involved to an ignorant patsy or participate.

The DA was now informed by the arresting officers, that his involvement was minimal if any? He was in the wrong place at the wrong time. He was going to visit someone and there was a misunderstanding about the address. Since he had never been to Queens before which was a lie.

He approached the wrong house shortly before they raided the place. And someone escaping shoved a package with money and cocaine in his hands, but he was the only person they were able to nab. The DA wasn't buying it totally. He saw too many holes in this scenario concerning the suspect.

Also it was brought to his attention, who his friend was, and his reputation as a celebrity? After the story was created by the arresting officers—about Lawrence being unfortunate, and Johnny Mc Ray was used as a reference. He was a close friend of the family and posted bail for him. His reputation allowed him some respect in court.

This was Lawrence's first offense of any kind. He is a productive citizen. He has a job, and was married recently. He hasn't been in any kind of trouble before.

From the quantity of drugs and money the DA wanted someone to go to jail. Since there was no one else arrested from the raid. So a deal was made for him. He would serve two years, and with good behavior. He would only do eighteen months, and three months community service.

Even though, he seriously was tempted not to take the deal. He was horrified of going to jail. He had no idea of how he would deal with his new life style.

Johnny explained to Lawrence, that the choice was his. But if he changed his mind, and decided to make a side deal with the DA. Or sell him out about where he received the items and money from, then he might as well commit suicide.

He wouldn't put a hit out on his friend's life, but he couldn't guarantee that the people who worked for him wouldn't find a way to take him out. Lawrence had to realize and understand that this business was the nature of their livelihood, also.

He would be taken care of as long as he kept his mouth shut, and took whatever time he had coming to him.

Johnny also knew people in the same prison that he would be escorted to. Who would keep an eye on him and take care of him. Lawrence didn't know what else to do, but after careful consideration and thought. He accepted the situation.

He was more afraid of turning on Johnny, and then getting whacked himself. It would serve no purpose to him now. After Johnny Mc Ray's high priced attorney completed his plea bargaining deal with the DA and the court.

Lawrence was sentenced to two years. He was a first time offender. He was a college dropout, with hopes of returning to complete his education. He was presently employed as a Model on the rise. And hasn't been in trouble in his life or with the law, and would do three months of community service upon his released.

Lawrence was relieved. He thought that his time was going to be much longer. He was still disappointed he had to serve time. He was hoping that Johnny could have pulled a few more strings with all of his power, but it didn't happen. He thanked him for all his help, and assured him he would do as he asked.

Lawrence hugged him, as Johnny watched his young friend being taken away by a court officer. His body-guards surrounded him, as he left the court house. They entered his Gold Escalade, which pulled up in front of the court house.

Lawrence had no idea concerning the powers that be? Johnny Mc Ray displayed a large smile on his face. It was a great accomplishment of his by orchestrating the whole event.

Nick and Janet were the two undercover cops, who were on his payroll. They received an extra bonus for their part in it, and a job well done. Johnny had a Co-op out in Queens. Where Detective Janet Segal resides. He is looking forward to seeing her tonight. The entire bust was a shake down, a classic set-up.

The real Bobby was tired up in a chair at the house. After Lawrence was taken away, Bobby's woman came from upstairs to untie him, while they attended to a second visitor who provided a replacement item to them from Johnny.

His objective was to offer, and give Lawrence a complete new sense of reality about his life now. Showing him that it was time for him to grow up, and be a real man where other people were concerned.

His days of trying to get over on other people are over. It's time for him to do something for himself, and assume some responsibility instead of expecting a hand out alone the way from someone else.

It's amazing how someone can feel they are entitled to something from you, because they feel they know you or they are a relative of yours

73

JOHNNY IS ALSO RELIEVED TO have Lawrence removed and out of his hair, and from the presence of Whitney and his business. Now he is going to have to watch out for his own privacy being invaded.

Johnny Mc Ray started laughing out loud. It was time for him and Whitney to get on with their lives. He went to see her. He told Whitney about Lawrence's present situation and misfortune.

She was surprised to hear the disappointing news. She was relieved in a tremendous way about Lawrence not being around to complicate her life, and her moment of weak judgment with him.

Johnny did everything he could to convince her it was their time from here on out. She also had to put the past behind her, even if Johnny was with Zoë.

He could never know about Lawrence and her being together, either. Just like Johnny didn't want her to know. He knew about Lawrence and her. He didn't blame her. He blamed Lawrence, but the matter was taken care of now.

"Whitney it is time for you to let it go about, Zoë. This is not the same woman you think you know?"

"And what is that supposed to mean, Johnny?"

"Well for one thing, have you been reading the entertainment section of the newspaper?"

"No. I haven't. And why should I?"

"Because if you did, you would see your former girlfriend is a Star now."

"What are you talking about, Johnny?"

"She has been receiving reviews and praise for her dancing. Not to mention, she is on Billboards all over the city.

"She is appearing at Avery Fisher Hall. Would you like to go and see her? What an incredible turn around, huh? You didn't say, she was that good a dancer, Whitney?"

She turned her head and frowned. If she was a dragon she would have fire coming from her mouth and smoke from her nose. She wasn't sure whether to feel angry, or jealous about her.

She realized it was time to count her blessings and let go of her vengeance. She had what she really wanted, which was Johnny Mc Ray all to herself. Whitney accepted in her mind, that perhaps she wasn't really the person she wished Zoe to be.

She denied things to herself that she was told by various people about Randall, which she didn't want to believe or accept. A part of her brother wasn't a good person when it came to women, and she was a woman.

The beautiful dancer she had always known her to be, like how she would thrill people with her dancing when they attended college, before she disliked her or became envious of her.

She had no reason to feel this way about her anymore. Now, that Johnny and her were looking forward to setting a date to be married. It was now her desire to find forgiveness within herself, or as well for Zoë.

It didn't mean she was going to invite her to her wedding, after hearing a voice in her mind. Or trying to find a psychic source of reasoning, as she stopped to think about?

****

Nine months later, Johnny Mc Ray appeared to be sad, and unhappy to receive the news about Lawrence in prison. He was dead. Apparently, after his first seven months of incarceration.

Johnny didn't keep his promise to provide the protection, that Lawrence believed he would be receiving, while he was in prison. But instead, Johnny left him hanging, like a man with no balls to fin for himself.

It was difficult for Lawrence, because he was abused, taken advantage of, and humiliated publicly. He didn't have any knowledge of prison life. He didn't know what was what? He didn't know any one he could definitely trust.

He cried many nights in his cell. When he was alone and didn't understand the position Johnny left him in. He was tired of people coming up to him, and whipping his ass because he was new, and didn't know the rules of the place.

He was determined to contact Johnny, when he was allowed to make a call. Unfortunately for him, Johnny was never available to receive his calls, but the messages were taken, and the messages were always the same, "Will you please come and see me?"

The only people to come, and ever see him was his mother and sister on two occasions. His brother refused to go to prison to see Lawrence. He was having a difficult time dealing with the issues of his disappointment, and embarrassment from his associates at work.

But then the abuse became worse. Because of a power struggle between several of the inmates regarding him. Then it happened, he was violated by being raped four times a week. It was horrible.

He was treated like he was dirt, that nobody cared for. Between the inmates and the guards, he was truly helpless and always in fear of his life. The first week he arrived in prison, he witnessed two men killed in front of him, and three more since then.

How ironic it was that he was being pimped out, like a whore because of his looks. The first time he thought about refusing. His jaw was broken in two places. The second time he refused. He was stabbed in the back. The third time he refused. He was gang raped.

So the power struggle for him continued, until one side won. Then he would receive notes every day, about where he would have to be, and at what time. So he would be molested sexually for whatever compensation the people in charge required for him.

After months of being controlled and the constant degradation. Lawrence could no longer deal with himself or his life. He didn't care anymore. It was time that he did something to change his circumstances. He could no longer continue accepting the pain he carried, that no one gave a damn about. When they look upon him with contempt.

He felt he had no choice left, but to stand up for himself and confront his worse fear. He went to see his inmate keeper, and told him about his refusal to continue, with the bullshit of what they were doing to him.

The man in charge look at him and smile. He then rolled his eyes at another inmate standing next to him. The inmate walked up to Lawrence, and split his throat before he could blink to realized, that it had happen. So much for Lawrence standing up for himself.

The group of men walked away like nothing had ever happened. It was more than sad. How different his life was when he was married to Sarah, and took her for granted. Since he didn't really want to settled down, and be a man to some woman to love.

However, he thought it was more beneficial to use them, and live his life the way he wanted to. It was too ironic how he lost Sarah. A good woman, a good wife, and a better person.

A month before she died, he was told about what happened to her. But other than the surprise of the news. He was more concerned about his present situation, and how he would be able to go the distance, before he was released.

How different his life could have been. If he could have given his situation with Sarah a real opportunity to excel in their relationship and marriage. But he was more involved with his ego, and the majority of his time was spend on him ego-tripping on his own bullshit.

All he had to do was give love a chance. No one is saying that it was the answer, but it would have been different for him. Yes, love comes with a lot of confrontations. But it is no different than the pain, the sacrifices, the struggles, the hurt, the disappointments, the betrayal, the lies, the setbacks, and the broken hearts to top it off with. But is there anything else other than this, that is different from love.

Not a damn thing, because everything else in life is a direct result of this, and all the shit you go through in life anyway. But now she is dead, and now he is dead from being another person's bitch. Like the same abuse that he displayed to women. Some people don't make sense, with sense, even if they have sense.

74

OLIVIA LEFT WORK EARLY. MARSHALL was on an incoming flight from Texas. It was her desire to be there for him by picking him up from the airport. He was surprised, pleased, and happy to see Olivia there waiting for him.

He spoke to her about the trip, but recalled they didn't make any plans in advance for her to meet him. They talked briefly in the car. Marshall was amazed at how good a driver Olivia was behind the wheel.

She could handle a car as good as anybody he had seen. She was a speed demon, but she was not reckless, and could skillfully drive her ass off.

He thought he could drive, when he participated in driving contest for his company, but Oliver would waste him and think nothing of it. It was like watching a professional race driver. Seeing her shift gears with her stick, and wearing her gloves, while maneuvering in and out of traffic was truly a sight to witness?

She wasted any car that was in front of her, on the side of her, or in back of her.

Marshall thought if he every decided to rob a bank, she would definitely be his getter away driver. Olivia smiled at him. He was home in no time. Her father was a race car driver. He taught her everything she knew about cars and driving. He had no idea she was also a grease monkey like her pop's.

She was that good. Her father was pretty good from the press clippings and winnings she revealed about him. But he was killed in a racing accident by another drivers mistake.

Olivia was going to turn pro, but decided not to after her father died. It wasn't the same for her anymore. So she gave up driving. He took her coat and made her a cup of coffee.

She hugged him tightly and kissed him. They lounged back on the sofa in each other's arms for a few minutes. He broke free of her to serve her coffee. She thanked him. She lit a cigarette.

"How are you Marshall? I know you and Sarah were close. I never met her. You were very forthcoming and candid about your relationship with her. I was very pleased about that." He gazed at Olivia as she took a sip of her coffee, and a pull from her cigarette.

Marshall wondered why Olivia even smoked. When she would hold on to a pack of cigarettes for months. She only smokes less than half a cigarette. He thought that was another story. She wasn't a real smoker. It was more like the idea of smoking. When you light-up, take a couple of pulls, and then extinguished three quarters of your cigarette.

She was serious, beautiful, and relaxed looking on the sofa. He thought about her being his "lovely one" at that moment. She returned her gazed back at him, with her large brown eyes of concern.

She pulled Marshall into her arms. She held him gently, as a child kissing every part of his face she could reach with her sensuous lips. Marshall remained relaxed in her arms for the time being.

"I want to thank you for picking me up at the airport, Olivia. It was a terrific surprise. I had no idea you would be there. I was happy to see you.

"I will miss her. She was good people to me. A sweet person, a thoughtful person, and a loving person," Olivia's eyes shifted.

"Her brothers were really okay. I never met them before. They were very considerate of my presence, and needs during the service prepared for their sister."

"I am sorry for their lost, as well as yours."

"Thank you, Olivia." He hugged her. "It will be okay." He rose up off of Olivia's body to turn his attention to her.

"In spite of that unfortunate event, I want you to know how much I have missed you."

"I know Marshall. I have never doubted that or your feelings for me. It's one of the reasons why I feel the way I do about you. I don't have to guess or wonder about you in spite of everything that is going on in your life.

"You wouldn't mistreat me for someone else, just like I know that you wouldn't mistreat someone else for me.

"You are not that kind of a person, but unique in your way."

They smiled at one another. Olivia leaned forward to kiss Marshall. The intercom ringed. It was security announcing, Marcus. Marshall was surprised by his visit.

He wondered how he knew that he was back and at home. When he didn't get an opportunity to talk to him before he left. He answered the door. They greeted each other, as if they had not seen each other in months.

"Marcus, how did you know?"

"Don't thank me. It was that beautiful woman's idea over there." Marshall looked at Olivia directly. She smiled at him.

"Since I didn't hear from you, I didn't know what was going on? She arranged it, booked it, and hooked it up. She didn't want you to be alone when you got back home. She felt that you should be surrounded by friends and love."

Marshall walked over to Olivia and kissed her big, with his arms around her. Olivia went to get her coat and was putting it on when Marshall turned to face her, after what Marcus explained to him.

"Are you leaving, don't?"

"Yes, I have to go unfortunately. However, I am leaving you in very good hands."

She moved in closer to his body to kiss him. Then she stared into his eyes and with vulnerability in her words.

"I would do anything to make you happy, Marshall. I love you. Please take care of yourself."

75

OLIVIA SAID GOODBYE TO MARCUS, and they embraced. Marshall opened the door for her as she left. He stood there touched by Olivia's thoughtful actions and words. He walked up behind her and turned her around before she reached the elevator, and kissed her meaningfully.

A center of nervousness was there in his body. He felt a sense of void that Olivia had left. He wondered whether or not, he was in love with her at that moment.

Then again, he wondered the same thing about Sarah too. The woman who was taken away from life, and never to be seen or heard from again.

"Are you okay, Marshall?"

"I am not sure anymore?"

"Then why don't you have a seat and we can talk."

Marcus expressed his concern for Marshall, and realized that, this kind of situation doesn't happen to everyone. He didn't envy Marshall's personal dilemma. The emotional ties to four incredible women in his life.

There was no question in his mind, regardless of whatever he and Jade experienced together, which led to their separation.

He still cared about her and loved her, but a lot of the intensity was diminished, because of the other women in his life.

Putting things back into perspective along with a man's pride? Once you go beyond a certain point. Then it's not about love anymore. It's about being a convenient fool for someone. The other person hasn't quite decided, if it's time to eliminate all the bull, that they are putting someone else through and do the right thing.

Since this ship has sailed once before. It was time for Marshall to get off of it, before he went down completely with it. This is why Marcus couldn't tell him what to do, but simply be there for him as a friend. It wasn't like he was going to tell him anything he didn't know, or hasn't heard before, or hasn't been through.

Marcus said, "That when a woman like Olivia comes into your life, with much quality, personality, and character. Then you have a decision to make. Granted she is married to someone else, which seems to be in clear sight her only fault?"

Oliver wasn't some kind of woman, with a stereotype axe to grind. She was no one's fool, or joke, and they knew that. She grew up with people of color in the South. She understood much about their livelihood.

This is why it became much more with her, than just being with her because she was a hot woman. You have to remember, hot women come a dime a dozen, and that means in all colors.

It was something she didn't try to hide about herself, or to anyone else, and was open about that fact in her life. Marshall wasn't trying to say, this made her black in anyway.

It was something in which, you had to acknowledge about her. It gave you a better idea of who the woman is. And the fact she cared, and was in love with Marshall only complicated things more for the both of them.

Marcus could see in her eyes, how much she desired to be with Marshall. He knew whatever her husband was doing was stupid. There was no doubt, he was certainly doing it wrong, with a woman like her, and screwing up on her account.

It was his choice. You can't leave a woman like Olivia alone to hang on a string, until you decide to come in from out of the rain, and want to give her some attention, and want to feel her up, and please her now.

She is not the kind of woman, who will settle for kibbles and bits. Just because a man wants to be cheap, and not explore his horizons in their relationship. She is a woman who requires a lot of attention. She gives a lot in return. It doesn't matter, what color she is. You just have to be sincere within yourself.

This is why Marcus understood what Marshall was going through. Then there was Sarah, no one would have predicted how close they would have become. It surprised them both and now she is dead. Then there is this mysterious new woman name, Zoë, which appeared out of nowhere.

Perhaps entering into his life. It's a bit much for anyone to deal with. It's not like he doesn't care about any of these women. Or he doesn't want to be with any of them.

The problem is, they are all more than any man could want. Whether you are ready for them or not. Marcus felt it wasn't a matter of what was right or wrong? It was a matter of what was right for Marshall, or right for them?

"When you called me to tell me about Sarah's accident, after you left on your trip. I saw the accident on Cable News. "All the people, the pilots, and flight attendances were killed. It had to effect Marshall, and not in the best way. Or put him in a good frame of mind. Whether anybody realized it or not, it was obvious to me. He was in a lot of pain."

Marcus told Marshall about what happened to Lawrence. Johnny Mc Ray believed that Sarah was made from homemade honey. She was so hot, with her buttered complexion. He thought about getting his lick on with her, but it was in good tribute to how sweet a person she was.

She was so gorgeous to him, that it would put him under. He was really sorry to hear about the news concerning her death. And when something like this happens, sometimes people just don't have any kind of luck in life?

Marshall was surprised to hear about the news of Lawrence. Since he was a constant pain in the ass to Sarah. She really didn't deserve it from him. And like Marcus said, "Lawrence got screwed real bad."

"Thanks Marcus. I appreciate your heads up on this matter. Outside of Jade, you are the only person who knows me as well as you do. I admit that things are starting to get scary."

"I know it's getting more complicated for you, and that is because, you genuinely care about all of these women, and they know this.

"Marshall I can honestly say, there isn't anything you wouldn't do for any of them. I think you need a little space to breathe now.

"Who was that who said, you shouldn't be to over anxious to get back on a horse again, after being thrown off from a hard fall in a relationship?

"Give yourself more time to reflect, and gather yourself again. So you can avoid from repeating the same mistakes again with someone else.

"You know exactly what I mean? The same situation but with a different woman. It only appears to be different on the outside because it's a new face you are with."

"I realized what you are saying, Marcus. I should have taken my own advice, but I didn't. So I'll have to deal with this as it is."

Marshall was tired of discussing the changes that lye a head for him, and wanted to change the conversation to inquire about Marcus and Dominique.

First, Marcus told Marshall about the charges still pending against Brenda Gentle concerning the assault on Dominique.

"She is out on bail. They are waiting for a court date." Marshall didn't know what to say or think about it. When Marcus told him about changing his mind about accepting the position to relocate?

He also had something else as a potential prospect for a new job lined up. His feelings have changed, and have grown much for Dominique. He is considering asking her to move in with him.

"When did all of this happen? How long have I been away?" He began smiling at Marshall.

"So you're falling in love, huh?"

"Yeah, I guess so?"

"So how long will it be before the two of you get hitched? Oh, I'm sorry. I mean married?"

Marcus and Marshall began laughing. He was elated for him. Dominique was a winner. "Let's not get too ahead of ourselves. I just want to take one step at a time," said Marcus.

"I still haven't forgotten what you're going through with women."

"Yeah, I know. But don't use that as an excuse to avoid the obvious, or make a true commitment to that beautiful woman of yours.

76

She came to see him alone and doubting about which twilight to center on. She quietly took her hand and placed it underneath the bed sheets. So that she could feel him in her dreams, as Jade thought to herself. Something disturbed her about herself. She acknowledged she always meant well.

It was about the love she had lost. Also she was two categories away from flipping out and wouldn't be the same.

Now, that more men were coming on to her. It breaks her heart to start over again, when she had it all. Or without Marshall. Or hope she could deal with someone else in her life, which is now marked by perfect fear? Since there were a lot of people who wanted to sleep with her. When she was approached by other people.

"It was like someone placed a hex on her," Jade said to herself. "But it was all good."

Now she had the same problem that other people had. Losing someone you love to lost, which she blames herself for? There was no one else, she wanted to satisfy her nude emotions with more than Marshall? Loving him wasn't enough already. Having him was much more important to her. Regardless of her Looney Tune state. Or with the magnitude of a smile not being abandon.

Or the first of it was not to be abandon. Or without a sabbath day for her desires—which was lost in another ugly person without her gifts. She couldn't forget about the lost in her new shelter?

But on the other side of her mind. There was a legitimate return to the asylum of a new person being in Marshall's life. Or the love they had for one another shouldn't have destroyed them, like in a song or in a mystery?

Jade was hurt more. When Marcus told her about the relationship between Sarah and Marshall. She couldn't believe it, or accept the thought of it when she heard of it in her denial.

She was more than stunned, but she was saddened by the news of Sarah's death. It was a real lost. The only reason why she didn't trust her is because she knew Sarah wanted Marshall, too, just like other women did.

She didn't blame her. She could see it in her eyes, and in her body language when she was around him.

Jade didn't care for Lawrence. She didn't like him. She was convinced that Sarah could be her equal, in spite of her mistake with Lawrence. She could make Marshall really happy. She saw this in her. How she beamed with enthusiasm for him.

Sarah just got stuck with a lemon in Lawrence. It happens a lot more to people than you think? Sometimes we go after what we really want and we are fortunate to get it, and sometimes we don't get what we really want, and have to settle for what we have.

Like we get stuck with someone we didn't know we would get stuck with. But as far as Marcus telling her about Sarah and Marshall. Jade continued to be hurt by the news. She didn't want Sarah to be experiencing any parts of him.

"Not like this? No, hell no!" Jade said to herself.

When she talked to him during the week. He explained to her after she asked him, what Marcus said about Sarah and him becoming fast friends.

Marshall stated that his emotions felt good with her, and he couldn't say if he was in love with Sarah. To her this was a relief. Obviously they were very good friends, with very good benefits.

Jade was jealous and personally envied Sarah, after hearing about this. She had an opportunity to be with him when she couldn't be with him.

Sarah was gone for good. Life is strange this way, but she was no fool. She knew that if Marshall is not one on one with someone. Then he is seeing more than one woman. This is what she knew?

Or was he putting distanced between himself and women, after she deeply hurt him? She was aware when he was good to someone, he was always good to someone. But when he is bad, then he is a good-bad boy. He is bad in a positive way not to harm himself or someone else.

She humbly thought about the other women, and how many were there? She didn't care because she dreaded to know that from here on out. She will move on with her life, but she will be there for him if he ever needs her.

She couldn't see herself competing for him with some other woman, after being with him for over ten years and to still be this young.

If it wasn't about him and her, then the hell with it, since it continued to hurt her. She understood and accepted what was going on since their separation. As much as she tried, she couldn't put her own mistakes aside. When there were two other men in her life besides Marshall.

Now she is recovering physically, emotionally, mentally, and from the fight she had with one of the men.

Hoping he will see her differently in the future. It may not change anything, but she needed to give him time away from her—which was something she painfully didn't want to do, as she recalled an old African Proverb that said, "Absences make's the heart forget."

She realized that it was still difficult for her to do this for herself. So Marshall can find out what he wants again, and discovers what he is going through. She had to travel alone. What she had to face with or without him, just like he was already doing without her.

77

THERE WAS NO DOUBT, OLIVIA was going to do what she wanted to do about her relationship with her husband, and no one was going to stop her or prevent this? This was another thing he failed to mention about her, she is damn head strong. He will have to make a decision soon. Whether or not to love her or lose her?

Olivia is very attractive and smart, but her husband shows her off as a trophy. They are financially comfortable individually. They have no children. Their only ties are their joint venture in buying a house together in Long Island.

They don't spend a lot of time together. Her husband shares most of his time at work with his friends, and other associates Olivia doesn't care for.

The kind that live in a material world. The type that has money and talks about their accomplishments, and about what they have and who they know. So you should be impressed with who they are? She didn't try to tell him, how to pick his friends. Or prevent him from doing anything he wanted to do with or without her.

He on the other hand, always wanted to put a time frame on her whereabouts. So he could know where she was at any given time. She didn't appreciate his double standard for their life styles apart.

Olivia was feeling intensified in her confidence and strength. When a person is growing and changing right in front of you, and you don't take the time out to notice it. It means that your ass will finally pay for it later. It was time for her to make many decisions she didn't labor about.

She loved Marshall this much. She didn't want to transfer her desperation of pain, hurt, and disappointment to him concerning her life with her husband.

It was something she needed to do for herself first, before she could think that far in advance about him and her. It took her some time to come around to her true emotions about everything. She didn't want to hurt her husband like this? Even though, she knew that he was getting his jollies off with someone else.

But she felt that love should be more about being open, and honest about your feelings—than being dishonest with a person. Because you want to spare them the pain of living a lie—and then for some ungodly reason you shatter their world. Because you don't feel the way that they thought you did—when the truth finally comes out.

In her heart, she realized that it was over, and there was nothing he could do to change this. If she was kissed by someone who kissed her with a tight kiss from his heart. Then it would tickle her and her emotions.

She describes him as unique for her, but he knew he had been touched by Olivia to recover from within his world. She was not only a good person for him, but she was also therapeutic for him—just like Sarah was, or Abby was?

Sometimes people have a wonderful way of showing you, the insight into your baggage from the past. Or providing you with a degree of civility unmatched by your past feelings or relationships.

They were both like this, they made each other feel better about themselves than they did before. And without feeling anything vague or nasty too. This is why all the women meant more to him than just a bed partner. She was dynamite, and extremely romantic.

She had a lot to offer a man, and with no superficiality about herself. She was just real, like death and taxes, and like death in another way to kill someone else. Which is what he appreciated about all three of them, that he didn't see in Jade after ten years, with her merry-go-round illusions.

He realized as a man, how difficult it can be to lose a woman like Olivia. He damn sure didn't want to be confronted with that situation at this time in his life. But a lot was changing and different for him now. It was all about serious decision making and soon.

People always have a way of putting up a front about their feelings in a relationship, and always trying to give other people the impression that it's no big thing. Until some unexpected shit hits the fan, and it's all out there about someone leaving you, or was cheating on you.

Now…all of a sudden, it's a problem about your emotions and the relationship. This is why he continued to go through some changes concerning the separation between Jade and him.

He really didn't give a damn, because it was real to him. He was hurt by it, and will always be hurt and disappointed when he thinks about them. There was nothing to hide or front about Jade. He loved her…plain and simple. Regardless of whatever, she claimed she felt for him.

He just knew that Jade appeared to be one type of person, when they were together. And then, she was another type of person when they weren't together. This is when her immaturity and irresponsibility would show about herself, which would confuse him about her.

No matter what is going down in his relationship with Olivia. She was very unhappy with her husband and their marriage. She was tired of being a fixture in their relationship.

It didn't matter whether he wanted to be with her or not. Or as much as she wanted to be with him?

Olivia believed that now was the time for her to make her move. A very strong part of her didn't care about the consequences of sleeping with Marshall getting out. Or the fact that they were involved with each another.

Missing him more, was like a spirit walking away from her. Or talk that comes before sleep, and not knowing which of her principals she would screw upon. She could see the laughter in her soul, and her body being computed daily in judgment of herself and her husband.

They have good jobs that pay well. A nice home together and was living comfortably. They drove expensive cars. They could afford the best things relatively in life. Her relationship and future with Marshall wouldn't change anything or produce a different life style financially.

Because Marshall and her cared more about each other than their financial situation, and just being together would prove that for them. They also realized how much of an emptiness they felt, with all the good fortune and success they were having individually. And yet, there was a certain loneliness they both felt. They knew that they didn't have the right person in their lives, like each other.

She was well aware of how people would be at times, regarding their relationship residing in New York. As if encyclopedias of a sudden death was a Bosom walk for her to explain, with a convenient smile toward family and friends.

She understood the type. They were people who were inspired by another life to be tortured, and her parents weren't from wealth. She didn't come from prominence with the usual privileges. Marshall and Oliver were from poor family backgrounds. Due to the hard work that they produced in their own lives, in order to accomplish, and achieve something positive from the limited opportunities that they had.

People would look at her differently, or look down on her for being with an African-American man. It was fascinating to see how people continued to be motivated by traditional racism and rumors.

Most people she knew from the South were tolerant up to a degree. When something went wrong with the opposite race. Then the racism would begin to prevail or emerge. So stereo-typing to her was still alive and doing well.

A year before Olivia met Marshall. She discovered her husband was having an affair with a woman who largely resembled her. But she was surprised the woman was Hispanic, and more or less described as a White Puerto Rican.

78

SHE WAS ATTRACTIVE AND HAD style, Olivia witnessed. How much could she try to love her husband, and save her marriage?

When she knew about his affair all along, before her affair with Marshall ever began?

This is why it was a surprise, when their relationship began. It wasn't her intention to get involved with anyone, after she discovered her husband's adultery. She did her best to deal with it for one month and confronted him about it.

He obviously denied everything and conveyed to her, that she get more involved in something meaningful, which required more of her attention and time.

Their relationship took a whole different meaning for her, while they became further distant from one another. So before she began thinking about getting a divorced. She met Marshall and her decision making was postponed. She decided to let whatever was happening between them develop. Her choice was the only relevant thing to her now.

Olivia was relaxed and ready to do herself fresh. She disagreed with the whole concept of where her husband was coming from. For her, there was just no more time, and no more patience in advance left for the results she wanted.

She thought about when you are living in a rubber room, and more than your life is bouncing off the walls. And how no one wants to hear about your problems? She tried her utmost to deal with it, and the situation with another woman.

Now that he had become a part of her life. She didn't feel compel any longer to continue a marriage with her husband. Her involvement with him gave her the courage she required to solve her own personal problems.

Not that he was the answer she was looking for, but their relationship offered her a different perspective on what she felt she was missing by being married to her husband. He continued to neglect her long before Marshall entered into her life.

Olivia was more than pleased with herself. She didn't allow herself to become pregnant by her husband, and start a family with him. He didn't like Black people, but he would date a Hispanic woman.

She didn't understand the difference in his logic? It was obvious, he understood little about the history of their races, and how much their cultures are connected to their heritage, she thought. Since he considered both of them to be lower than him, and Hispanic's even lower?

He was a good provider, but she was a good provider. He wasn't a good husband and she didn't see him any better as a father. As far as the "Good Wife" was concerned, he could kiss her ass. She wasn't going to spend her life playing this kind of role for him, or for anyone else.

She didn't want her children to be mixed up racially with her husband's views. Color should not be a factor in determining someone's character as a person. A bad person comes in any race or in any color, and basically people know this from all races. No matter how much they want to deny this, or deny that?

So there is no superior race, unless they come from another planet. Her husband's view point was different from hers. She didn't judge him for this?

She respected him for the most part, but not where color was concerned. It was something which did hurt their relationship. She didn't like being married to a racist behind closed doors.

Olivia's emotions were different with different viewpoints, and was about being who she was, open and sincere. She didn't feel intimidated by African-Americans or Hispanics people. Or feel uncomfortable in their presences or environment. She always had a mutual interaction with people of color and herself.

Marshall saw this, and he recognized this in her, and he realized that women of color and Olivia clicked. It was self-explanatory, when you observed them and each other. There was no pretense when they would just get into it with each other.

She diligently talked to her husband about the state of her emotions concerning their life and marriage. A chance for him to correct his mistakes, but he took her for granted. So when this other man named, Marshall, came into her life and everything changed for her.

Before Olivia and her husband were married, he was all over her and on her like any other man would be. Who was trying to take something away from him. Then after they were married and relocated to New York. He behaved like he owned something she knew nothing about, and he could have anything he wanted due to the changes in his life style.

She became sick and tired of his constant lack of attitude about things. He always pointed out to her what he wanted her to do, and what he thought was best for her. He didn't have any idea what she needed from him as a man in their relationship, or to make this thing work and survive between them?

Also on her assessment of the situation. He wasn't a very intelligent cheater either. But a man who didn't appreciate and enjoyed the finer things in life, or everything that he had.

Or a man who loves women now? There were so many in New York City. Who were available for one reason or another? It pleased him coming from North Carolina.

He claimed that he loved her and his family. He cared for them and took care of them first, and still had the time to have as many affairs on the side as he chooses to. It's pretty much like a man who is a bigamous, with three wives and had a family with each wife.

He had an ability to maintain himself and everyone else around him with happiness, while manipulating and incorporating all of this back and forth for years to come. While no one is the wiser, until some unforeseen event finally happens.

You have to give the man his hype and credit for being such a clever cheater for so long, she thought. While his wives and family were happy with him; enjoying the life that they had together.

Olivia believed that an intelligent cheater was too complex for her husband's character to deal with. He was more of an intentional cheater. Someone who would pursue someone else on the down low.

Someone who wanted to maintain whatever he had, but was able to create the possibility of other relationships with other women? Who he could offer something to for taking a risk with him, as she often wondered?

What was her husband trying to offer this Hispanic woman he was cheating on her with? The woman who was trying to pass off as white. So she could move up easily and unrestricted within his circle, and be a part of his crowd.

Olivia wished her well with her hidden identity crisis. She knew that her deception wouldn't last very long, especially among his kind of people. The woman was better off just being herself and who she was. If she is cheating with another person's husband.

She definitely had what it takes to move up in his world, but her problem is that she doesn't want to work for any of it. Olivia misread her husband and thought that he wouldn't cheat with just anyone, but she was wrong when it came to his choice.

Like the neighbor next door, or the baby sitter, or your sister, or your best friend. You are aware of the type, anything that has a split between their legs. It gets worse from there on out. She recalled vividly, like it was that kind of a day she thought about concerning her husband.

Olivia and Marshall agreed that they would no longer continue to see each another, until she completes her business with her husband and their marriage. She believed that it was too unfair for him to be free, and for her to still be a married woman who wasn't free.

It was time for a change. It was what she wanted as she expressed it to him. The next time Olivia sees Marshall. She said, "That she wanted to be free also. Free of her husband and free of her situation with him."

It was a risk she felt strong enough to take. Realizing that he may not be available when this happens. He assured her that for the time being, he would be there to explore the possibility with her?

If it was still her desire to be with him. He wished her well on what she was trying to achieve. He knew then, it didn't matter if he was free or not. She didn't want to be with her husband anymore, and she wasn't going to be with him too much longer from what he could see. It was just a matter of time for them.

79

SIXTEEN MONTHS LATER, ZOË AND Marshall have been talking to each other over the phone. She continued to be on the road with her dance performances. After this time tonight, they decided to romance each other, with the presences of their company in private together.

He was beginning to feel her, like a few steamy sins about to happen. Now he could believe in anything, that kept him on the edge of eternity. Somehow without consciously realizing it, Zoë and Marshall were developing a relationship with one another over the phone.

Although, there was no phone sex. It was still a long distance affair, but it was happening because she was away from time to time. But with time being allowed, she would call him every opportunity she could get. She was now feeling him stronger than ever, like a hidden promise within herself.

She wanted them to make love to each other, so she could have it for tomorrow. She never felt this way, especially about a man before. She was surprised she believed, and thought she could feel this way where a man was concerned.

Like she couldn't believe, how much she was falling for him. She sprayed another whiff of perfume on.

Tonight was a big night for her. She felt like a high school teenager going out on her first date with a boy. After recalling what happened in her relationship with Randall. Who was her first love, and took her virginity, and who broke her heart all at the same time. She wanted to do things differently for herself in regard to a man.

But she apparently learned, that Randall had no patience with her or for her. When she waited for the right man to come along, and they would be engaged to be married. Everything went wrong because of him.

Marshall was no boy to her, but a man with a unique character and personality. He represented everything that she hoped for in a man. This is what she told him once. Whenever they talk to each other, they showed a need to listen to each other. It helped their communication to be fast and easy.

Not too many people you meet in life will listen to you. They will always tell you about what they know, or about what to do, rather than listen to what you are trying to say to them.

Or how you should do this, or when you should do this, and why you should do this, but they will hardy ever listen to you. No one can say for sure, but the music in Marshall is one she hasn't heard of as yet, and she wants him to play it for her.

It could be described as foolish fun like Jack and Jill. Who didn't go up the hill to fetch a pale of water, but went down the hill to look for a jumbo coconut, while giggling with their eyes on each other, as they continued to search for some privacy under a big tree secluded down the hill, she thought.

Jade, was a major concerned for Zoë. For reasons of her own, she wasn't concerned about the other women in his life, which she knew about now, as much as she was concerned about his ex-wife.

She thought that from a woman's point of view. Jade was still there hovering about, like a Bee who was lurking, seeking, and wanting more honey from Marshall. In spite of her wrong doings, while they continued to be friends, which meant they still cared for one another.

Or anything could possibly happen between them. In spite of their present circumstances. She believed that this was her competition if there was any?

She didn't want to talk about it. It was the other women such as her. Who were competing for Marshall and his time in his life. She made it plain and clear, she wanted him in her life. He was like everything to her, and all rolled up into everything. A friend, her man, and her family, but you can't wait around like a lame duck for it to happen either.

She preferred being a peepshow offering herself, as the last rites to make a play for him.

It was better than walking alone after hours, or dying for someone to love her like him. She became very happy because of her trust in him. He was direct and honest with her because no one else had been, accept Ms. Peters. And the beautiful young kids of all races she continued to help and encourage.

It was time, she called a cab. He offered to pick her up, but she refused. She wanted to come to him. She moved to the upper West side of Manhattan. She was much closer to him now.

He was finished and everything was ready for their evening together. Soon she will be here. The last time he saw her was six months ago, and that was only briefly. She was being mobbed by her fans outside of the theater.

When she arrived, it was like he was looking at another woman he first met.

It was rendering to see her in his environment. He hasn't seen her like this before. He didn't think of her this way before he became attracted to her. He didn't think they would be together intimately since he met her.

She came up behind him and hugged him, after he hung up her coat. He turned around to face her and they gazed deeply into each other's eyes. Her eyes were much prettier and lighter than he recalled.

She said that her eyes have a tendency to change colors in the light or depending on what she was wearing. Her smile was tainted with cause and passion. Her clear skin was a vision of light keeping her active.

She asked, "Is there anything wrong?" He replied, "Absolutely not. You are just an unbelievably beautiful woman."

He had never taken the time out before to admire the femininity of her beauty as a woman. She was more stunning than he cared to say, and her body captivated his attention and excited him more.

When he first met her, it was like she was trying to down play and hide who she was, and didn't want someone to know what she truly looked like.

Since she didn't trust men, or had any interest in them at the time. She didn't want the attention from them. It was obvious she had physical attributes. Sometimes you don't notice what's right in front of you, until it is too late, or you are not looking at it that way?

"You act like you haven't seen me before, Marshall? I hope that I am not making you uncomfortable?"

"I am sorry. I know it seems like that, but it seems like I am seeing you for the first time.

"You appear to be so different, since I saw you last."

"Is that good or bad?" She asked.

"It's all good and more, Zoë."

He admit that he was taken by her outer beauty and presence. She commands power about her when she is all dressed up. She was still warm, gentle, affectionate, and generous. He was surprised by the gifts from her when she was on the road. They were expensive and touching to him.

He felt powerless when he was losing Jade. There was a feeling of power returning within him, when he encountered Abby. He didn't feel the same power with Olivia or Sarah. He felt other things concerning Olivia, and he felt different things about Sarah.

Yet maybe because they were married. He wasn't sure what it was at this stage. A maturity had already claimed itself concerning their friendship. They were flowing unexpectedly, like in a marathon race. They felt a growth in their communication with each other, after her traveling and the phone calls. A certain type of flow, that she and he had. Unconsciously, they acted as though they had been doing this for a while. She moved closer to him. He felt her breath up on him, as her lips came closer to touch his. Her kiss was soft and wet, and then there was no air to breath. The kiss became long. He couldn't breathe as he released the oxygen through his nose.

80

He was excited. He was hot and bothered by her too. When he was kissing her, he began thinking about when you first meet someone, that you are obviously attracted to.

There is this feeling of excitement, mystery, and wonder? As time begins to speed up for the two of you. Then various comments are made to each other in order, to know more about each other: the unique experience you begin to share together, that describes what you are doing to each other.

Then you begin to gradually change your life with this person. Then you find yourself falling deeper for this person. Then the intimacy goes further, and develops into a deep closeness.

Which now, gives you a feeling of invincibility together, before anything, and everything else in the world decides to go wrong? But not for you, because you have met someone new you are in love with, and all is good in life.

When you are in love, you see what you want to see. Because this is what you and the other person created in your relationship for each other to be.

And you see less and less of what the truth is in something, before it becomes denial with your drama, which makes you blind to it as love is. What you see is not what you are getting, What you are getting is what you are not seeing.

Since knowing, and believing becomes two different things, which neither one, you can actually depend on for the accuracy of your emotions.

You will never know when that time will come for you, because of everything you endured with someone in a relationship. When it will come to an end for you, which always surprises the hell out of you, when it comes.

Especially, when deception has become your new best friend, and now your worst enemy. Or perhaps you do know? Since you are the one, who is on the other side of the lies, and make believe.

It's true, it does take two people to bless a relationship to work. Although however, it only takes one person in that relationship to screw it up, or simply fuck it up. It was one of the blind spots that Marshall realized after his separation from, Jade. When one person you love is two different people you love.

So when this starts to happen again, you become helpless beyond words. The situation changes for you and this person? Then it becomes one of the most painful things you would imagine in life, or a misunderstood event that hasn't happened to you before?

When his lips and hers parted, they continued to hug each other to end the beginning on a wet tip of air. He escorted her into the kitchen. He seated her comfortably, with a glass of wine next to her. Placing it on an elegant smoked glass table top, with a Butcher Block designed base?

When he returned and looked back at her, she felt the electricity between them. But he felt that was her objective to put him on alert. It was natural and strong, but overwhelming for the both of them at the moment.

He looked at her sitting at his kitchen table looking awesome, and with a body that cries out for him to save hell? He couldn't do it, and he didn't think that anyone else could do it, or save her body from hell?

If there was something else in a relationship, other than love? Then you could relate to in a way of touching instead of feeling. Then maybe you could take a tangible element of something, and make it real—like when you die.

Will it honestly be forever or when the day you were born? He still wondered whether people really wanted to be in love, with another person for the rest of their lives.

He thought further about the possibility of a relationship between them. They looked up at each other like they had an agreement. He walked over to her and kissed the back of her neck, as he held her around her waist, while she sipped on her wine with the other hand and trembled.

He started to set the table for dinner. She stood up to assist him. She knew which items to place where on the table for their dinner, like she knew in advance what he was preparing for them. They instinctively stopped and turned to kiss. They smiled and repeated kissing again.

"Have we done this before, Marshall?"

"No, Zoë. But it seems like it is second nature to us?"

They sat down to have dinner by candle light, after she lit the candles. The room was filled with music from John Legend's CD. She graciously shook her head, as her long dark hair fell back into place up on her shoulders.

Her sensuous eyes and lips were like trying to fake an orgasm you just couldn't do. She was making him feel weak inside from the truth. The more he looked at her, the more he began to want her.

They had charming conversation for the duration of their dinner. And then in the course of what was about to help him lose his mind up in here?

She sat there more relaxed with much ease, and with him being manipulated by a switch feeling from inside. He knew that love had no real time to save a heart for you. When you need to know what is going to happen before and after to your heart?

So with a wet and erotic kiss of touching lips, and with the taste from the wine. The feeling was like carrying an infant baby on his back. It was an incredible feeling. So why do relationships always end up on the same note of a lie, a deception, or a betrayal?

He thought about her sitting there looking like something out of a dream. It was an unexpected surprise of romance. He felt his blood boiling with fire for her now. He was feeling a sense of strong need for her.

Then he realized after viewing her and her body. She isn't going to get too much competition from anyone else, except someone who is her given equal. She was looking quite rare and that's difficult for a woman to be. When it's rare to see another beautiful woman stand out from other beautiful women.

She returned a passionate look at him, while they continued to eat, drink, and talk. She expressed something interesting about him, as he expressed the same about her. He removed himself from his chair to walk over to her, and take her hand again. He wanted her to take a walk with him. She kissed him and was encourage by the suggestion.

The weather was brisk, and mildly cold. After a twenty minute walk through the neighborhood, which she was enjoying? He stopped at a restaurant so they could have a cup of coffee, but she preferred hot chocolate.

As they talked and laughed for forty-five minutes before walking back home. She held on to his arm as they walked through the brisk cool weather, and smiling at him all the way as they approached the facade of his building.

They entered the building. A woman walked toward them. He didn't recognize her at first, because of the difference in her appearance. She changed and looked differently and better, which he didn't think was possible. It was Jade. He was engaged in conversation with Zoë.

Jade leaned over to kiss him on his cheek, and he returned a kiss to her cheek.

"How are you? Is everything okay?"

"Yes, I was at the high school."

81

JADE VOLUNTEERS HER TIME TO the community by tutoring kids, after school in one of the neighborhood high schools. She has serious computer skills.

"Since I was in the neighborhood for a hot minute, I was going to stop by and say hello. I have another appointment to go to after this.

"I am dealing with another project through my job as well."

"It sounds like you are keeping busy."

"I am very busy. I didn't know you had company, or I wouldn't have stopped by."

"We just had dinner. Then we had a cup of coffee and a walk," said Marshall.

"Oh, I' m sorry. Zoë this is my ex-wife, Jade. And this is a friend of mine, Zoë."

They both extended their hand to shake, while they respectfully checked each other out. They were impressed with what they saw from each other. Jade asked her, "Do I know you from somewhere?

Zoë replied, "I don't think so?"

Jade suddenly recalled. "You are the Dancer. Who had an article in *The Sunday Newspaper*, Zoë P. Ames?

"Yes, that's me."

"It's nice to meet you."

"It's nice to meet you too."

He excused himself from Jade to talk with Zoë.

"Here are my keys to the apartment. I will be with you shortly. I am going to walk her to her car."

Zoë wanted Jade to see where she was coming from immediately, and to let Marshall know as well. She hugged him, and then kissed him on his lips with heat. At the same time, Jade tried to act like she didn't see the embrace or the kiss, and how she was playing it off in public.

Zoë left no room for doubt at this point where she was going with this, Jade thought. She tried to hide behind her denial. She knew in her heart there would be other women, but that was insignificant to her. It didn't mean that he was in love with her or them.

Zoë escorted herself up to the elevator and to Marshall's apartment, while she prepared herself to wait for him comfortably. She didn't walk away with the Sun at her back either, or with a strange manifestation in her conscious mind.

Jade wasn't the Mona Lisa to her, but she was a touch of immediate contact for Marshall, Zoë thought. She was coming back from everything she had been through with herself. She felt strong and confident again.

She was wiping the past off of her, like you wipe bad stuff from the bottom of your shoe. The smell is gone along with everything else. It was his sadness without her that convinced Zoë to regard Jade with extreme caution, because no one heals overnight, she knew.

Zoë was selling Marshall a novel about love, and death in her life and indicating pleasure to him all the way. So now she can recreate it all differently for them, because he was touching her with his heart. He was renaming her for her emotions.

Jade and Marshall arrived at her car. She leaned over to hug and kiss Marshall with passion. He looked into her eyes, before she entered her car.

She replied, "Call me some times, when you get a chance? It will be nice to hear from you."

Then she drove off. Marshall watched her for thirty seconds, as her car disappeared and blend into traffic.

Jade asked herself? "Was there a sunset being felt in his life with this other woman? Did she bring him to life? Or was he still empty inside trying to fulfill himself again, but without her? Or like time that becomes the sound of her voice.

"I yearn to kiss him with so much passion, but I cannot touch his lips the way I want to make contact with him and lose myself.

"The love I once saw as a guiding light is dimming further and further away, even though he is there. Now I can no longer feel what was there, and see a ray of hope other than our friendship.

"I wonder, will it ever return for us? How long will I miss him?

"I will wake up tomorrow with a unique picture of loneliness, because I didn't see a shooting star across the sky the night before to help me make a decision. So that it will help me to grow like a flower from the sunshine, I once felt with him."

When he returned to his building, he thought about her. How he loved her. It was like falling off of, or jumping off of a water fall over a steep rock. And yet, she felt angelic to him as a ball of fire from the intrigues of life, and there is always a glitch that will come from love.

It is the hollow cavity that craves to be fulfilled, with an arrow of obligation and pain in the heart right away? He tried to give Jade total kisses on her jugular vein. So it will be a feeling released from a warp sense of love; to be unified without another man in her life.

He knew absolutely nothing about this point in the sky that is directly over his head. It will never be any wonder, that you can't explain it as something moving, or shaking, or often associated with a commitment. Because now trust could be a thing of the past.

Zoë told him that he received two calls on his cell phone, after he entered the apartment. She noticed that the missed calls revealed on his cell phone screen, because the phone was directly in front of her on the table.

One was from Olivia and the other was from Abby. She had no idea who they were or what it was in reference to.

When he retrieved his cell, he swiped the screen and saw who the missed calls where from. He tried to put this all into perspective again, while he was still involved from being in the mix. You must always remember, he thought. When love is in your mix, then it's the same for everyone else who is in the mix. It's just that their mix, now becomes more shit attached to your mistake.

CPSIA information can be obtained
at www.ICGtesting.com
Printed in the USA
FSHW011247030321
79100FS

9 781648 017223